ONE, TWO, THREE—INFINITY!

Lancer accelerated outsystem to meet the incoming rebel fleet that now lay revealed on Basil's displays.

They'd all heard about all the warships that the rebels had gained with the shockingly sudden collapse of Imperial authority in their sectors, but they had to be running on skeleton crews and relying heavily on automated systems. Had to be. And yet . . . there were a *lot* of ships coming at them. Basil made himself relax.

As he did so, hellfire awoke on his readouts. "Incoming . . . multiple!" he shouted. The tactical display had already processed the automatic download and the main screen showed the converging energy bolts, crawling toward a seemingly stationary *Lancer* at lightspeed.

"Stand by," Captain Vladek called out calmly.

With no more warning than that, the universe turned to noise and chaos as the ship shuddered and a secondary explosion ripped through the bridge's port bulkhead. Basil saw Lieutenant Perrin hurled from the comm station with such force that her securing straps practically cut her in two. Vladek was lying back, motionless. In the erratically flickering tactical display Basil saw a rebel ship altering course to vector on *Lancer*.

Suddenly, he *knew* what must be done. It was as though he heard a stranger speak, "This is the bridge. On command, disengage the drive."

"*What?*" Komen's voice almost broke into a squeak. "Who is this? Let me speak to the captain!"

"No time! Here comes a three-count!" he shouted, as a second bolt of death crawled at lightspeed toward *Lancer* from the rebel ship. . . .

"One!"

ALSO BY STEVE WHITE:

The Disinherited
Legacy
Debt of Ages

With David Weber:
Insurrection
Crusade

PRINCE OF SUNSET

STEVE WHITE

BAEN

PRINCE OF SUNSET

A Baen Books Original

Baen Publishing Enterprises
P.O. Box 1403
Riverdale, NY 10471

ISBN: 0-671-87869-7

Cover art by Gary Ruddell

First printing, March 1998

Distributed by Simon & Schuster
1230 Avenue of the Americas
New York, NY 10020

Printed in the United States of America

To Sandy, with love.
And to Lo Kuan-chung, with apologies.

CHAPTER ONE
Nyjord (Nu Phoenicis IV), 3889 C.E.

Afterwards, Basil Castellan was always certain that it had all begun the day he'd been rescued by the dragon.

Oh, it hadn't been a *real* dragon, of course. So he hastily assured everyone to whom he told the story. Only . . . it *had* been a real dragon. He would never share that particular knowledge with anyone but Sonja and Torval.

His feet started to slip as he mounted the trail, such as it was, and he scrambled to compensate, grabbing at the slender trunk of a sapling. He felt a sense of kinship, for its species was a Terran import like his own; and the tree evidently agreed, for it held. He pulled himself upright and regained his footing, then resumed hiking uphill.

The ridge line couldn't be too much further. Not that he could see it yet, for he'd walked upward into a low-lying cloud that enveloped this region of the Kraaken range, into an enchanted world of pearly mist made subtly iridescent whenever the afternoon light of Nu Phoenicis came streaming through the occasional rift.

Then, abruptly, he was above the clouds, and the ridge line was just ahead. He hastened his steps and soon was at the summit, standing under a crystalline blue sky in which Nyjord's small, intense white sun rode serenely with only a few fleecy high-altitude clouds for escorts. He stood breathing heavily, but only for a moment. He was a healthy young man of fifteen years (local years, of course; eighteen of the standard years of faraway Earth in which people's ages, as well as history, were generally measured), and exertion in this thin mountain air was more exhilarating than exhausting. He turned slowly in a circle, automatically shading his eyes against a slightly more ultraviolet-rich sunlight than they'd evolved under.

Below and to the east, whence he'd come, the wooded mountainside sloped down into the clouds that rested against it like an ocean lapping against a breakwater. But elsewhere all was dazzling clarity, and he could see forever through air that had never known large-scale burning of hydrocarbons. Northward and southward the mountains curved away into infinity, while to the west a whole series of upland valleys spread themselves verdantly at his feet. Beyond them the further ranges of the Kraaken rose, range piled upon enormous range. Dark forests clothed the lower slopes, but above the timberline the peaks rose through snow and glaciers to altitudes where no life could exist.

After a while he dragged his eyes from those god-remote titans and gazed down at the valleys below, checkerboarded with fields and dotted with curious little towns where a few pure-blooded Old Nyjorders still spoke the language their ancestors had brought from a part of Earth called Scandinavia. The sun was warm, but his jumpsuit's molecularly engineered material responded to his sweat by breathing more copiously, and no discomfort distracted him from the view. He was still in familiar territory, for he'd come to this crag many times in the course of his youth, sometimes in the company of friends but more and more often alone. Here, with what seemed like the entire continent on display far below, he'd always felt an irrational but nonetheless real sense of isolation; his problems were down there in those distant valleys and plains, and couldn't touch him. Which was why he'd come today, for what would probably be the last time. He'd already taken a long look through the window of his old room at a familiar panorama that had suddenly seemed strange, and disposed of certain objects which he'd somehow never quite gotten around to throwing out; but this seemed the right place to complete the relinquishment of boyhood.

He shook his head, irritated with himself. It must, he decided, be the thinness of the air. His mother, a planetologist by profession, had explained it long ago. "Nyjord is a relatively massive world, compared to Old Earth," she'd clipped, in lecture mode.

"Is that what they mean by 'one point thirteen gee'?" he'd piped up, eager to display his precociousness. How old had he been that day?

"Don't interrupt. And yes, that means that our gravity is stronger than Earth standard. At the same time, our atmosphere is somewhat thinner. That's all right at sea level, or even on this plateau. But the gravity causes the atmospheric density to drop off faster with altitude—you might say the atmosphere is shallower and 'harder.' Anyway, that's why the higher peaks of the Kraakens are lifeless; they're in near-vacuum." She'd indicated the distant pale-blue mountains to the west that seemed to float above the cityscape beyond their back garden. "And it's why you and your friends have to be very careful hiking, even on the established trails. As you climb higher, the air can get dangerously thin before you know it."

He'd stopped listening, for his eyes had followed her finger toward the mountains and stayed there. "Is it true," he'd asked softly, "that a Luon lives up there?"

"Well," she'd replied, slightly ill at ease, "there are always stories. Nobody knows how many Luonli are left on this world, if any—certainly not more than a very few. Some people claim to have seen one in this part of the Kraakens. But they were probably just imagining things. Luonli are hardly ever seen unless they want to be seen."

"Why? I mean, if they're so big . . . ?"

Her unease had deepened. "It has to do with telepathy."

All his resolve to seem grown-up and sophisticated had fled, leaving him alone with the childhood fears that were part of his culture's legacy. "You mean . . . you mean they can control your mind . . . ?"

"Don't be silly! The theory is that they can, ah, implant certain suggestions . . . including the negative one that you *haven't* seen something." She'd taken a deep breath and turned severe. "Don't bother your head with such things! Even if there *are* any Luonli left on Nyjord, they keep to themselves just as they do on all the worlds where they live."

"But," he'd protested, "if nobody ever sees one, how do we know they even exist? My friend Ivar says they don't." But Ivar hadn't said so very loudly.

"Oh, they exist," she had said, smiling and nodding slowly. "If they didn't, we wouldn't be living here."

Later, he'd learned what she had meant. And whenever he'd walked this trail he had strained his eyes against the intense sunlight, hoping for just a glimpse in the royal-blue sky. But none had been granted him. And, it seemed, none was going to be today.

He stretched and rubbed a finger across the sun-browned skin of the back of his left hand. The imprinted circuitry glowed to life and showed him the time. He really shouldn't go any further, not if he wanted to return the way he'd come. But he could always summon the aircar he'd parked down below—it was quite capable of flying itself and seeking out his wrist communicator's homing beacon. Normally, neither he nor any of his friends would be caught dead taking advantage of any such unworthy expedient. But now, on the eve of his departure for Sigma Draconis, he was above all that. Wasn't he? He sighed. Maybe he *should* start back now. He began to turn, then paused for a last look at the vista which, like so much else, he was leaving behind.

It was then that a metallic-seeming glint of reflected sunlight in the high deep-blue vault of heaven caught his eye. It didn't register at first; surely it must be a high-altitude aircraft, although few such flew above this region. But no, the glint wasn't really metallic, for it was not quite coppery and not precisely golden, and as he focused on it he could make out the impossibly slow beat of vast wings. . . .

"A Luon," he breathed, fearful to shatter the crystalline fragility of the moment. Then, as he watched, the Luon caught an updraft and snapped its wings out to full extension, swooping into a southward glide, and was gone from sight.

The lateness of the hour was forgotten. He *had* to get another look. He looked to his left. The trail led upward as it followed the ridge line to the south. Perhaps the Luon was headed to its home among the higher crags. Nobody really knew where they lived, but it was well known that they liked mountains, and his imagination conjured up a titanic eyrie where the Luon perched—or whatever—in lonely majesty. Without hesitation, he started upward. It was steep, and the trail seemed little used. He paused to pick up a fallen limb that was the right length to make a walking stick. He made good time with its aid, leveraging himself up the increasingly steep trail and dismissing his occasional, annoying dizziness with a headshake and a deep breath. In his eagerness, he didn't notice that he was having to do so more and more frequently.

The woods were thinning, leaving the view obstructed only by a few stunted trees. Soon, surely, he must catch another sight of the Luon. The thought made him glance upward, and he momentarily lost his footing. He muttered a word that even now would have drawn a rebuke from his mother, irritated by the way his head spun as he steadied himself. Then, up ahead, he saw that the trail narrowed as it skirted the righthand side of a crag. To the right of the trail, a sheer cliff fell away. There'd be a matchless view from there, he thought as he resumed his heavy-breathing progress.

The trail was rough as well as narrow as it wound around the crag. Fortunately, he'd never been afflicted by a fear of heights. And the view was even more spectacular than he'd expected. He rested his back and looked around for a sight of the Luon.

There was no flash of reflected sunlight anywhere in the

sky. But maybe the Luon had left some trace of its habitation nearby. He leaned forward, using the stick to support his weight, and peered southward.

With a sharp *crack*, the stick snapped.

His oxygen-deprived brain responded with nightmarish slowness as he began to topple forward. He tried to throw himself back and regain his balance, but then his feet began to slip and in a timeless instant of terror he was over the edge, scraping his back against the lip of the cliff as he fell. He flailed his arms wildly, seeking something to grab. As he did, his left wrist smashed into the cliff face, and he felt a stinging pain. Then he was in free fall . . . but only for a sickening moment. With an ankle-wrenching impact, he landed on a ledge. Then he began to slide off it, but this time his windmilling arms caught the stunted trunk of one of the dwarf trees—*not* of Earthly origin—that grew through cracks in the rock at these altitudes.

For a time he simply hung there, feet dangling above the abyss, breathing in great gasps. Then, slowly and painfully, he pulled himself back up onto the little ledge. Only then did he yield to the shakes.

At last he could think clearly, if somewhat sluggishly. *All right. No problem. Call the aircar.* He brought his left hand up to speak into the wrist communicator . . . and then he remembered the pain in that wrist.

The communicator's plastic casing should have held. He must have hit it against the rocks in exactly the right way— or, rather, in exactly the wrong way. For a while he just looked at the shattered device, ignoring the cuts made by jagged little fragments. They were the least of his worries. Finally, for lack of anything better to do, he tried to activate the communicator. The result was precisely what he'd expected: a brief crackling sound and a flicker of dying molecular circuitry seen through the breaks in the casing, then nothing.

After a while he became aware that the sun was almost touching the peaks to the west as Nyjord's 19.3-hour day drew to a close. His jumpsuit would compensate for external temperature changes, up to a point. But in this thin air the nighttime drop in temperature was extreme, and a slight chill was already invading him. He looked up and saw that the trail from which he'd fallen wasn't too far above his ledge. Given anything at all to get a handhold on, he would have tried to climb the cliff wall. But there was only sheer stone.

He tried to think constructively, if only to avoid leaving a vacuum for despair to fill. But all that came was resentment of the Luon for having lured him into this. He rejected it angrily as the irrational petulance he knew it to be, but it wouldn't go away; he couldn't get it out of his head. . . .

And as he thought about it, something else came into his mind, something he had never felt before, something that seemed to swell like an expanding sun until for a moment its glare filled his consciousness, filled the universe. . . .

Then he was warily approaching the edge of the rock outcropping on all fours. (Odd, he'd never been afraid of heights before.) He looked down the sheer cliff at the wooded valley below. And all at once he forgot to breathe.

He'd only gotten the briefest, most distant glimpse of the Luon before. Now, in all its immeasurable splendor, it swept along almost skimming the tops of those trees so far below. Then, in a maneuver that its thirty-meter wings couldn't account for, it banked and flung itself upward, all that mass arrowing straight up toward him at a velocity that must surely carry it past and on up into the darkening sky.

Then it was level with him, and thrust its wings outward in a violent braking motion that brought it to a sudden stop with a thunderclap sound that flung him physically back from the edge, stunned. He scarcely noticed, for he was face to face with a visage conjured up from myth, gazing into enormous amber eyes in whose depths he saw the source of that which had seemed to burn its way into his mind. . . .

The cold wind brought him back to consciousness. Then his situation began to register, one impossible impression at a time.

The sun was setting and he was above the corrugated landscape of the eastern Kraakens, headed south. He would surely have yielded to hypothermia had it not been for the warmth emanating from the great flying body against which he was being held. What was holding him was one of the four specialized arms between the wings and the head. Aft of the wings, he knew, would be four more limbs: the legs and two that could function as either legs or arms. All these limbs, including the two that specialized as wings, were arranged in pairs. The Luonli might not be vertebrates— evolution had produced something far more flexible than a spinal column on their unknown homeworld—but they were bilaterally symmetrical.

Just ahead of him was the great head that a native of Earth might have characterized as vaguely crocodilian in a lighter-jawed sort of way until he saw the eyes. One of those eyes—their settings were wonderfully flexible—turned to gaze at him.

"Ah, you are conscious." A sensation of relief accompanied the bell-clear words into his mind, but then came concern at the cultural phobias that had come roaring to the surface of his consciousness. "Please set your mind at rest. I am, it is true, communicating with you telepathically. But your innate resistance to such communication is such that I can only detect consciously organized surface thoughts, such as those that a non-telepath such as yourself formulates in the process of speech. A certain sensitivity to emotions is an unavoidable concomitant, but with that exception your mental privacy is as secure as it is when you are conversing with a fellow human."

Basil knew about his own psi-resistance, for like everyone else he'd been tested for such talents at an early age. Of course, there was no knowing how effective it would be against an alien's powers. . . . But somehow it never occurred to Basil to doubt the Luon's words, or to suspect that his lack of doubt was a result of mental manipulation. He could only ask, "Where are you taking me?" in a voice that the wind whipped instantly away into inaudibility but which the Luon "heard" perfectly.

"Since night is falling, I thought it best to take you to shelter before the temperatures fall to a level that is dangerous to you. In the morning, I will convey you to the nearest human habitation, unless you have a specific destination in mind."

"My aircar," he muttered. For a fact, the wind was biting into him cruelly and his eyeballs were starting to ache. But he felt oddly detached from all such sensations, as detached as he was from fear.

The stars were coming out and one of the moons was rising as they approached a cliff. For a moment of panic, Basil thought the Luon was going to crash into it. But then the great wings went into braking configuration, and the Luon lost velocity with an abruptness that almost stunned its human passenger. Very slowly, they continued to approach that rock wall.

"Prepare yourself," said the calm, asexual pseudo-voice in his head.

The moonlit sky around them and the world beneath vanished.

Basil had no opportunity to lose his sanity, for without the passage of any time at all they were in an interior that seemed too vast to be indoors, landing with a bone-rattling thump, and the Luon was using its legs and dual-purpose limbs to come to a running stop. *Conservation of momentum*, he thought with a brain that only wanted to gibber.

The irresistibly strong arms released him and he sank to the stony floor, content for the moment to let the sudden warmth soak into his bones. Presently, his surroundings began to register. He could see clearly, although the artificial lighting's source was obscure. But it was difficult to make out the vaulted ceiling and soaring walls, for his initial impression of immense space had not been exaggerated. His intellect insisted that spaces designed to accommodate Luonli must be vast as a matter of simple practicality; the rest of him knew he stood in the Hall of the Mountain King.

The chamber was carved out of solid rock, and he had

not the slightest doubt that it was inside the mountain they'd been approaching. It must fill most of it, and he wondered how, and when, the Luonli had scooped out a mountain's insides.

The thought made him turn and look at his rescuer. The Luon had its legs drawn up under it and its other limbs extended to prop it into a sitting position, and it gazed down from a height of only about half its total length—slightly more than three times Basil's height. Its wings were folded, although there was plenty of room to flap them in this titanic hall. The odd illumination, indefinably different in quality from electric light, shimmered on the fine scale pattern of its hide.

"So you can teleport, too," Basil heard himself say. Something about the acoustics made his voice seem less tiny than it should have in this hollow mountain.

The Luon didn't physically nod its head, but a sensation of nonverbal affirmation touched Basil's mind as the soundless words came in their unhurried way. "The technique is inherently limited, but it has its uses." (*Concern.*) "Are you hungry? Our species' dietary requirements are not identical, but there is considerable overlap, so I can offer you sustenance."

"I have my own food." Basil indicated his pouch and canteen. He wasn't hungry, but he found he was suffering from a bad case of dry-mouth. He took a swig of water from the canteen, wishing he'd brought something stronger. "Thank you for saving me," he continued belatedly. "Why did you do it?"

(*Puzzlement.*) "You were obviously in distress, and would hardly have survived the night. I followed an elementary ethical imperative. And besides . . ." For the first time, there was a perceptible hesitation in the Luon's telepathic cadence. "I knew your great-grandfather Boris Marczali."

Basil's lulled apprehensions awakened. "What? But you said you could only read the thoughts I actually vocalize— and I haven't told you who I am!"

"Compose yourself. I know you as the son of Arabella

Marczali-Castellan and the late Lysander Castellan because I know of your mother—a noted student of my species. Which reminds me: a moment ago, you observed that we could teleport *too*. May I ask what you meant by that particular phraseology?"

"Well," Basil began, not noticing that the subject had been deftly changed, "the first humans to encounter you were unable to account for your ability to fly. It was a manifest impossibility for beings as massive as yourselves."

"Approximately three-quarters of a metric ton, in your terms," the Luon interjected.

"It was clear that you must be able to somehow neutralize, or shield against, gravity. At first it was theorized that you had some kind of contra-grav generator—not that anyone had any notion how to build one then—surgically implanted in your bodies." Basil wondered fleetingly if the Luon could sense his distaste and embarrassment. "That was back when people used to do that sort of thing a lot, you see. So the idea naturally occurred to them. But it didn't make sense. You wouldn't have evolved in the wild as flyers if you couldn't fly without advanced technology. So after Antonescu established the scientific basis of psi phenomena, it was suggested that maybe you used psionic levitation for lift, and that the wings are for lateral movement only. My mother has always favored that theory, even though it doesn't seem to make evolutionary sense either. . . ." He trailed to an abashed halt as the Luon's amusement communicated itself nonverbally to him.

"I see that you have come to share your mother's interest in us . . . and also, perhaps, the characteristic academic tendency to lecture." The Luon paused, whether thoughtfully or for effect Basil couldn't tell. "In point of fact, she is correct."

Basil grew aware that his mouth was hanging open. In the sixteen—or was it seventeen?—standard centuries since human interstellar explorers had first set unbelieving eyes on a Luon, the aliens had never evinced the slightest hostility toward humankind. But neither had they volunteered any solutions to the mysteries implicit in their existence. They had simply remained aloof, living out their unimaginably long lives in solitary splendor—never had two of them been seen together—amid the mountainous terrain they seemed to prefer. Only rarely did they deign to notice their small, ephemeral supplanters.

"But," the Luon broke into his thoughts, "why do you say this violates evolutionary logic?"

Basil ordered himself not to stammer. He didn't know why he was being singled out to receive such knowledge, but he *had* to prolong this unique moment as long as possible. This flow of revelations *must* be made to continue. "Well, er, a species' evolutionary history occurs before it becomes sentient—that is, before psionic powers become possible. It's like the notion of the implanted contra-grav device; evolution wouldn't have prepared you to exercise a capability you weren't going to acquire until later."

"Your logic is faultless. But your premises are not. You see, our evolutionary ancestors acquired an elementary form of psionic levitation while still presentient."

Basil's mouth started to open, but in his mind he felt the equivalent of an upraised, forestalling hand. "Yes, I know: psionic phenomena are a concomitant of neural activity above a level of complexity which is normally associated with sentience. But our brain structure, like our physiology, is the unique product of an equally unique series of evolutionary accidents—what I believe you would call an evolutionary 'hothouse plant.' We became aware of this when we left our homeworld."

"I suppose," Basil began hesitantly, hardly daring to ask for more information than he'd already been given, "that's why you engaged in so many terraforming projects."

"Leaving aside your ethnocentric terminology, the answer is yes." (*Renewed amusement.*) "I perceive that this accounts for the interest your mother—a planetologist, not an exobiologist—has shown in us."

"Yes. Planetology is an offshoot of astronomy, and astronomers used to be conditioned to think in terms of a lifeless universe. But then we started to learn something

about the planetary systems near Sol, and that stopped being
possible. . . ."

Epsilon Eridani had been the first.

That K2v star, only eleven light-years distant, had once
seemed one of humanity's most promising neighbors. Less
massive than Sol, and burning with a relatively cool orange
glow, it nevertheless belonged to that narrow range of main-
sequence stars that could conceive and nurture a world at
an orbital distance where liquid water was possible, neither
tidelocking such a world into dual hells of searing and frozen
hemispheres nor consuming it prematurely within the fiery
envelope of an expanding red giant. Even before the first
landing on Earth's moon, electronic ears had been cocked
in Epsilon Eridani's direction, hoping to hear the voices of
other radio users.

Then, in the last decade of the twentieth century, the
realization had sunk home: Epsilon Eridani was rotating
at the undignified rate of a young star. It hadn't existed
long enough to slow to the more sedate spin of stellar
adulthood. Any planets it possessed would be barren at best,
molten at worst. The quest for life had turned elsewhere.
Only in a spirit of curiosity about earlier stages of planetary-
system formation, and as a matter of distinctly low priority,
had the twenty-first century's space-based instruments been
turned toward Epsilon Eridani.

They had found the spectral lines that meant free oxygen,
and therefore life.

Somebody, it seemed, had been up to something.

"The astronomers never recovered, according to Mother.
Some of them simply denied the findings until the first
interstellar probes confirmed them. By then, other living
worlds that shouldn't have existed had come to light—
including this one. When the first colony ships reached those
worlds, they found various species that were identical or
nearly so on all of them."

"And, on some of them, us." For a time there was silence

inside Basil's skull, beneath which he thought to detect a brooding undercurrent. Then the Luon resumed, at first with seeming irrelevance. "Our development differed from yours. For example, since we *knew* psionic phenomena to be possible we were able to attain an understanding of them at an earlier stage. At the same time, space travel was quite out of the question for us as long as payload mass remained a limiting factor, given our physical size and psychological need for living room." A motion with two right arms indicated the vast hall. "By the time we left the surface of our homeworld we had reached an overall technological level that your species would not attain until the Unification Wars period, but were far more advanced in the application of psionic effects—for which, unlike the vast majority of humans, we had a considerable natural aptitude."

"You must have been like gods," Basil breathed.

"But vulnerable gods. It was only when we ventured away from our birthworld that we came to realize how precisely we were attuned to it." *(Irony.)* "Once, when your race was still so new to the scientific world view as to be susceptible to pseudoscientific quackeries, there was a theory that human behavior was controlled by *biorhythms*. It was nonsense as applied to humans. But something analogous was altogether too real for us. Only rare individuals could survive away from the homeworld, with its particular orbital and rotational periods.

"We resolved to colonize as many planets as possible with those individuals, to assure the continuity of our species. It proved to be easier to establish a biosphere from scratch than to alter an existing one, so we were attracted to those planets which were capable of sustaining life but were as yet too young to have given birth to it." The Luon's features remained as expressionless as ever— what evolutionary need had a naturally telepathic race for a face which served as a communications device?—but Basil sensed an almost embarrassed hesitancy. "Naturally, the worlds with highly developed native biospheres were of greater intellectual interest—especially yours."

"You mean," Basil said faintly, "Earth?"

"Earth," the Luon confirmed. "One of only three worlds where we encountered tool users."

"We've *never* found any, besides yourselves—at least not in Imperial space." Basil wondered how far the Luonli had explored. But his rescuer continued before he could put the question.

"I perceive that you are not particularly surprised that we visited the human homeworld. It had been my impression that this was not a matter of general knowledge."

"Well, not exactly *knowledge*—no actual proof. But we've surmised it ever since we first encountered you. After all, it would account for an old legend of ours."

(Dawning recollection.) "Ah, yes: dragons."

Basil nodded. "They appear in the myths of various old Earth cultures, always looking similar but with strangely different personalities."

"Yes, it all comes back to me now: the benign if not always reliable *lung* of China versus the evil treasure-hoarding monsters of Europe and the Near East." The verbal symbols evoked fairly meaningful images in Basil's mind, even though his knowledge of Earth's geography was sketchy. "There is no great mystery here. An officially sanctioned scientific expedition, to the extent that such a concept has meaning for us, established itself among the Neolithic tribes that would one day become the Chinese. At the same time, western Eurasia became the field of operations for a group of . . ." *(Acute embarrassment.)*

"Uh, enemies in a war?" Basil prompted.

"Oh, no. Divided sovereignties were quite unknown to us."

"Pirates?" Basil suggested, unable to keep the incredulity out of his voice.

"Not precisely. I believe the closest social equivalent would be certain associations of humans who use one- and two-seat open contra-grav vehicles to cruise the traffic lanes in large groups, committing assorted illegalities, abusing psychoreactive substances, and indulging in obnoxious and threatening behavior."

"Huh?" Basil's imagination reeled. "So you mean . . . you're talking about a Luonli *gravbiker gang?*"

(Slightly huffy defensiveness.) "Any race of social beings is bound to have its social deviates. And the most infallible way to bring out the worst in those deviates is to give them access to a culture so far behind their own as to be helpless. When a sufficiently wide technological gulf separates two societies, the fate of the weaker depends entirely on the morality of the stronger."

"But, but," Basil stammered, horrified by the implications, "couldn't your government—your police, or whatever—do something?"

"Oh, something was done in the end—something rather drastic. But not before things had occurred which left permanent scars in the folk-memories of the afflicted regions. You see, we had no 'government' that you would have found recognizable as such. Large, permanent organizations do not come naturally to us, descended as we are from solitary animals which formed temporary unities-of-convenience around charismatic leaders. The suppression of the aberrational individuals who had taken refuge on Earth was not so much a law enforcement operation, in your sense, as it was a—" *(Uncertainty as to whether meaning is being, or can be, accurately conveyed.)* "—feud of honor. Delays were unavoidable. It was a matter of our racial peculiarities."

"It would seem," Basil said, carefully keeping his surface thoughts as emotionless as his voice, "that we humans paid a high price for these . . . peculiarities."

"Oh, so did we." *(Bleak melancholy.)* "So did we. For there was no widespread union to coordinate efforts at survival when our homeworld fell victim to a catastrophe beyond any possibility—even for us—of a technological solution."

Basil's capacity for astonishment finally reached the overload point as he realized that he was about to be given the answer to yet another mystery: the fate of the mighty prehistoric civilization that had scattered the Luonli among the stars. "What happened?" he asked in a small voice.

"Our home sun was an atypical one, unduly massive for its spectral class—seemingly too massive to have remained stable long enough for sentient life to evolve. But our inexplicable good fortune could not continue forever. As the star aged, freakish internal changes overtook it and it flared with almost no warning, wiping the homeworld clean of life."

"But," Basil protested, obscurely resentful of the Luon's matter-of-factness in describing transcendent horror, "you were already established on many other worlds, the worlds you'd terraformed."

"True. But, for the reasons I have explained, there could be no mass migration to join the few individuals able to adapt to those worlds. The fate of the species was in those individuals' hands."

"Shouldn't they have been enough? One thing we've learned about you is that you're fully functional hermaphrodites."

"Yes, even one individual per planet should have sufficed. Our lives are very long by your standards, and births are infrequent among us—an evolutionary necessity, for no ecosystem can support very many beings such as ourselves. So a long time passed before we came to the realization that we were even more finely attuned to our native environment than we had supposed. For our equivalent of your germ plasm began a slow deterioration, or unraveling. We gradually ceased to reproduce. We began to die out."

Basil waited, conscious of the inadequacy of words, as the Luon sat in a brooding mental silence which held the suggestion of an emotion beyond human capacity to define or feel, just as the tale it was telling was beyond mere tragedy.

"Few of us are left now," the Luon finally continued. "I am the only one on this world. On certain other worlds, we have died out altogether. But our lives are very long. The process of extinction takes an inordinate amount of time. We have watched with interest as you humans rose to civilization and later set out to colonize the stars in slower-than-light ships—astonishing, considering the brevity of your lifespans." *(Slight but unmistakable bitterness.)* "Indeed, our amazement at your species' determination almost exceeded our envy of its adaptability. We watched as you finally learned to outpace light and used that knowledge to form a federation. We watched as that federation devolved into interstellar states whose wars grew ever more brutal as technology advanced and imperial ambitions awoke. We watched as an empire finally arose and enforced peace."

"And now," Basil cut in bleakly, "you're watching as the Empire dies."

"Ah, you speak of the 'New Humans,' as I believe they call themselves." *(Bemusement.)* "I am afraid we have a great deal of difficulty with the entire concept of ideology. And *their* ideology is particularly incomprehensible to us—as is the allure it holds for humans."

"Not *all* humans are taken in by it!" Basil protested hotly.

"Enough, though, to have gained political control of several Imperial sectors," the Luon gently reminded him. "To the extent one understands the concept of the 'state'— admittedly foreign to my race—one must question the survivability of a state which allows a political movement inimical to its very existence to function."

"The Solarian Empire has never interfered with individual worlds' internal forms of government, as long as they acknowledge the Emperor's sovereignty and keep the peace. That's why it's worked. The Draconis Empire tried to rule as a vast, uniform anthill-state. And it collapsed! People accepted Anton the Great's restoration of it under a new name because he pledged to respect the right of the various worlds' cultures to be themselves." All at once, something slumped inside Basil. "Yes, I suppose you could say that caused the Empire to lack antibodies against this particular virus. We'd thought totalitarianism was safely tucked away in dusty history books."

"The New Humans indignantly deny any resemblance between themselves and the late unlamented Draconis Empire," the Luon pointed out.

"Sure," Basil snapped. "They're not trying to set themselves up as a master race and genetically engineer the rest of us into specialized subraces. Oh, no! In *their* version of Utopia, everybody will be equal . . . and alike!" He stopped abruptly, wondering why he was pouring out his anger to this alien.

"Such vehemence in one so young!" The Luon's mental tone held none of the sarcasm or condescension for which Basil suspiciously searched. "You obviously feel strongly about these matters. This must be why you sought admission to the Imperial Deep Space Fleet Academy."

"Why, yes. I leave for Sigma Draconis tomorrow. How did you know?"

"As I indicated before, I knew your great-grandfather."

"Yes, you did mention that. But it doesn't explain how you know so much about *me*. And . . . and why have you been telling me all these things? Things that humans have been wondering about since—"

(Silent laughter.) "Patience! All these questions can wait. For now, you need to rest. We must return you to your aircar early tomorrow. It would hardly do to miss your departure on such a momentous journey."

Basil became aware that he was, indeed, desperately weary. It hadn't even entered his consciousness before, any more than hunger had. But now he could barely keep his eyes open. . . . He blinked them angrily. "No! You've got to tell me—"

"Sleep now." The Luon's pseudo-voice tolled in his head like a bell, and he could only obey.

Again the stinging wind brought Basil awake, clutched against the Luon's side in flight. But this time his eyes were dazzled by the rising sun, for they were headed east.

"Your pardon. You were deeply asleep, but I thought it best to start without further delay lest you be late for your departure." Even as it thought these words, the Luon began circling downward. Soon Basil could make out his aircar below.

"How did you know where . . . ?"

"Given the trail on which you were hiking, this seemed the logical landing area." The Luon's placid tone quieted Basil's arising suspicions. Then they landed, and the Luon gently set him down.

He looked at the familiar aircar, and the sight seemed to trigger an oppressive awareness of how hungry he was, of how gummy his mouth felt, of what his mother would say when he finally called in, and of all the dreary, mundane things his consciousness had held no room for since the previous afternoon. Like one awakened too suddenly from too vivid a dream, he felt a leaden depression tinged with vague anxieties and nameless apprehensions. "Uh, thank you for everything," he mumbled.

"No thanks are necessary. Farewell." And with that curt thought, the Luon rose with a thunderous beat of its vast wings.

Basil watched his rescuer gain altitude and turn toward the west. And as he did, his mind seemed to abruptly regain its ability to function and all the questions he'd wanted to ask came crashing back into his awareness as one. He took a deep breath and opened his mouth to shout after the Luon . . . but there were so many questions, and for some reason he couldn't seem to frame any of them. Infuriatingly, all that came out was: "But I don't even know your name!"

"You may call me Shenyilu." The strange syllables came as a mental whisper as he watched the Luon recede against the distant mountains, gleaming coppery-gold in the morning sun. He watched until that gleam grew tiny and vanished. Then he returned to his own world, where his rescue by a Luon created a sensation that he left behind when he departed for Sigma Draconis. But he didn't tell anyone the things he had learned. Indeed, he felt an odd disinclination to do so, and the memories grew dim and confused in his own mind. And so it remained for a long time.

CHAPTER TWO

Prometheus (Sigma Draconis II), 3891 C.E.

"Now, then." Professor Gramont stroked his silvery goatee and surveyed the second-term Imperial History class with a benevolent gaze which fooled none of his students. "We have reached a period less than one and three-quarters standard century in the past. Which means that we have, in the eyes of a few purists such as myself, practically left history behind and emerged into the sordid realm of current events. Nevertheless, we must persevere.

"As a few of you may recall, when we last met we completed our discussion of the Empire's deterioration in the middle and late thirty-seventh century. To recapitulate: Armin II, a no-nonsense pragmatist disinclined to tolerate the inefficiencies and irrationalities of the Empire's traditional laissez-faire approach, had pursued a policy of centralization which his military successes seemed to validate. It was precisely that centralization which led to the decline following his death. Do you recall why . . . Cadet Castellan?"

As usual, Gramont had let his voice trail off soporifically before striking like an adder with the name of his current victim. But this was an easy question. Basil came to a seated position of attention, as they all unhesitatingly did for this elderly civilian. "Because, sir, it made the Empire's health more dependent on having a strong, capable emperor on the throne."

"Yes . . . and that happy eventuality was rare to the point of virtual nonexistence in the century following Armin's death."

Even this late in the course, there was a faint rustling sound of unease in the room at hearing the Empire's past treated with the irreverence that Gramont habitually displayed. But everyone admitted to the Academy was of unimpeachable loyalty, verified by registered psis. (The military was, as ever, an exception to certain fundamental rights.) So liberties could be permitted here which were unthinkable in the secondary school settings to which they were accustomed. And there was a persistent rumor that the urbane old man acted as a kind of agent provocateur to aid in the ruthless winnowing of the first- and second-term classes. Whatever the truth of that, he clearly enjoyed himself to the hilt.

"But now," he continued, "we've come to the final outcome of that period's trends: the Rajasthara Usurpation. You have, of course, completed the assigned reading and therefore are conversant with how Delmore Rajasthara, an Imperial minister, came to power and attempted to found his own dynasty. You are also aware that his fifteen-year reign was an uninterrupted disaster. You would be aware of that even if—nonsensical assumption!—you hadn't done the reading, for this is one of those rare instances where the popular perception of history is accurate. The question we must now consider is *why* Rajasthara was such an abject failure."

This time Gramont didn't pose the question to an individual but paused to invite volunteers. The cadets squirmed and exchanged nervous glances, for no one was quite sure what Gramont was up to. The answer was so self-evident that there *had* to be a trick lurking behind it. The silence stretched before a hand finally shot up. Gramont smiled. "Ah, I knew I could count on you, Cadet Rady."

Sonja Rady ignored the sarcasm. She swept her auburn hair back in a characteristic gesture and answered the question without preamble. "Because, sir, he was . . . he was a *usurper!* A damned traitor! He deposed the infant emperor for whom he was supposed to be acting as guardian. Then, when the legitimate successor vanished, he set out to loot the Empire for his own profit. The wonder is that it took as long as it did for a rebellion to break out against him. *Everyone* knows that." With the last words she glared at Gramont as though she found such an obvious question insulting.

There was a collective hiss of indrawn breath as the other cadets awaited thunderbolts and tried to pretend they were somewhere else. But Basil gave Rady a glance of admiration for her guts. He knew her by sight, as a fellow Nyjorder and for having a temperament as fiery as her hair. Now, though, he wondered if she might have gone too far. But Gramont only smiled.

"*Brava*, Cadet Rady! You have forcefully expressed the view of Rajasthara that practically all Imperial subjects take for granted. Indeed, it is so obvious to most that they find it difficult to put into words." He gave Rady's classmates an arch look. "Unfortunately, it is also quite wrong."

Rady started to open her mouth, but Gramont raised a forestalling hand. "Do not misunderstand me. Rajasthara was undeniably a usurper. But he was not an opportunistic adventurer looking only to line his own pockets. He was, in fact, something far more dangerous: an idealist. He firmly believed that the first two and a half centuries of the old Solarian Federation represented the high point of human history to date. He was, of course, hardly alone in this. The early Federation's success in keeping the peace caused those who lived in the war-torn centuries that followed to think better of that era than it perhaps deserved. By now, idealization of the period has fossilized into consensus. But Rajasthara went beyond idealization. He sought an actual return to the institutions of the twenty-eighth and twenty-ninth centuries . . . as he conceived them. Those last four words are crucial, for he was an historical ignoramus. His notion of the early Federation actually bore a closer resemblance to its predecessor, the

United Nations of Earth. Ah, you have a question, Cadet Bogdan?"

"Yes, sir." The rumbling basso came from the back of the room, where Torval Bogdan filled a desk. He was a heavy-planet type, thick of bone and muscle. But he wasn't short like most natives of such worlds, which meant his home must orbit far from its sun, where size had been an advantage in resisting cold. None of the other cadets were certain just where that home was, for none of them had gotten to know him well. He wasn't really hostile, but his size and obvious strength were somewhat inhibiting, as was the fact that he was several years older than the rest of them. A former enlisted Marine, he had a double row of decorations that contrasted with the others' virginal tunics. Quite simply, his classmates had little in common with him.

"I don't quite understand, sir," he continued. "Last term, we learned that the Federation arose in conscious opposition to the U.N."

"Quite so, Cadet. Nevertheless, the two had become an inextricable muddle in Rajasthara's mind. To him, the solution to the Empire's problems lay in the socialist economics which the U.N. had continued to espouse throughout its seven centuries of existence. In particular, he rummaged up an ancient sage named Marx whose version of socialism had been the intellectual community's established pseudo-religion in the twentieth century when the U.N. was founded."

Bogdan's face—wide across the cheekbones, as muscular as the rest of him—took on a frown, and his eyes became slits of concentration. "I gather, sir, that this Marx's economic philosophy had a historical record of success."

"Oh, no. It failed with awe-inspiring consistency. In fact, states based on it had begun to collapse even before the twentieth century was over, leaving the corpses of scores of millions of people they had found inconvenient, and the untold human wreckage of destroyed societies."

Bogdan shook his head slowly, like a man certain he must be missing something. "Then, sir . . . why was he a 'sage'?"

Gramont smiled benignly. "My dear Cadet Bogdan, you obviously have the good fortune to be unacquainted with the intellectual community—the 'herd of independent minds' as someone called it long ago. I, for my sins, know it from the inside. But a full explanation would take longer than I am allowed by the curriculum. For now, the point is that an ideology's catastrophic failure in the practical arena merely demonstrates its Higher Truth to its anointed. And, more importantly, the anointed's ability to perceive that Higher Truth proves—to their own satisfaction, at least—their moral and intellectual superiority to the common ruck which allows itself to be deceived by mere facts. Their right to control the lives of that common ruck—for its own good, of course—follows as a natural consequence."

"Like the New Humans," Rady said quietly.

Dead silence fell in the room, partly because they were supposed to avoid all mention of current politics (and especially of the conflict whose inevitability was still officially denied), but mostly because Rady had done the unforgivable by speaking without being recognized by the instructor. But Gramont only smiled his alarmingly gentle smile.

"That is outside the scope of this course," he said quietly. "I'll only leave you with this thought: I've often reflected that we might learn more from history if it didn't bore us to insensibility with its repetitiousness."

Then he proceeded briskly with his lecture. But Basil wasn't listening. He made eye contact with Sonja Rady across the room. It only lasted an instant, but in that silent instant he felt a sense of kinship that needed no words.

The moon Atlas was nearly full, and its red-infused light rippled on the darkened water as Basil crossed the footbridge into Oporto.

Ahead, the district that existed for the sole purpose of separating cadets from their money was a garish blaze of light. Its growth had kept pace with the Academy's over the past decade or so, as the Empire's traditionally modest military establishment had expanded. The Academy wasn't

even the sole source of commissioned officers for the Deep
Space Fleet any more, only the most prestigious. And the
hereditary scions of the old professional officer class were
now lost among the socially miscellaneous parvenus who
swarmed among the new buildings that spread in circle
after ever-more-characterless circle around the cluster of
soaring towers, cloistered courtyards and spacious parade
grounds which in the popular mind *was* the Academy.

Socially miscellaneous parvenus like me, Basil thought
wryly. His academic record alone would not have sufficed
to secure him this appointment. He still wasn't altogether
sure what *had* sufficed, although he knew his mother's family
had included Fleet officers a few generations back.

He quickened his step. Soon he was off the bridge and
amid the gaudy raucousness of Oporto. Here, he reflected,
was as good a place as any to feel rootless. The standardized
nano-grown structures housing the bars, restaurants,
gaming houses, "escort" agencies and all the rest disguised
their sameness behind a diverse array of decors. But the
staffs of all the establishments, however bogus-exotic their
costumery, generally belonged to the local populace, whose
diverse original genotypes had long since blended into a
recognizable type. The cadets and other Fleet personnel
thronging the streets showed a far greater variety of
features and coloring above the collars of their uniforms,
although two centuries of the Unification Wars and the
Draconis Empire with their wholesale forced population
transfers, followed by four centuries of freedom of
movement, had pretty much robbed the old ethnic
stereotypes of whatever resemblance to reality they had
ever possessed.

He ran a finger around the inside of his collar in a vain
effort to reduce its discomfort. Prometheus was a coolish
planet, but this was in its subtropics. With the onset of spring
the uniforms' imprinted circuitry had turned them white
and their memory fabric had rearranged itself into the more
open weave that regulations prescribed for summer
planetside wear. But this was a muggy night and he wished

he could have worn civvies. Out of the question, of course, for an underclassman. Only now, in his second term, could he get liberty at all.

He walked a short distance along Fulgham Road, turned right, and entered the Friend in Need Pub of Gamma Pavonis ("Authentic Tandoori cuisine of Olde England"). He passed through the restaurant that fronted the street and ascended a short flight of steps to a bar paneled in what purported to be wood, where he ordered a pint of what purported to be "bitter." He waved away a professional hostess and looked around. The room's windows of many small panes overlooked the river with its reflected Atlas-light. Seated at the bar and the tables were a number of cadets; it was fairly early in the evening, but the Friend in Need had a reputation as a good place for preliminary lubrication before commencing serious slumming further up Fulgham Road. He wasn't sure he was in the mood for that—its novelties had worn thin earlier in the term. Indeed, he wasn't certain what had brought him over the footbridge tonight, beyond pure restlessness and the usual cadet conviction that it was somehow *wrong* to not take liberty when one had the chance. He chuckled to himself, tossed off his beer and ordered another as a couple to his right stood up and moved away from the bar.

"Well! I'd know a Nyjord accent anywhere."

He glanced sharply to the right, where Sonja Rady sat three stools away. He wondered how he could have missed her auburn head even in this dim light. "Right," he said, drawling out the word to indicate the accent. "Not many of us here. Mind if I join you?" He indicated the now-empty stool next to her.

"Suit yourself. The stool's empty." Her usual surliness seemed moderated a trifle. "Why not? Coming from a backwater like Nu Phoenicis, we'd better stick together." Her eyes narrowed as he shifted seats. "I know you. Castellan, from old Gramont's ImpHist."

"Right," he said again, certain that she'd really recognized him from the first. "I thought you'd gone over the line with him the other day."

She snorted and chugged at least half of her beer. "That supercilious old gasbag! I don't know why I let him get to me. Still, anybody who can keep me awake in a history class must be doing something right." She gave him another close look and changed the subject. "What part of Nyjord are you from? It took me a while to recognize your accent."

So she *hadn't* only just noticed him after all, he thought, inordinately pleased. "Central Vaasaland, the high plains just east of the Kraakens. And unless I miss my guess, you're from the Seabreak Islands."

"Not bad," she acknowledged. "Although my mother came from closer to your part of the planet, on the northwest coast of Vaasaland."

"Aha! That explains it. I thought you looked like you might be part Old Nyjorder. Not many of them in the Seabreaks."

"Small chance of anybody thinking that in your case," she said, eyeing him.

He acknowledged the point with a wry expression. In contrast to her auburn-haired, straight-featured, blue-eyed looks, he was dark olive of complexion, with wavy hair of a brown so dark as to be practically black. His eyes were little lighter than his hair, and he suspected that his nose was going to develop a decided hook as he got older. Only in his tallness did he resemble the Nyjorder of traditional popular image.

"A maternal great-grandfather of mine was from off-world," he explained. "His family were some kind of political refugees during the Rajasthara Usurpation."

"So that's why you were right off the mark with Gramont's first question the other day. He was talking family history for you. You must have gotten the inside story on it directly from your great-granddad."

"Hardly. I never met him. Besides, he was just an infant then. The rest of his family got killed in the fighting and he was adopted by the Marczalis, who didn't exactly belong to the original colonial stock themselves—any more than the Castellans did. But that's all right," he added with a grin. "By now we're more Nyjorder than the Nyjorders—

even by the standards of the Vaasaland high plains!"

"Right! Where men are men, women are scarce, and sheep are nervous." She finished off the rest of her beer. "Let's get out of here. This dump is so close to the Academy it might as well be the Club. Hell, this whole part of Oporto is practically a Fleet franchise! Maybe things are a little more interesting further up Fulgham Road." Without waiting for a response, she inserted her credcard into the slot in front of her stool. Then she slid to her feet with a lithe motion and headed for the door without waiting to see if he was following.

All right, Basil thought, *so she needs to play the tough cookie.* At least she took his mind off whatever it was that had been preying on it. He paid for his beer and quickly followed her out.

Things did indeed get, if not more interesting, then at least less phony as they proceeded along Fulgham Road. Fleet whites grew sparser, and the buildings grew older and more eccentric. Most had originally been homes, of a distinctive half-timbered style dating centuries back in this part of Prometheus, but had been converted to commercial use. As was typical in these latitudes, they were generally surrounded by flowering plants and trees of both local and imported gene-engineered Earth origin. (The Academy's schedule was based on the standard Earth year, but by sheer coincidence these waning days of the term corresponded to local spring.)

Sonja was unimpressed. "Here we are," she complained, "in the Sigma Draconis system itself, and they had to put the Academy next door to this piss-hole town!"

He knew what she meant. So towering was this system's role in human history that many people had difficulty remembering whether Homo sapiens had evolved under the light of Sol or that of Sigma Draconis. In the popular outworld imagination, Prometheus meant the apotheosis of technological civilization: exciting cities seemingly wrought of solidified light, awesome relics of a millennium and a half of history . . . and, at night, the blood-infused light of

Atlas as a constant reminder of that history's grimmest pages.

But the last was all that the cadets generally got to see.

"Yes," he agreed, "this is about as out-of-the-way as you can get and still be on Prometheus. The closest we get to the interesting stuff is looking down at it when we arrive." He would never forget the moment when the orbit-to-surface shuttle had crossed the terminator from day to night, and all at once the continental outlines had become easier to pick out, for they were ablaze with light. "When we only get liberty for one day at a time—" (one of the 37.6-standard-hour local days, but still . . .) "—it's not worth the trip, and wouldn't be even if money was no object." He grinned. "Now if we just had a Sword Clans teleporter to flick us there instantaneously—"

"Don't tell me you believe in *that* shit! All my life I've heard about the super-powered technology the Sword Clans are supposed to have, out there wherever they live. You name it, they've got it!" She snorted. "I suspect they're really just one more bunch of ragged-assed Beyonders. But people need to believe in miracles."

"Well, the stories make a kind of sense," Basil argued as they emerged into a kind of square or plaza, surrounded by larger structures which mostly held restaurants and entertainment establishments. "I mean, if they've spent centuries locked in war with nonhumans who copied their own early-Federation-era technology, they've had a pretty good incentive to innovate. And, being outside the Empire, they're free of the Society's influence."

"That's another thing I wonder about. How much influence does the Society *really* have? Do people just *need* to believe that we'd be more advanced than we are if it wasn't for these sinister old men manipulating everything behind the scenes because they want us all to go back to our 'natural state' of being subsistence farmers? Maybe that and the Sword Clans crock are just variations on a theme: imaginary technological fixes for all our problems, lying either far out in space or in the realm of things that were prevented from happening." Unconsciously, but not unnoticed by Basil, she'd let her habitual rough-surfaced defensive shell slip, revealing the questing intelligence beneath. "Ever think about how our civilization is haunted by things we know very little about except that they exist? The Society, the Sword Clans—"

"The Luonli?" It was out of Basil's mouth before he had made a conscious decision to say it. The memories had almost blended into the mists of old dreams, and he wondered what power they could still have over his voice.

But Sonja stopped, turned toward him and gave him a level blue regard. Her mouth started to open. . . .

Then her eyes focused on something beyond him, and her parting lips formed the words, "Oh, shit!"

He turned around and followed her gaze. Streets debouched on the square from four directions, and from one of them a column of marching figures was emerging, carrying signs and torches. They all had the same close-cropped hair and wore the same plain gray garment of loose trousers and tunic, both designed to deemphasize the differences between genders and individuals.

"Shit," Sonja repeated. "I've heard that there were New Humans—or New Human imitators—even here in the Sigma Draconis system, but I assumed they were all in the big cities."

"Certainly not here in this Fleet town," Basil agreed. "Of course, these might be imported. . . ." He watched as the white-clad Fleet personnel in the square drew back in an angry wave. The demonstrators, sensing an advantage, pressed hard, waving fists and screaming slogans. Most of the local civilians in the square scattered, but a fair number clustered with the Fleet uniforms. The New Humans might not be unknown on this world, but they were far from popular.

Basil grabbed Sonja's upper arm. "Let's get out of here. This looks ugly, and you know what happens to cadets who're involved in any sort of politically-related brawling, regardless of who started it."

She gave a tense nod, glaring in the direction of the

demonstrators, and let him pull her back the way they'd come. But then things began to get out of hand.

Basil couldn't tell who had made the first move, for the scuffle in the middle distance was already under way when he first heard the change in the shouting's timbre. All at once, as though by some spontaneous chemical reaction, fights were breaking out all over the square. The demonstrators surged forward in a tide that pushed the figures in front of them back until he and Sonja found themselves in a press of struggling, screaming bodies.

A swung sign knocked Basil off balance and a gray-clad body crashed into him, breaking his hold on Sonja and grappling with him. Practiced mental exercises allowed his combat training to take over, directing his movements from a calm storm center. He freed his arms with a well-executed breaking technique and delivered a short punch to the side of his attacker's head. Then he looked around in the chaos until he spotted Sonja, just in time to see her deliver a viciously accurate kick to a demonstrator's crotch. He plowed through the crush toward her, and had almost reached her side when a female demonstrator appeared in his path, clawing for his face. He stopped to fend her off with a sweep of his arm. But the pause allowed a fresh knot of attackers to crash into him and Sonja, bowling the two of them over by sheer weight of numbers. He tried to go into fetal position, curling protectively around his vitals, but arched his back with a gasp of pain when someone punched him from behind in the kidneys. Then all he could see were the figures that covered him, and all he could feel were their blows. . . .

Suddenly, he could see the night sky over the square from where he lay, for two of his attackers had been pulled, no, *lifted* bodily off him. Then their heads were brought together with a definitive *clunk*. Torval Bogdan, who had been holding one with each hand, dropped them unceremoniously and turned his attention to another demonstrator. He parried a blow with his right arm and brought the left around to deliver a punch that drove his massive fist wrist-deep into the fellow's midriff. As the demonstrator doubled over with a whistling expulsion of air, Torval brought a knee up into his face, sending him flying over backwards trailing a spray of blood, to rebound from a wall and lie still.

Then two more demonstrators landed on Torval's back and started to topple him forward. Basil shook the pain and confusion out of his head and staggered to his feet. He grabbed one of Torval's attackers and swung him around until they were both off balance. He pivoted on his right heel and delivered a side-kick that sent the New Human staggering backward . . . into Sonja, who dropped him with a precise chop to the base of the neck from behind. Basil was thus able to get a good view as Torval heaved his second attacker up over his head and hurled him against the nearest wall.

It was enough for the remaining New Humans in the vicinity. They proceeded to put as much distance as possible between themselves and the massive heavy-planet man. Basil, Sonja and their rescuer were suddenly alone as the riot moved on. "Come on," Torval said in his bass rumble, motioning toward a side street. "The Patrol will be here any time, and they've got no sense of humor about a little light exercise like this."

As though on cue, a contra-grav personnel carrier dropped from the sky in a blaze of stroboscopic lights. Its wailing siren drowned out the protests of its overstressed impellers as they braked it to a halt just short of the pavement. Its sides fell open and impact-armored men sprang out, plying their weapons. Those weapons produced no sound, and no light except the pale flicker of laser guide beams, but people began to fall in swathes of immobile bodies.

"They're paralyzing everybody," Sonja gasped.

"Come on," Torval repeated, giving them each a shove in the direction of the side street. "I've got a slider parked down this way."

Cadets weren't supposed to have private vehicles, but Basil was in no mood to worry about that. He let Torval's push, which the other probably thought of as gentle, propel his battered body out of the square. "But," he blurted, "they'll be watching the approaches to the Academy . . ."

"Who said anything about going straight back? We'll get out of town and head downriver to a place I know. We can lie low there for the rest of the night and get back in time for morning muster. We can also get something to drink there. You two look like you could use it."

Basil and Sonja needed no further persuading. The three hurried along the narrow street, past an old building whose windows were curtained behind iron grates, muffling the sounds of music from within. The noise from the square diminished behind them.

"Up ahead." Torval pointed toward a battered-looking civilian slider parked under one of the street's inadequate lights.

It was at that moment that a harsh glare bathed them from above, and a whine of impellers announced a descending aircar.

"Shit!" Torval rumbled. "They must be sealing off the approaches to the square. Come on!" He turned to run.

"Stop." Basil didn't really raise his voice. But the massive ex-Marine stopped, so abruptly that Sonja, who had started to break into a run, bumped into him. "They must have already seen us. If we run, they'll just paralyze us with no questions asked."

Torval gave him an odd look. "They might just do that anyway."

"Maybe. But maybe we can brazen our way through this."

Neither Torval nor Sonja said anything more, because it was too late to run. The Patrol aircar—smaller than the personnel carrier in the square—settled to the street between them and the slider. Its gull-wing doors swung upward, and its two occupants got out and advanced toward them.

Sonja and Torval looked silently at Basil. He wondered what they expected him to do. *Execute your brilliant plan, of course,* he gibed at himself. He fell into a stance of innocent nonchalance and called out to the Patrolmen in a voice he hoped sounded tipsily casual. "What's the matter? Trouble over in the square?"

The rating in charge didn't raise his weapon. He sounded bored. "All right, you three, get into the aircar. We're rounding up everybody involved in the riot."

"Huh? What're you talking about?" Basil shifted to righteous indignation. "What riot?"

" 'What riot?' " the Patrolman echoed sarcastically. "Don't gimme that. We saw you coming from that direction."

"Uh. . . ." Basil's brain thrashed about frantically inside his skull. *What am I supposed to say? What else is down there?* Then an idea came, and his voice acted on it without waiting for his mind to fully formulate it. "Well," he said, shifting tone and expression to embarrassment, "actually, the truth is . . . we were at the house back there." He jerked his chin back the way they'd come, at the old house with the glowing, curtained windows." Hastily: "Yes, I know it's off limits, but *everybody* goes there!"

It was a pure shot in the dark. He didn't know for certain that the building was one of the whorehouses that catered to cadets of both genders. He held his breath until his head spun . . . then gradually released it as he realized that the Patrolman, who doubtless knew this district well, was thoughtfully silent.

"Hmm . . . I dunno. You look roughed up, like you've been in a fight."

"Hey," Basil protested, "have you *seen* some of those girls in there?"

The face inside the impact armor's open visor grinned briefly. Then the regulation police-issue expression was back in place. "Still, I'd probably better take you in. Come along quietly, and we won't have to paralyze you." This time the weapon-muzzle did rise slightly.

From behind him, Basil could hear the faint sounds of his companions shifting stance. Would the fiery woman or the combat-trained heavy-planet man try something crazy? Possibly. He stood a little straighter and looked the Patrolman directly in the eye. The fellow was pretty young, and only a second class petty officer.

"You have no probable cause to arrest us," Basil said in a

quiet voice into which something new had entered. "And we don't require an escort back to our quarters. Let us pass."

For a moment, the tableau held. Cadets were technically in the fifth enlisted grade, but strictly for purposes of the pay scale. That was one of the first things made clear to them in their indoctrination—they weren't in anybody's chain of command, including and especially members of the Patrol. But the impact-armored figure stood silently, his face a battleground of conflicting emotions—resentment of educated young twits, apprehension bred of the knowledge that those twits would one day be commissioned officers, and . . . something else. Basil pressed what he hoped was an advantage. "Besides, you ought to hurry. They probably need your help in the square, rounding up the people *really* responsible: the New Humans."

All at once, Basil knew he'd won his gamble. The Patrolman's expression at the words "New Humans" suggested regret that he was armed with a non-lethal weapon. His eyes slid away from Basil's. "All right," he growled. "Just keep moving on out of this area. And—" a final face-saving assertion of authority "—stay away from places like that in the future. Come on." The last was addressed to his subordinate. The duo stalked off toward the square.

Basil turned to his companions. They were both looking at him with the same odd expression Torval's face had worn earlier. "Wait till they're out of sight," he cautioned. "Remember, the slider's non-reg."

"Right," the ex-Marine nodded. "Hope they hurry, though. Now *I* need a drink."

The slider soon left Oporto behind, its vectored impellers keeping it a few inches above the riverside road as it sped south. The river widened, residences thinned out and the mixed semitropical vegetation grew thicker before they entered a stretch of riverbank where fishing and recreational boats lay tied to docks, swaying gently in the Atlas-light.

Soon they came to an arrogantly shabby building in the old local style, extending out over the water on pilings. A holo sign announced PEACHY'S TAVERN in glowing midair letters.

This was unfamiliar territory to Basil, who had never gotten outside Oporto's Fleet district, and the lack of Fleet uniforms in the tavern did nothing to allay his unease. But there were no signs of hostility from the clientele as they entered, and Torval was obviously known here.

"Peachy is an ex-Marine," he explained after they'd been seated on the verandah that overlooked the river and were supplied with a bottle of good-quality local whisky (which meant good-quality anywhere) at an amazingly low price. "He and I went through a few things together. He got out, while I let my CO talk me into applying to the Academy. Peachy thinks the idea of me as an officer is a real knee-slapper. Gives me a hard time about it whenever I'm here." He gave a fatalistic shrug and raised his glass. "At least he doesn't water his booze."

Basil gave his own glass a slightly apprehensive look— Torval hadn't even ordered ice. But . . . he raised it, Torval gave a toast in what was presumably the native language of wherever he came from, and they all drank. Basil didn't choke, to his pleased surprise.

"Uh, it's a little belated, but thanks for your help back there in the square," he said.

"Think nothing of it. I recognized you two from ImpHist, and I happened to be in the right place at the right time. Besides . . . I've never had all that much use for New Humans."

"These tonight were just local twerps dressing up like them and mouthing their slogans," Sonja opined. "If suicide was currently chic, they'd be cutting their wrists." Her expression suggested that she wasn't convinced this would be an altogether bad idea.

"Probably. Still . . ." Torval's voice remained level, but his ruddy face clouded and he took another pull on his drink. "When the movement was just starting, they set up one of their communes on my homeworld. I saw what they were doing to people who dared to disagree with them . . . and the families of those people. I got mad enough to get in some trouble—I was just a kid then, you see. Anyway, things reached the point where it seemed like a good idea to leave. I knocked around awhile, then joined the Marines."

"Well," Sonja observed, "I guess you're the only one of us who has a good, sound, personal reason for hating the New Humans. With me, it's . . . well, just a feeling. A damned *strong* feeling—revulsion, in fact, at the whole notion that human individuality must be crushed out of existence because it doesn't fit some half-assed theory. But still, just a feeling. Same with you, I suppose," she added, turning to Basil.

He didn't reply at first, for he was recalling a dragon to whom he had poured forth his anger. Then he blinked away the awakened memories and smiled at Sonja. "Yes, I suppose so. But it's *not* just a gut reaction. History shows—"

"Oh, shit!" Sonja tossed off the rest of her drink and reached for the bottle. "Might have known we'd get a history lecture. Word is that old Gramont wants you for his honors program next term."

Basil refused to be distracted. He leaned forward and spoke with an intensity that got their attention. "But it's true. And here on this world, of all places, we can't ignore it. Not with *that* in the sky." And he pointed at the near-disc of Atlas in the sky, veined with red like a bloodshot eye in a pattern that nature had never wrought.

Atlas, like Old Earth's Luna, was technically not a moon at all but rather the lesser component of a binary planet system. But Atlas was more obvious about it, with its almost-half-Earth-standard gravity, its thin nitrogen-and-carbon-dioxide atmosphere and its feeble but measurable plate tectonics. In almost any system but Sigma Draconis it would have been a prime candidate for terraforming. But with the marvelously Earthlike world of Prometheus available, to say nothing of the system's fabulous asteroidal riches, why bother? By the time Prometheus had gotten crowded, its people had had much else to occupy their minds—like breaking free from, and then overthrowing, the U.N., and organizing the Solarian Federation.

Later, after Prometheus had felt the kiss of thermonuclear fire in the course of an attempted coup and the Federation had gone to Old Earth to grow old and then dissolve into a wraith, the governors-general of Sigma Draconis had dusted off old terraforming studies. Still later the founder of the Draconis Empire, whose name most people still could not bring themselves to pronounce without a conscious effort, had rushed their plans to completion. He had, after all, had unlimited resources. He'd also had a purpose: to build his capital city in the lighter gravity of Atlas which would, he had believed, remove restraints from his architectural fancies and extend his life span.

He'd been right about the first, but as for the second, the low gravity had proven as unavailing as the anagathic treatments to which he, like about six percent of the human race, had not been amenable. So the Founder had had a palace dwarfing most of history's cities in which to let the fear of death gnaw away at his vitals and finally kill him. And the intriguers who swirled around his feeble successor had wiped his recorded consciousness from the great computer into which it had been downloaded even before the rebels had arrived to sweep that successor into oblivion. Those rebels had then vented a decade and a half of rage on the world from which he had ruled. Their fleet had hung in orbit around Atlas, tearing at its surface with antimatter long after every living thing on it was dead, blasting its atmosphere into space, breaking open its crust in a cataclysm that had left its entire surface a pattern of cracks through which hellfire still glowed after four centuries. The stories about the number of days it had seemed to burn in the skies of Prometheus were doubtless exaggerated.

"Afterwards," Basil concluded, "four years of civil war among the rebel leaders was enough to remind people of why they'd once been willing to accept the unity the Draconis Empire had offered. But that had turned out to be a cure worse than the disease. And yet nobody really wanted a restoration of the old states; that would just have started the whole nightmare of the Unification Wars all over again, until some state or other wiped out all its rivals and founded *another* Draconis Empire. Unity was needed to prevent that—a unity that didn't try to impose any one pattern on the various societies and cultures. That's what the Solarian Empire is about. That's what the New Humans have forgotten."

Sonja looked troubled. "We also can't ignore what's happened to the Empire since then. The corruption, the waste, the growth of the Great Houses' power and wealth at the expense of everybody else, the influence of the synthetics at court . . ." Her two companions unconsciously winced at the last, for it was a very sore point. The Draconis Empire, with its super-soldiers and other specialized castes, had burned into the human soul an almost superstitious abhorrence of vat-grown artificial persons created from modified human genetic material. But over the centuries they had made a stealthy comeback, for they had their uses— especially as court functionaries. After all, no one had to worry about them as rivals for the Imperial title. But that, of course, left them with nothing to do except plot to wield power behind the throne from which they, like all such clones, were absolutely barred.

"All that," Sonja continued, "is what the New Humans claim their movement has arisen in opposition to. They couldn't have gotten as far as they have if there wasn't some grain of truth to it."

"Oh, yes," Basil said—absently, for he couldn't take his eyes off the face of Atlas, an ill-fitting puzzle through whose cracks the blood of the billions the Draconis Empire had exterminated seemed to ooze. Then he shook himself, took a gulp of whiskey and looked Sonja in the eye. "Nobody can deny that the Empire is corrupt. But even its corruption is a *human* thing. The Empire is the summation of human history—all the variety, all the glories . . . yes, and all the mistakes, which carry with them the opportunity to learn. The New Humans would wipe the slate clean of all that's been accomplished and learned in seven thousand years of recorded history, and leave only the scribblings of that half-educated neurotic Montrose! No matter how rotten the Empire has gotten, they *can't* replace it because it has . . . I know I'm not saying it very well, but it's got something *real* behind it and all they've got is a crazy dream!"

He stopped abruptly, conscious of the way they were looking at him, and once again he recalled a time he had faced a dragon and let his innermost feelings gush out. He half-opened his mouth to tell them about it . . . but the details were so hard to remember. Then Torval shifted in his chair, which creaked alarmingly.

"You two," he announced, "are half drunk. There's only one solution: you'll have to get completely drunk." He picked up the bottle, eyed the level of its contents critically, and bellowed for a waiter.

But Basil, oddly enough, didn't feel drunk in the least. What he did feel was a sense of something he couldn't put a name to, although the word *immanence* touched the surface of his mind. "No," he said slowly, "I don't think we are drunk. I think we're . . . Let's face it, the three of us are closet idealists." Sonja made a rude noise with her mouth—but only half-heartedly, as though she knew it was expected of her, and her eyes never left his. And he knew, without having to be told, that she felt the same indefinable thing he felt at that moment. "We all believe, very deeply, in the *idea* of the Empire, however tarnished the reality has become and however little we like to openly admit our belief."

Torval's eyes also made contact with theirs. "I don't know anything about history," he said, and if possible his voice seemed to have grown even deeper than its basso norm. "But I know that a war is coming. Never mind the official bullshit. Whenever one side's determined that it's going to have its way no matter what, there are only two possibilities: war, or surrender by the other side. And unless the Empire is even further gone than I think it is, it's not going to passively accept its own dissolution." He smiled slightly. "I think I know a little more than you two about times like those that are coming. And I'll tell you this: in bad times, you need people you can count on. I mean *absolutely* count on. Like family, but in times when your real family—if any— is nowhere around."

"And who better," Basil's voice seemed to speak for him, "than other people who know those times are coming, and why they're coming, and why they're worth enduring?" He took the bottle and emptied its meager contents into the three glasses equally. Then he rose in the blood-infused light of Atlas, which was about to vanish behind a cloudbank blowing in from the west. And he spoke in a voice he didn't recognize. "I have a feeling—don't ask me why—that in the years that are coming our fates are going to be closely tied together. And I want us to swear that we'll be true to each other. Because I also have a feeling that there are very few others we'll be able to count on."

Sonja stood up. "They say drunken talk is cheap. But . . . you know, I don't feel drunk at all."

"Neither do I," Basil said.

Torval rose to his full height, at least equal to Basil's and twice as broad and thick. "I'm with you," he said simply.

When the waiter arrived with the whiskey bottle Torval had ordered, the three of them were still standing. But they were no longer standing in the light of Atlas, for it had vanished behind the clouds.

No doubt about it, the waiter reflected. *A storm is coming.*

CHAPTER THREE
The DM -27 14659 system, 3894 C.E.

"Approaching Chen Limit, sir."

"Thank you, Mister Castellan," Commander Vladek acknowledged. Then she turned toward the helmsman. "Prepare to disengage the drive, Mister Imamura."

"Aye aye, sir," Lieutenant Commander Imamura replied with a crispness reflected by the rest of the bridge crew. HIMS *Lancer*'s brain was conducting the approach under the human supervision tradition demanded, and everyone on the bridge took traditions like that seriously—especially with Vladek watching. The Fleet had long ago learned the dangers of overdependence on artificial intelligence, and all ship captains were procedural sticklers, even in the course of a relatively routine maneuver like this.

Lieutenant (j. g.) Basil Castellan let his eyes stray to the main viewscreen. The orange light of the K0v star DM - 27 14659 was, as expected, waxing at a seemingly impossible rate. Then, dead ahead, a tiny reddish dot appeared out of the surrounding blackness and the starfields, growing into a ball that hurtled directly toward them as though released from a star god's sling.

All at once, with no physical sensation save a tone shift in the background sounds, *Lancer* resumed experiencing time at the same rate as the rest of the universe. In the viewscreen, the onrushing sphere seemed to come to an

43

instantaneous halt . . . but not really a halt, for it continued
to grow into a rusty planet as *Lancer* approached, her
impellers worked to kill her not-inconsiderable intrinsic
velocity.

Damned show-off, Basil thought venomously in the
direction of Imamura's back.

The helmsman showed no ill effects, confirming what
Basil already knew about his own lack of active psi talents.
Indeed, as the neurohelmet rose from Imamura's head with
a faint hum and settled into its niche in the overhead—no
need for the direct neural linkage that made the ship an
extension of the helmsman's own body, not for a mere orbital
insertion—the facial expression it revealed was one of pure
self-satisfaction. "Drive disengaged, sir," he reported
unnecessarily.

A smile flickered across Vladek's lips. "Very good, Mister
Imamura. But I believe you overlooked the customary practice
of deactivating the inner field at the time approach to the
Chen Limit is announced, thereby avoiding disconcerting
optical effects and also effectively enhancing your own
reaction times."

"Sorry, sir. Won't happen again." Imamura's deadpan
contrition fooled no one. Had the crew spaces been subject
to the same accelerated time as everything else inside the
drive field with which the ship surrounded itself, the
approach would have been too easy. More to the point,
looked too easy. The inner field had to stay on, slowing time
down for the crew as the drive speeded it up for the ship
as a whole, if everyone was to appreciate his virtuosity. He
and Vladek understood each other. In combat or any other
real emergency, he would instantly kill the inner field without
waiting for orders. She knew this, just as he knew that if
he didn't he'd spend the remainder of his Fleet career on
some disagreeable planet, cleaning up the nano-constructors'
residue with a whisk broom.

Still, Basil thought, the skipper was being more than
usually tolerant of the helmsman's grandstanding. Perhaps
it had something to do with the current state of the ship's

morale. They'd been abruptly ordered to this system, with a lack of explanation which would ordinarily have left a vacuum for Rumor Central to fill. But there had been a strange *lack* of rumors, for they'd all known what must lie behind their change of orders, with a knowledge that had made rumor superfluous. So the transit had passed in an odd kind of embarrassed depression, with eye contact avoided and conversation shunned. Faced with this state of mind, Vladek had probably decided they could use all of the usual banter they could get.

Seeking refuge from the thought, Basil looked again at the viewscreen. The ruddy and obviously-lifeless planet was filling more and more of it, and an irregular cluster of orbiting objects had emerged off to the side. As *Lancer* drew nearer, the cluster resolved itself into two main components: the irregular junk-sculpture that was Krasna Prime Station, and the vast silvery parasol shape that was the real source of this system's importance. *The real reason we're here*, Basil amended in his mind.

And not just us, his thought continued, for as the distance closed a swarm of smaller objects grew from iron filings into warships, glinting in the star's orange light. And he felt a curious gloomy satisfaction at the final confirmation of his most pessimistic assumptions. He turned back to his sensor station, for those ships and *Lancer* were already swapping recognition codes. He didn't need to formally report this exchange, for it was being automatically downloaded to the command chair just as it was to his terminal—comm was the primary recipient. But he had his curiosity, and he ran down the list of ships. A couple of old *Impregnable*-class battleships, no longer fit for front-line service. Five of the new *Indomitable*-class battlecruisers, with no more defensive strength than an ordinary cruiser except the greater punishment-absorbing capacity that sheer size conferred, but far more heavily armed. And then the roster of cruisers of *Lancer*'s class or essentially identical ones: *Hussar, Dragoon, Hoplite, Ghazi, Sepoy, Chasseur . . .* and Basil's heart thudded, for Sonja was holding down a weapon station aboard *Chasseur.* Torval, he already knew, was here with Krasna Prime's Marine detachment.

Sonja had been right: for once, drunken talk hadn't been cheap. The three of them had stayed in touch since graduation, as much as that was possible across the light-years. They'd all been promoted inside a year—not unusual, given the Fleet's accelerating buildup. And now fate, or whatever, had brought them back together.

Lieutenant Perrin, the comm officer, broke in on his thoughts. "Captain, we're being hailed by Krasna Prime."

Vladek frowned with a puzzlement the entire bridge crew shared. They'd received and responded to the routine challenge some distance out, as per doctrine. What was the problem, now that they were in visual range of the station? "Put them on, Lieutenant."

The slowly growing panorama of Krasna Prime vanished from the viewscreen, to be replaced by a face that brought Vladek upright in her command chair. "Why, Admiral Tadesco, sir, I—"

The haggard-looking elderly man in the screen gestured her to silence. "Yes, I know, Commander: my presence here isn't generally known. Neither is our mobilization in this system. You were summoned in response to the latest escalation of tensions. But within the last few hours, we've received word that . . . well, actually two messages, in rapid succession . . ." The old man's voice trailed off into vagueness, and he looked all of his century-and-a-half-plus despite the government-financed anagathics to which his rank gave him access. Then something inside him seemed to firm up. "The first message informed us that the New Human-controlled worlds of the Iota Pegasi, Psi Capricorni and Beta Aquilae Sectors have seized control of the Imperial administrative apparatus in those sectors and declared the formation of the 'People's Democratic Union of New Humanity.' They have also declared the Empire dissolved and called on all members of their movement everywhere to rise in rebellion." The silence on the bridge was a palpable presence, not a mere absence of sound. But Tadesco's voice continued to gain in strength as that which he had always been forbidden to publicly discuss marched forth at last in ordered ranks of words.

"The second message came from Fleet HQ at Sol, in top-security code. It seems that, as we suspected, this rebellion has been carefully planned for a long time. In addition to the warships they've seized at the Fleet bases in their sectors, the New Humans have been clandestinely arming merchant ships, and upgrading their drives to military standards, for years. Their plan is an immediate drive on Sol, to bring the Empire down before it can organize to oppose them." Tadesco's face set into even grimmer lines. "It would be superfluous, Commander, to tell you or any of your personnel that this system will lie squarely in the path of that drive."

"Quite a difference from Peachy's," Sonja remarked, with a gesture that took in the Krasna Prime Officer's Club and the panorama beyond its clear armorplast wall.

The orbital station was built around the immense cavity that was its maintenance dock, open to space at one end, and the club was just inside one of the walls that defined that vastness. Its current occupants looked out on the comings and goings of far more ships than the station had ever been intended to accommodate, moving with ponderous majesty through the swarms of shuttles, utility tugs and other small craft in the glare of the great lights. As the three of them watched, a *Norden*-class frigate glided silently past the transparency that separated them from airlessness and weightlessness. Its liquid-crystal skin was currently set for the Fleet's regulation light gray, with the bronze-gold dragon emblazoned on its flanks. *Odd*, Basil reflected irrelevantly. The Solarian Empire, so careful in most ways to de-emphasize all resemblances to its predecessor, had kept the Draconis Empire's symbol. A symbol which, the more one looked at it, bore less resemblance to the supernatural beast of Old Earth legend than to a Luon. . . .

He shook his head free of disturbing half-memories and turned back to his companions. They were all in space service

dress: comfortable jumpsuits which, with the addition of
gloves and flexible transparent hoods, became light-duty
vac suits at need. His and Sonja's were deep blue, white
and gold; Torval's was Marine black, white and silver. Torval
had gotten them a good table, offering a panoramic view
from just inside the mezzanine railing.

"So," Sonja said to the massive Marine, "bring us up to
date. *Chasseur* hasn't been here much longer than *Lancer*,
and neither of us got much news in transit. Just a couple
of mail drops."

"And what we got was pablum," Basil amplified. "But
you . . . well, there's got to be *some* advantage to being
stationed at a communications nerve center."

Torval smiled in appreciation of the gallows humor. "Right,
to make up for having your butt in the center of a target!
But yes, we got the news as fast as it broke. The New Humans
claimed that the Fleet moved into the rebelling sectors and
tried to intervene in the planetary governments to, uh,
'thwart the will of the people' or 'halt the irreversible
progress of humanity toward its next stage of social evolution'
or something."

"Ha!" Sonja took a quick pull on her drink. "If only the
Imperial government was that decisive! It can't even decide
whether to stick its head in the sand or up its ass."

"It's hard to sort out what really happened," Torval
continued, giving her a cautionary frown. "Considering how
long they've obviously planned this, I imagine they staged
an incident or two. But one way or another they got their
pretext, complete with colorful atrocity stories."

"Naturally," Basil sighed. "I gather that the Imperial
authorities in those sectors were taken completely by surprise
by the rising. Our Intelligence types obviously failed to
predict the New Humans' timing."

"Why am I not surprised?" Sonja sneered, to a growl of
agreement from Torval.

"Still, Intelligence must have done *something* right." Basil's
companions' body language couldn't have made their feelings
much more obvious. Most line officers' attitudes toward

intelligence work began with revulsion and proceeded
downward from there. It was an open secret that field agents
were bionically enhanced, and *cyborg* had been as great a
swear word as *synthetic* ever since the Unification Wars
and the Draconis Empire. But Basil pressed doggedly on.
"After all, we evidently knew in advance about this plan
for an all-out drive on Sol."

"Then why didn't the Empire *do* something?" Sonja flared.

"It did," Torval said quietly. "It put us here."

They were all silent for a moment. Then Basil absently
laid his left forearm on the table and spoke a command to
his wristcomp. Its holographic display-projection awoke,
and above the table appeared a multicolored spheroid, a
little over ten inches in average diameter but with bulges,
that represented the Solarian Empire.

On this scale, where inches substituted for tens of light-
years, individual stars could not be displayed. Instead, sectors
glowed in different colors. Basil pointed to three irregular
expanses, like half-melted lozenges of green, yellow and
red, that made up one flank of the representation.

"The database is slightly out of date," Sonja remarked
drily. "It's still showing the rebel sectors as part of the
Empire."

"Yes, but at least it makes clear why this system is crucial."
Basil spoke the system's name, and a tiny pinpoint of light
appeared. On one side of it, beyond a region that was empty
of color because it was empty of planetary systems, lay the
regions that had suddenly become *the enemy*. On the far
side lay the only other star symbols in the display: Sigma
Draconis and Sol.

"From what I hear," Sonja said, "their call for an Empire-
wide revolution has gotten enough response to keep most
of the Fleet's units pinned down where they are, stomping
on minor uprisings before they can spread. Typical of the
New Human leaders, to encourage their supporters to stage
suicidal uprisings. And typical of the supporters, to go along
like silly sheep!"

"But while those uprisings last," Torval rumbled, "they'll

keep us spread thin, instead of concentrating here against the main offensive."

Sonja looked uncharacteristically hesitant. "I suppose the offensive doesn't absolutely *have* to come this way."

"Oh, yes it does," Torval said flatly. He turned his head to look out through the transparency toward the open end of the docking area, and his companions' gazes followed his. There, against the starfields, the silvery parasol of the tachyon beam array was visible.

Theoretical physicists continued to stoutly deny that tachyon communications were *really* instantaneous. But no one had ever succeeded in measuring any time lapse between transmission and reception, whatever the distance. In theory, the device's range should have been effectively infinite like its speed of propagation. In practice, problems which non-specialists found it easiest to visualize as "focusing" imposed certain limitations. For one thing, the location of the receiver had to be known *precisely*; ships in transit could receive messages as long as their occupants' time rate was synchronized to that of the outside universe, but in order to do so they had to arrive at certain prearranged coordinates at prearranged times—"mail drops." More importantly, interstellar-range transmission required a physical array of such size that it could only be constructed in orbit, a kilometers-wide prairie of costly exotic alloys. And the requisite surface area of the array went up exponentially as the range increased. As a practical matter, no transmitter of more than ten light-years' range had ever been built. So messages had to be relayed, and the great orbital arrays were strategic pearls beyond price.

Which explained why one of them was in this economically unimportant young system. Located on the edge of the gulf of nothingness between the centers of civilization and several outlying sectors, it enabled Fleet HQ to exercise command-and-control throughout the regions which had risen in rebellion.

"You're right," Sonja acknowledged, nodding slowly. "This has to be their first target. And if they're as well-prepared as they seem to be, what we've got here can't possibly hold them."

"We shouldn't have to," Torval reassured her. "Word is that everything that could be spared has been organized into a fairly serious task force at Sigma Draconis, and that it's on the way now."

"Right," Sonja muttered skeptically.

"Who's in command of it?" Basil inquired of Torval.

"Vice Admiral Medina."

"Well!" Sonja perked up. "That's the first good news I've heard yet."

"I suppose so," Torval said in his deliberate way. "Of course, Medina's not everybody's cup of tea—"

"Snobs!" Sonja snorted. "Just because his grandfather was a Beyonder! I tell you, we can't let ourselves worry about things like that. Not now, when the Empire is collapsing around our ears."

"It's not just his ancestry," Torval insisted. "I've heard some disturbing things about him from people who've served in headquarters outfits directly under him."

"All right, admittedly he's ambitious. But, again, can we really afford to worry about that just now? He's the one real man in a high command full of ineffectual dodderers like Tadesco." Both of her male companions shot her warning glances this time. But she'd kept her voice low, and now it dropped even further, even as it took on a challenging note. "Well, am I wrong? Maybe the Empire can't live with Medina's ambitions in the long run. But we can't live with the New Humans in the *short* run!"

Basil spoke up, quietly and almost diffidently—and the other two fell silent to listen, as they'd been more and more inclined to do over the years. "I think Sonja may be right. There's an old saying: 'Beggars can't be choosers.' And if Medina really is the man who can salvage this situation. . . ." His voice trailed off into an embarrassed laugh, and a white grin split his dark face. "Will you listen to us? Anyone would think we were settling the fate of the Empire!"

They all chuckled ruefully, but those chuckles held an

odd nervous brittleness . . . which the PA system shattered.

"Attention! General quarters! All personnel report to your duty stations! All ships' companies report to your ships! Repeat, general quarters! All personnel . . ."

"They weren't supposed to be here this soon, were they?" Sonja's voice and features were just a little too composed, in the way of those who have never seen combat and are determined not to show it.

"No, they weren't," Torval remarked with the kind of calm fatalism she was striving for. He got to his feet, then paused and lifted his glass. "Sin to waste this; the damned serving robots will just dump it."

"Soulless bastards," Basil agreed. "Here's to our next drink, when we *all* meet here again."

"I'll tell 'em to hold the table," Torval grinned.

They tossed off their drinks, then joined the maelstrom of running figures that the club had become.

Lancer accelerated outward until Krasna Prime and the tachyon beam array shrank to metallic toys against the backdrop of Krasna's Planet and then vanished, and the planet itself was only a little dirty-orange ball. Then they crossed the invisible line called the Chen Limit, where the world-lines were flat enough to allow the warping of time. Vladek nodded, Imamura engaged the drive, and Krasna's Planet seemed to drop away behind them at the same impossible relative velocity with which it had hurtled toward them when they'd arrived.

But Basil had no eyes for the view aft, even had his duties permitted his attention to stray to it. The real spectacle was spread out before him, here at his scanner station.

Starships disobeyed no physical laws inside the bubbles of accelerated time with which they surrounded themselves, and therefore could interact with the outside universe from which standpoint they seemed to be flouting those laws. Which meant that they could be detected by normal sensors. This wasn't particularly helpful if the sensor was limited to lightspeed, for the starship would arrive long before the signal of its detection. But the treated antineutrinos of modern sensors could, by various tricks, be given transluminar acceleration. They weren't instantaneous like the tachyon beams that were useless for sensing purposes, but within their not-inconsiderable range they effectively provided realtime detection. Thus it was that the pickets out in DM -27 14659's Oort Cloud had given them enough warning to scramble outsystem to meet the oncoming rebel fleet. And thus it was that that fleet now lay revealed by the ship's sensors on Basil's displays.

They'd all heard about the windfall of warships that the rebels had gathered in with the shockingly sudden collapse of Imperial authority in their sectors. But the consensus had been that they wouldn't be able to employ those ships anytime soon, for lack of politically reliable, trained personnel. But now, looking at the phalanxes of former Fleet ships that formed a hard forward carapace for the mass of armed merchantmen that followed, Basil came to the sick realization that the New Humans' preparations must have included clandestine training of crews. Of course, he told himself, those crews couldn't possibly be up to Fleet standards in either quality or numbers. They had to be running on skeleton crews and relying heavily on automated systems.

All of which was undoubtedly true. And yet . . . those were a *lot* of ships coming at them. Such an armada, launched at the heart of the Empire so soon after the rebellion had been declared, spoke of planning that had begun long before that declaration, and made nonsense of the New Humans' talk of Fleet provocation. He found he was clenching his teeth, and made himself relax. With a force of overwhelming size bearing down on them, political mendacity was probably the last thing he should be getting upset about.

He turned his attention to the disposition of the loyalist forces. Tadesco had organized his resources into three divisions, now approaching the invaders from as many different directions in an effort—thus far completely unsuccessful—to distract them from their objective. Looking at the display, Basil frowned at the icons of the *Indomitable*-class battlecruisers, scattered among all three divisions. Concentrated in a squadron of their own, they could have been used as they were intended to be used, employing their speed and maneuverability to stay out of range of anything that exceeded them in defensive strength while overwhelming ordinary cruisers with superior firepower. But Tadesco had felt he had no choice but to use them as command ships for his divisions, for he had nothing else that could match their command-and-control capabilities. Basil wasn't sure he was right . . . but, for some odd reason, nobody had asked him.

At least the *Impregnable*-class battlewagons were together, in the First Division under Tadesco's personal command, directly in the path of the invaders. They couldn't match the newer ships' sophisticated combat systems, but they were big enough to carry the weapons that now appeared in Basil's display.

To function at all in faster-than-light combat, missiles had to carry their own drives and sensor suites, to say nothing of sentience-level computers—in short, they had to be starships in their own right, crewless to be sure but too expensive for lavish deployment and too large for any but the largest warships to carry. Now Tadesco was expending them prodigally, as desperation overcame his conservative instincts. They sped ahead of their mother ships as overloaded impellers pushed them to tremendous accelerations within their drive fields. Basil watched, fascinated, and spat out periodic reports as the robot suicide ships entered the range of the rebels' weapons and began to die. But some got through, and the enemy ranks began to waver as ships initiated evasive action.

Then, as though in response to a central will, the rebels' formation began to firm up again, into a rigidity which held even as a certain number of ships began to fail under the intolerable energies of the bomb-pumped lasers the missiles died to create. Basil caught himself nodding slowly as his supposition was confirmed: the rebels, with hastily thrown-together crews of inexperienced personnel, could not trust individual ship captains to take independent action. They had to treat their fleet as a single, massive unit whose defensive strength and sheer momentum could bull its way through any obstacle. And for that approach to work, their formation's integrity must be maintained at all costs. Besides which, the very notion of individual initiative was ideologically unacceptable to them.

But then the Second Division to which *Lancer* belonged, and the Third which included *Chasseur*, swept in from the flanks, Imamura cut the inner field, the viewscreen switched to tactical display, and they were engaged.

The formations slid together, and energy pulses (the ancient term *laser* was still common, although these weapons used the X-ray wavelengths rather than visible light) began to cross the intervening space at what seemed to the bridge crew—existing as they were in the state of vastly accelerated time induced by the drive, without the compensating inner field—to be a snail's pace. The initial exchange was indecisive, for the rebels were holding formation and both sides' drives were, of course, speeding up time to the highest factor permitted by current technology. Both sides lost a few ships, but the rebel formation continued on. Second and Third Divisions curved around to keep pace with that formation's flanks as it drew into energy weapon range of First Division. Tadesco immediately ordered the obsolescent *Indomitables* away from the scene of action, where they would be helpless against the newer ships . . . but he should have done it sooner. The rebel command must have recognized that those ships would be formidable defensive platforms once the battle moved inside the Chen Limit of Krasna's World where no one's drives could function, for lances of energy fire impaled the two great old ships.

The basic, brutal fact of deep space warfare was that for ship-to-ship combat to take place both ships' drives must be able to accelerate time by the same factor. Otherwise it wasn't combat—it was an execution Thus it was that all warships were designed for the same drive strength: the maximum possible one. Any speed differentials among them were a function of the thrust of the impellers that actually moved them. The *Indomitables*, products of an earlier era and never upgraded by the parsimonious peacetime Fleet, shouldn't have been here at all, and wouldn't have been save for the fact that their missile capability couldn't be spared in the Empire's present extremity. Now they became death traps for their crews as energy beams struck them with an intensity enhanced far beyond their own drives' ability to spread that energy out. Their answering beams might as well have been searchlights for all their potency against the rebels' up-to-date drive fields. Basil was glad he couldn't view the holocaust that lay behind the tactical display's dry symbology, the boiling clouds of volatilized matter that were the funeral pyres of those gallant old ships.

The rebels began to interpenetrate with First Division, whose elements scattered and came around to join the running battle, pouring fire into the ships on the periphery of the rebel formation which they didn't dare enter lest they be demolished by the converging fire of several opponents. But that formation continued inexorably on insystem, toward Krasna Prime, to whose watching occupants the entire battle so far had occupied less than a second of incomprehensible violence.

Tactical analysis so far was confirming Basil's suppositions about the relative fighting quality of the two sides' units. The Imperials' fire was a good deal more effective, ship for ship. But the rebel numbers began to tell more and more, with several ships concentrating their firepower on a single target, as the battle approached the Chen Limit.

A lurch brought Basil abruptly out of the deep concentration with which he had been regarding his readouts. Deep in the ship, alarm klaxons were whooping.

"Damage control, report!" Vladek snapped.

"Nothing critical, sir," came a voice after a moment. "Life support functions on delta deck, radians seven through twelve have had to go to standby. But nothing affecting propulsion or weapon systems—"

Something caught Basil's eye from the corner, and all at once hellfire awoke on his readouts. "Incoming . . . multiple!" he blurted—unnecessarily, for the tactical display had already processed the automatic download and the main screen showed the converging energy bolts, crawling toward *Lancer* at lightspeed.

"Stand by," Vladek called out calmly.

With no more warning than that, the universe turned to noise and chaos, as the ship shuddered and a secondary explosion ripped through the bridge's port bulkhead. Basil, existing in a state of protracted time that had nothing to do with the drive field, saw Lieutenant Perrin hurled from the comm station with such force that her securing straps practically cut her in two. Blood bubbled forth as the artificial gravity momentarily lost its hold, only to fall to the deck in a grisly spatter as weight returned. Imamura's neurohelmet seemed to explode in a pyrotechnic shower of electric-blue sparks, and he came bolt upright with arched back before collapsing. A stench of burnt meat told Basil that he wouldn't want to see what remained of the helmsman's head. Then consciousness wavered . . .

"Bridge! Come in, bridge! Anybody!"

The executive officer's voice brought Basil back to intolerable reality. He staggered to his feet and looked around the darkened, smoke-swirling ruin that had been the bridge. *Amazing*, he thought with a strange calmness, *how much still works.* Like the main screen, and the communicator in the arm of the captain's chair, from which Commander Kronen's scratchy requests for acknowledgment continued to come. But Vladek was lying back, motionless. Basil heaved himself upright and staggered over to the skipper's side . . . and once again the black wings of unconsciousness beat around the periphery of his vision, and his gorge rose.

The roughly triangular segment of torn metal had sliced into Vladek's body at God-knew-what velocity, pinning her to the command chair and cutting open heart and viscera. The chair, tilted backwards by the force of the impact, was

like a bowl of blood and other fluids in which Vladek reclined,
staring sightlessly at the viewscreen.

"Bridge! This is the executive officer. Damage Control
is on the way. Is anybody alive up there? Please respond!"

Basil shook horror from his head and looked around. He
could hear low moans and see feebly stirring bodies, but
he was clearly the only member of the bridge crew fit for
duty. And the XO needed to know that, so he could assume
command and fight the ship from his auxiliary command
center in Engineering. Basil licked his lips and opened his
mouth to respond . . . but then something caught his eye
in the erratically flickering tactical display.

The maelstrom of battling ships was approaching the Chen
Limit of Krasna's World. *Lancer*, without a human command
to do otherwise, was still on course, dogging the left flank
of the rebel formation, part of which was slightly ahead of
her. And a rebel ship was altering course to intercept her.

Suddenly, standing in that scene out of hell, he *knew* what
must be done.

It was as though he heard a stranger speak, using his voice
at the deepest pitch he could manage. "This is the bridge.
On command, disengage the drive."

"*What?*" Kronen's voice almost broke into a squeak. "Who
is this? Let me speak to the captain!"

"No time!" Basil snapped. Later, he reflected calmly in
some inner storm center, there would be time to let the
enormity of what he was doing register. "This is a direct
order from the captain. I'll give you a three-count. One!"

"Damn it, I want that order authenticated! Who in—"

"Two!" Basil's universe had narrowed to that segment of
the main screen where the battle's leading edge was creeping
up to the Chen Limit, almost touching it. He didn't even
notice the bolt of death that was crawling from the
approaching rebel ship toward *Lancer* at mere lightspeed.

"All right! But after this is over I'm going to get to the
bottom of—"

"*Three! Disengage!*"

Things happened quickly.

Lancer's time scale crashed back into synchronicity with that of the normal universe. Perhaps a femtosecond later, on that time scale, the rest of the warring ships did the same as they crossed the Chen Limit. At essentially the same instant the enemy beam, computer-directed to intersect the point in space that *Lancer* would have reached at her previous effective velocity of incredible multiples of *c*, stabbed through emptiness far ahead of the cruiser. Still further ahead, the battle raged on, moving toward Krasna Prime at the combatants' intrinsic Einsteinian-space velocity.

"Commander Kronen, sir," Basil almost whispered into the communicator, "the captain is out of action. You have the conn." He slumped to his knees, almost too weary to breathe. But he managed to do two things. First he scanned the computer's roster of friendly units . . . yes, *Chasseur* still lived. And he reached past that which had been Imamura and switched the screen from tactical to visual.

Kronen didn't even acknowledge, for he had instantly understood.

Another fundamental fact of deep-space warfare was that ships moving far more swiftly than light—as far as outside observers were concerned, at any rate—could outrun the beams of directed-energy weapons. Therefore, a ship under drive could not be attacked from astern. Tactics and ship designs alike reflected this. And now, practically dead ahead, lay the rebel ship that had sought to intercept *Lancer*, presenting to its erstwhile prey a stern unprotected even by the deflector screens that were the ships' only passive defense inside the Chen Limit where their drive fields could not form.

Basil could feel the thrumming through the deck under him as Kronen ordered the impellers up to full thrust. Basil gazed at the screen, not really expecting to be able to see the enemy ship before . . .

The screen's automatic glare-reduction function saved him from blindness as a brief sun erupted. Kronen had taken the rebel ship "up the kilt" with every beam weapon that could be brought to bear.

Basil found he was on his feet again, no longer drained, screaming a wild war cry that welled up from he knew not where. As he stood bathed in the light of fusionfire, some impulse made him remember the woman who lay dead in the command chair beside him. And he switched the screen back to tactical so that any part of Vladek that had not yet departed this place might watch as Kronen drove *Lancer* on, seeking another target, and another, and another, knifing through the rebel formation like some elemental principle of destruction.

But there were still a lot of rebels between them and Krasna Prime. And he saw that assault shuttles had begun to converge on the station.

Another explosion shook the deck, making the voice in Torval's helmet communicator superfluous. "Prepare for visitors, Lieutenant Bogdan."

"Aye aye, sir," he responded, most of his attention on the readout of his powered armor's integral sensor unit, which formed the suit's left "hand."

"Twenty hostiles," he told his squad. He didn't need to tell them that the hostiles were encased in battlesuits comparable to their own. Nothing less well-protected had any business in the firefight that was coming. There were more sophisticated strength-enhancing technologies—flexible form-fitting suits whose machinery was molecular, for instance. But they couldn't match the sheer defensive strength of the traditional armored exoskeletons which the Marines still favored.

Torval spoke a command and the sensor unit began to change shape, its nanoplastic components flowing and writhing as it reconfigured itself into a laser weapon. With his right hand he hefted a plasma gun designed for powered armor. Then he glanced left and right at the line the Marines had formed across this vast empty storage space behind an improvised barricade. Satisfied, he settled in to await the boarders.

Krasna Prime, huge and without the need for drive

machinery, mounted deflector screen generators beyond the capacity of any starship. But deflector screens' strength was in direct proportion to the kinetic energy of incoming attacks. They were most effective against energy weapons, fairly so against high-velocity material projectiles. But the small, slow assault shuttles could push their way through as though against a stiff wind. This type of attack was costly, for the station's weapons took a toll on the shuttles. But they only had to get close enough to disgorge their cargoes of power-armored troopers, who proceeded on to the bare metal walls and cut their way through with laser torches. Now, like bacteria invading an organism, they were working their way inward, eating their way through all obstacles . . . of which this chamber's walls were the latest. Torval braced for an explosion.

But none came. Instead, the bulkhead began to spout leprous patches of dissolution, and gaps began to grow as the metal sagged downward in slow gray streams of a substance that was obscenely unidentifiable as organic or inorganic.

"Lieutenant," the panic-stricken voice of Corporal Nash quavered in his helmet communicator, "they're using dis!"

"Belay that!" Torval snapped, though demons came shrieking up from the depths of his own acculturation to gibber at him. One of the weapons that had lent the Unification Wars their peculiar horror was aerosol-delivered disassembler: clouds of nanomachines which broke all matter down at the molecular level, turning it into an undifferentiated grayish goo. *All* matter, including living flesh. Would even the rebels flout the prohibition, so long-standing as to have attained almost religious stature, against using it on humans? "Stand fast," he continued, as much for his own benefit as for his men's. "I've read about the stuff. It's expensive as hell—too expensive to use on individual opposition. I'll bet they're expending it on the bulkhead just to make us wet our pants and run crying to momma. They must think we're Fleet Security."

A collective wolfish laugh submerged the incipient panic.

The men knew that Torval was ex-enlisted, no ninety-day wonder, so "lieutenant" wasn't a term of belittlement in his case. And what happened next seemed to confirm his words. A shower of grenades came sailing through the space where the bulkhead had been, to lie in impotent sparks and sputters. This time the laughter in the comm circuit needed no prompting from Torval. The rebels must *really* think they were facing second- or third-drawer opposition, which would now be helplessly in the throes of hysterical fear or morbid depression or whatever emotion it was that these psi-grenades induced. Surely they knew that Marine combat helmets incorporated mind-shields as a matter of course.

Then the hostiles were through the breached bulkhead, and nothing was funny anymore. But the Marines, now facing mere bolts of superheated plasma and streams of hypervelocity metal, had steadied, and gave better than they got in the hermetically-closed segment of hell that the compartment had become.

Torval pivoted away from his part of the barricade just before it was blasted into a howling inferno of flame and showering molten metal. Then he swung back around in a practiced motion and sent a plasma discharge roaring down its guide beam in the general direction of the opposition, accompanied by a rapid-fire discharge of laser pulses from his reconfigurable integral weapon. But the laser—visible-light frequency for this work, for atmosphere absorbed X-rays—was becoming less useful in this smoke-filled environment. He spoke a command . . . and, in that instant of distraction, an enemy battlesuit crashed into his with a clang that would have deafened unprotected ears had any been present.

The two of them went over together, with faceplates in contact, but of course both were opaque and Torval couldn't see the enemy face that was mere inches away. He could, however, see the contact plasma discharger that the rebel was bringing inexorably closer to his helmet. . . . But then his integral weapon completed its reconfiguration, and a thick metal blade, humming with the current that caused it to vibrate thousands of times a second, jabbed up from under the rebel's armpit, and inward.

With their helmets in contact, Torval heard the man's scream for a split second before he arched up and flopped over sideways, the battlesuit's myoelectric "muscles" amplifying his thrashings. Torval thought he ought to put him out of his misery . . . but then he remembered dis, used against a bulkhead that *might* have had humans huddled against its far side, and he moved on, advancing against a pair of rebels who were just entering the compartment with anti-armor rocket launchers. He took them by surprise, for they hadn't expected opposition at such close range. He smashed one aside and sliced another's launcher across with the vibroblade before dispatching him with a point-blank plasma blast. The man he'd knocked off balance came back at him and attempted to grapple. Torval blasted one leg out from under him and, after he'd crashed to the deck, brought one battlesuited foot stamping down on his helmet, flattening it—and its contents—like a tin can. Then he paused, for the din had ceased, and saw that his men had mopped up the remaining rebels.

"Compartment Delta-26-M secure, Major," he reported over his helmet comm. Then, with a cockiness he'd thought he'd long since outgrown: "Bring on the next wave."

"Outstanding, Lieutenant Bogdan," the battalion CO commended, then paused. "Remain on alert, Lieutenant, but . . . there may not be a next wave. Word is that something's going on out there to disrupt their attack. We'll keep you advised."

"Hey, Lieutenant," somebody called out, "could it be that the blue-backs are doing something right for once?"

Torval joined in the general chuckles. But . . . *It might even be true. After all, Basil and Sonja are out there.* He roughened his voice. "All right, cut the comedy. You heard the man: we're still on alert. Until further notice, stand ready to kill anything that comes through that bulkhead."

❖   ❖   ❖

The medics insisted on giving Basil a thorough going-over where they found him. So he lay on the bridge alongside the seriously injured, within sight of the still-functioning tactical display, and felt depression wash over him as he saw that they were done for after all.

The rebel command had finally awakened to what was loose amid their over-rigid formation, and the battle had dissolved into a chaos of individually battling ships. Then a pattern had reestablished itself, with the outnumbered Imperials clustering around Krasna Prime in a defensive hedgehog that was gradually being worn down by overwhelming rebel fire. Tadesco had died with his flagship and even the divisions could no longer function as units; command-and-control was down to the individual ship level.

He caught sight of an auxiliary comm screen where, doubtless by oversight, Kronen's voice could be heard, and the features of the senior surviving officer of the nearest friendly ship were displayed over an identifier: HIMS *Chasseur*. The man in the screen shook his head wearily.

"No, Commander. Our orders don't give us the option of trying to break free and run, however hopeless the situation we find ourselves in. . . ." Basil heard no more, for in the background view of *Chasseur*'s bridge he had caught sight of a lithe female figure topped by auburn hair.

"I appreciate all that," Kronen was saying. "But I call your attention to General Directive 43-22a, which gives commanding officers the latitude to decide—*what in God's name?*"

Basil became aware that the bridge had suddenly grown quiet, and that every pair of eyes except his were on the tactical display. Incredibly, impossibly, the rebels were disengaging as rapidly as tactical wisdom allowed—in some cases more rapidly than that—and seeking the Chen Limit at the highest acceleration their impellers could provide.

Before any voice could break the stunned silence, the display vanished, to be replaced by Kronen's sweat-soaked face. But Basil knew what he was going to say before he opened his mouth, for he had glimpsed the first icons of

Imperial ships that had begun to appear in the viewscreen's extreme upper-left-hand corner—the system-scale display.

"Attention all personnel," Kronen rasped. "Admiral Medina's advance elements have arrived in this system—"

Whatever else he said was drowned in a storm of cheers. But Basil could hear one voice above the hubbub, from the direction of that neglected comm station. For Sonja had elbowed her way to the screen pickup, and was looking out with a grin that, for him, banished the rest of the universe.

"Hey, Basil," she yelled, "if you're there, aboard *Lancer* . . . what did I tell you?"

The three of them—grimy, sweat-stinking, in a manic state beyond exhaustion—met in the great entrance bay of Krasna Prime's maintenance dock, where shuttles were moving slowly through the atmosphere screen and wheezing down onto their landing jacks. Torval and Sonja had to push through a crush of others around Basil, for the stories had already begun to spread.

"Basil!" Torval roared, bulling his way through with Sonja in his wake. He was clad only in the nondescript skintight gray garment worn inside a battlesuit, and thus looked better than Basil in his ruined Fleet uniform. "What's this I hear about what you did out there?"

"Yeah," Sonja added, hugging him soundly. "Can't I let you out of my sight for even a minute? Everybody's talking about—"

"Lieutenant Castellan!"

"Yes, looks like everybody is," Basil muttered. He came to attention along with everyone else present—except those who were hastening to get out of Commander Kronen's way. *Lancer*'s acting skipper advanced until his nose was mere inches from Basil's.

"Lieutenant Castellan," he repeated, this time in a grinding rasp rather than a bellow. "I have just concluded an impromptu investigation of precisely what happened at the time the bridge was hit and immediately thereafter. Am I, or am I not, correct in believing that Commander Vladek was already dead at the time you communicated to me what purported to be an order from her?"

Academy habit reasserted itself, and Basil picked out precisely three hairs on the back of someone's head in front of him. He kept his eyes fixed on those three hairs as he responded. "Sir, that is correct. Under the emergency circumstances that existed at the time—"

"Then your cotton-candy ass is mine, Lieutenant!" Kronen blared. "I'll see you court-martialed! I'll see you brainwiped down to the level where you can't even figure out how much saliva to drool! I'll—"

"Attention on deck!" The loudspeaker drowned out even Kronen. "Relief Task Force, arriving." At the same instant, the station's most senior officers emerged in a group to meet the shuttle that was nosing through the atmosphere screen. Under the Imperial dragon on its side were the three flaring sunbursts of a vice admiral.

"We'll continue this later, Lieutenant," Kronen told Basil. But, like everyone else, he turned to watch as the shuttle settled down and its exit ramp extruded itself. And like everyone else he broke into a cheer for the figure that came down and advanced through the steam of the landing jacks.

Vice Admiral Yoshi Medina was clad in the space-service uniform of his rank, complete with the white cape that was an optional accessory, usually reserved for formal occasions. Under these circumstances, it was a touch of flamboyance that seemed somehow right. It was also a striking contrast with his dark face, with its high cheekbones, slitted black eyes and thin slash of a mouth under an equally thin, slightly drooping black mustache. Commodore Tzin, the station CO, greeted him with a formality which promptly gave way to handshakes and renewed cheers.

Basil watched, his problems momentarily forgotten, as Tzin motioned Medina toward a hatch. But the newly arrived admiral paused. "Wait a moment, Commodore. I've heard some odd stories since arriving here, about the cruiser

Lancer, which evidently broke the momentum of the rebel attack. Is her CO present?"

Tzin looked around and noticed Kronen. "Here, Admiral. Commander Kronen was her XO, and assumed command after the skipper was killed."

"So I've been given to understand," Medina acknowledged, as he stepped forward and received Kronen's salute. "Outstanding work, Commander. If it hadn't been for *Lancer*, this station probably would have fallen before my arrival."

"Thank you, Admiral," Kronen stammered. But Medina went on in his deep voice.

"I've also heard that a very junior officer who was the only one alive and conscious on the bridge took some . . . shall we say, unorthodox steps. In fact, if the reports are to be believed, *he* gave the order to disengage the drive at that precise moment."

"Yes, Admiral. In fact, this is the man right here." Kronen gave Basil a sideways smile of vindictive glee. "I was just dealing with him when you arrived."

Medina stepped slowly in front of Basil, who tried to weld his spine into an even stiffer position of attention. The admiral's thin mouth was a slightly downturned line of grimness, and his eyelids drooped slightly as he studied Basil's name tag. "Is that true, Lieutenant . . . Castellan?"

"Yes, sir," Basil got out through a constricted throat. Visions of his probable future came crowding back, and he thought he was going to be sick.

"Well, Lieutenant," Medina said, in a voice like the deep purr of a large cat, "this is serious business. You usurped command for a brief period—arguably mutiny."

"Yes, sir," Basil croaked. His vision began to tunnel, and he wasn't sure how long he was going to be able to stay on his feet.

"Bad business indeed, Lieutenant," Medina went on. "In fact, you're putting me to a great deal of trouble. After actions such as yours, it's going to take some doing to justify the decoration and accelerated promotion I'm going to recommend for you."

"Yes, sir," Basil repeated automatically. Then the admiral's words began to penetrate his private universe of despair . . . and he stole a look at Medina's swarthy face, which was split in a sharklike grin.

It was too much. Basil would have collapsed had Medina not slapped him on the shoulder, the kind of sensation that was needed to bring him back into awareness of the physical world. Everyone else looked as stunned as he felt, and Kronen seemed to be experiencing difficulty breathing.

Medina turned his predatory smile on *Lancer's* acting CO. "Oh, don't worry, Commander. You're also to be commended. You displayed initiative and flexibility in taking advantage of an opportunity—the opportunity that Mister Castellan created."

"But . . . but . . . Admiral . . ."

"Yes, I know. Not exactly according to The Book, was it?" All at once, Medina's face was set back into the harsh lines that seemed natural to it. "Well, Commander, it's time you—and everyone else here—adjusted to the fact that things aren't going to be the same. Not ever again in our lifetimes." He raised his voice until it filled the cavernous space. "We've won this battle, we've thwarted the rebels' plan to bring the Empire down with a single stroke. But that just means we're entering into a time of protracted war. A time when *nothing* will matter but survival. A time when the people with the brain and the stomach to do it will have to take whatever actions are necessary to preserve the Empire. *Whatever* actions . . . regardless of what traditionalists and legalists may say. The Fleet—the entire Empire—will have to accept this or go under!"

In a heartbeat or two of silence, an odd disquiet ran through the crowd, for Medina was speaking of the dissolution of familiar things, things that had formed the backdrop of their lives. But his voice seemed to hold the metallic clang of destiny as it reverberated around the great entrance bay, and the order of things they had known seemed to recede into the past, beyond the boundaries of present reality, leaving them stranded in a strange new world where nothing could be taken for granted and the only way to cope with change was to embrace it wholeheartedly. And they cheered again, but the cheers held a subtle new note that Basil could not define, even though he heard it in his own voice as well: an odd blend of reckless excitement, unacknowledged fear, unrecognized sorrow, and need for a leader to follow into this uncharted new country of the future.

Medina turned back to him. "I don't imagine you'll want to stay aboard *Lancer*, Lieutenant. I'll arrange a transfer. I want you under my own command anyway. You see . . . I think I recognize a man who's like me in many ways." He smiled wolfishly. "So I'll want to be able to keep an eye on you." Then he was gone, leaving Basil gaping after him, unaware even of Sonja's embrace and Torval's back-pounding.

They were at the same table in the just-reopened officers' club, although like the rest of the clientele they were a good deal less spiffy than before. They were, Basil thought, probably running on pure adrenaline, and he wasn't sure what the result of an alcohol admixture would be.

Torval didn't seem to be letting it worry him. He tossed back half his drink, settled back and loosened the collar of the service dress he'd gotten back into. "Well, Sonja," he said, "I'm surprised you haven't already started telling us you told us so. About Medina, that is."

Sonja drank too, but her face wore a subdued expression Basil had never seen on it. "Yeah, I suppose so. It's just . . ." She took another drink. "There's just something a little . . . disturbing about him."

"What's the matter? Isn't he what you expected?"

"Yes. Maybe that's the problem. Now I'm not sure that what I expected is what I really want."

"I don't think we have much choice," Basil said. They both gave him sharp glances, for his grimness was as out of character as Sonja's hesitancy. "Oh, I know what you mean. When he spoke, it was like an axe blade cutting us off from our past and leaving us in a future that I'm not sure I'm going to like. But, you see, he's right. Most of the rebels got away, and what we've won is—let's face it—a defensive victory that we're in no position to follow up on. Not with rebellions breaking out all over the Empire like a rash." He held their eyes. "We're heading into what may be the worst period since the Unification Wars. We *have* to support Medina."

Torval gave him the thoughtful look that few besides himself and Sonja were ever allowed to see. "So you think he's the man who can impose order?"

"Yes . . . even if it's only the order of his own will. But the alternative is chaos." Basil studied the amber depths of his drink. "He worries me too . . . he even frightens me. But the oath we swore to each other implies a commitment to whatever or whoever it takes to hold the Empire together."

"You're right . . . I think," Sonja said. And they all raised their glasses and drank. They refilled in haste, as though to banish their own doubts.

CHAPTER FOUR
Hespera (Mu Arae II), 3908 C.E.

"Attention on deck!"

The officers around the table rose to their feet in response to the chief of staff's quiet announcement as Vice Admiral Castellan entered the room.

"As you were, ladies and gentlemen," Basil said, with an authoritativeness he still had to consciously put into his voice at age thirty-seven. The fact that he had only just gotten his third sunburst, and was the youngest person in the Fleet to have it, didn't help. Such rapid advancement had been unheard of in the old days. So many things had been unheard of in the old days. . . .

He dismissed the thought and sat down at the head of the shiny-topped oval table, and everyone else followed suit. The ensuing moment of chair aligning gave him and his new staff a chance to study each other. They saw a man who looked even younger than he was. Flag rank had brought with it access to the anagathics that the Castellans—academics of no enormous distinction—had never been able to afford. His response had proven to be about average: his aging would be slowed by a factor of roughly two and a half, as long as he continued to receive the treatments on an annual basis.

"I'm sorry we haven't had a chance to get to know each other better," he began. "But, as you're all aware, this task force is being put together in some haste. Only recently has Grand Admiral Medina been in a position to undertake the offensive we're going to be a part of—the offensive that will put an end to the rebellion." He studied the staffers' reactions. Some were oddly ambivalent. Most of these people, like him, were young for their ranks by the standards of the old peacetime Fleet. The youngest had come of age with the New Human rebellion, and probably found the idea that it could ever end slightly unreal. As unreal as he would once have found the notion that it would still be going on after fourteen years.

"Please turn your attention to the packets Captain Silva has already distributed. These documents contain the basic operational concept that Grand Admiral Medina submitted to His Imperial Majesty for approval." He eyed them narrowly, but no one cracked a smile. There was a snapping of security seals and a soft clicking as datachips were inserted into the tabletop terminals. "Captain Silva, please summarize."

"Thank you, Admiral." The chief of staff, an obvious native of a low-gravity planet of a hot sun, reminded him of Torval Bogdan simply by being so precisely his opposite. She was taller than the average man but elvish slender, and her skin was ebon black although her features reflected a mixture of races. Her willowy look concealed a wiriness acquired over a professional life spent mostly on heavier planets and aboard ships that maintained the Fleet's standard one Prometheus gee. She touched a control, and a holographic star diagram appeared over the table. It covered the three sectors that had broken away fourteen years ago, mostly still in rebel hands, and the nearer regions of the Empire, including Sigma Draconis. "Up" and "down" were defined by the traditional ecliptic plane of Old Earth.

"You will note," she said, "that the Mu Arae Sector's isolated position makes it, from the rebel standpoint, a potential base for us to create a new front. This, of course, explains their early efforts to gain control of it through internal subversion." They had all seen the scars left by the fighting in the rebellion's early days, when control of this small, out-of-the-way sector had fluctuated. "Grand Admiral Medina's plan is for us and a task force from Sigma Draconis to advance toward the rebels' core systems simultaneously. The Sigma Draconis force will allow itself to be driven back rather easily, leading the rebels to believe that we represent the main thrust. But in fact there will be a second, stronger wave from Sigma Draconis under Grand Admiral Medina's personal command, timed to enter rebel space just after they have realigned their forces to confront us.

"Obviously, this plan will require us to face the main rebel fleet for a short time—hopefully a *very* short time, before they realize their mistake and try to fall back to protect their capital system. The objective is to catch that main fleet between ourselves and Grand Admiral Medina and crush it, thus effectively ending the rebellion as a military force and making the individual rebel planets accessible to us. Of course, the rebels have had a long time to fortify those planets—"

Yes, a very long time, Basil thought bleakly. *Longer than anyone would have dreamed, fourteen years ago.* He stopped listening as Silva proceeded with the order of battle, which he already knew—indeed, he'd helped formulate it. Instead, he thought back over those fourteen years.

As Medina had foretold, they'd been in no position to exploit the initial victory at DM -27 14659, with rebellions erupting all over the Empire. Regional admirals had been given extraordinary authority to deal with those rebellions, superseding an Imperial administrative structure that had been reeling toward dissolution anyway. As time had passed, those admirals had tended more and more to behave as quasi-independent warlords. And they had seethed with resentment of the corruption and incompetence among the inner court circle which had hampered every effort to reconquer the three seceded sectors. Fortunately, in the aftermath of DM -27 14659 the "People's Democratic Union" had been like a wounded dog, growling at the hamstrung giant but unable to spring for its throat.

Then, in 3899, old Emperor Armin IV had died—and the synthetics who had surrounded and dominated him overplayed their hand. Tradition permitted the Emperor to choose his successor from among his own blood relatives, and Armin's choice had fallen on Josef, the younger of his two sons. But the synthetics had installed Andrei, the elder, whom they deemed more controllable. The governmental apparatus, long accustomed to being excluded from the Emperor's person by his household administration, had been paralyzed by indecision . . . all but Prime Minister Morava. She had summoned available Fleet forces to Sol, hoping to overawe the synthetics with the threat of a military coup and thereby avoid its actuality. Unfortunately, the forces first able to respond to her call had been those of Admiral Kleuger, who by virtue of his unrivaled ability at murder and slaughter had gained control of the Sigma Draconis system. Unfortunate, too, that Morava herself had been assassinated by the synthetics shortly after those forces had arrived. Kleuger had sent his Marines down onto the Old Earth city where the court had currently been in residence. (What had it been called? New York? New Delhi? Something like that. One of the capitals of one of the old civilizations whose remains overlaid Old Earth like geological strata.) They had exterminated all the synthetics they could catch. Then they'd exterminated all supporters of Andrei the False. Then they'd exterminated everyone whose support for Josef's claim to the throne had been insufficiently vociferous. Then they'd exterminated everyone whose face they hadn't liked. Somewhere along the way, they'd managed to take Andrei alive; and Kleuger, in one of his more rational moments, had accepted his abdication. (His subsequent death, the Empire was solemnly assured, had been a natural one.)

Then, threatened by a coalition of rival freebooting admirals, Kleuger had taken the newly crowned Emperor Josef to Sigma Draconis "for security reasons." For the next two years, he had claimed universal authority in the name of his puppet Emperor. Finally, by 3902, his behavior had reached such a psychopathic level of violence that his own officers had thought it prudent to assassinate him. The Imperial court had existed in limbo until 3906, when Yoshi Medina had seized Sol and declared himself protector of the Empire. He ceremoniously brought Josef back from Sigma Draconis and reinstalled him on Old Earth amid such of his ancestors' accumulated glories as Kleuger hadn't plundered. Then, armed with the prestige which the Emperor could still confer on his military commander-in-chief, Medina had brought most of the renegade admirals to heel. Only Kang still remained evasively recalcitrant in the Serpens/Bootes region—a group of frontier sectors with imperfectly assimilated populations. Medina deemed him ignorable for the present, preferring to put a final end to the New Humans before dealing with Kang and those other admirals of whose subservience he still wasn't altogether certain.

Basil grew aware that Silva was concluding her presentation. "Thank you, Captain," he said, hauling his mind back to the present. "As you can see, ladies and gentlemen, the task force still exists largely on paper. Major elements have yet to arrive—notably Rear Admiral Rady's battle group and Major General Bogdan's planetary assault forces. In order to meet the target date, we will have to begin preliminary staff work immediately, while they are still en route. Captain Silva has full authority in this matter until I return from my inspection tour." The nearby red-dwarf system of DM -48 11837 was the staging area for the first of the new *Implacable*-class battleships which had been assigned to this task force—Medina was still skeptical of the Mu Arae system's security, and he wanted the *Implacables* to come as a surprise to the rebels when the offensive commenced.

There was a brief flurry of questions, and then Basil was off, ascending a lift tube to an even higher level of this urban tower and emerging onto a flange where his personal aircar waited. It was night, and as the aircar lifted off he got a spectacular view of Bronson's Landing, the metropolis of Hespera, with its dazzling array of towers. Nanoconstructors could make repairs very quickly, and the cityscape showed no signs of the ravages of civil war. Basil wondered if the same was true of the society that dwelled inside these gleaming buildings.

He dismissed the thought, to make room for his more usual anxieties—notably, the length of time it was going to take Sonja and Torval to get here with their respective commands. He had asked for them and gotten them, for Medina had learned over the years that the three of them formed a whole that was more than the sum of its parts. As Basil had risen as Medina's protégé, the other two had risen with him.

The aircar approached the spaceport, its vast field an oasis of darkness in the light-blazing cityscape. Mu Arae had never had a Fleet base before the rebellion, just a small headquarters at this civilian facility. Now the entire spaceport was under military administration, and Basil's *Courier*-class speedster lay alongside a secondary terminal which had always handled such small vessels. As the aircar settled down beside the terminal and Basil stepped out, a quartet of guards emerged from the darkness and fell into a diamond-shaped formation around him. They were Fleet Security, and Basil smiled at the thought of what Torval would have said. But this sort of duty was, by tradition, Security's job. No need to step on people's toes unnecessarily.

They proceeded toward the *Courier*. It was streamlined for rapid atmosphere transit, which gave it a look of fleetness which could have been completely spurious as far as the interstellar long haul was concerned but wasn't. It was near the lower limit of size for a viable interstellar craft, built for speed and little else. Its sleek sides reflected the meager light—this was a poorly illuminated area—and Basil couldn't make out the features of the uniformed woman who emerged from the hatch. It must, he decided, be his aide, who would share the Spartan accommodations with him and the crew of two. But wait, wasn't this woman a little tall for Lieutenant

Commander Markova? And who was that coming out after her . . . ?

The woman walked briskly forward and, without breaking stride, brought up a hand weapon. There was the harsh humming of a sonic stunner, and the guard in front of Basil collapsed. By sheer chance, the guard fell backwards, into him, and he lost his balance. He saw the other guards go down—their impact armor was designed to stop solid projectiles, and offered no protection against sonics. Only the point man's body had shielded Basil. Looking up from under the immobile form, he saw the two figures come closer, stunners lowered—they evidently thought him unconscious. A third, silhouetted against the *Courier*'s hatch, called out, "Take him—quick!"

The woman approached. Basil pulled his legs sharply up and, using them and his arms, propelled the guard's limp form into a collision with her. As she stumbled, he sprang to his feet and charged her companion, seizing him by both wrists before he could bring his stunner into play. As they grappled, Basil took a deep, gasping breath and yelled with the maximum volume he could manage. "Guards! Anybody! Help!"

He wrestled the man to the ground and spared a quick glance at the woman, who had regained her feet. She was pointing her stunner but seemed hesitant to try a shot, which would almost certainly stun both of the struggling figures. Then he heard the sound of running feet on the tarmac from the direction of the small-craft terminal. *Ah, they heard me, or saw what was going on. About goddamned time . . .*

There was a brain-rattling impact behind his right ear, and the universe exploded into whirling galaxies of stars before going out.

He awakened into an infinity of pain and nausea, far beyond what a simple hit on the head, even if combined with sonics, could account for. He couldn't even escape from his nightmare of inability to move, for he was lying on his back strapped tightly to a narrow bunk in what he recognized as a *Courier*'s cabin. And he could hear and feel the very faint thrumming that was unavoidable aboard even the best-built spacecraft under drive.

Movement at his bedside penetrated his fog of agony. He turned his head slightly and saw a woman—the one from the spacefield?—stand up and pocket the injector from which she'd presumably dosed him with whatever had brought him around. She moved aside, revealing a man in nondescript civilian clothing with a paralysis pistol holstered at his side, sitting cross-legged in a chair—a thin man with a long narrow face and a long narrow nose down which he gazed impersonally at Basil with pale-gray eyes. There was a guard standing beside the compartment's door, but Basil spared him only an instant's glance. The seated man was the one who counted.

The pain in his head gradually made room for the reality of his situation. With it came the slate-gray knowledge of what his duty was. Without further thought, he probed with his tongue for a certain tooth . . . only to find a gap, and awake a shooting pain that momentarily rose whitecap-like above his sea of misery.

The thin-faced man's mouth twitched upward in a half-second's amusement. "Don't bother, Admiral Castellan. We're aware of your suicide devices. We haven't removed the explosive implant, since we lack the equipment to do a proper job and we didn't want to risk damaging your brain. We have, however, extracted the artificial tooth with which it is activated."

Basil hadn't even noticed the pain of the rough-and-ready dental work, for individual pains were hard to differentiate. And he didn't really notice even now, not in the face of the despair that eclipsed even his physical agony. He opened his mouth with some effort, for his lips seemed to be glued together, and when he tried to speak he realized how dry his mouth was. "Water!"

The thin-faced man gestured, and the woman stepped forward and offered Basil the drinking tube of a plastic bottle. The rarest and most fabled vintages were reduced to insipidity by comparison with the room-temperature water . . . which, with another gesture from the man in the chair, was withdrawn.

"Not too much at once. We've kept you unconscious for some time. An awkward process, but this craft lacks cryogenic suspension facilities."

"How long?" Basil croaked.

Again the thin lips moved in a tic of momentary amusement that had no humor in it. "Cautious habit prevents me from answering that question, Admiral. It might enable you to estimate the distance from Mu Arae to the destination at which we are about to arrive."

"I'm hardly in a position to make use of the information."

"True. But security procedures are best observed at all times. We need only look to your side for illustrations of the consequences of failure to do so."

Either Basil's headache was ebbing or he was getting used to it, for speech seemed to be coming with less agony. "I suppose you're referring to your knowledge of my movements. And the fact that you were able to infiltrate the Bronson's Landing spaceport and take control of this vessel."

"And also take control of the small craft terminal," the thin-faced man nodded. "Which allowed us to escape from the system before anyone was aware of what was happening."

Basil wasn't too surprised. They'd known there was still a functioning New Human underground on Hespera. Evidently they hadn't taken it seriously enough. "So your local people held that terminal long enough for you to make your escape. I imagine they're all dead by now," he added with calculated malice.

"Indubitably." There was no sign that Basil had succeeded in shaking his captor's composure. "By the way, I am Felix 3581-2794. We have, you see, done away—"

"With surnames," Basil finished for him. "Part of your overall policy of destroying the family."

"Of course. It must be eradicated along with all other institutions which interpose themselves between the State and the individual. Only then, with the individual's insignificance revealed plainly enough for even the stupidest to see, will the majority of humans be sufficiently controllable to be led into the next stage of social evolution, in which individuality is transcended. But I digress." Felix stood up and stretched. "We are arriving at our destination. Which is, of course, the reason you've been awakened."

Of course, Basil's mind echoed dully. *It's necessary that I be conscious.* In some periphery of his mind that was not immobilized by knowledge of what was to come, he became aware of that subliminal change in background sensations that told an experienced spacer that the ship had come out of drive.

Felix gestured, and his two subordinates proceeded efficiently to release Basil's straps. Then they grasped him by the arms and hauled him up into a standing position that his long-unused muscles couldn't have sustained unaided. A thousand tiny needles seemed to prick his legs and feet as blood circulated back into them, and a wave of nausea and dizziness washed over him. Before he had time to be sick they marched him through the door and along the *Courier*'s short central passageway to the bridge.

It was a small bridge, with the pilot-captain's and helmsman's chairs and their attached control panels and neurohelmets extending out into the concavity formed by a bowl-shaped viewscreen. That screen showed only the star-strewn blackness of interstellar space.

Felix observed Basil's puzzlement and gave his brief half-smile of humorless amusement. "Tactical," he ordered the pilot-captain, and at once the viewscreen ceased to reproduce what unaided eyes would have seen through a transparent hull. Instead, an array of multicolored symbols appeared, bewildering to anyone who wasn't trained to read it. But Basil was so trained. And his despair deepened as he gazed at the serried ranks of ships that had no nearby light source to reflect in the visual display.

These weren't the converted freighters that had made up the bulk of rebel strength in earlier years. They were warships of every class. Swift, lightly armed frigates. The cruisers and battlecruisers that were the backbone of every fleet. And battleships comparable to the Empire's new *Implacables*. This new-construction armada must represent a fanatical production drive by all the worlds in all the sectors of the breakaway "People's Democratic Union."

Basil grew aware that Felix was looking at him. This time the faint smile held an unmistakable element of malice—the first real emotion Basil had seen his captor display.

"Where are we?" he asked, not expecting an answer but needing to fill the silence.

"We're orbiting a rogue planet at the maximum radius at which it can hold objects in a stable orbit—it's quite invisible to the naked eye at this distance. As for the location of that rogue planet, I'll only say that the force you see before you will be in a position to launch itself at the Imperial core systems as soon as those have been denuded of ships by your Fleet's offensive."

Basil knew his jaw had gone slack, and couldn't help it. Felix's expression was now unmistakably one of gloating. "Oh, yes. We know, in general terms, about the offensive planned by the butcher Medina—your mentor. We've known for some time. You really have no idea, do you, how deep the rot goes in the Imperial system? It goes far beyond security leaks on Hespera. Some of the synthetics in the Imperial court itself have been in our pay!"

Basil wasn't really surprised. The synthetics' corruption was well known to everyone except the Emperors, whose trust in them had repeatedly proven to be misplaced. It was an abiding Imperial blind spot. Living in a court pervaded by intrigue, the Emperors *needed* to believe that someone around them was free of ambition. So they made intimates of synthetics, believing that ambition was simply out of the question for beings who had nothing but Imperial protection standing between themselves and the universal loathing and contempt with which they were regarded. So went the theory. But in fact the synthetics were quite capable of avarice . . . and of a sheer malice born of desire to hurt and punish the society of natural humans that had brought them into existence.

"I don't imagine," Basil heard himself saying, "that they've been much help to you lately." Kleuger's berserk pogrom of the court synthetics had been followed by Medina's careful, systematic one.

"True enough," Felix admitted. "We've experienced a certain drying-up of our sources of information, and therefore know about the offensive only in broad outlines. Which is why we were prepared to go to great lengths—including the sacrifice of our surviving organization on Hespera—to capture you, Admiral."

Basil met his gaze in silence, for there was no reply to make. After a moment, Felix glanced back at the viewscreen. "I believe we're now in eye-range of our destination." The pilot-captain took the hint and switched the viewscreen back to visual display. At first Basil could make nothing out except a small shark-shaped segment of blackness, occluding the stars. Then a ship began to take form and grow, feebly reflecting the stars and the *Courier*'s spotlights.

"A frigate specially equipped for intelligence-gathering purposes," Felix explained. "Naturally it carries mind-probe equipment."

"Naturally," Basil echoed in what he hoped was a conversational tone. He made himself relax, hoping that the two who held his arms would loosen their grips correspondingly. Felix probably wasn't a fast-draw artist, and at any rate he wouldn't use his paralysis pistol here, where an accidental hit could play hob with electronic systems.

"Let no one assert," Felix philosophized, "that technological advancement has not fundamentally altered the human condition. For one thing, it has eliminated much of the need for torture—at least as an aid to interrogation, in which capacity it was never particularly reliable anyway. Indeed, to a limited extent it has eliminated the very process of interrogation, in the old sense."

And, Basil thought sickly, watching the frigate swell in the viewscreen as they approached rendezvous, *along with torture has disappeared the possibility of resistance to torture.* Determination, courage, honor, loyalty . . . all counted for nothing. Even extreme gestures like biting out one's own tongue, once effective against the old "truth" drugs—which at any event had only been able to access what the subject *believed* to be the truth—could no longer suffice to withhold information. Nor could suicide, for even the freshly dead mind could be made to yield its secrets.

But that mind had to be housed in an intact brain. . . .

Basil made his muscles relax even further as the frigate continued to wax in the viewscreen and its docking bay yawned before them like the mouth of hell. His captors, with no resistance to overcome, grasped his arms a little less tightly.

As suddenly as he could manage in his weakened, just-awakened state, he performed a textbook breakaway maneuver—first forcing his arms upward in a movement that those holding him instinctively pushed against, then downward. Then he thrust his momentarily free arms straight outward to each side, shoving the startled rebels off balance. Felix yelled something, but Basil hardly heard, for with everything he could summon up from his stiffened limbs he was springing forward toward the open space between the two control chairs, through which he would leap headfirst into the viewscreen.

It might have worked, had his body been functioning at its normal pitch, and had the pilot-captain and helmsman been mind-linked with the ship and thus oblivious to their bodies' immediate surroundings. But the former had his neurohelmet raised, and responded instantly to Felix's shout, throwing himself sideways out of the chair against Basil's sluggishly pumping legs. The two of them went down in a tangle from which Basil was hauled by his two guards. They yanked his arms painfully upward behind his back into a position from which he couldn't even attempt to extricate them save at the cost of dislocation.

Felix stepped slowly forward into Basil's field of vision. Abruptly and with no appearance of passion, he slapped

his prisoner across the face twice. Basil tasted the saltiness
of blood from a cut lip, and consciousness wavered. Behind
Felix's head he could see the viewscreen. The frigate's
docking bay was swallowing them.

"Typical," Felix observed. "Theatrical heroics are only
to be expected from a servant of a system rooted in archaism.
I remind you that while use of the probe requires that you
be conscious, it does *not* require that you be willing . . . or
comfortable. Any further recalcitrance will be punished with
nerve lash." There was a faint jar as the *Courier* settled
onto the docking bay's deck. "And now, let us proceed."

Basil went without resistance. He didn't really think Felix
would use nerve-lash, which while technically non-lethal
(although it carried harsher penalties for unlawful use than
most deadly weapons) sometimes resulted in its victim's
death as the nervous system seized up in response to
unendurable agony. But he had no desire to take the
chance. There was a brief colloquy in the docking bay
between Felix and an officer in the nondescript gray
uniform of the People's Democratic Union. Then they
proceeded through labyrinthine corridors where people
stepped aside deferentially at Felix's approach despite his
civilian dress. They came to a hatchway where a sentry
admitted them to a small compartment.

The room held the same clutter of cabinets and overloaded
shelves as such rooms anywhere. But its centerpiece was
an ironically comfortable-looking reclining couch. Overhead,
ready to be lowered down over the head of the couch's
occupant, was something that looked not too unlike the
standard neurohelmet used in ordinary forms of direct
human-machine interfacing, but which Basil recognized for
what it was. Off to one side was a desktop-sized device
including a viewscreen he couldn't see, connected to the
chair by cables. Behind the desk, under a still-raised helmet
identical to the other, a gray-uniformed woman sat. Her
head had the same stubblelike haircut that all New Humans
affected (black in her case; Felix's mingled the colors of
sand and dust), but Basil could tell that she was a woman.

And, for no particularly good reason, that made it even worse. His mind ran frantically back over things he had seen, heard, felt, smelled and tasted in the last three months.

"And now," Felix said, "just to assure that there will be no further nonsense. . . ." He drew his paralysis gun and fired at a range at which he couldn't miss.

The pair holding Basil's arms kept him upright as he abruptly became incapable of any voluntary muscular action. They put him on the couch, manipulating his limbs with the impersonality one might bring to the hanging of a carcass from a meathook. Then they lowered the slightly peculiar-looking helmet over his head. His consciousness of all this was horribly unimpaired, and he found that he could, with great effort, turn his eyes in their sockets. Thus he saw the woman from behind the desk approach from his right and, without granting him even the most passing of glances, roll up his sleeve. First she inserted an IV tube—probably to continue feeding him nourishment, for this might take a while. Then she pressed an injector to his upper arm. Then she was gone from his range of vision, and Basil heard a faint hum which, he knew, meant that her own helmet was lowering into place.

Felix stepped in front of him. "As you are doubtless aware, the process is physically painless. And your innermost mental privacy is quite secure, for the probe reads not actual thoughts but sensory impressions—*all* of them, for the last three months or so, regardless of your ability to consciously recollect them. Of course, most of these will simply be skimmed over by our operator, a highly skilled—and professionally detached—technician." The thin face was as immobile as ever, but Basil detected a slight gleam in the pale-gray eyes, and he decided his initial impression of emotionlessness had been mistaken. Felix enjoyed his work. "We are, after all, only interested in what you have seen and heard that pertains to the planned offensive," the dead-leaves-dry voice went on. "And, to repeat, your actual memories will be inviolate—for now. Afterwards, when we've taken you to a core system of the People's Democratic Union where full-scale hospital facilities are available, it will be time to consider downloading your consciousness."

Basil, whose immobilized larynx could not form a scream, just looked at him. The thin mouth formed one of its momentary half-smiles. Then Felix moved aside, and it began.

Basil lay on the hard, narrow bunk in the room without windows or doors, looking up at the featureless ceiling. His soul looked up from the bottom of a black well of hopelessness.

With the usual absence of warning, a doorway appeared in one of the smooth walls as the nanoplastic reconfigured itself. Felix, now in uniform and carrying a briefcase, stepped into the room, followed by two powerfully built guards with paralysis guns. Behind them, the wall became unbroken again.

"You are well, I trust. Evidently the rations agree with you, as I understand you've been eating voraciously."

Basil's stomach had shrunk during the period when he was being intravenously nourished, so he hadn't experienced any hunger pangs until after his first normal feeding. Then he'd ravenously attacked food that he normally would have found about as appetizing as dampened chalk. Now he wordlessly swung himself up into a sitting position on the bunk's edge.

Felix evidently hadn't expected a reply, for he continued without a break. "You will be interested to know that your probing was a complete success. As expected, most of the material was of no value to us—all the everyday tediousness and sordidness. But some of the auditory input exceeded our most sanguine expectations—"

Like Medina's voice, and my own, and those of his staffers, as we hammered out the operation, Basil thought bleakly.

"—as, to an even greater extent, did some of the visual images, which as you know can be recorded by ordinary means as they appear on the probe's screen."

The operations people were so proud of their detailed,

multicolored hologram of the entire plan, Basil's bleak thoughts flowed sluggishly on. *Nothing would do but that I view it from every angle and voice appreciation of every aspect.*

"I have the datachip containing the visual recording here," Felix continued, patting his briefcase. "And now, the time has come for us to depart for Unity."

Curiosity overcame Basil's disinclination to speak. " 'Unity'?"

"A planet of the People's Democratic Union. It used to have another name, of course—now abolished like all holdovers of the past. Our transportation should have a comforting familiarity for you, for we're taking your personal *Courier.* Its swiftness is such that the journey should not be a tedious one."

"Will I be kept unconscious again, lest I occupy my time calculating distances?"

"I don't believe that will be necessary, Admiral. You will, however, be closely guarded to prevent any attempts at self-destruction."

"Why bother, now? You have what you want, don't you?" But then a recollection broke the surface of Basil's consciousness. "Unless you really meant what you said about . . ."

Felix nodded. "The downloading. Yes. You'll find I never say anything without meaning it, Admiral."

"I'm flattered, considering the expense."

The ability to record the memories that made up a human awareness dated back to the thirty-fifth century, when it had been heralded as offering a kind of immortality through imprinting copies of one's consciousness onto the blank brains of one force-grown clone after another. But that hope had run aground on the hard facts of organic chemistry; the process took too long for a living brain to accept the input. Computer software, though, was another matter. A very complex computer, purpose-built at staggering cost to accept the very specialized data-storage media involved, could run a recorded personality as a self-aware program.

"It *is* expensive," Felix acknowledged. "But with your knowledge of Imperial operations, we fully expect it to justify its cost."

"What makes you think a copy of my mind will have any more inclination to cooperate with you than I do myself?"

Felix's tiny smile lasted longer than usual. "Oh, I think you'd be surprised, Admiral. The downloaded consciousness can be given whatever stimuli we desire. And there is no physical body to go into shock, so the traditional limitations of torture do not obtain . . ."

"Weren't you the one who was lecturing me about the obsolescence of torture?"

"For certain information-gathering purposes—*not* for purposes of enforcing obedience. However," Felix continued after a barely perceptible pause, "I have high hopes that such regrettable expedients will not be necessary. You see, we have been experimenting with subtle modifications of the recorded personality, at the basic motivational level. Such as, for example, instilling a devotion to the principles of New Humanity without adversely impacting the memories and abilities. The preliminary results are quite promising. And, of course, the research is expedited by the availability of additional copies of the original copy, in any number desired. We need not hesitate to test a recorded personality to destruction. So I have every hope that it will be possible to avoid the cruder forms of coercion."

"Thank you," Basil said drily.

Felix spoke like one reciting doctrine. "Gratitude, Admiral, is a disease of dogs—as a very great man once said, very long ago."

"Lenin," Basil muttered automatically.

Felix raised one eyebrow. "Ah, yes: I remember now. You are a history enthusiast. I was one myself, in my former life." Basil recognized the New Human jargon. "And I have been allowed to continue to refine my knowledge of it, in accordance with the policy that permits persons of demonstrated reliability to pursue forbidden areas of study which may have practical applications. It is one of the reasons

I look forward to working with you, Admiral . . . or, rather, with a download of you, when a satisfactory one has been produced. After which, of course, you yourself will become disposable."

Felix gestured to the guards. They hauled Basil to his feet and fastened neural shackles to his wrists. He made no attempt to struggle against the physically flimsy restraints, which would deliver a nerve-lash effect in response to any such attempt. Then Felix turned on his heel toward the wall, whose sensors detected his genetic pattern. The doorway appeared again, they passed through, and the wall resumed its confining seamlessness.

CHAPTER FIVE
Unity (DM +7 4052 II), 3908 C.E.

Unity had been called something else—Nueviberia, a worn-down form of the name its original colonists had bestowed on it long ago—when it had been the capital planet of the Empire's Psi Capricorni Sector. Basil could already see that the name wasn't all that had changed.

Certain of his fellow officers had always regarded his interest in the New Humans as an eccentricity, as well as a waste of time that might otherwise be devoted to more fruitful and potentially career-enhancing fields of study like the power politics of the contending regional admirals. But he'd persevered, mindful of the incredibly ancient adage, "Know your enemy." And now he had an opportunity to compare what he'd learned with reality, as he rode a slider with Felix and two guards from the spacefield toward Montrose City, as to whose former name he had no idea.

"Quite an honor for this planet, isn't it?" he asked Felix. "Having its chief city named after the originator of the New Human ideology. How is he, by the way?"

"Quite well," Felix said shortly. Fleet Intelligence had deduced that Montrose was now certifiably insane and addicted to a remarkable variety of drugs, and that his public persona was a computer simulation, aided by a very sophisticated robotic double whenever a physical appearance was required. But Felix ignored Basil's mischievousness and changed the subject. "Unity is, after all, an important planet of the People's Democratic Union, second only to Equality, the capital world. The naming of this city merely reflects that importance."

"No doubt. Still . . . I thought you'd done away with surnames."

Felix refused to be baited. "There are always exceptions—or, at least, there will be until all vestiges of the past's irrational clutter have been obliterated from the very memory of a New Humanity which has become universal. Delmore Montrose had his great revelation while still a former person, and therefore the surname is still associated with his work. The inescapable fact is," he added parenthetically, "we *all* used to be former people. Except, of course, those born in the last fourteen years."

"How very fortunate for them." Basil was all blandness.

"Actually," Felix went on, "it is hoped that eventually the use of all individual names can be discontinued, and that humans, as well as planets, cities, geographical features, and so forth can be identified purely by alphanumeric designators. Personal names of all kinds, with their more or less blatant historical associations, carry underlying assumptions of exceptionalism. Indeed, language in general is permeated with the stench of the past. Ultimately, for true equality to prevail, the existing tongues must be replaced by a rational language created as a phonetic analogue of binary logic. A language in which it will be *impossible* to express ideologically unacceptable thoughts."

"What a magnificent vision."

"Yes," Felix said softly, either oblivious to sarcasm or deliberately ignoring it. More and more, Basil was coming to suspect the former; Felix was armored in the absolute humorlessness of the ideologue. And he was even more given to lecturing than Basil himself. "Unfortunately, not everyone can perceive its magnificence. Most require . . . guidance. And there are always recalcitrants."

Basil began to see the implications of Felix's words as they swooped along the highway from the spacefield. To their left was the Naiad Ocean, beyond sand dunes with patches of mutated sea oats. Ahead, the towers of Montrose City—or whatever—still sought the sky, for the new regime still needed this system's economic infrastructure in place. But as they neared what had once been the suburbs, those towers were lost to sight in the press of shoddy residential blocks, newly run up by nanoconstructors working from the most elementary programs. Everywhere, the residue of unprocessed raw materials lay about in heaps that the inhabitants, sulking about in dispirited crowds, showed no inclination to remove. Sewage disposal clearly hadn't been part of the plan for these warrens, for streams of foul runoff flowed in the gutters, where skinny half-naked children played in a desultory way. The stench that penetrated the slider's enclosed cabin made Basil wonder what it was like outside.

Felix gestured at the masses of human misery beyond the cabin's armorplast bubble. "Former rural inhabitants of this continent," he explained in an offhand way. "They have been relocated to central locations like this so their labor can be more rationally organized for the war effort. Also, removal from their accustomed environs makes them more socially malleable. In the past, they have displayed a certain stubbornness in clinging to obsolete societal patterns, notably those associated with the family."

"I see they're still being brought in," Basil remarked as they passed a large open area in the midst of the high-density squalor. A bulky contra-grav transport had grounded there, and crowds of people were shambling out under the gaze of uniformed guards with nerve lashes.

"Yes . . . and there appears to be a disturbance. Stop here." The slider came to a halt in obedience to Felix's command. The bubble raised, and Basil forced his rising gorge down as the outside air flowed in. This was a fairly cool day; he wondered what the hot ones were like.

Felix, showing no reaction to the miasma, got out and walked toward a knot of struggling figures. Two guards were restraining a wild-eyed woman from touching two children being pulled away by other guards. A junior officer was running up, but came to a sudden, exaggerated position of attention at the sight of Felix. There was a brief exchange that Basil couldn't make out, then Felix said something to one of the guards.

With a sudden movement, the guard touched his nerve lash to the base of the woman's neck. Her back arched convulsively, and she rent the air with a scream fit for the ultimate torments of hell. The guard withdrew the lash, and the woman collapsed, convulsing—but Felix gestured, and the guard, after what might have been a fraction of a second's hesitation, thrust the lash back into contact with her, and kept it there. The screams rose to a level that must have lacerated her throat, drowning out the children's wails, but they didn't last long.

Felix, without troubling to determine if she was dead or merely unconscious, turned to the children. He glanced only momentarily at the girl, five or so, who was standing in unblinking shock, sucking her fingers. But his gaze lingered longer on her nine- or ten-year-old brother, a slender olive-complexioned boy with regular features. Then Felix spoke a few words to the junior officer, who saluted and spoke to the guards. The two children were taken off in separate directions, screaming anew and reaching for each other. Felix, without a backward glance, returned to the slider.

"What about . . . ?" Basil gestured at the crumpled heap of the children's mother, carefully keeping his voice level.

"Unimportant. Even if she's alive, the neural damage she's sustained would render her useless for any form of labor. The detritus will be cleaned up by morning." As the slider proceeded in response to his command, Felix gestured at the instant slum around them. "What happens to these people is of no concern. As I indicated, they are just rural trash, inherently incapable of appreciating the truth of New Human doctrines."

"Such as that of human equality?"

"Precisely. I'm gratified—and surprised—that you understand the situation so well."

"Still," Basil ventured, "some of them evidently are less useless than others. The boy and girl, for instance?"

"Ah, yes." Felix's eyes took on a faraway look, and he unconsciously licked his lips. "The girl is fit only for labor—and later, perhaps, as recreation for the male laborers. But the boy will be attached to my household staff, in which capacity he will be able to render more important service to the State."

They rode in silence as the shoddy forced-labor housing gave way to the old city. Here, the crowds were marginally better dressed and better nourished, and basic services seemed more or less functional despite an overall air of run-down shabbiness. And there was one altogether new municipal utility: on every major street corner, a holoprojector ran a twice-lifesize image of Delmore Montrose, declaiming his precepts for the edification of small crowds that collected at each such corner. The members of those crowds alternated between vociferous exclamations of admiration for the sage's words and surreptitious glances over their shoulders to see if any uniformed personnel were watching. The answer was almost invariably yes, for every fourth individual seemed to be wearing a uniform. Those uniforms weren't all that different from the standardized gray garb that everyone wore. But the sight of the rank and branch insignia on cuff and shoulder was enough to reduce civilian gait to a kind of shuffling cringe.

They proceeded through the city to what was obviously a long-established residential district. Soon, with the abruptness of a giant's axe stroke, the old tree-shaded homes and the landscape produced by centuries of careful tending ceased, for the slider had entered an area that had been recently cleared with brutal thoroughness and surrounded with a security fence. After a while they came to a gate in the fence and turned down a long driveway between rows of recently planted saplings that hadn't had time to grow into shade trees. Beyond, a vast manorial residence rose at the far end of a reflecting pool. Basil, whose knowledge of classical schools of architecture was sketchy at best, recognized only a few of the elements that had entered into the grandiose eclecticism.

"Most impressive," he remarked neutrally.

"It is the residence of this sector's Coordinator. He found the old Imperial governor's palace inadequate to his needs. Naturally, the local populace was overjoyed to contribute to the expense of construction, for they realized—after suitable instruction in correct doctrine—the gratitude they should feel toward those of us who are leading them out of the Empire's archaic class structure into a new age of democratic equality."

"So I can see," Basil muttered, gazing around at the extensive grounds. Here and there, humans—presumably cheaper than robots—labored at gardening chores and tried to make themselves inconspicuous whenever the armed guards strolled by.

The slider curved off to the right of the reflecting pool and bypassed the main façade, coming to a halt at a side entrance. "When I based my intelligence-gathering operation here," Felix explained, "the Coordinator was good enough to place a wing of his residence at my disposal." Then one of the guards nudged Basil out of his seat, and they passed through the doorway into a long high-ceilinged entrance hall from which hallways extended in three directions. Here and there, a number of fine-featured young boys were in evidence, and Basil decided he had been correct in certain assumptions about his captor.

Felix turned to face him. "You will be housed in comfortable quarters to await the procedure we discussed previously. Unless . . ." He stretched the pause to the snapping point. "Unless you decide you would rather cooperate with us voluntarily."

"I gather you'd prefer that." Basil spoke in a voice whose steadiness surprised him.

"It's possible that you will be more useful to us in your organic form. So, to that extent, the answer is yes. But, more to the point, I would think *you'd* prefer it. You'll have

a while to consider the matter, as preparations have to be
made in any case. Besides which, I have plenty to occupy
me at the moment." With what passed for a theatrical
flourish, Felix indicated the briefcase he was carrying. "I
must supervise the harvesting of the rich crop of information
your probing yielded."

Once again despair engulfed Basil—or, rather, his dulled
awareness of its presence flared up anew. Yes, the datachip
that held all the images that had impressed themselves on
his eyes, right up through his capture to the point where
he had been taken into that little chamber after seeing the
rebel fleet . . .

All at once, he knew what the cliché "blinding realization"
meant.

*After seeing the rebel fleet . . . with the stars spread out
behind it . . .*

He struggled to keep his face blank, without total success.
But Felix never saw his expression, for he turned on his
heel and departed. Basil was hustled off down a side corridor.
He scarcely noticed the guards' frequent shoves, for his
thought processes had suddenly acquired a new intensity.

"Comfortable" was a generous description of the austere
semi-subterranean bed-and-bath with its shallow, barred
windows near the ceiling. But at least the sanitary arrangements
were civilized, and the rations were measurably better than
the synthetic shipboard paste. And they didn't keep him there
long.

He was lying on his narrow bed, propped up into reading
position, when the door slid aside—this was a traditional
residence—to admit Felix and a pair of guards. "Ah, Admiral,
I see you're using your time wisely," Felix remarked
approvingly, with a glance at the book he was reading.

Basil put the condensed anthology of the works of Delmore
Montrose down without commenting that it was the only
reading matter that had been made available to him—which
Felix already knew anyway. "Yes. Most illuminating. But I've
also been using the opportunity to do some thinking."

"Ah." Felix seated himself on a chair, leaving the guard standing in a watchful attitude. "Thinking about what I said when we arrived, I presume."

"Yes. I've come to the conclusion . . . well, I can see no real alternative to cooperating with you."

"Ah," Felix repeated, and gave his quick near-smile. "Am I to understand that you have become a convert to New Humanity?"

Basil laughed harshly. "If I claimed that, you'd probably have me downloaded without further delay, and then kill me."

"Quite true, Admiral; I don't respond well to having my intelligence insulted. So what *are* you saying?"

"It's simple enough. If I don't cooperate, I'll be killed—but only after you have my download under your control, so my death would accomplish nothing."

"Very rational, Admiral. Only . . . I can't rid myself of the suspicion that this particular manifestation of rationality is slightly out of character." The pale-gray eyes grew even colder. "As you've probably gathered, I've made something of a study of you. In addition to your stubborn loyalty to the outworn trappings of Imperialism, it is my impression that you value the good opinion of your peers highly. Too highly to be able to endure the thought that they might learn of your treason."

Basil met the almost colorless eyes with a glare that was as tightly controlled as the bitterness in his voice . "Oh, you're right . . . more right than you can know. The thought *is* unendurable. But the fact is, I'm going to *have* to endure it, aren't I?" He gestured at the spy cell high on a wall. "The visuals you have of me should provide the raw material for a very sophisticated holo simulation, which you'd be able to trot out in conjunction with my recorded personality. So my side is going to think I'm a traitor regardless of what I do. Once again, my death would mean nothing."

"I see." Felix looked pensive. "Perhaps my estimate of you requires modification, Admiral. I'm not in a position to verify this change of heart, as I have only one telepath and she almost certainly isn't strong enough to penetrate beneath your active surface thoughts, given your powers of telepathic resistance—oh, yes, we know about that, too. Still, much can be done with drugs—"

"Wait! You haven't heard my conditions."

Felix's head snapped up in annoyance at the interruption, and the guards tensed. " 'Conditions'? I don't think you're in any position to be talking of 'conditions,' Admiral."

"You'll have to be the judge of that. It's all a matter of how badly you want the added benefits and lesser expense that will come with my voluntary cooperation. But you'll have to hear them before you can decide, won't you?"

"Very well. Proceed."

"First of all, no drugs. And no poking about in my mind by some powerful telepath or group of telepaths working in concert until *after* you've met my second condition."

"Which is?"

"I want to talk to higher authority than you. Higher, in fact, than anyone this side of your capital world."

Felix raised one sandy eyebrow. "You *do* think a lot of yourself, don't you? What makes you think anything you have to tell us would be of sufficient interest to earn you immediate access to anyone higher than me? Especially in light of the fact that we already have the most important information you can provide. Thanks to the probe, we know in detail the plan for the coming offensive."

"Do you?" Basil asked, very softly.

Felix's mocking expression suddenly froze into the worried frown of a man wondering if he's missed something obvious. After a second or so, his face cleared and he gave his head an annoyed shake.

"Of course we do! It's all there: everything you heard yourself and others say, transcribed by the probe operator; and everything you saw, recorded from the screen in conventional video media."

"But *not* what I *know* about what I was hearing and seeing. The probe doesn't read thoughts and memories, just sensory impressions."

"But those sensory impressions are *real* ones. . . ." Suddenly, Felix's pale-gray eyes ignited with anger. "Are you actually trying to convince me that you and other highly placed people, up to and including Medina, have spent the last three months play-acting, to feed us false information?"

"Oh, no. But what you don't seem to understand is that while Imperial security has its leaks—in fact, the court is one vast sieve—it is *very* tight where Grand Admiral Medina is in direct charge. And the possible capture and probing of someone with access to highly sensitive information has been taken into account."

Felix's frown was back, along with a slight sheen of sweat on his brow. "Meaning . . . ?"

"Of course the staff can't communicate in code at all times. But for quite a while—considerably longer than the last three months—certain protocols have been in effect, designed not just to obscure information but to actively mislead the uninitiated. You know what I heard and saw . . . but you don't necessarily know what everything *meant*. You just think you do."

"Tell me about these 'protocols.'"

Basil shook his head. "No. This is too important, and from what I've seen of this place I don't trust its security a bit." Felix's eyes flashed again, but Basil pressed on. "Besides, if I'm going to turn my coat, I may as well do it *right*. I want to oblige the most powerful people I can."

"So," Felix said in a voice whose quietness was, Basil somehow suspected, deceptive, "I'm not a prominent enough patron for you?"

"Oh, don't take it personally. In fact, there's no reason why we can't share the credit."

"What do you mean?"

"Your capital system—'Equality' I think you called it; I can't remember what it used to be called—is only a short hop from here for a speedster like my *Courier*. You could take me there; and en route, with no security worries, I could go over the visuals and transcriptions with you and explain in detail the discrepancies between apparent and actual meanings. You could present your superiors with the information, as a fruit of your success in recruiting me. We'd both benefit: kudos for you, unassailable credibility for me."

As he'd spoken, Basil had noticed Felix's tongue making its little unconscious lip-licking motion. In any other circumstances, he would have been amused at his captor's efforts to keep up an emotionless façade. "On reflection, Admiral, I believe that your conditions are acceptable, and that the course of action you suggest has much to recommend it. In fact, I suggest we leave for the spaceport at once."

They retraced their route through the city to the spaceport, but this time Basil noticed nothing, for he was deep in thought.

Unsurprisingly, Felix had appropriated the admiral's stateroom on the *Courier* for himself. Basil found himself housed in the secondary cabin in which he'd been kept unconscious after his capture. The other secondary cabin held the one guard Felix had brought along. The two-man crew had its own quarters.

They had barely passed Unity's Chen Limit and engaged the drive when the guard came and escorted Basil to the admiral's stateroom, gesturing with a nerve lash for emphasis. Felix was waiting there, amid the stateroom's relative spaciousness. The compartment was largely unchanged; its new occupant hadn't removed any of Basil's personal objects . . . including an odd sculpture of some crystalline material, on a side table to the right of the data terminal. Basil sternly ordered his body and features not to sag with relief.

"And now, Admiral Castellan, let us proceed." Felix seated himself before the data terminal and inserted a datachip. Then he turned to Basil and motioned him to stand beside the chair.

"So that's a visual recording of my probe?" Basil gave the guard at his elbow a sideways glance. The fellow, who hadn't spoken to him except in monosyllables, had a holstered sidearm besides the nerve lash; Basil recognized a standard Fleet issue bead gun.

"It is. And don't concern yourself; this man is absolutely trustworthy."

"What about the crew?"

Felix shrugged, and fingered certain controls. "This stateroom is now locked, and surrounded with a privacy shield against the highly unlikely eventuality of eavesdropping by the crew members."

"But . . . is this necessary?" Basil indicated the nerve lash that the guard was holding unsettlingly close to his side.

"It is," Felix stated in a flat, cold voice. "You see, Admiral, I still don't trust you. This room has been checked for any conventional booby traps you might have had installed here. And you're not a telepath, so you can't trip any hidden psionic switches. So I feel secure allowing you here in your old stateroom. But *not* unguarded. And any attempts at prevarication will be instantly punished by nerve lash. If I come to the conclusion that you've been deceiving me from the beginning, the punishment will be prolonged to the edge of permanent neural damage—this guard has much experience in judging when that point has been reached. And now that your position has been made clear to you, let us proceed." He activated the screen.

Basil stepped forward. "Let's begin at the beginning. I assume your probe operator edited out everything that was obviously of no interest."

"Of course. And the operator's recitation of your relevant auditory input accompanies it." Felix pressed keys, and a corridor of Fleet Headquarters on Prometheus appeared on the screen, as viewed by a tall man walking along it.

"Speed it up some. A significant sequence should be coming up soon." Basil leaned forward as though to look over Felix's shoulder. The latter, secure in his knowledge of the guard's presence and absorbed in the sights unfolding on the screen, was oblivious to his captive's movements. And not even the guard found any cause for suspicion when Basil rested his right hand on the curious crystalline sculpture.

It portrayed a tiger lizard of Selagore, a world of the Serpens/Bootes region where life had arisen independently and the higher land animals were hexapods. "And damned ugly hexapods," he'd remarked when Torval, who'd served on Selagore, had presented the grotesque thing to him as a birthday gift.

The big Marine's ruddy face had formed a grin in the beard he had taken to cultivating—it was chestnut rather than dark brown like his hair—and his hazel-green eyes had twinkled. "Has its uses, though. How much do you know about Selagore?"

"Not much. Ex-Beyonders, incorporated when the Draconis Empire expanded in that direction but never completely assimilated."

"Right. And like a lot of Beyonder societies, they'd become backward in most ways but advanced in odd directions in a few others. In particular, they're real craftsmen with psionically active materials. Some of their artworks have more to them than meets the eye."

"I'm relieved," Basil had said drily, continuing to eye the sculpture with scant favor.

Torval had chuckled in his seismic way. "Listen. The thing about these Selagore psi-crystals is, you don't need to be a telepath; they're sensitive to the right thought from anybody who makes physical contact and concentrates. Here, touch it and—"

It had made quite a party trick, and Basil had kept the thing with him. Now, with his hand resting on the head of the sculpted beast, he thought of the actual tiger lizard—neither a tiger nor a lizard, of course, but with attributes worthy of both in its scale-armored, razor-fanged, massive-jawed presence. . . . which suddenly appeared in the middle of the stateroom, a quarter-ton of ill-natured carnivore rearing up on its two hind pairs of legs and using the front pair to slash the air with cutlasslike claws. It opened its cavernous, slavering mouth to emit a roar which the holoprojection couldn't reproduce but whose volume Basil did his best to approximate with a full-throated scream.

The guard would have been more than human if he hadn't used the weapon in his hand to fend off that nightmare apparition whose sheer impossibility hadn't had time to register. With a strangled cry he swung the nerve lash away from Basil and thrust it at the gaping fang-lined jaws, a movement made clumsy by panic.

But Basil, who had known exactly what to expect, moved swiftly and surely, chopping at the guard's wrist in a manner summoned up from academy vintage memories of karate training. The impact sent the nerve lash falling and sliding across the floor. Simultaneously, Basil used his left arm to catch the guard's head in a choke hold, followed by a vicious neck-breaking sideways twist. Then, dropping the still-twitching guard, he flung himself in the direction the nerve lash had gone . . . only to collide with Felix, who had come out of his paralysis and dived toward the same goal.

They fell to the floor in a struggling heap, rolling into the side table and sending the sculpture toppling onto the floor where it shattered into a thousand crystalline shards. The phantom tiger lizard abruptly vanished, but the two men didn't notice as they strained to reach the nerve lash while grappling with each other. Basil brought a knee up into an impact which caused Felix to gasp and loosen his grip. Taking quick advantage, Basil gave a forward heave which brought his fingers curling around the nerve lash's hilt. With another heave, he got on top of his opponent and jabbed the nerve lash into contact with Felix's cheek. He didn't activate it, but Felix's struggles ceased abruptly, and sweat broke out over the long narrow face.

Basil gasped for breath and then spoke levelly to his motionless opponent. "And now, Felix, you will order the crewmen to leave the ship under computer control and go to their quarters. Any tricks and I'll use this."

Felix gave the smallest possible nod. Basil pulled Felix's left wrist up behind him, raising him slowly to his feet while keeping the nerve lash in position, and walked him over to the intraship communicator. Felix gave the command in as steady a voice as could have been expected. Basil toyed with the thought of indulging himself in a brief application of the nerve lash anyway, but only momentarily. Instead, he reversed the device in his hand and, with the base of its handle, struck Felix a precise blow behind the ear, then lowered the limp form to the deck. Next he turned to the guard's body and drew the bead gun, a heavy pistol-shaped weapon with a magnetic accelerator coil around its barrel. He made sure the weapon had a full magazine of the little glass spheres that gave it its name. Then he went to the door and studied the spy cell. No activity in the short passageway; the pilot-captain and helmsman must already be in their bunkroom. He touched a key, and the door slid open with the faintest of hums.

As he stepped out into the passageway, it occurred to him that he hadn't really thought things through. The *Courier* wasn't designed to transport prisoners; these hatches couldn't be locked from the outside, for no one had ever visualized a situation in which it would be desirable to keep their occupants from getting out. Felix was such a valuable prisoner that he'd be worth keeping physically restrained for the whole trip, even if it required nursemaiding him. But two others, when there was only one of himself . . . ?

Then the question became academic, as the two crewmen appeared in the bridge hatch at the far end of the passageway, firing paralysis pistols.

Basil didn't waste time wondering why the rebels equipped space crew with the electronics-disrupting weapons. He just flung himself back through the hatchway. It wouldn't have been enough, save for the paralysis guns' narrow-beam effect. He wasn't quite fast enough to keep his right foot out of the fringes of a beam, and all at once it felt as though he'd spent motionless hours with that leg curled up under him. Luckily, rising to his feet was neither necessary nor desirable just now.

I'm not a trained combat soldier, he told himself. *I haven't fought with anything except my brain for years.* He did, however, have the knack of letting immaterial thoughts run their course while his body carried out the necessary action. (Torval had once told him he would have made a pretty good Marine corporal. He'd decided to take it as a compliment.) Ignoring his tingling foot, he rolled to the hatch, thrust the bead gun out into the passageway at floor level, where his opponents didn't expect it—they weren't trained combat men either—and pressed the firing stud at full automatic setting.

The gun accelerated the crystal beads instantaneously to six thousand meters per second with a faint plasma flash as their ferrous coating met the air at that velocity, but they didn't have enough mass to impart much recoil. So Basil was able to momentarily hold the weapon more or less on target. That was enough. One of the rebels fell backwards with a scream and a spray of blood, ruined arm flapping from the strands of red muscle that still connected it to his shoulder. The other stayed upright for a fraction of a second longer, as Basil started to lose control of the pistol. But the upward-swerving stream of glass beads crossed his forehead, and his skull exploded upward from overpressure as hydrostatic shock took its course.

Limping as he dragged his barely-functional right foot, Basil stepped onto the bridge, imposing mental discipline against the gore. Fortunately the armless man, whom he'd been prepared to put out of his misery, had at least lost consciousness. So he examined the controls. Bead gun projectiles were valued for shipboard use because they inflicted only limited damage on anything except unarmored flesh, shattering on impact with hard surfaces; but there was no telling what the out-of-control beams of falling paralysis guns might have shorted out as they swept across the bridge. He seated himself at the pilot-captain's station, ignoring the neurohelmet—he did not belong to that minority of humans with the specialized form of mental discipline needed for direct computer interfacing—and applied himself to the keyboard. Piloting a *Courier* wasn't his job, but he'd spent enough time aboard the little ships to acquire basic familiarization from pilots who'd been flattered by the high-ranking interest.

A few minutes' work convinced him that all was not well. The *Courier* was still proceeding under drive on its preset course toward the rebel capital system, but he was far from confident of his ability to persuade it to change that course. Then he remembered Felix, and decided there would be time enough later to worry about navigational problems.

He picked up one of the crewmen's paralysis guns and limped back to the stateroom. Felix was beginning to stir, and his eyes registered despairing surprise at the sight of Basil in the hatch.

"How did you give them the warning?" Basil asked conversationally. "I'm damned if I caught it."

"That," Felix said with a glimmer of returning animation, "would be telling."

"You didn't do them a favor," Basil continued. "I would have accepted their surrender, and figured out a way to keep them prisoners until we got back to Mu Arae. But you don't give a shit about your own people's lives, do you? Any more than you do about any others. And before you can read me a tract on the meaninglessness of individual human life . . ." He raised the paralysis pistol and Felix froze into immobility with his mouth half-opened. *No insects here to fly into it*, Basil thought regretfully as he dragged the motionless form into the cabin where he himself had been held captive and secured it on the bunk. Then he returned to the bridge.

It was difficult to pinpoint the problem, for there was little physical damage. And the computer, like those of most military ships, was not designed for voice communication, which might have led to confusion in the heat of battle. Basil had to sweat his way through on the keyboard, a job for a specialist. It was with a shaky sigh of relief that he sat back two hours later, watching the stars precess across the viewscreen until Mu Arae lay dead ahead.

He was punch-drunk with exhaustion, but sleep was out of the question until he had satisfied himself on one point. He returned to his stateroom and ordered coffee from the little autogalley. Then he seated himself at the data terminal, which still held the digital video recording of his mind probe.

He sped through ninety percent of what Felix and his technicians had deemed important, hoping frantically that they hadn't edited out what he needed. Then he was up to that last staff meeting on Hespera before his capture. . . . *Yes!* After that, they hadn't bothered with further editing. Conceivably, Felix had wanted the Basil's-eye view of the capture preserved as a testament to his own cleverness. Basil fast-forwarded through the confused fight at the spaceport, his awakening and initial conversation with Felix, the two guards manhandling him down the passageway to the bridge . . .

Weak with relief, he watched what his own eyes had seen: the stars in the viewscreen, just before Felix had ordered tactical display that had revealed the rebel fleet. He backed up, and recorded those few seconds' view of the firmament, then settled back with a long sigh.

Interpreting those star configurations to determine the observer's location in space was no job for the *Courier's* little nav computer, even had it been in the best of health. But back on Hespera, with the base's great molecutronic brains and encyclopedic astronomical databases available . . .

He was still thinking about it when sleep finally took him, still seated at the data terminal.

CHAPTER SIX
The DM -17 954 system, 3908 C.E.

It happened while Basil was securing Felix after a meal.
The *Courier*'s lack of detention facilities, combined with
the fact that he was alone with his prisoner, had proved an
even greater headache than he'd anticipated. On a ship with
a real sickbay, he would have put the rebel intelligence officer
in cryogenic suspension for the voyage. As it was, the strain
was beginning to tell.

"I need to use the facilities," Felix said—*after* Basil had
finished strapping him back into the bunk.

Basil glared. "It isn't time," he said shortly. His captive's
incessant mind games didn't help, especially after he'd spent
a tedious half hour standing over Felix with the paralysis
gun while the latter ate—a procedure whose single virtue
was that it was better than keeping Felix bound and feeding
him by hand. He could always *use* the paralysis gun as a
last resort—but the weapon's effect only lasted twenty to
thirty minutes, and they both knew its charge-pack would
run down if overused. As a *real* last resort there was always
the nerve lash. But Basil disliked using the thing, even on
Felix, who unfortunately knew that. "You'll hold it or lie in
it."

It was then that the harsh buzzing came through the open
doorway.

Basil started. The ship's brain was under instructions

to give the noisy alarm upon certain occurrences, none of them good news. He finished securing Felix—whose face had taken on an oddly complacent smirk that he didn't like—then hurried to the bridge, where the buzzing was almost deafening. He cut it off, and scrutinized the viewscreen. Nothing, of course: it was set for visual, and the only notable object was the yellow star DM -17 954 off to starboard, outshining every other star. He switched the viewscreen to tactical display. Still nothing. He added long-range sensors.

For a long while he stood motionless, staring at the scarlet icons. They had the flicker that indicated objects at the extreme edge of sensor range, and nothing could be inferred about what ship classes they represented. But it scarcely mattered, for the least of warships would effortlessly vaporize a *Courier* once it got within range—where these ships' purposely converging courses would inevitably bring them.

The question was, he thought in an oddly calm sort of way as he calculated probable time to intercept, just how they happened to already *be* on those courses. Just as his vessel had only now detected them, they should have only now detected him; they might well mount more capable sensors, but the *Courier* was a smaller target. As he thought about it, a suspicion solidified into certainty.

He returned to the secondary cabin. Felix was still wearing the same smirk.

"Is there something you haven't been telling me?"

"Whatever do you mean?" Felix's expression wavered momentarily as Basil drew the nerve lash, but then composed itself. "You won't use that. I know you too well; your values are mired inextricably in the past, among obsolete notions such as 'compassion' and 'human dignity' and other archaic holdovers of individualistic—" His didactic voice suddenly drowned in a scream and his back arched upward against the restraining straps as Basil jabbed the nerve lash against his upper arm for the barest instant.

Then he withdrew it and leaned over until his expressionless face was mere inches above Felix's twitching, sweat-drenched one.

"It seems," he said quietly, "that you've made a convert of me after all. Congratulations." He brought the nerve lash into another fleeting contact, ordering his ears to ignore the screams and his nose to ignore the stench of evacuated bowels. "And now, tell me about the ships that are pursuing us."

Felix didn't hesitate, except to take a few gasping, shuddering breaths; people generally didn't, after nerve lash. "As a precaution, I had a sensor beacon installed in this ship. It enhances the ship's sensor return as long as the drive is operating. You can't deactivate it without disabling the drive itself. No!" The last was shouted frantically as Basil began to make a move. "I'm telling you the truth! A fully equipped specialist with plenty of time might be able to—but you can't possibly."

"Even so, how did these ships just happen to be within any possible sensor range of us, out here in the middle of interstellar space?"

"By now we must be approaching the Union's frontier. And this region is heavily picketed." A trace of Felix's wonted smugness was beginning to creep back—a remarkable recovery, under the circumstances. "I gather from your behavior that interception is unavoidable. Let me remind you that all of your own rationales for cooperating with us were quite valid, however mendaciously you may have adduced them, and are still as valid as ever. If you surrender now, I will assure that your surrender is accepted, and do my best to minimize the consequences of your actions in attempting escape. . . ."

Basil found himself totally at a loss for words. He also found himself feeling certain urges concerning the nerve lash—an unwelcome bit of self-discovery. Without a word he stood up, raised the paralysis gun and pressed the firing stud while Felix was in mid-wheedle. Then he returned to the bridge and flopped down into the pilot-captain's chair.

The sensor display was too depressing, so he switched to visual.

His options were limited. He could cut the drive here and now—it made ships easier to detect even without Felix's beacon device. But even if they lost sensor lock on him, they'd simply proceed to his last recorded location and search until they found him. Besides, he wouldn't live long enough to get anywhere at sublight speeds, even if his supplies were unlimited, which they weren't.

Other alternatives were even less attractive. He had no idea how to go about blowing up the ship, or even if it was possible, but he could certainly destroy himself in any number of ways. But even the prospect of taking Felix with him didn't make him relish such a course of action.

Glumly, he let his eyes wander to the star-spangled depths of space in the viewscreen. The gleam of DM -17 954 drew his gaze like a magnet. The *Courier*'s course had brought it within a standard light-year of the yellow star, and it showed a perceptible drift in the computer simulation. Seeking mental refuge from his dilemma, he reviewed the data on that uninhabited, long-ignored system.

Technically a main-sequence star of spectral class G1v, it was oddly massive for that class and obviously had a history of instability. At some astronomically recent date, its inner planets had been scorched clean of whatever atmospheres and life forms they might have possessed. With its lack of habitable real estate and its potential for further stellar misbehavior, it had been bypassed by the colonizing waves of humanity. But it had an extensive outer system, including a gas giant more than four times the mass of Sol's Jupiter—which still set the standard for planets of its class, just as Old Earth did for life-bearing worlds—and therefore a borderline "brown dwarf" or failed star. This body, the fifth in orbital order, ruled its own extensive subsystem: moons, rings where moons had been unable to coalesce, and assorted cosmic rubble. . . .

Basil found himself calling up more and more data, requesting details on that subsystem. And, as though actuated by a spontaneous will of its own, an idea began to take form.

It wasn't much of an idea, as ideas went. But he couldn't for the life of him think of anything else to do. Abruptly, he began giving the computer instructions, knowing even as he did so that the plan's meager merits didn't justify his sudden enthusiasm for it.

"This is absurd," Felix said, not for the first time.

After a certain point, Basil had decided that he was going to be too continuously busy to take trips aft. So he'd secured his prisoner very tightly in the helmsman's chair, and occasionally fed him small portions of a low-residue diet. So now Felix sat before the viewscreen and looked out at the spectacle through which they were gliding.

DM -17 954 V filled a third of the bowl-shaped screen, off to the left. Curving around from behind that stupendous orange sphere was the outermost ring; it looked like a fairy bridge in the distance, but immediately "above" them its etherealness dissolved into myriad component particles of ice and rock. Off to the side hung several moons, glowing like fat, dim lanterns with their primary planet's reflected light. He didn't let himself think about the radiation with which the brown dwarf flooded the space surrounding it; if the *Courier*'s protective force field failed for even a moment, its material hull would give him and Felix no protection worth mentioning.

"Absurd," Felix repeated when no response was forthcoming.

"Not too absurd to have worked so far," Basil said absently, devoting most of his attention to nav hazards. There had been a satisfying delay in the rebel ships' response to his sudden course change, probably resulting from sheer incredulity. But then they had followed him to DM -17 954 V, maintaining their sensor lock until he'd reached the Chen Limit—a distant one, for so massive a body. Then, with his drive disengaged, they had lost him as he'd hoped. But they had closed in on the brown dwarf and commenced a methodical search.

"Let us suppose," Felix said, ostentatiously reasonable, "that you can continue to hide in all this cosmic junk indefinitely—unrealistic though that supposition is. Your supplies won't hold out forever, you know. And if you imagine that our people will simply grow bored with the search and go away, you're very far afield." He drew a deep breath, emboldened by Basil's lack of response. "I remind you that the option of surrender is still open to you. I also remind you that we are still in a position to be useful to each other, in light of which I am prepared to forget the incidents of the recent past."

Basil swung his chair around to face his captive, and spoke in the quiet tone at which Felix had learned to feel alarm. "I remind you that the only reason I've gone to the not-inconsiderable trouble of keeping you alive is your value as a prisoner, which makes it my duty to take you back with me. The moment you succeed in convincing me that I have no hope of *getting* back, you will become—and I quote—disposable." Then, with Felix silenced as effectively as the threat of the nerve lash would have done, he turned his attention back to the nav plot.

There was nothing to see, for his orbit had carried him into a relatively clear region.

So he switched to the intermediate strategic display he'd had the computer set up, which showed Planet V's entire subsystem. The scarlet icons of rebel ships were still moving in the same deliberate search pattern. The nature of sensor technology was such that its target could not detect the fact that it was being scanned. Thus the *Courier* could keep tabs on its hunters without giving away its position. By the same token, if they detected him, he'd have no direct indication of it—only indirect ones, like sudden course changes as they converged on him like stooping falcons. . . .

He shook the thought out of his head and switched back to visual. Still nothing to see, for the grandeur of the brown dwarf and its attendants had long since palled. As his tightly focused attention eased, he realized how tired and tense he was. He started to stretch.

Then he saw it. Or thought he saw it.

Weariness forgotten, he hunched forward and gazed narrow-eyed at the patch of space where, for the barest instant, Planet V's edge had seemed to waver or shimmer. Nothing. He shook his head again, deciding it must be eyestrain. But then something made him squint in that direction again.

There! That ever-so-slight distortion in the otherwise hard-edged line where DM -17 954 V met the blackness of space. He never would have noticed it against the backdrops of space or the brown dwarf, but at that particular point where they met and thus gave a frame of reference . . .

"Did you see that?" He was too preoccupied to wonder why he put the question to Felix—the closest approach to camaraderie in the voyage so far.

"See what?" Felix blinked with incomprehension. For just a moment, they were simply two humans, alone in an unknowable vastness.

Basil didn't really hear the reply. Without conscious thought, he found himself keying the commands into the computer to train a thorough sensor search on those coordinates.

The sensors reported absolutely nothing. He sagged back in the chair, ignoring a sharp glance from Felix. Then he straightened at the keyboard again. With flying fingers, he ordered a grav scan of the coordinates.

Grav scanners, which inferred the presence and characteristics of masses by the curvature of space they caused, had been starships' primary means of interpreting their surroundings before being superseded by modern sensors. They still had their uses, and were routinely included in the sensor suites of even small vessels like the *Courier*-class. Very short-ranged, and limited to lightspeed . . . but quite equal to the task at hand. And they, too, reported nothing.

Exasperated, Basil reached out to terminate the whole fruitless business. But then an idea entered his mind, from he knew not where. He ordered the computer to measure the distance to Planet V's surface, using grav scanners directed through the region he'd been scanning. Then he had it do the same thing, but at a slightly different angle. Then he sat for a long time in a silence Felix knew better than to break, studying the two figures. They should have been the same. They weren't, quite.

The silence stretched and stretched . . . and, with a stomach-dropping start, Basil realized that he had, in his preoccupation, forgotten his regular check of the strategic display. He hastily activated it, and his stomach sank again. For the red icons were no longer following a standard search pattern. They were converging with unmistakable purpose.

He shot a glance at Felix. The prisoner remained silent, but the gleam in his eye was so eloquent that words would have been superfluous. Basil met those eyes for an instant, then turned back to the viewscreen and a universe whose vastness and diversity had suddenly narrowed to two choices: surrender or death.

He was never sure whether the idea sprang full-armed into his consciousness a split second before or a split second after his hands started keying the commands. But the impellers awoke from their station-keeping level of thrust and sent the *Courier* surging ahead before he had fully formulated the plan.

Mystification proved stronger than the desire to gloat had, for this time Felix broke his silence. "What are you doing?" he blurted.

"I'm proceeding," Basil said absently, "toward a certain region of space." Most of his attention was devoted to ordering the computer to do a rapid-fire series of ranging grav scans of the planet's surface, all around that region. By observing where each of the two disparate figures resulted, he was able to map out the outlines of the phenomenon, whatever it was. It appeared to be a sphere of several hundred kilometers' diameter, in a slightly lower orbit than the one he'd been following.

"What do you mean?" Genuine alarm was beginning to

awaken in Felix's voice. "Are you, by any chance, talking about whatever optical illusion you thought you saw earlier?" Basil's silence confirmed it, and Felix's nerve lash-induced caution dissolved into the recklessness of desperation. "This is insane! Surely even you can see that surrender is your only viable option! You cannot trust your life to some figment summoned up by an exhausted brain from wishful thinking, or some sensor anomaly—"

Basil tuned him out, for he was fully engaged in piloting the *Courier* toward no visible goal. But most of the detail work was done by the ship's brain, which only needed to apply a little impeller thrust to carry out its orders. It was just a matter of matching orbits with the unknown. They would enter the enigmatic region at a leisurely relative velocity. The interorbital hop was not a long one.

"We should," he said, talking over Felix's ongoing tirade, "be crossing into the affected area just about—"

In mid-word, both of their voices halted, leaving a silence in which the bridge's faint background hum seemed deafening.

"—now," Basil finished in a near whisper, because he had to fill that silence with something human. Felix said nothing. They both stared at the viewscreen.

There had been only the briefest warning as the *Courier* had drifted through a boundary region where the space distortion he'd only glimpsed before had enveloped them, causing the universe to waver. Then they'd passed through and emerged into this eerie realm where the harsh orange glare of Planet V had become a swirling ash gray, and the moons and the stars glowed murkily in the same non-color as though through a gauzy film.

After a time, Felix licked his lips and spoke. "Perhaps something is wrong with the visual pickup."

"Something that would account for *that*?" Basil pointed dead ahead with a finger that was no steadier than Felix's voice.

It grew in the viewscreen as the *Courier* drew slowly closer. At first it seemed a featureless bead of crystalline silver, but details gradually emerged—meaningless alien details that gave no clue as to its size. But Basil was sure it must be kilometers across. And it had a gleaming hard-edged clarity quite unlike the darkly blurred unreality of the universe outside the borders of this strange region they'd entered.

Time crawled by in silence, and the mysterious construct—for such it clearly was, though it looked to have been not so much built as woven, or perhaps grown—filled more and more of the viewscreen. Suddenly, they felt a faint bump.

"Tractor beam," one of them said. Basil, using only a tiny part of his mind, cut off the impellers, which had only been keeping the *Courier* on course anyway. He knew with absolute certainty that it would be pointless to try to escape from this thing. And he was equally certain that he didn't want to. Fate or inevitability or whatever, just as surely as the tractor beam, was drawing him toward that vast oblong opening, so obviously a docking bay, which he was quite sure hadn't been there a moment before. He knew he wasn't in shock—as Felix evidently was—and therefore should be gibbering. But he felt only a strange calm.

The portal had swallowed them up, and the *Courier* had drifted into a world of spun silver, before it occurred to him that he ought to be trying to communicate with the masters of this place. He was starting to reach out toward the console when his head filled with a great pseudo-voice whose like he'd "heard" once before.

"Greetings, Admiral Castellan. You are expected."

Basil didn't notice the strange look Felix was giving him. After almost two decades the maddening half-memories had suddenly firmed up and now stood forth in his mind as clearly as yesterday.

He walked along a corridor proportioned to accommodate Luonli, with someone else's sense of direction to guide him.

The tractor beam had moored the *Courier* without a bump against the end of what had seemed a spire of the curious silvery pseudo-metal extending from the wall of the vast cavity into which they'd drifted. After securing Felix (whose questions he'd stolidly ignored), he had followed the telepathic voice's instructions and exited into the spike's tunnellike interior. It had led into the interior of this . . . station? Ship? Fortress? Perhaps he'd soon find out, for up ahead the corridor seemed to debouch on an open space.

The area was circular, and its diameter wasn't enormous by the standards of this place. But it had no floor or ceiling that could be seen; it was a well of seemingly infinite depth. Emerging from the corridor, Basil found himself on a wide balcony cantilevered out from the entire circumference of the curving wall. Other corridors opened out on the balcony, and between those openings the wall held large rectangular panels . . . or, Basil decided as he gazed at one, they might really be windows, for the effect of what he was seeing was unmistakably three-dimensional: a velvety blackness of indefinite extent which held a myriad of floating lights, moving in a stately pattern that his mind could not grasp.

It was all very interesting, but . . . first things first. "Before we go any further, I must remind you that my ship is being sought by enemy warships, which had detected it before my arrival here. By now they are probably approaching this region of space, where they got their last readings."

(Calm reassurance.) "Have no fears on this score. This installation is, as you will have noted, surrounded by a field which renders it undetectable to all sensing techniques, including sight."

"Yes, I certainly 'noted' it, although how it works is beyond my understanding."

"In grossly simplistic terms, the field creates a kind of warping effect which causes radiation of all frequencies, including that of visible light, to 'bend' one hundred and eighty degrees around it. Thus, there seems nothing to detect. And, to anticipate your next question, the device incorporates a compensation feature which enables you to see out of it in a darkly blurred, colorless way."

"Still," Basil said dubiously, "I was able to infer the presence of *something* here. If I could do it, maybe my pursuers can."

"Again, set your mind at rest. The only reason you were able to notice the slight distortion caused by the refracting effect was that the field had been expanded to its maximum practical diameter of several hundred kilometers, as is possible for a short time at a substantial energy cost. Now it has been contracted to its normal dimensions: just large enough to encompass the physical installation—which is *very* small indeed in term of the vastness of space. Rest assured, Admiral Castellan, that you would never have detected anything out of the ordinary if you had not been allowed—indeed, encouraged—to do so."

It never occurred to Basil to take umbrage at this arguably insulting assessment, for it reminded him of another of the myriad questions roiling in his mind. "Yes, you said I was 'expected,' didn't you? What did you mean by that? And . . . and who *are* you? Why can't I meet you? Why have you directed me here?"

"Before leaving your ship, you expressed a desire to meet me face to face." (*Amusement.*) "I am afraid this is the best I can do."

"What?" Basil blurted. "You mean you're not a Luon? But you must be! I mean, the quality, the tenor of your thoughts—"

"Your reaction is to be expected. Your conversation with Shenyilu has been your only experience with telepathic communication—except certain instances of the crude verification techniques used by human telepaths, which hardly count. Naturally you would be unable to perceive the subtle indications that you are not communicating with an actual, organic Luon mind." (*Condescension.*) "Do not be overly concerned. After all, in this case the indicia are very subtle indeed, inasmuch as my creators were, in point of fact, Luonli. Inevitably, they imparted to me many of their . . . Admiral Castellan, are you quite well?"

Basil was not, for the obvious fact had belatedly crashed into his consciousness: he was in telepathic communication with an artificial intelligence. And for the moment his mind had no room for anything but shock, revulsion and fear.

For almost half a millennium, humans had possessed the ability to build computer hardware which could be given psionic capabilities as "programs." But they never did so—and not just because of the hideous expense. To a civilization which regarded both artificial sentience and psionic phenomena with fear and distrust, the two in combination represented a kind of ultimate in abomination, invested with the full force of a cultural taboo. . . .

(*Amusement.*) "But not to my creators. For them, it was just ruinously expensive. In fact, I am the only example they ever built."

Basil brought his thoughts and emotions under control, and forced himself to speak levelly. "It seems quite a coincidence that I encountered you, then. By the way, what should I be calling you?" For a jocular instant he thought of stereotypical macro-computer designations like "Alpha Prime" and such. It became clear that he was dealing with a more capable telepath than Shenyilu, for once again his unspoken thought was picked up.

(*Renewed amusement.*) " 'Omega Prime' would be more appropriate in my case, as I suspect you'll come to agree. But what is the 'coincidence' to which you refer?"

"That a unique . . . entity such as yourself should be here in this particular system."

"To the contrary. I am, in several respects, the Luonli's ultimate creation. It is therefore to be expected that I would be found here, in their home system."

"You mean . . . ?" Basil began faintly.

"As their sun began to misbehave, the Luonli created me. Actually, they already had a cybernetically-run station in orbit around this planet, but they upgraded it to such an extent that I cannot feel any continuity of identity with it. They also moved it into this close orbit so that the planet's mass would help shield it from what they knew was coming.

They were wise to do so, for if the planet had not happened to be between me and the sun at the crucial moment, even my very formidable defenses might well have been inadequate. Those defenses, by the way, account for much of the mass of the station. Alone, I would not require nearly so large an installation—even though my size requirements are abnormally great, for a variety of reasons, of which my psychotronic capability is only one." (*Graveness.*) "Another reason for its size is that it had to be made accessible to the Luonli. But permanent occupancy by them was, of course out of the question, because of . . . But you've already heard all that from Shenyilu."

"Yes, that's right—you've mentioned Shenyilu once before. Are you telling me that it's been here in the nineteen years since it rescued me?" As always when discussing Luonli, he felt vaguely uncomfortable with the neuter pronoun. But what else to use for a hermaphrodite? "How did it get here?"

"It used a very old space vessel which the Luonli had long ago abandoned in the outer reaches of the Nu Phoenicis system. The ship was in bad repair, and Shenyilu wasn't really a qualified pilot. Its voyage here was an act bordering on recklessness. But it had become obsessed with learning the full truth of its heritage, so it—"

"But," Basil cut in, "how could Shenyilu have brought such a ship to Nyjord and then taken it outsystem without anyone noticing? Granted, Nyjord isn't exactly one of the nerve centers of the human universe. But we *do* monitor space traffic. Especially in the last fourteen years, when the whole Empire has been on a war footing."

(*Long-suffering patience.*) "You are making the unwarranted assumption that Shenyilu's journey took place after your encounter with it. As I was about to explain before you interrupted, Shenyilu departed during the fighting associated with the end of the Rajasthara Usurpation, as you call it. The confusion provided a priceless opportunity to depart undetected."

Basil shook his head in exasperation at the unanticipated

communication problem. "You're not making sense, uh, Omega Prime. Rajasthara died, and the legitimate dynasty was restored, in 3733! How do you know about my meeting with Shenyilu if you talked to it then? How could Shenyilu have known anything about that meeting—or anything else about me—if it came here well over a century before I was even born?"

"It couldn't and didn't, of course. But, you see, I had expected its visit, from future references. And so—"

"Excuse me," Basil interrupted weakly. " 'Future references'?"

"Just so. But I perceive that a pause for an explanation would be in order."

"Yes," Basil managed. "You might say that." He'd begun to suspect that Omega Prime had, quite simply, gone insane in the unthinkable eons of loneliness. Only . . . in his experience, psychosis in sentient computers left them incapable of functioning at all, much less functioning at the level of competence that Omega Prime had displayed. "Yes," he repeated a little more firmly, "perhaps I need some background familiarization."

(*Didacticism.*) "You must understand that my Luonli creators were seeking to preserve the maximum possible volume of information about themselves—their history, their accomplishments, their aspirations. The quest for greater and greater data storage capacity led them into realms of tachyon physics far beyond what your civilization has so far explored. To make a long story short, they extended my data storage volume into an added dimension: that of time."

"Uh . . . I beg your pardon?"

"To put it more accurately, they extended my capacity to access data into the temporal dimension. Thus, any time I run out of data storage capacity I can simply use the same capacity again—at a different time. In practice, this means erasing everything and starting over. Because, you see, I can access any data that I *ever* held, including erased data."

"Wait a minute, Omega Prime. I'm not sure I'm following you, but unless I'm mistaken you seem to be talking about *time travel*. Which is *impossible!*" Basil found that he was growing angry, which was so idiotic that the realization made him angrier still. "Absolutely, incontrovertibly impossible! It would violate a whole array of fundamental natural laws . . . conservation of matter and energy for starters. And it would upset causality and result in all sorts of paradoxes—"

"Compose yourself, Admiral Castellan. You are quite correct about time travel in the usual sense in which humans have used it as a fictional device: physical transposition from one moment in time to another. That, you can rest assured, is not what we are discussing here. I cannot send myself— or you, or anything else—into the past. I can merely shift data about within my own tachyon-based . . . 'circuitry' will have to do."

" 'Merely,' " Basil muttered. He still wasn't certain Omega Prime was insane, but he desperately *wanted* to be certain of it.

(*Studied imperturbability.*) "You will appreciate that with this innovation my creators attained their objective of effectively infinite data storage. But as is often the case— in humanity's history as in that of the Luonli—a dying civilization failed to grasp the full implications of its own ultimate achievement."

"Uh . . . what 'full implications'?"

"Their failure—and yours—is understandable, inasmuch as I myself did not come to the realization until much later. Although, in retrospect, it should have been obvious all along as a natural corollary of my ability to access data which I had held in the past. You see, I can also access data which I have not stored yet . . . but *will* store. Any data I will *ever* store."

There was a very long pause, during which Basil opened his mouth and shut it again several times. Finally, he managed to form words. "Omega Prime, correct me if I'm wrong—*please* correct me if I'm wrong!—but you seem to be claiming that you can *foretell the future.*"

"Only in a strictly limited sense. The only information about the future I can access is that which I myself will at some point learn. And since I cannot know in advance what that information is, or will be, there can be no question of a systematic search. I can only scavenge at random for knowledge and then try to make sense of what I find." (*Annoyance.*) "And the last is the greatest problem of all, for these . . . messages from the future lack *context*. For example, I was quite unable to make any sense out of *this* conversation when I first perused it—or, rather, the précis of it which I shall record shortly, when we have concluded."

Basil clung tightly to his sense of reality as the mental "voice" went inexorably on.

"Later, after Shenyilu's arrival—which, to repeat, I had anticipated from future references to it—matters became clear . . ."

"Wait a minute, Omega Prime!" Basil's voice held a note of desperation. "You lost me some time ago. Let's take this slowly. I gather that you're building up to an explanation of what you said when I first arrived here: that I was 'expected.' "

"An astute conclusion. You see, when Shenyilu came here on its quest for the truth about the Luonli race's past, I had long conversations with it. I freely admit I used it as a source of information as much as it used me. In particular, I wanted information about you."

"Me? But Shenyilu couldn't have known anything about me, so long before we met—before I was born, even!"

"No, it didn't. But, on the basis of the yet-to-be-recorded references to you which I had accessed, I inquired about Shenyilu's activities at the time of the Usurpation, a decade and a half before its visit. It had, you see, played a rather vital role."

"What? How?"

"You will recall from your history that the Emperor whom Rajasthara deposed was an infant at the time, so there was no one in the direct line of succession. And the Imperial relative with the best claim—also an infant—vanished."

"Yes. But it's generally supposed that he didn't just 'vanish' but died."

"Yes—a supposition which Rajasthara encouraged, not just for the obvious reasons but also because he believed it himself. You see, certain loyal officers spirited the youthful heir-presumptive off Earth in the confusion surrounding the coup, and took him to the out-of-the-way system of Nu Phoenicis."

"Nu Phoenicis! But I grew up there, and I never heard any such story! And how did Shenyilu know about this?"

"To address your points in order, the infant's presence on Nyjord was shrouded in strictest secrecy, for the legitimate heir could expect only one fate at Rajasthara's hands. And Shenyilu was very much involved; it assisted in concealing the child, for it knew one of the officers in question—a certain Captain Ivar Marczali, who had been stationed in the Nu Phoenicis system and who had relatives there."

"But . . . but, Marczali is my mother's—"

"Despite all security precautions," Omega Prime went on without a break, overriding Basil's weak attempt at interruption, "the rescuers were found out and tracked to Nu Phoenicis. Captain Marczali and his confederates left the heir with Shenyilu and staged a hopeless attempt to escape from the system, under circumstances designed to lead their pursuers to believe that the heir was with them, en route to yet another sanctuary planet. So when their ship was vaporized, he was assumed to have died with them, and the search was called off.

"The heir had been left with Shenyilu for safekeeping to await an Imperial restoration, when he could claim his heritage. In fact, Captain Marczali, who had discovered the ancient Luonli ship in the outer system of Nu Phoenicis years earlier, had made it known to Shenyilu in the anticipation that the Luon would use it to take his charge outsystem when the time was ripe. But Shenyilu had, over centuries of observation, acquired a somewhat dour view of human affairs. It also developed an oddly sentimental affection for the human infant in its care. It resolved that despite its friendship for Captain Marczali—and its gratitude for the ship, which it was eventually to use for its voyage here—it would shield the child from the potentially fatal knowledge of his ancestry. It arranged for an adoption by Captain Marczali's relatives, who for security reasons had been led to believe that the child belonged to a family of middle-level loyalist officials who had died in the fighting.

"So, Admiral Castellan, it will now be apparent to you why Shenyilu was knowledgeable as to your background."

Basil shook his head. "I have no idea what you mean, Omega Prime. Shenyilu never mentioned anything about these events. All it told me about that era was . . ." As though with the lifting of a fog, Basil's memory seemed to clear. "Yes, that's right. Shenyilu kept telling me it had known one of my maternal great-grandfathers. But what does that have to do with . . . ?"

In the cleared skies of his mind, a fusion bomb seemed to explode.

"No," he heard himself whisper. He found himself sitting on the floor, slumped against the wall, with only Omega Prime's soundless words to keep him from losing consciousness.

"Yes, I perceive that you have grasped the truth. Now you know who your great-grandfather Boris Marczali really was—which is more than he himself ever knew. And you will understand why I told Shenyilu to return to Nyjord and, in the course of rescuing you in 3889, insinuate a compulsion to seek out this system."

Anger brought Basil at least partially out of shock. "So Shenyilu lied! It used telepathy to tamper with my mind . . . probably while I was asleep."

" 'Tamper with your mind' is a bit strong. As you humans have realized for over a millennium and a half, psionics is not sorcery. The 'compulsion' of which I speak involved no mental enslavement, no brutal overriding of free will. It merely predisposed you to favor courses of action that would lead you here over those that would not, if such a choice ever presented itself. And, under the circumstances that brought you here, a certain gratitude would seem in order."

Basil started to speak but fell silent as he remembered his oddly single-minded enthusiasm for his idea of seeking refuge in this system, even though he'd recognized it as a forlorn counsel of desperation. He suppressed a shudder of distaste and forced himself to speak levelly. "Yes, I suppose I should be grateful. But I don't understand *why* you did it. First of all, if you already knew that I was going to come here and have this conversation with you—"

"But, you see, the references to your arrival indicated that it would take place as a result of the predisposition which Shenyilu would implant on my instructions. Therefore, I had to give those instructions. What could be clearer? Of course, my subsequent recording of the message that I myself have already accessed will be based on my knowledge that the message itself was what caused me, years ago, to act as I did."

"Uh . . . yes." Basil shook his head to stop it from spinning. "All right, never mind about that. But in the *second* place . . . why were you even concerned? Why did you even *want* to ensure that I'd come here? What am I to you?"

For the first time, there was a pause before the indescribable "voice" filled his head. "Surely you understand the implications of what I have told you about your ancestry."

"Yes, unless you're mistaken or lying—neither of which I've ruled out, by the way. But even if really I am related to the Imperial family, even if I . . . if I . . ." Basil swallowed and tried again. "Even if I have a claim of some sort to the Imperial throne—"

"Arguably a better one than the present emperor. Your great-grandfather indubitably had the best claim in his own lifetime. It is an interesting legal question whether the claim you inherit from him overrides the—"

"Even if all that's true," Basil pressed grimly on, performing the difficult feat of ignoring a telepath's interruption, "the question remains: why do you care? What does the rightful succession to the Solarian Empire matter to you? You're not even human. Your *creators* weren't even human! The Luonli are the only organic beings whose fate ought to matter to you."

(*Bleakness.*) "The Luonli are a dying race, and have been since long before humanity left its cradle world. I will mourn them, with a sorrow beyond your imagination. But I cannot undo the fact that they belong to the past. I can only use the capabilities that they gave me, including that of self-motivation." (*Mental tone that precluded any thought of interruption or protest.*) "I cannot—or, if you insist, will not—answer your question concerning the precise reasons for my actions. Not now, and perhaps not ever; the data I have gleaned from the future are inconclusive on this point. You must simply accept that my intentions are benign, and that when you find yourself in need of help I will provide it, within certain very definite limits—limits which I myself must delineate. In particular, I will not grant you any specific foreknowledge. And the words 'I will not' are meant literally, not just as a statement of intent: I *know* I will not."

Basil had been skirting the edges of exhaustion from the strain of his escape even before he had ventured out of his ship into these ancient corridors. Now, with what he had imagined to be reality lying in ruins around him, he could barely think, much less attempt to understand all he had been told. But he lashed his mind into awareness of what he was apparently being offered. "Uh, I believe I'm clear on what you won't do, Omega Prime. But can you give me some notion of what you *will* do? What is the precise nature of the help you are, for whatever reason, prepared to give me?"

(*Dry humor.*) "To begin, I can and will inform you of the battle that is commencing in this system even now."

"*What?*"

"Yes. A fairly substantial Imperial naval force has come into sensor range of the rebel units which were in search of you. They are frantically seeking to exit this system, but are about to be intercepted. If you wish, I can deactivate this installation's sensor-distortion fields so that you can observe the outcome, and communicate with your rescuers, unimpeded."

"Yes! Do that!" Basil shouted as he ran down the corridors, fatigue gone as though burned away by a triumphant flame.

He got to the *Courier's* bridge just in time to see the destruction of the last rebel picket. Then he hailed the Imperial flagship.

Oddly enough, he wasn't even surprised when Sonja's face appeared on the comm screen.

"We arrived at Mu Arae just after they snatched you," Sonja explained. "It's possible that I may have made kind of a nuisance of myself there while we were waiting for word from you."

"Just barely possible," Torval deadpanned. Basil hadn't been particularly surprised to see the big Marine emerge from the shuttlecraft that had docked—if that was the word—alongside the *Courier* in this station's womblike interior. He was coming to believe, more and more, that there was such a thing as inevitability.

"Then the message from your drone arrived," Sonja continued, not deigning to notice the interruption. "I managed to get myself put in charge of a rescue expedition out Aquila way. I'm still not quite sure how this oversized cargo item got himself included." She flashed a grin in Torval's direction. "It's a little untraditional for a task group's senior Marine to outrank the CO—as he does me, if you want to get fussy about dates of rank. And we haven't got enough Marines along to need a major general to order them around."

"You never know," Torval intoned, "what's going to come up."

"But," Basil interposed, "how is it that you're here this quickly? There simply hasn't been time for the drone to have gotten all the way to Mu Arae—much less for it to have gotten there *and* for you to have organized this task group and brought it here!"

"Oh, the drone is still on its way to Mu Arae," Torval affirmed. "But it happened to encounter one of the flotillas picketing the frontier. As you know, they've got ships with collapsible tachyon beam arrays. So the message got to Mu Arae almost immediately. And we'd already been organizing a rescue expedition." He gave Basil a slightly aggrieved what-did-you-expect look. Basil didn't notice, for the word *inevitability* was again tolling in his mind.

"So," Sonja resumed, "we proceeded, behind a screen of scouting frigates. Their sensors picked up nothing until we reached this system—which we knew was lifeless, but which was the first star of any size along our direct route. The rebel pickets' activity brought us here, But then, of course, after we'd dealt with them . . ."

Her voice trailed off, for she could no longer avoid what had happened next, against which her fieriness and Torval's stolidity were barricades. Omega Prime had dropped all concealment as Basil's call had gone out, and the station had seemingly materialized from empty space. It had been only the first of the shocks awaiting them, for Basil had told them the nature of that which dwelled here. They had taken his word without the need for direct communication from Omega Prime, and they continued to let Basil handle all such communication—the phobias ran deep and strong. Basil wasn't dissatisfied with this arrangement, for there were things he hadn't told them.

Now the three of them stood on a kind of terrace overlooking the vast atmosphere-screened docking bay. The shuttle that had brought Sonja and Torval lay alongside Basil's *Courier*, the two craft emphasizing by their tininess the immensity of the otherwise-empty space. The rest of the task force still hung in orbit, for there had been no telling how its personnel would have reacted to this place and its occupant. The only other Imperial craft to enter had been another shuttle, to which Basil had thankfully transferred custody of his prisoner.

"Well," he said to Sonja after a time, "I suppose we ought to be departing. It's going to be pretty tight as it is, getting back to Mu Arae in time for the commencement of the offensive."

"In time for the . . . ! That's right; I never told you, did I? We're not just a rescue expedition. We're the offensive's vanguard—of which you're now in command, of course."

"*What?* But . . . but it's not time yet!"

"Medina moved the date up," Torval explained. "When you were captured, he knew that the plan had been hopelessly compromised. So he decided to strike early, rendering obsolete whatever information they would have gotten from you. Everything's now in motion."

Basil fought down sickening panic. "But it *can't* be! I told you about the rebel fleet poised to launch a counterstroke once our fleets are committed. We've got to return to Mu Arae, alert Medina to abort the offensive, then pinpoint the rebels' location and organize a preemptive strike."

"It's too late for that," Sonja stated. "Torval's right; the fleets have started to move, from Mu Arae and Sigma Draconis. It's too late to halt the offensive, Basil. All we can do is proceed with our part of the plan and hope that—"

"Wait." Basil's tone stopped her short. But he didn't fill the silence he'd created. He just stood for several heartbeats in absolute concentration which the other two left undisturbed. Then his eyes focused and he spoke in a loud clear voice.

"Omega Prime."

"Yes, Admiral Castellan," came the not-sound in his head. His companions could not conceal their discomfort at what they knew was occurring.

"Omega Prime, let's resume our earlier discussion. This help you're prepared to offer me . . . would it extend to answering a certain astrogational question?"

"Quite possibly. And this question is . . . ?"

"If I show you a visual image from a certain point in open space, can you locate that point?"

(*Blandness.*) "Why, of course. The problem is conceptually elementary. It would involve identifying certain individual giant stars from their spectra. The rest would be a matter of mere geometry."

Basil commanded himself to not slide down a slope of relief into unconsciousness. "Good, Omega Prime . . . very good. The imagery is on standard visual media. I suppose you'll need for me to—"

"My proxy devices can take care of everything, Admiral, if you will permit them access to your craft and its main computer."

"Yes, of course."

"Furthermore, Admiral, I perceive that you are at the edge of exhaustion, and were even before your compatriots arrived. And I daresay they themselves are in need of rest. Why not retire to your ship, which is more comfortable than their shuttle?"

"Yes . . . yes, that's a good idea." Omega Prime's thoughts had brought him back to an awareness of a fatigue that adrenaline could no longer hold in check. He turned to his friends. "I need some sleep or I'm going to collapse. Omega Prime will take care of everything."

"Take care of *what?*" Sonja asked with some asperity. "We only heard your half of that conversation, Basil. Tell us what's going on here."

Basil was almost too weary for his face to form a smile, but he managed it. "What's going on, Sonja, is that *we* are going to be the preemptive strike!"

Sonja and Torval both regained the power of speech at appreciably the same instant. Her "But all we've got is a task group!" interpenetrated with his "But our orders don't give us that kind of latitude!"

"We're looking at facts that Medina didn't have available, Torval. As on-scene commander, I'm making the command decision to respond to those facts. The responsibility is mine alone. And, Sonja . . . our force will just have to be big enough, won't it? Our tactics will have to *make* it big enough." For a moment, with a final effort, Basil thrust back the enveloping arms of exhaustion and held their eyes.

"You're crazy," Sonja finally said . . . softly, and with an unwontedly gentle smile.

"Yeah," Torval affirmed, and grinned in his beard. "And I like it."

In the end, all three of them slept aboard the *Courier*, for Sonja and Torval had more accumulated stress than they'd admitted.

They all had odd dreams, which they found they had no inclination to share on awakening.

CHAPTER SEVEN
The fringes of the Beta Aquilae Sector, 3908 C.E.

Rogue planets had once been thought to be extremely common. After all, the theory had run, objects' frequency in the universe seemed to be in inverse proportion to their mass, from supergiant stars at the top of the mass rankings to hydrogen atoms at the bottom. So it seemed to follow that bodies of substellar mass should be even more numerous than red dwarf stars, drifting alone or in clusters through the great cold dark, unlit by any sun.

The reasoning had proven fallacious. The interstellar medium, it seemed, did not normally condense into isolated planet-sized masses. Instead, such masses were byproducts of stellar formation, spun off from the great balls of coalescing hydrogen destined to ignite into fusionfire by the heat of their own gravitational compression.

But there were always exceptions, for certain of the stellar children wandered off beyond their parents' ability to hold them. It was such a body that the People's Democratic Union was using as a gravitational anchor for its secretly constructed and stealthily assembled striking force.

"You're sure about this?" Sonja asked irritably.
Basil nodded. They were standing on the great balcony

that was HIMS *Intrepid*'s flag bridge, overlooking the wide-curving main screen. Below them, men and women moved in purposeful activity among the control consoles that formed a crescent facing the screen, ignoring the panorama of the stars. The nearer of those stars drifted aftward with a stately but nonetheless perceptible motion, for *Intrepid* was still under drive.

"Yes," Basil affirmed. "Omega Prime was quite positive about it. We're heading for the point in space where I saw the rebel fleet before . . ." His voice trailed off into a momentary silence which Sonja and Torval were disinclined to break, for they knew how little he liked to speak of his probing. "When our sensors established that there really is a rogue planet there, it was all the confirmation we needed."

"Our sensors haven't actually detected any ships."

"Of course not. We're still too far out, given that they're not under drive, or even under power except the minimum necessary for station keeping and life support."

"Still . . ." Sonja was in an odd mood, and Basil knew why. The entity whose physical housing she had seen at DM - 17 954 still haunted her thoughts even though she had never entered its mental presence; watching Basil do so had been bad enough.

Torval laughed, and stroked the chestnut beard that suited him so well. "Come on, Sonja. Basil's right: the planet itself is confirmation enough for me." He stretched hugely—actually, he did *everything* hugely. "I'm going to scan some late reports on the exercises—the *few* exercises—you've given us a chance to conduct under way."

"Why bother?" Sonja asked with an attempt at snappishness that didn't quite come off. "If everything goes according to plan, there won't be any boarding actions. If it doesn't . . ." She left the thought unspoken.

"There's a very old saying about battle plans and initial contact with the enemy," Torval rejoined with massive dignity. "But I probably won't keep at it. We've been up too long. I need some sleep. So do you two."

"Thank you, Mother."

Torval chuckled, impervious as always to Sonja's shafts, and departed, leaving the other two almost alone on the off-watch flag bridge.

"He's right, you know," Basil said. "There's nothing we can do here. Not now."

"I know." But neither of them made any move to leave.

"Tactical," Sonja said abruptly. The screen transformed itself, displaying the other ships of the task group in their own bubbles of accelerated time. Five other battlecruisers of *Intrepid*'s class. A dozen lesser cruisers. The swarm of frigates, holding close formation because there was no need for them as scouts. The supply ships, sheltering behind the warships whose operating range they extended.

"So you really think we can pull this off?" Basil knew that Sonja's rhetorical question held none of the skepticism that some might have heard in it. She only wanted reassurance. But he had little to give, for he couldn't reveal the real basis of his confidence.

"Yes, I do," he said simply.

"But," she persisted, "we know the size of that rebel force from the recorded look you got at it. And we may not be right in assuming that they're still in the same configuration they were then. And—"

"Sonja, you've got to trust me. I have . . . reason to believe that this is going to work." No, he decided anew, he wouldn't share that reason. For if he did, she'd probably think him mad. And, actually putting it into words, he might well agree with her.

She gazed at him thoughtfully, then nodded. "Yes. It's something to do with that . . . with 'Omega Prime.' Something it told you."

She had never lost her ability to surprise him, in all the years since their lives had become linked. And as he met her eyes, all his resolve vanished as though it had never been.

"I told you," he heard himself saying, "about Omega Prime's ability to access data it hasn't recorded yet. I also told you about its vague half-promise to help me in ways which don't involve revealing the future. But, you see, in a sense it *has* revealed the future, simply by making the offer of help after going to the trouble of arranging to predispose me to come to that particular system. It must have grounds for believing that I *have* a future. Otherwise, I wouldn't be worth bothering with!"

He braced himself for a snort of derisive laughter. But her features remained grave, and she said only, "So you believe in this business of . . . shifting data around in time?"

"I have to. That's the only way I can account for some of the things Omega Prime knows, and has done. And the remark Omega Prime made about the future data's 'lack of context' makes sense. Suppose that, say, twenty years ago you had been able to see one of the message chips you've gotten from me in the last few years. You wouldn't even have known who I was, much less the background of the events I was talking about. How could you have possibly made sense of it? I imagine Omega Prime is acting carefully, sifting through the mass of meaningless information and trying to build a coherent picture by correlations. I got the impression of a very cautious temperament."

Sonja blinked a haunted look from her eyes. "So it follows that Omega Prime never actually takes any action without being very sure of its grounds. And so it further follows that it must be very certain that you live to be 'worth bothering with.' Which means that you, and presumably the task group, will survive the coming battle." Her voice still lacked all mockery, and the blue eyes that held his dark brown ones were entirely serious. "Has it occurred to you that this kind of thinking could lead you into a very bad case of overconfidence—to say nothing of megalomania?"

"Of course I've considered that. I want you to kick me, hard, the first time I seem to be relying on this . . . destiny I seem to have. And I plan to tell Torval the same thing. A kick from *him* would carry conviction!"

"It seems to me that you're already 'relying' on it. You've staked the lives of everyone in this task group on it."

"Not altogether," Basil argued. "Does it seem to you that I've slighted any aspect of the planning of this attack?"

"No," she admitted. "Nobody could fault your operational groundwork. In fact, all of us are pretty much used up from the hours we've been keeping."

"Well, does that suggest anything to you?"

" 'The future helps those who help themselves,' " she misquoted. "Yes, I can see that. But there's still something I don't understand. Even assuming that you do survive, why are you so important?" She paused with an abashed laugh. "Sorry. I'm sure there must have been a better way to put that. But you know what I mean."

"Yes, I do." Basil hesitated a long time before resuming. "Omega Prime gave me an indication—something I didn't tell you and Torval about at the time. And I can't tell you now. Even this—" he indicated the mostly empty flag bridge "—is too public."

"Then let's get more private," she said in a voice in which she was clearly exerting a conscious effort to keep level. "I suggest my quarters."

There was a long silence, in which he stared at her against the backdrop of slowly streaming stars and saw her anew. Like him, she had gotten access to anagathics with the attainment of flag rank and therefore looked in her early-to-mid thirties. Her features were as clear-cut as ever, her auburn hair only slightly faded. On any standard except one which demanded curvaceous vapidity, she was a striking woman. For the first time it occurred to him that some might think it odd that they had never consummated their relationship sexually. He'd never felt the need to explain it, to himself or anyone else, and he could think of no explanation now except that it had always seemed unnecessary—superfluous, somehow.

He wondered why it no longer seemed so.

They held each other's eyes for a few more heartbeats. Then, without words or the need for words, she walked toward the hatchway. He followed.

❖   ❖   ❖

"So," she said drowsily from the bed, "how should I be addressing you? Your Imperial . . . 'relative-ship,' maybe?"

He glanced over his shoulder at her and snorted. The armorplast transparency that was a prerogative of Flag quarters arched over the bed, and they had created their own universe of ecstasy there under the stars, stealing some of the divine fire from those remote pinpoints of light. Afterwards, he had told her everything, unconsciously getting up and pacing as he spoke. Now he stood silhouetted against the starfields, and within her armor of jocularity Sonja suppressed a shiver, for part of her was Old Nyjorder and as she'd listened her blood had remembered the Norns.

But now he gave her a grin that gleamed white against his dark face in the starlight. "Actually, now that you mention it, that's not such a bad idea. About time I got a little respect . . ."

She made a noise that wouldn't have been appreciated in a crowded elevator and flung a pillow at him. He caught it and was about to retaliate, but then he saw what was in her face—an underlying seriousness that few others would have recognized. He sat down on the edge of the bed and waited for her to speak.

"You're going to tell Torval," she said. It was not a question.

"Of course. I can't imagine not telling him, now that I've told you. That's always the way with us, isn't it?" And had been, he reflected, ever since that night at Peachy's, in the moonlight whose bloody tinge had proven so prophetic.

"Of course," she echoed. "But, Basil . . . aside from him, I don't think you should tell anyone."

"What? Oh . . . of course. I understand. Nobody would believe me anyway! And I've got no more desire than anyone else to undergo psych probing. Especially given the kind of mind-ream it would require, given my defenses—"

"No." She shook her auburn head and sat up in bed. "That's not what I mean. What we've got to worry about is the possibility that someone *would* believe you. Or think others might believe you."

"Huh?"

"Basil, in case it's escaped your notice, the Empire has become a snake pit of military strongmen intriguing for supreme power. Right now Medina's the titular leader because he's acting in the name of the legitimate emperor, and the others have enough sanity left to keep their infighting within limits as long as the New Humans are still a threat. But the minute we succeed in removing that threat—"

"I don't give a damn about any of that! You know I don't have any political ambitions."

"Yes—which makes you pretty eccentric these days. So much so that I doubt if anyone who doesn't know you will believe it. If it becomes known that you have some kind of claim to the throne, a lot of ambitious people are going to see you as a danger."

"I make *no* claim to the throne! The whole idea is preposterous. I'm totally loyal to the dynasty, which is in enough trouble without having the succession thrown into question."

She grasped him by the ears and pulled his head to within inches of hers. "Basil, I know what you want to be: an apolitical guardian of the Empire. Only . . . there's no such thing any more." Her eyes took on a kind of wistful tenderness. "The world you want to live in is a *better* one than today's real one, I'll give you that. But if you want to serve the Empire as it now is, you've *got* to do it in the arena of power politics. And, by the way, if we win tomorrow you'll be in that arena whether you want to or not, because you'll be a hero. If you're also a hero *with a claim to the throne*, you'll . . . well, you'll simply have a target painted on your forehead."

"I gather," Basil said slowly, "that that would matter to you."

"I suppose you could say that," she allowed, her old self bobbing back to the surface with a twinkle of blue eyes in the starlight.

He was silent for a moment, because that which filled his heart was beyond his ability to verbalize. Then he stood up abruptly and started pacing.

"But the whole thing's so ridiculous! Even if I did have any ambition for the throne—which I don't!—my 'claim' barely qualifies as a joke! Let's say that Boris Marczali really was the legitimate heir at the time he was spirited off Earth. That was three generations ago! To say that I have a better claim than the present emperor would be to negate the legitimacy of all the emperors since the Restoration!" He shook his head with a kind of self-reassuring emphasis. "At most, I'm a distant relation of the Imperial family."

"I don't pretend to understand Imperial succession law," Sonja said. "But I know what everybody else knows: that Josef is childless. If he dies that way . . ."

That halted Basil's pacing.

"So you see," she pressed her advantage, "why the predators contending for power will see you as a threat to their schemes if this becomes common knowledge."

"Yes. And . . . and you know, they may be right! A member of the Imperial family with some military prestige might just be what's needed to prevent the Empire from being torn apart by competing warlords." He strode back to the bed and gripped her by the shoulders. "Sonja, this must be why I'm so important to Omega Prime's plans!"

"Me and my big mouth," she breathed.

He laughed. "Oh, don't worry. I'm not going to tell anyone but Torval—for now. I'm going to bide my time and hold this knowledge in reserve, to be revealed only when the time seems right" —("When *and if*," Sonja muttered, unheard.)— "and when the Empire is in desperate need."

"Would it be impolite to remind you that before you can save the Empire you have to win the battle we're going to be fighting in a few hours?" Beneath her asperity, Sonja felt a rising hatred for the artificial Luonli ghost that had somehow known exactly how to tempt this man: not with power or wealth or limitless sensual indulgence, but with the opportunity to live up to his own ideals in an age that was not friendly to them.

But she fought that hatred down, because Omega Prime's help, whatever form it took, was precisely what might enable

Basil to survive the seemingly fatal course on which he was now so eager to launch himself. The tempter was also potential savior, and Sonja was perforce its unwilling ally. She wondered if that, too, was part of the plan.

Basil laughed again, a laugh that was exultant and defiant without—she thought hopefully—quite straying over the line into recklessness. "Oh, yes, I know. And we ought to be trying to get some sleep. But . . ." He took her in his arms.

They made love again under the starry firmament, and Sonja commanded herself to ignore her feeling that Basil's thoughts weren't entirely there.

The rebel ships orbited outside the rogue planet's Chen Limit, so that they would be able to go immediately into drive when the time came to launch themselves at the Imperial heart worlds. Basil received confirmation of that with relief, for it was one of the things that made his plan workable.

Still further out, the Imperial task group disengaged not just its drives but also its impellers and coasted inward toward the invisible cosmic wanderer in a hyperbolic orbit that would intersect with the massed enemy formations. In free fall, the task group was effectively undetectable. It *could* have been detected as it had approached under drive, had any rebel sensors been turned in the right direction. But none had been. Why should they? The axis of approach was nowhere near the Imperial frontiers.

Now Basil sat on *Intrepid*'s flag bridge and gazed fixedly at the main screen, where the sensors' report of the rebel fleet was displayed.

"They're still in the same formation you saw," Sonja observed from her seat by his side. He recognized her studied calm for the façade it was. She felt the same hunter's eagerness that sharpened his senses and held at bay all the hours of sleeplessness.

"Stands to reason," he replied. "Their plan is to launch the counterstroke after our fleets are engaged with their frontier forces. Now that Medina's offensive is under way they're expecting the word any time; this is no time for any maneuvers or training exercises." It had been another of the foundations of his plan, and he carefully kept the relief out of his voice.

Still . . . he studied those readouts, unable to keep his eyes away from the enemy force totals. Nine battleships. Twenty battlecruisers. Thirty-five cruisers. The lighter warships and the tenders didn't matter. In major combat units the task group was outnumbered more than three and a half to one. In tonnage the disparity was six to one. In firepower, comparisons were meaningless because the rebel force included battleships and theirs didn't. Those battleships weren't the equals of the Empire's *Implacable*-class, but that was cold comfort at the moment.

Sonja met his eyes, reading his thoughts. She seemed about to speak, but then the task group chief of staff arrived, needing some decision made, and she had to tend to it. Basil was in overall command, and the plan was his, but he had left Sonja in effective operational command of what was, after all, *her* task group. These people had all heard of him, but they didn't know him as they knew Sonja, and he had no desire to tinker with a smoothly-humming machine. (He had legalized the arrangement by organizing—subject to Grand Admiral Medina's approval, of course—a task force, commanded by himself, consisting of only the one task group.) There had been some tactful suggestions that the two of them should perhaps go into battle aboard different ships, lest the Imperial force be decapitated by a single lucky hit on *Intrepid*'s flag bridge. But they hadn't even considered it. Whatever destiny they had bound themselves to that night at Peachy's so long ago was about to come to a climax, and they would face it together. So would Torval, who had muscled his way into a general-quarters station on the command bridge.

Time passed, with excruciating slowness to men and women accustomed to outpacing light. Basil wouldn't let himself reach out for Sonja's hand, not here on the flag bridge. But their eyes met, and no physical touch was needed.

"Ten seconds to contact point, Admiral," the chief of staff reported.

"Thank you, Commodore," Sonja acknowledged levelly. She gave no commands, for the entire task group was gathering itself in cadence with the countdown, in accordance with the plan. Her work, and Basil's, was done— except for the uttering of one final command. . . .

"Execute Operation Dragon!" she snapped as the count reached zero, in a voice that broke slightly in spite of her best efforts.

Within what would have been visual range of the rebel ships had there been any light for those ships to reflect, the task group's drive fields awoke, speeding time within them by a factor of tens of thousands. But the impellers which actually moved the ships were *not* activated, and it was fundamental drive theory that momentum was conserved within the field; it was only acceleration while the drive was activated that was subject to the time multiplier. So the Imperial ships continued free-falling at the same velocity relative to the outside universe. Likewise left deactivated were the inner fields. So the occupants, existing in the accelerated-time state, watched the massed rebel formation inch closer with impossible snaillike slowness.

Not even the most routine sensor watch on the orbiting ships could have failed to detect those awakening drive fields at that ridiculously close range. But there was no time for the rebels to react, for the Imperials' intrinsic velocity swept them the rest of the way into the carefully calculated orbital intersection in an eyeblink of time.

But for the Imperial crews, that eyeblink lasted long enough to permit painstaking targeting calculations and unhurried preparation as the two formations seemed to crawl into their closest approach, and the moment finally came when Sonja gave the command to fire.

Coherent energy in the devastating extreme X-ray

wavelengths lashed out at the naked metal hides of rebel ships that lay in the imagined safety of secrecy. The beams themselves were invisible. But when they struck their targets the hellfire of energy transfer flared. It was the stuff of every space officer's most bloodthirsty fantasies, for one of those beams' targets received in a single microsecond all the energy that the beam generator, existing under accelerated time, could pump out in tens of thousands of microseconds. Under such an attack, those ships weren't damaged—they were volatilized.

To the Imperials, the rebel formation seemed to flare into a series of explosions, like a star cluster dying in a whole series of supernovas. Even from within the drive fields, that cataclysm had nothing of slow-motion stateliness about it. Basil, bathed in the light that the main screen automatically stepped down to what human eyes could stand, reflected that to the surviving rebels it must have seemed as though the universe had exploded.

Then, in a short time even as *Intrepid's* clocks were measuring it, they were past the point of orbital intersection and the next phase of the plan went into effect. Sonja snapped another command, and the task group engaged its impellers and flashed ahead at the incredible apparent acceleration the drives made possible, an acceleration which would shortly have sent them past the velocity of light as viewed by outside observers. It didn't immediately, of course, and they didn't outrun the eye-searing light of the conflagration they'd wrought. Nor did they outrun their sensors' ability to assess the damage they had inflicted. The battleships on which they had concentrated their fire had ceased to exist. So had six of the battlecruisers. As he read the figures that appeared in midair over his swing-out command console, Basil didn't let himself waste time wondering if his little force had just struck the heaviest single blow in the history of space warfare.

He couldn't spare the time, for the sensors also reported that the rebels were swarming in pursuit like denizens of a fire-seared beehive.

"They're moving sooner than we anticipated," Sonja observed levelly.

Basil nodded, trying to imagine the superhuman efforts it must have taken for the surprised rebels to get their drives energized in so short a time on the orders of whoever had succeeded to command after the death of their flagship, which must have been one of the battleships. The ragged order in which they were coming could scarcely be dignified by calling it a formation. But they were all on the same heading, which would converge with the Imperials' course. And the fact that they were moving from a standing start meant nothing. The intrinsic velocity the Imperials had kept was insignificant under these conditions; only the drive-multiplied acceleration that both sides' impellers were now piling on mattered.

"Are we going to have to alter our plans?" Sonja asked.

Basil stared intently at the flag bridge's holo display, in which the rogue planet showed as a hard point of purple light surrounded by a pale lavender sphere representing the extent of its Chen Limit. Skirting the edge of that sphere was an emerald string-light: the hyperbola the Imperial force was following like a bead sliding down a string. He studied the rebels' newly-awakened ruby icon, converging from the right, and needed no mathematics to tell him that it would intercept the green icon before it reached its closest approach to the Chen Limit.

"I think we're going to have to turn inward sooner than we planned," he decided. For answer, Sonja summoned her chief of staff. As always, the sight of Commodore Delarouche awakened in Basil a feeling of regret—which he knew to be as unfair as it was futile—that he didn't have Lenore Silva here. But Delarouche was competent, and very shortly the orders went out that sent the task group swinging to starboard in the direction of the rogue planet's Chen Limit.

At first the rebels kept coming, and Basil permitted himself a moment's grim satisfaction at their obvious indecision. But then the ruby icon began to turn in the holo display, mirroring the Imperials' course change.

"Their bewilderment is understandable," Sonja remarked drily, echoing Basil's thoughts. Inside the Chen Limit neither side could use its drives, so no advantage would be conferred on the Imperial force, which was still outnumbered and outmassed by about two and a half to one.

"Yes. They must wonder what we're up to. But they have no choice except to turn with us." The reason went without saying. The Imperials' turning movement had threatened to take them across the rebels' course. In space combat, with both sides under maximum time acceleration, "crossing the T" was as valid a tactic as it had been in the days when floating warships had sought to send each other to the bottoms of Old Earth's oceans.

"At the same time," Sonja observed, "there's some doubt as to whether they'll close to within range of us before the Chen Limit." Her voice held no reproach.

"It'll be close," Basil admitted. Then they fell silent and watched as the two icons followed their converging courses in the holo display. The curving wall of lavender crept closer.

The two icons were almost touching when Sonja gathered herself with a movement that Basil noticed out of the corner of an eye. He started to open his mouth and shout that it was too soon, that they were still too far from the Chen Limit. But then he clamped his jaws shut. This was Sonja's task group, and he would not interfere. And besides . . .

"Enemy units closing to extreme beam weapon range," Delarouche reported.

So there was no more time after all. But Sonja only nodded, waiting for an inner sense of the precise moment. Basil realized that he hadn't breathed in some seconds. *To hell with it,* he thought, and reached out and grasped her hand. And it was as though some galvanizing energy flowed through that contact.

"Disengage drive," Sonja sang out like a clarion. The command flashed to the other Imperial ships and, as one, they dropped into synchronicity with the outer universe.

Far too fast to be seen, the rebel ships flashed past them and were ahead, screaming toward the Chen Limit. And,

one by one, the safety cutoffs hardwired into those ships'
brains began to cut their own drives—entering a body's
Chen Limit with drive activated was never good for the
drive, and sometimes the results were enough to put a ship
into the repair yards. But they didn't do so on command
and in unison as the Imperials had, and as one ship at a
time resumed its intrinsic velocity, the formation their leaders
had been trying to nurture during the pursuit dissolved
into chaos.

Basil and Sonja released each other's hands and sank
backwards into their command chairs. It was out of their
hands now. The individual ship captains knew what was
expected of them at this point. Now it was up to those
captains to take advantage of the opportunity that Basil and
Sonja had created for them.

The rebels had only been under acceleration over the
course of the short pursuit. The Imperials, however, had
been accelerating while under drive en route from DM -
17 954, then had added a little more velocity while falling
inward toward the rogue planet, and then had resumed
acceleration. So the intrinsic velocity they now resumed
was far higher than that of the rebels, who now lay ahead
of them in a badly shaken and disorganized state.

The Imperial captains were now released for autonomous
action, and they responded as Basil had hoped they would.
Plunging ahead on impellers, the Imperial ships took the
rebels from behind, each ship picking out a helpless target
and vaporizing it with energy weapon fire.

It was sheer murder . . . but it couldn't last. The impellers
might slip through a loophole in the laws of the ancient
sage Newton, but they weren't magic, and they didn't
eliminate inertia. And now they had to go into full braking
mode lest the Imperial ships simply fall onward down the
rogue planet's gravity well, leaving the rebels behind. At
the same time, the rebels awoke from their stunned paralysis
and began frantically changing course. The battle became
a twisting maelstrom of ships, rending and tearing at each
other with energy weapons.

The rebels still had the advantage of numbers, but that was the only advantage they possessed in this kind of fight. They were still reeling from two very severe shocks in rapid succession, and a tactical doctrine which had to accommodate itself to New Human ideology discouraged ship captains from even considering the possibility of acting on their own initiative. Against badly shaken enemies clearly unused to taking independent action, the Imperials—riding a wave of *élan* after momentum of the devastation they'd already wrought and inheritors of a tradition which valued dash—were wearing them down. Basil and Sonja could see it in the holo image of the battle as a whole and also in the constant reports of *Intrepid*'s exchanges of fire with successive rebel ships.

They were closing to optimum range of an enemy battlecruiser when the flag captain broke into their concentration with a report from the command bridge. "Admiral, a second hostile has broken free of the engagement and is converging on us. Tactical analysis predicts that it will bring us within range while we're still heavily engaged with our present target."

"Acknowledged, Captain," Sonja spoke, and summoned up a secondary hologram of their particular segment of the battle. There was no mistaking the purposefulness of the new enemy's course. She and Basil exchanged a worried look; given the free-for-all nature of this fight, the rebels' computers couldn't possibly have deduced the identity of the Imperial flagship and marked it for destruction. The new threat must be mere coincidence. Which somehow wasn't very comforting, especially given the absence from the hologram of any readily available help that could be summoned.

"Fight your ship, Captain," Sonja said tightly.

The range closed, and the ships began to pour coherent energy into each other's deflector screens. Sometimes those screens would fail, and the alarm klaxons would whoop as damage control teams would be summoned. But battlecruisers were large constructs, capable of absorbing a lot of damage. *Intrepid* fought on, and seemed to be giving better than she got.

Then the second hostile drew into range, and the calls for damage control grew more frequent as did the shudders and nauseating lurches as the artificial gravity momentarily lost its grip.

There was no warning when the flag bridge bucked with a violence that flung them against the restraints of their crash couches and a bellow of rending metal brutalized their ears. Shaking his head to clear it, Basil could barely hear the bass voice from the intercom. "Basil? Sonja? Damn it, come in, flag bridge!"

Basil glanced at Sonja. She was still struggling up out of disorientation. He activated the intercom. "Torval, it's me! What's your situation?"

"Captain Ho is dead. I've assumed command of the ship. Yes, I know: I'm not exactly in the chain of command. But I'm the only commissioned officer left alive and conscious on the command bridge. I've gone to computer override for most command and weapons functions, so I can continue to fight the ship for a while. But I'm ordering everybody else to abandon ship. Get to a lifeboat fast."

"*What?* And leave you here to die? You're crazy! We'll stay here and—"

"And what? At this point, you're nothing but a high-ranking spectator." The voice shifted to the tones of the Marine drill field. "As acting captain, I *order* you to abandon ship! Now get Sonja to that lifeboat. Move!"

Basil moved, half-lifting Sonja out of her crash couch and guiding her off the flag bridge and along corridors, moving with nightmare slowness as the ship's brain called the "abandon ship" over and over in a voice like a cybernetic god's. She was fully functional by the time they reached their assigned lifeboat. A ragtag group of other survivors was already there. The boat's pilot was not.

"Does anybody here know how to pilot this thing?" Basil demanded in rising desperation.

"I do," boomed the massive figure that filled the hatch

and squeezed through just before it automatically closed and sealed.

"Torval!"

"Yeah, me." The big Marine went on talking as he strapped himself into the pilot's couch and ran his eyes over the controls. "You don't *have* to be crazy to be a Marine. It helps, but it's not required. I set the brain for fully autonomous control of the ship. It can't do much, given the limitations hardwired into it. But it can continue to shoot back for the minute or so it's got left. And it can release the powerplant's antimatter from its containment fields. . . . Hmm, this isn't quite as similar to an assault shuttle's controls as I thought. But . . ." His hands ran over the manual control panel, and a virtual viewport awoke in front of him just in time to show the lifeboat bay's hatches rolling aside to reveal the heavens.

"Stand by!" There was a brief surge as the boat launched, and the starfields revolved sickeningly.

"We're free," Torval announced. He shifted the screen to view aft, where the visibly ravaged *Intrepid* receded rapidly into invisibility. "Should be any time now . . ."

Abruptly, the screen automatically cut down its light sensitivity by orders of magnitude. So they were merely dazzled and not blinded as they watched what wasn't so much an explosion as an *event*.

"Stand by for shock wave," Torval said quietly.

Then the wavefront of the cloud of infra-debris that had been a battlecruiser caught up to them, and the lifeboat staggered and tumbled. Basil, flung brutally against his restraints, had only a second's awareness before blackness took him.

Sickbays are very standardized, and Basil suspected that rebel ones weren't all that different. So as soon as his surroundings swam into focus he ignored the danger of triteness and croaked, "Where am I?"

"HIMS *Defiant*," came a voice which almost sent him back into unconsciousness with relief, and Sonja's face entered his field of vision. "Some people have all the luck. You were out the whole time we were waiting to be picked up. It was boring as hell!"

"The battle . . . ?" He had to ask, although Sonja's expression had already answered the question.

"Over," came Torval's bass as the Marine joined Sonja. "It wasn't cheap. We lost five cruisers, and two battlecruisers including *Intrepid*, and practically every surviving ship has some damage. But the rebels are finished. You can scan the details later. A few of their lighter units managed to evade pursuit back out to the Chen Limit and got away. A few others surrendered. Otherwise, they're plasma."

Basil started to sit up, wavered as the universe spun, then completed the movement. "You know what this means, don't you? The rebellion is finished! They'd committed all their new-construction ships to this secret strike force. All that stands between Medina and the rebel planets are light forces that weren't even intended to be able to stop him."

His eyes held Sonja's and for at least a heartbeat her expression was a supernovalike blaze of joy that, like a supernova, the universe wouldn't allow to burn for long. Then she was her old self again. "Yes, I imagine Medina will be willing to overlook a few little irregularities we've committed lately," she drawled. But her eyes and Basil's remained locked.

Torval looked from one of their faces to the other, and his own wore a shrewd look that neither of them noticed. "Well," he said with gusty heartiness, "you know what they say: wars come and go, but paperwork is forever. I've got things to do. Try and get some rest." He sauntered away, then paused. "Oh, yes; Sonja, remember to tell him about the statistics of who was rescued from *Intrepid*." Then, with a wave, he was gone.

"He's right," Basil said shamefacedly. "I should have asked about that."

"Why? You're not the skipper. Anyway, most of the crew got off. The point is . . . well, what he means is . . ." She shook off the uncharacteristic hesitancy and sat down on the edge of the bed. "Remember the shuttle we sent to pick up your prisoner from Omega Prime? Back in the DM -17 954 system, while the rest of the task group stood off at long range?"

"Yes, of course."

"Well . . . the crew of that shuttle were *not* among those who got off *Intrepid.*"

"Oh."

There was an awkward silence. Sonja broke it.

"Are you thinking what I'm thinking?"

"Yes . . . and I'm ashamed."

"I know what you mean." She hung her head for a moment and then rallied. "I really *do*, damn it! It seems almost ghoulish. But the deaths of those people are a *fact* now— a statistic of war. And we can't ignore this further fact: no one alive besides ourselves—you, me and Torval—has any real idea of what was in that system."

"They'll have talked to their friends, of course," Basil, mused. "But spacefarers never take each others' tall tales very seriously. There'll be rumors, but that's all." Then an unwelcome recollection brought him up short, and his eyes widened. "Except for the prisoner himself! What about him?"

"Oh, yes: Felix whatever-he-called-himself." Sonja looked like she'd bitten into a bad pickle. "He survived. Figures, doesn't it? But how much does he really know? How much did you tell him?"

"I told him nothing at all after I'd actually met Omega Prime. But he knows there's something decidedly out of the ordinary in that system; he saw what's in low orbit around the fifth planet." Basil gave his head a dismissive shake. "But what difference does it make? Omega Prime is quite capable of concealing itself from detection. Remember, *I* only detected it because it wanted me to."

"Well, that's something. Still . . ." Sonja looked him unwaveringly in the eye. "The records of who got off *Intrepid* are still being sorted out. And mistakes do get made . . . and accidents do happen."

Basil met those level blue eyes for a moment before

shaking his head. "No, Sonja. I know, it's a real temptation—especially in the case of a totally contemptible piece of human slime like that. But . . . he's still too valuable a prisoner. A probe of him will yield information Medina can use in the mop-up campaigns on the rebel worlds."

"That's just rationalization, isn't it?"

"Yes, it is. I think you know the real reason, as I do. And even if I hadn't known it before, coming in contact with *him* would have made it clear to me. If we think we have a right to destroy inconvenient human life, how are we any better than him?"

Sonja shook her head. "I suppose I may as well get used to the fact that you're too good for the universe you were born into, Basil." A long, eye-averting moment passed before she resumed. "I suppose that's part of the reason I love you."

For a long time they embraced tightly, as though each was trying to shield the other from unnameable fears.

CHAPTER EIGHT
Earth (Sol III), 3909 C.E.

A gust of cold wind caught Basil as he emerged from the shuttle. His uniform protected most of him—it was the bulky winter version of court dress that was worn when the Emperor was in residence here, in a style that tradition associated with the ancient nation whose capital this city had once been. But his face stung from the cold, even though he'd grown up on Nyjord, which wasn't a warm planet.

Torval's homeworld was even less so. "Feels good," the big Marine approved. "Bracing."

"Not exactly the word I'd use," Sonja grumbled.

"Well," Basil said, "we're in the high latitudes, and it's the tail end of winter here in the northern hemisphere." Then he fell silent, and so did his companions, quieted by the common experience of all colonial humans landing for the first time on this undistinguished planet of an undistinguished star: the body's sudden adjustment to the indescribable *rightness* that suffused everything. The gravity, the air's density and composition, the distance to the horizon, the smells, the color of the setting sun . . . All was as his chromosomes told him it should be.

Basil pulled himself together and looked down at the field below, at the honor guard and the group of officers who were stepping forward to the base of the ramp. "Well," he said, a little too emphatically, "let's go on down. The reception committee's coming, and . . . my God, it's Medina himself!"

Without further ado they marched down the ramp and saluted like cadets. The Grand Admiral returned the salutes with a smile that creased his dark, flat, hard face. That face, with its thin drooping mustache, hadn't changed much in the fifteen years since they'd first set eyes on it, and it somehow belonged under the fur cap with flaring side-flaps that was part of the current regulation court dress. Light snow flurries were falling, and captured flakes momentarily gleamed like tiny diamonds against the fur's sable black, before the heat of the uniform's environmental circuitry melted them.

"Welcome to Earth," he greeted. "I know you weren't expecting me. But I couldn't pass up the opportunity to personally present the three of you to His Imperial Majesty—who, by the way, is beside himself with eagerness to meet you. So let's proceed at once. It's unseasonably cold even for this damned Imperial residence, and it's going to get *really* cold when the sun goes down."

A slider carried them through a stretch of woods—Basil recognized the slender white birches, whose species had been transplanted to Nyjord to find a niche in the ecology the Luonli planetary engineers had established. The sun had set by the time they entered the city, but they had no trouble seeing the well-lit preserved or reconstructed areas, dominated by what Basil recognized as ancient religious structures in a colorful and distinctive style he couldn't quite place. Then they were crossing a bridge over a frozen river, where ice skaters took advantage of the floodlights illuminating the large structure—or walled compound of structures—that loomed on the far bank to the right.

"Impressive," Sonja remarked. Basil, gazing at the high-peaked towers overlooking the crenellated walls and the inner buildings with their onion-shaped golden domes, was inclined to agree.

"It's called the Citadel," said Medina. "No, I keep forgetting; to be correct, you should call it the *Kremlin*, which meant 'citadel' in this city's classical language. Every city of this culture had one in the medieval era. Apparently they needed them for defense against one of those old conquerors: Genghis Khan or Hitler or somebody like that."

"I think Hitler came a little later," Basil said absently, eyes still on a spectacle whose like could be seen on Old Earth alone.

Medina's dark eyes narrowed slightly at the omission of military courtesies. But then he resumed, obviously not sharing Basil's enthusiasm for history. "Anyway, it's now the Imperial residence—or at least the outer crust of it—whenever he's here, in his capacity as 'Tsar of all the Russias.'"

"How many 'Russias' were there, sir?" Torval asked, curious.

"Haven't any idea," Medina admitted offhandedly. "It's just one of his titles. Too bad you didn't arrive while he was being the Son of Heaven or the Grand Mughal or the Hereditary President of the United States or something else that takes him a little closer to the equator. Now, what I *really* like is when the court is at Versailles. . . ."

Basil nodded unconsciously. After centuries of total war, social disintegration and the unapologetic rule of unrestrained military force, culminating in the nightmare tyranny of the Draconis Empire, thirty-sixth century humanity—what was left of it—had been in desperate search of continuity and governmental legitimacy. So the Solarian Empire's first Emperor had acquired a genealogy which linked him with every royal dynasty that could be rummaged up from Old Earth's pre-spaceflight history. How seriously the people of that era had taken it was impossible to say at this late date. But it had sufficed, for it had filled the general need to believe that the final victor of the civil wars ruled by some right other than his monopoly of the weapons that could incinerate worlds.

To strengthen the linkage with the past, and to sever any linkage with the Draconis Empire, the capital had been moved to Old Earth. There, the Emperors had come to follow a prescribed yearly round, holding court in the ancient capital cities of their "ancestors" in accordance with forms laid down before the first starship had departed or the first artificial intelligence had awakened.

The slider came off the bridge and turned right, emerging into a large paved expanse defined on one side by the walls and towers of the medieval fortress. Brightly floodlit at the far end of the plaza, or whatever—Medina identified it as "Red Square" although its shape wasn't really square—stood another of the ancient religious buildings. But this one was a wild architectural fantasy that either epitomized the style or parodied it, Basil couldn't decide which.

Medina observed his fascination and smiled his predatory smile. "An omen if ever I saw one, Admiral Castellan. That's a very old cathedral, called . . . Saint Basil's."

Before Basil could think of a reply, they were through a gateway and into the enclosed courtyard. The slider came to rest before an honor guard, arrayed in the dark-green Imperial Guards court dress for this residence. Running his eyes over the geometrically perfect ranks that brought their gauss rifles to present, Basil was struck by the similarity of those faces, as though they all belonged to one of the relatively unmixed ethnic genotypes that had existed on Earth millennia ago—presumably the one that had characterized this region, with light skin, high cheekbones, and straight hair mostly in shades of brown or blond. But it was only to be expected, for the faces were part of the uniform. These were synthetics, genetically designed to fit the historical masquerade.

Basil suppressed a shiver of distaste and returned the salute of the guard's commander. He, like all the officers, was of course true-human. But he resembled his troops—which, again, was no surprise. When money was no object it was a straightforward matter to inject the body with nanomachines which rewrote the genetic code in such minor respects as features and coloring . . . or gender. Basil wondered if the commander had originally been a woman, modified to harmonize with a milieu whose soldiers had been by definition male. This sort of alteration was as frowned upon as it was expensive. But where the Imperial household was concerned . . .

Then they were inside one of the ancient buildings and Medina was leading the way toward an incongruous drop shaft. Artificial gravity whisked them down, and down, and down into the working levels which nanoconstructors had hollowed out under the old fortress without disturbing it. They emerged from the shaft at a level where vaulted corridors stretched away further than the eye could see in four directions. Chamberlains, majordomos, valets and other assorted flunkies converged on them. Mostly synthetics, Basil noted—you could always tell. Medina had banned them from the Emperor's household except for the ornamental Imperial Guards units. Evidently they were making a comeback.

Medina sloughed off his greatcoat and tossed it in the general direction of the nearest flunky, not even slowing as he headed down a corridor. "Come on," he called out as he swept off his hat and threw it over his shoulder. "Can't keep His Imperial Majesty waiting."

"His Imperial . . . ? You mean we're going to meet him *now*?" Basil felt the bottom drop out of his stomach, leaving a void through which panic came roaring up. "But sir, we were given to understand that the presentation is tomorrow . . . that we'd have time to prepare—"

"You're thinking of the full ceremony. Yes, that's tomorrow. Tonight is just an informal reception. But as I mentioned earlier, he's eager to meet you. Also, he wants to be the one to spring some news on you; he does love his little secrets. Ah, here we are."

The Grand Admiral halted before a doorway flanked by a pair of the custom-grown ceremonial guards. The highest-ranking flunky they'd seen yet gave him a small bow. Medina ignored it and turned to inspect the trio who'd hurried up behind him. They'd all managed to shed their outer garments and stood self-consciously in their stylized court dress. He gave a curt nod. "You'll do. And now—"

"But, but sir," Sonja stammered, "we just got here. We

haven't had time to . . . you know, freshen up." Basil mentally applauded her, for his bladder was about to burst.

Medina misunderstood. "I told you this is casual—he insists on it. Be yourselves. Believe me, the three of you can do no wrong just now." He gestured to the flunky, who bowed again and opened the doors. He strode through, and they could only follow.

It immediately became apparent that the Imperial definition of "casual" differed from most people's. The reception room was of vast extent, and heavily ornate in the prevailing local style. The lighting simulated that of massed candles, and it flickered off mosaics whose style seemed to suit the architecture. The crowd, mostly attired in variations of military dress, fell silent when Medina entered, and parted for him as he proceeded down the length of the room with his three juniors in tow.

Too much had happened, and Basil had seen too much, in too short a time. His need to urinate was his only contact point with reality by the time they emerged from the forest of glittering uniforms into a clearing occupied by a single man. That man was of middling stature and slight build. He wore the court dress of the Imperial Guards, but his narrow pale-olive face did not fit the mold into which the Guards officers had been modified. And his shoulder boards bore no rank insignia, just a small golden dragon.

Basil found that his body had locked itself into a position of attention. Moving like a robot, he imitated Medina's stiff bow from the waist.

"Your Imperial Majesty," Medina was saying, "allow me to present—"

"Vice Admiral Castellan, of course!" The long, somehow melancholy face formed a smile which Basil sensed was all too rare. "And your companions must be Major General Bogdan and Rear Admiral Rady. At ease, and welcome to Earth. And . . . 'sir' is quite sufficient."

"Thank you, your . . . sir." Basil forced himself to relax a trifle, and stole a glance over his shoulder. Sonja seemed to be recovering her aplomb, but Torval had only gone to parade rest.

"Admiral Castellan and his subordinates have only just arrived, sir," Medina said. He laid an odd stress on the last word, and it occurred to Basil that the Emperor's gentle admonition on modes of address might have been taken as a rebuke of the Grand Admiral. He decided he was better off unaware of the undercurrents he could dimly sense in this place.

"You must be quite fatigued from your journey." The deep-brown Imperial eyes reflected nothing but genuine solicitude. "Here, have some refreshment." The Emperor made no perceptible gesture, but a waiter—human or very expensive synthetic—was at Basil's elbow instantaneously with a tray of snifters. He sipped, blinked, then sipped with greater relish.

"Georgian brandy," the Emperor enlightened him. "From an estate of ours to the south of here, near a lovely place called Sochi. And now," he continued with a smile, "I want you to be among the first to hear the latest news from Admiral Noumea."

Basil was instantly alert at the mention of the officer Medina had left in charge of mopping-up operations in the rebel sectors. "She reports," the Emperor went on, "that the defenders of the planet Lusitania, or 'Equality' as it has been called since becoming the capital world of the self-styled People's Democratic Union, have surrendered. There may be more small-scale fighting to do on isolated worlds, but" —a dramatic pause— "the New Human rebellion is now over as an organized force."

After a heartbeat's silence, the reception room began to fill with applause which, it seemed to Basil, had a quality of pro forma politeness even at its loudest. He suspected that he himself and his two friends were the only people present who hadn't had advance knowledge of the Emperor's announcement. And he found, to his surprise, that even he was strangely ambivalent about news he'd dreamed of hearing for a decade and a half. It might have been an equivalent of *post coitum triste*; or it might have been a nagging realization that the rebellion had, for some time, been less dangerous than the forces called into being to suppress it.

The Emperor seemed oblivious to the brittle artificiality of the applause, for he beamed at Basil. "This is, of course, not yet a matter of general knowledge. But we intend to announce it openly tomorrow, at the ceremony where the three of you receive the recognition you so richly deserve. There could be no more fitting moment for the announcement, for it was your miraculous victory which made this great news possible." A sound of rapturous agreement ran around the room.

"Sir," Basil annoyed himself by mumbling, "we did no more than our duty."

"Kindly permit us to be the judge of that, Admiral. You did far more than merely your duty—at a time when all too many high-ranking officers are doing far less." All at once the gentle brown eyes hardened, and seemed to flicker in Medina's direction. "Indeed, we began our reign in the midst of a monstrous sedition—"

"Kleuger received his just deserts years ago, sir," Medina said in the patronizingly reassuring tone of one seeking to humor exaggerated concerns. Basil sucked in his breath sharply, but no one else seemed shocked that the Grand Admiral had interrupted his sovereign. He thought he heard, barely above the threshold of audibility, a subliminal growl from Torval's direction.

The Emperor's face darkened a shade, but his voice remained level. "We are aware of that archtraitor's richly merited fate, Grand Admiral. Unfortunately, the indiscipline and outright lawlessness infecting the Fleet's higher echelons did not die with him. Even now, when the final extinguishment of the rebellion should occasion universal celebration, the high command seems unable to impose its authority on various insubordinate admirals in outlying regions."

Medina's voice took on the deep purr of a large, predatory cat. "Due to the exigencies of combating the rebellion, sir, we've had to allow local commanders an abnormal degree of autonomy. Now, of course, I intend to reestablish the Fleet's traditional policy of firm centralized control. Any of the sector admirals who cannot or will not accept this will be dealt with."

"We are reassured." The Emperor's thin voice seemed overmatched, his sarcastic tone futile. But his eyes met Medina's for an instant before he turned back to Basil with a smile. "Still, it is a great comfort to know that there are those such as yourself, Admiral Castellan, who are still mindful of where their proper loyalties lie."

"I . . . I only sought to do my duty, sir," Basil stammered. His eyes darted around the ornate room with its lighting like molten gold and its richly arrayed crowd, all of it still so unreal to him. He took refuge in another sip of brandy, and all at once he felt an impulsiveness so foreign to his usual nature as to be alarming.

"Indeed," the Emperor was continuing, "it is no exaggeration to say that the dynasty owes its continued existence to you."

With those words, Basil's defenses against the unaccustomed impulses he was feeling crumbled. He felt his facial muscles forming a reckless smile, and heard himself speaking words he'd never intended to utter this night. "I'm only glad I was able to be of service, sir. It seems the least I could do, inasmuch as I have reason to believe I'm distantly related to the Imperial house."

The Emperor, preparing to deliver further pleasantries, froze openmouthed. At the same instant, all sound in the reception room ceased. Medina's expression congealed into absolute unreadability.

"I beg your pardon, Admiral Castellan?" the Emperor finally asked in his mild voice.

Basil felt the oddly liberating sensation of having placed himself in a position from which there could be no retreat. So he pressed forward. "At the time of the Rajasthara Usurpation, sir, the infant heir-presumptive was believed to have been killed—"

"Yes, yes. This is well known." The Emperor's voice held a curious eagerness.

"—but in fact was spirited off-world out of danger. He was eventually adopted by a family of Nyjord, in the Nu Phoenicis system—my mother's family. On that side, he was my great-grandfather."

The Imperial face wore the first genuine happiness Basil had seen on it. "But this is splendid!"

"If true." Medina spoke with studied mildness. "Admiral Castellan, this assertion is new to me. May I ask on what you base it?"

The enormity of the step he'd taken belatedly caught up with Basil, and he reined himself in short of any further unintended revelations. "Well, sir, there's a, uh, family tradition—"

"Which can be easily verified," the Emperor broke in with uncharacteristic firmness. "Can it not, Admiral Komos?"

"Indubitably, sir," said an elderly gent wearing medical branch insignia, presumably the Imperial physician. Under modern conditions, genetic comparison was simple, noninvasive and absolutely conclusive.

"Then let us do so at once! Everyone else, please excuse us. We and Admiral Castellan must attend to this without delay. We must confirm that there is yet another piece of glad news to be made public tomorrow." The Emperor proceeded toward the door, trailing a wake of bowing dignitaries. Basil started to follow him but felt a touch on one arm.

"We weren't exactly expecting this, you know," Torval rumbled softly.

"Neither was I," Basil admitted. "Believe me, it wasn't planned. It just . . . well, it just seemed right."

"Some people," Sonja muttered darkly, "will do anything to get out of here and go to the head!"

The next day was less cold, and the sun was as dazzling as it must have been when this ancient city was young. It was decided to dispense with an environment screen—the

Emperor liked things as natural as possible—and the wind nipped at Basil's cheeks.

He stood before the dais that had been nanogrown in front of the splendidly gaudy cathedral with the ominous name. The Emperor, arrayed in full court dress that included a sweeping cape and topped with a bulbous jewel-encrusted crown, had bestowed the Order of the Empire. But the decoration that now hung from a scarlet ribbon around Basil's neck—a golden dragon with its wings folded protectively around a planet—was less difficult to adjust to than the fact that he'd just gone from being the Fleet's youngest vice admiral to being incomparably its youngest full admiral. The rapid promotion would have been impossible in the old days. But, he recalled, with a glance at Medina where the Grand Admiral stood behind and to the left of the Emperor, so had a lot of things.

The Emperor had launched into his announcements—the New Human surrender and the discovery that the hero of the hour was a long-lost Imperial relative—with the help of a throat amplifier that sent his reedy voice booming across the openness. Basil let his eyes do some wandering. The court stood on the dais behind the Emperor and his Grand Admiral, arrayed in military-style finery as befitted the Empire's beleaguered state. Behind Basil stretched a double row of synthetic Imperial Guards, holding back the throng that crowded the square under the looming medieval walls and the blue vault of heaven. And, flanking him, stood Sonja and Torval, wearing their own new decorations.

Finally the speech was done and all the invited guests were trooping through a side gate into the Kremlin compound, leaving behind the thousands in the square, the millions around Earth who had been viewing the ceremony on the planetary datanet, and the billions who would shortly do the same throughout Imperial space by grace of tachyon communications. Inside the walls, a transparent environment-controlled pavilion had been set up for a reception. Basil had dreaded an endless round of introductions. But most of the courtiers seemed more

interested in politicking. He, Sonja and Torval were able
to devote themselves to the free-flowing wine, doubtless
from the Imperial estates. *Yes*, Basil thought as they settled
in, *not bad . . .*

"Admiral Castellan! Permit me to offer my congratulations."

Basil began to groan, but there was something familiar
about the voice. He turned around, and almost dropped
his wine glass.

"Professor Gramont! Why . . . what brings you to Earth?"

"Oh, I live here now." The elderly academic was clearly
relishing his former students' stupefaction. His trademark
goatee was a lighter shade of silver now, but otherwise he
seemed unchanged—obviously one of those for whom the
anagathics took well. "I retired from teaching at the Academy
years ago. Now I devote myself to writing."

"I imagine no planet offers as much historical inspiration
as this one," Torval ventured.

"No, not even Prometheus. And no area as much as the
Mediterranean Sea, south of here, where I have some
property on an island called Corfu. When I heard that three
of my favorite students were to be honored, I couldn't stay
away."

Sonja nearly choked on her wine. "Favorite?" she finally
managed to gasp.

"Why, of course." Gramont was all benignity. "Couldn't
you tell?"

"Still," Basil opined, "it must have taken some doing to
get in here." He indicated the surroundings.

"Fortunately, I still have a few friends at court, and I called
in some favors. . . . Ah, Grand Admiral! Congratulations on
the glad news His Imperial Majesty just revealed to us."

Medina smiled through his mustache. "Thank you, Doctor
Gramont. But if you will excuse me . . ." Before Basil could
inquire as to the nature of his acquaintance with Gramont,
Medina turned to Torval. "General Bogdan, there are some
very important people who would like to meet you. If you
could spare a moment . . . ?"

Torval met his friends' eyes. Even more than they, he

knew an order even when it wasn't phrased as one. "Of course, Grand Admiral," he rumbled, and allowed himself to be led away.

"I think I'll circulate some, myself," Sonja said. "I'm about to dry up and blow away." She departed, homing in on a waiter.

"So, Admiral Castellan," Gramont said, interrupting Basil's efforts to define Sonja's mood, "what is your impression of Old Earth?"

" 'Basil,' please. Well . . . I haven't had a chance to see much of it. I only arrived yesterday, and was rushed straight here."

"Of course. Still, you must have formed some impressions of the court itself. And of Grand Admiral Medina's role in it."

Basil gave Gramont a sharp glance, for his voice had taken on a slight but unmistakable edge. But the goateed face was as bland as ever.

"What do you mean, Professor?" Basil tried to imitate the older man's expressionlessness. He was suddenly very aware of how far from home he was, on this planet of unimaginable antiquity and unfathomable subtlety, and apprehension slid along his nerves.

"Oh, nothing," Gramont said airily. "Only . . . it occurs to me that you might find it helpful to have someone to confide in—someone who has known this world for longer than he cares to admit." He produced a card. "Here: my address on Corfu. Any time you'd like to talk, feel free to drop in. And now," he continued briskly, "I really must run along and greet some old friends. Once again, my most heartfelt congratulations."

"Uh, thank you, Professor. It was good to see you again." Basil was left alone in a sunshine that had grown chill, thinking disturbing thoughts that were soon interrupted by a wine glass being thrust into his hand.

"What did the old humbug want?" Sonja inquired.

"I don't really know. I'm not sure I want to know."

❖   ❖   ❖

As viewed from the upper storeys of the Grand Kremlin Palace, the modern towers rose like pillars of light under the stars beyond the fortress walls and the restored old city that huddled around them. Josef II, holder of so many titles that a large-capacity database was necessary to remember them all, gazed out through the French doors and recalled that there was no need to keep those doors closed—it wasn't as though he'd *really* let in the March night air. He flung them open, stepped out onto the balcony and let the hologram surround him. Chill breezes could have been provided, but there was no need to go overboard with authenticity.

For a few seconds Josef took in the view that was being faithfully transmitted from far above. Then he turned on his heel and went back inside, into the labyrinth of the subterranean Imperial quarters. Soon he entered the hall he sought, dimly lit at this hour. He advanced its length under the holographic eyes of the life-sized figures that lined it, finally pausing before the one in the especially prominent alcove at the far end.

Anton the Great, first Emperor of the Solarian Empire— he was never called the "founder," for that title was reserved for he who had founded the Draconis Empire, as a substitute for the name everyone preferred not to pronounce—looked down at his distant collateral descendant. Josef sometimes wondered if the image had been doctored. Probably not; if it had, the stocky figure would have been stretched and the jowly countenance chiseled into something more aristocratically heroic. No, this was the obscure local official who had turned against the Draconis Empire and emerged as one of the leaders of the rebellion that had brought it down in a storm of fire and a torrent of blood. Afterwards, in the cold dawnlight after the final victory celebration, the rebel leaders had come to the realization that each of them had his or her own idea of what should take the fallen tyranny's place. In the ensuing civil wars, Anton—who'd maneuvered his way into control of the all-important Sigma Draconis system—hadn't so much overcome his rivals as outlasted them.

Josef would have liked to consult with the old bastard. But of course it wasn't possible, for Anton had never had his consciousness downloaded. Rumor had it that he'd feared the software holding his memories might one day be persuaded or coerced into telling the true story of the civil wars. Not even his most fulsome hagiographers claimed he'd been a great warrior, and there were persistent whispers about his conduct. But whatever truth lurked behind those whispers now lay buried under the pedestal of the Imperial edifice he'd erected, for his no-nonsense pragmatism had been just what the times had required.

"A man for his times, no question about it."

Josef turned and gave his father-in-law a weary smile. "My very thoughts, Rovard. How, I wonder, would he have coped with these times?" He turned to his wife, who'd entered at her father's side, and gave her a quick peck on the cheek.

"We're not likely to know, are we?" Rovard Mondrian rasped. He wasn't looking well, and hadn't for years. But at his son-in-law's insistence he hung on as Grand Secretary, largely a ceremonial sinecure these days but one of the few positions which carried automatic access to the Imperial person. Josef sometimes felt guilty about it, for the old man was aging alarmingly—the anagathics had only limited efficacy for him. The same couldn't be said for his daughter; Elena was older than Josef but retained the unmistakable aspect—youth without the awkwardness—of those who'd had access to the fabulously expensive age-retarding regimen from the earliest age at which it could be usefully administered and who took to it very well. Of course, there were always the side effects . . .

Josef couldn't claim any great originality for noting, as people had been doing for almost a millennium, the irony in the fact that the same hypercomplex chemical combinations that slowed the aging process also depressed fertility. It would have been humanity's salvation from hideous overpopulation had the anagathics been generally available. As it was, with their scarcity restricting them

to the super-rich and those who'd placed the state in their
debt, its most important effect was the notorious fragility
of the Imperial succession. The issue didn't arise as
frequently as it had in previous ages when monarchs—
like everyone else—hadn't lived as long. Still . . . Josef
had grown genuinely fond of Elena in the years since
their political marriage, and he often wondered which
of them was at fault. It was a question never spoken aloud
between them.

"No, we'll never know," Rovard answered his own
question. "He's dead and we're alive in this damned age—
which has suddenly acquired a new complicating factor."

"Ah, yes: our long-lost relative, who also happens to be
a popular hero. Could he be a possible ally for us?"

"Or another potential usurper?" Elena asked in her brittle
voice. "One who differs from the others by having a claim
to legitimacy?"

"The answer to both is almost certainly no," Rovard
answered in measured tones. "Everything we know about
him suggests that his loyalty is absolute, and he's never
displayed dangerous ambition. But he's been a protégé of
Medina's since the beginning of the rebellion. I don't dare
approach him."

"Ah, well." Josef sighed. "A pity. I'd hoped to enlist his
support. But you're right, of course. Compromising ourselves
to him would be too risky. We can't count on being able to
wean him away from Medina."

"It might be possible," Elena said in a voice almost too
small to be heard.

"What do you mean?" Josef asked. "How?"

"By offering him the ultimate reward." Her voice remained
small, but it did not waver. "Offer to declare him your heir."

For several interminable heartbeats there was silence as
the Solarian Emperor looked into the eyes of this childless
woman, still physiologically young enough to entertain hopes
of conceiving, and tried to imagine what her last sentence
had cost her.

Rovard finally broke the stillness with a heavy shake of

his gray head. "No. It wouldn't work. He'd never be able to trust it unless you announced it publicly. And by doing that you'd sign his death warrant, given Medina's iron control of this planet."

"You're right, as always. Well, I suppose we shall have to do without Admiral Castellan, won't we?"

"At least we can dare hope he'll support us after his mentor Medina is out of the picture."

"Perhaps. But for now, we can only proceed with your plan. So . . ." Josef took a deep breath. "See to it."

"Your Imperial Majesty." Rovard inclined his head as the Emperor turned and started for the door. Elena began to follow him, but paused and spoke to her father in an undertone.

"You may have already said too much in his hearing."

"Yes. This had better be our last meeting for now. I'll tell Doctor Komos to go ahead."

They followed the Emperor out, leaving the hall to the holographic ghosts of the past.

The conference room was long, dark and austere, dominated by a holo display screen which currently showed the golden Imperial dragon. Between that and the massive double doors at the other end extended a table topped in a gleaming synthetic that simulated silver-veined black marble. Three heatless glowglobes hung above it, casting their light on the faces of the people seated around it. From the head of the table Grand Admiral Yoshi Medina studied those faces.

It was, he reflected, damned inconvenient when he had to be here on the ceremonial capital world, and not at the Fleet's nerve center on Prometheus. But tachyon communications enabled him to keep *au courant* with the important developments from his Old Earth headquarters, here far beneath the titanic masses of this mountain range called the Caucasus. And he had his top advisers with him, here around the table in regulation service dress—they were away from the play-acting court—except for two who wore civilian clothes. One of those was speaking.

"As a claim of right, it's sheer fantasy!" Dugald Dalross spoke so emphatically as to set the wattles beneath his chin quivering, as though delivering a summation in court. "It passes over three intervening emperors and their descendants."

"All of which might be relevant if he were asserting a claim." The sarcastic observation came from the other civilian. "But he hasn't, and he loses no opportunity to assure everyone who'll listen of his loyalty to Josef."

Dalross's florid face darkened to a near magenta and he glared through slits in his fat. Like everyone else at the table, he resented the second speaker as a Johnny-come-lately as well as loathing him for the sheer venomousness of his nature. Medina studied the man—a striking contrast to Dalross in his thin colorlessness—as he would have studied something disgusting in a plate of food. But he had his uses . . . and the strongest possible motivation to continue making himself useful. So Medina kept his detestation concealed behind hooded eyes as he leaned forward, bringing discussion to a halt.

"I agree that Castellan is probably not dangerous. He's served me well throughout the rebellion." Several of the military people rumbled affirmatively. "And his almost archaic loyalty to the dynasty assures his continued support, as long as I'm ruling through the legitimate Emperor."

"Still," Dalross muttered worriedly, "the way he announced his relationship to the dynasty, without first clearing the matter with you . . ."

"That took me aback," Medina admitted. "But on reflection I think it was just a case of spontaneity, typical of his nature." *Which I've never really understood,* came the worrisome thought. "No, I regard Castellan as an opportunity rather than a danger. Given his status as a popular hero—which I don't think he fully appreciates—he can be an invaluable support for us. I intend to make every effort to cultivate him."

"May I offer a suggestion, Grand Admiral?" the second speaker asked diffidently. Medina nodded. "Admiral

Castellan cannot be understood without reference to his special relationship with Rear Admiral Rady and Major General Bogdan. It is a unique friendship which dates back to their early adulthood and involves an extraordinary degree of mutual loyalty on which they all rely." He spoke like a xenobiologist discussing an alien form of life. "Anything that weakens this support system would render Admiral Castellan more controllable."

"I believe I understand." Medina kept his voice mild. "And which of them would you propose as the . . . target?"

"Inasmuch as all three of them are heterosexual, I take it as a given that Rady's link with Castellan includes the added dimension of sex while Bogdan's does not. I therefore suggest that the latter relationship is probably more vulnerable to being subverted. Also, my analysis of Bogdan suggests that he is the artlessly honest sort who expects artless honesty from others." The second speaker paused and essayed an insinuating smile, as though inviting Medina to share his amusement at such childlike weakness.

The Grand Admiral's face remained immobile. The very characteristics which made the fellow such a worm also assured his dependability. Given his past, Medina had only to open his hand to drop him into the pit. Loyalty was as alien to him as every other decent impulse, but he was fully amenable to fear. Medina owned him, body and (highly problematical) soul. *Yes, it was probably a good idea not to have him shot last year, even though it would have been hugely satisfying and actually* legal.

"Very well," Medina said aloud. "There is undoubtedly much in what you say, given the special knowledge of Admiral Castellan you acquired in . . . the past." The second speaker's face grew even paler than its wont at the unsubtle reminder, and Medina permitted himself a thin smile. "We will proceed along the lines you suggest."

Felix Nims, who had been called Felix 3581-2794 in the past to which Medina referred, inclined his head graciously and concealed his relief.

❖   ❖   ❖

Old Earth's northern hemisphere had passed into full spring, and the court had moved on to another ancient city. Basil had liked this one better than Moscow since the first time he'd ridden a slider down a tree-shaded thoroughfare toward an Imperial residence lacking all trace of the sinister, fortresslike atmosphere to which he'd become accustomed.

"But why don't they call the residence 'London Palace'?" Sonja had quibbled. "After all, the city isn't called 'Buckingham.' " She'd become convinced that Old Earth's inhabitants were addicted to inscrutable eccentricities. Basil hadn't been able to argue the point. He'd only known that this city, with its labyrinth of crooked streets and its air of incredible antiquity washed clean by the chronic rain, spoke to something deep within him.

He wondered how much of it was genuine and not reconstructed. Most, probably; the General War had been fought under an unwritten, unacknowledged agreement to spare population centers whenever possible, which was why it had wiped out a mere quarter of the human race and not all of it as the twenty-second century's weapons had been quite capable of doing. Torval hadn't worried about that aspect; he'd merely declared the place the home of some of the best beer he'd ever tasted.

The thought of Torval brought a frown to Basil's face as he watched the uniformed throng in the senior officers' lounge. He and Sonja had been summoned from London for this reception for Admiral Noumea, who'd come to report personally to Medina on the progress of a mopping-up operation that could now be safely left to her subordinates. So they'd flown from London to the Fleet's Earth headquarters, passing over lands with names from the fairy tales of Basil's childhood . . . but Torval hadn't been with them. He was elsewhere in the Solar System, heading a project to chose a replacement for the standard assault shuttle. It was one of the many juicy assignments Medina had given him of late, and Basil was happy for him. But they hadn't seen much of him for a while.

Medina emerged from the crowd and joined him at the bar. "You seem preoccupied, Admiral Castellan."

"Just thinking about General Bogdan, sir. The last time we spoke, he couldn't overstate his gratitude to you for putting him in charge of this project—it enables him to implement some long-standing pet ideas. I've been meaning to thank you myself for all the things you've been doing for him."

"No thanks are necessary; he's been doing a superb job. In fact, I wouldn't be surprised if there's a promotion to lieutenant general in his future." Medina gave a broad wink and turned to the live bartender for another drink— something called "bourbon," whose acquaintance Basil had only recently made. The Grand Admiral had already had several, but was only subtly showing it. "Get yourself another and come with me." He led the way to an alcove. They sat down on couches at a virtual window currently set to show a dazzling nighttime cityscape on Prometheus. Medina took a sonic privacy field generator from his pocket and activated it. The background buzz of conversation ceased.

"This isn't general knowledge yet," the Grand Admiral began without preamble. "But Admiral Mordan in the Zeta Draconis Sector has disobeyed a direct order to report to Prometheus and answer charges concerning his administration of the sector. What's worse, Serafini, who relieved you at Mu Arae, will support him if—*when*, that is—we take direct action. This, in spite of the fact that they've always detested each other." He paused, took a pull on his bourbon, and eyed Basil narrowly.

Basil took a drink himself, partly to stall for time as he framed a reply but mostly because he needed it in the face of this news, which hadn't even reached Rumor Central yet. "Uh, why are you telling me this, sir?"

"No formality," Medina said, waving a hand negligently. "And to answer your question, I'm telling you because I want to hear your evaluation of the threat this poses. And, for that matter, of *all* the threats facing us."

"Without having had time to review the intelligence evaluations, I'm hardly in a position to—"

"No false modesty either." Medina tossed off the rest of his drink, eyed the empty glass critically and said, "Two bourbons" into his wrist communicator.

Basil gathered his thoughts and visualized the Imperial sphere. "Well, Zeta Draconis isn't all that big or rich a sector, isolated down there below the core worlds. But by the same token there's nothing much between it and the Sol and Sigma Draconis systems—which cuts both ways, since it's an advantage for whoever takes the offensive. And Mu Arae is the closest sector to it, so Serafini's help could be a genuine factor." He stopped as a waiter entered the privacy field's dome of silence with a round of drinks.

"No, no," Medina said with a headshake as soon as they were alone again. "I'm not talking about the astrographics of the situation. I want your informal evaluation of the *people* we're dealing with. Be frank."

Basil finished off his first drink and launched into what he hoped was what Medina wanted. "Mordan has been able to entrench himself at Zeta Draconis. There was a strong New Human element there, so he could justify almost any measures he wanted to take. And he's a good defensive tactician. He'll be hard to root out of there."

Medina laughed his deep, purring laugh. " 'Defensive tactician' is exactly the right pair of words. He's got all the offensive spirit of this couch. And he's always been weak on grand strategy. He won't grasp the fact you pointed out, that he's positioned for a bold stroke against the capital systems. And even if he did, he wouldn't be able to execute it. He'll just try to hold onto the little fiefdom he's got now. And, like all people who're unwilling to risk anything, he'll lose everything. What about Serafini?"

"You can't call *her* a stand-patter. She's always been one to take risks, seize the initiative—"

"Oh, yes; she'll rush in every time she sees a momentary advantage, losing sight of her long-term goal, if any. Whenever I'm ready to deal with her, all I'll have to do is dangle some kind of bait in front of her nose." Medina drank deeply and gave a belch of satisfaction. "Now we come to the *real* problem: Kang."

"He can't be taken lightly," Basil opined cautiously, "given the sheer volume of space he controls."

"True, although most of the worlds in that volume are thinly populated by a motley collection of half-assimilated Beyonders."

Basil carefully kept a straight face. "Also, he's shrewd. He hasn't openly defied your authority. He's just stalled and pleaded circumstances beyond his control, and asked for one 'clarification' after another any time he doesn't happen to like an order."

"Yes . . . and there have been an amazing number of tachyon beam array malfunctions out toward the Serpens/ Bootes frontier." Medina scowled briefly, then resumed the smile of a cat who was, if not yet full of canaries, anticipating that happy condition. "You're right: he's the cleverest of the lot, besides controlling the greatest resources. But he's also the oldest. That's important, because it means he's mired in old-fashioned thinking. He set up on his own out there because, like all of us, he was disgusted with the court's obstruction of our efforts to deal with the rebels. But now, when he's in a position to secede outright or else try to take control of the Empire, he can't bring himself to do either. He'd like to continue as he is now, officially a loyal Imperial officer with 'special emergency powers' but in practice independent. He can't see . . . Are you all right?"

"So you really think," Basil asked sickly, "that Kang could . . . usurp the throne?"

"Oh, probably not; more likely just seize the actual power. That is, take *my* place. But you see," Medina went on, oblivious to the expression Basil quickly wiped from his face, "he won't really try, because the status quo is the limit of his vision. He doesn't realize that people who only want to freeze the present into permanency are doomed to failure. The universe won't let them succeed." Looking pleased with himself for this insight, he sank back into his couch and took a deep drink.

Basil sipped more cautiously. "You seem to have eliminated all the possible contenders."

"Yes. Isn't it fortunate that we're dealing with such limited people?" Medina leaned forward, and his voice lost its bantering tone. "The rebellion may have lost, but it succeeded in putting an end to the Empire as it was before. Nothing will ever be the same again. Everything is in a state of flux; and any able, advantageously placed individual with the vision to see that could mold the future in his own image."

"Well, then,' Basil trusted himself to say, "let's hope you're right, and that no such genuinely dangerous person exists."

"I didn't say that. In fact, I believe there are two."

Basil wondered if Medina had actually let himself get drunk. "But you dismissed everyone we discussed."

"We didn't discuss the two I'm thinking of: myself" — Medina paused and held Basil's eyes with a gaze the younger man couldn't break free of— "and you."

The moment stretched and stretched until an impudent *beep* from Medina's wristcomp popped it like a bubble. The Grand Admiral muttered irritably about people who were authorized to interrupt him at any time, and began to speak inaudibly into the comm while Basil sought to collect the shards of his self-possession behind a tightly controlled façade. Amid the swirling chaos of his thoughts, one realization tolled in his head with funereal certitude: *Medina sees me as a threat*. He'd been on Old Earth long enough to have a fair idea of what happened to people Medina saw as threats.

The Grand Admiral talked and listened in silence for a long time, then smiled at Basil with a carnivore's innocence. "Matters have arisen which require my personal attention, Admiral Castellan. If you'll excuse me . . . But no, you're part of the power structure that runs the Empire now, and you may as well get a look at how it operates. Collect Rady and come with me." He stood up and strode across the lounge. People got out of his way.

Basil got Sonja's attention and followed. They hurried to keep up as Medina led the way down a corridor to a drop shaft that took them even deeper beneath the Caucasus. Here armed guards came to attention. "Deactivate the scanner," Medina told their officer. "It hasn't been programmed with Admiral Castellan's and Rear Admiral Rady's genotypes yet, and they'd find paralysis inconvenient." The officer obeyed, and Medina proceeded on toward a blank nanoplastic wall in which an opening appeared just in time for him to walk through.

They were in a large, dimly lit chamber, somehow theaterlike even though it held only a few seats. These faced a transparent hemisphere about three times a man's height in diameter. Around its base clustered assorted machinery, among which Basil thought to recognize a small deflector shield generator. He kept his puzzlement to himself.

Sonja, however, could no longer restrain herself. "What's happening, sir?"

Medina sank into one of the cushioned seats and gestured to them to do the same. "A few days ago Fleet Security—specifically, a newly formed unit which looks after the Grand Admiral's personal safety—uncovered a plot against my life," Medina explained matter-of-factly. "Oh, we've had hints of its existence for some time. But now the individual who was to actually implement the plan has been apprehended. He's been brought here from London."

"London?" Basil echoed faintly.

"Yes. They went ahead and probed him there, so the results would be available for me. They also tried telepathic interrogation, but he's got the same kind of resistance you do—doubtless one of the reasons he was chosen for the job. So we're left with the probe results—and that's the problem. Ah, here he is now."

A conventional door slid open beyond the transparent hemisphere. Silhouetted against the door's rectangle of light, two impact-armored figures emerged, leading a third figure moving like an old man in pain. One of the guards pointed a remote-control device at the hemisphere, and a man-sized portal appeared. They thrust the prisoner through it.

The man looked at his surroundings through the again-unbroken transparency around him. His eyes finally settled on Medina and his two companions. Those eyes evinced no emotion when they met Basil's. It might have been sheer fatalism and resignation, or else genuine non-recognition. But Basil recognized him. Not immediately, given the condition of his face—Medina's 'special unit' of Security had not been gentle—but the soiled remnants of a medical branch vice admiral's uniform were a giveaway.

"So, Doctor Komos," Medina spoke toward an audio pickup, "it seems you and your fellow plotters were very careful. You never actually met or talked to any of the principal conspirators—with one possible exception—within the last three months. I'm quite sure you did earlier, and that your timing took into account the probe's inability to access perceptions earlier than that." He paused as though inviting a response, but the Emperor's physician gave him none. He only stared impassively back from within the transparent dome.

"I want their names," Medina resumed in a voice which had acquired an edge. "I want the names of all the conspirators. *All* of them . . . including the one who, I'm sure, isn't aware of your role at all."

Komos started at that. Basil didn't understand why, but he'd stopped hoping—or wanting—to understand any of this.

Medina also noticed Komos' reaction. "Ah, you take my point," he purred. "Tell me their names, Doctor."

Komos licked his lips and croaked in response. "I'll only tell you what I told your thugs, Medina: I acted on my own, to cut a cancer out of the body of the Empire. I'm only sorry I failed. Now if you're going to kill me, go ahead and do it."

"Of course I'm going to kill you, Doctor." Medina spoke as though urging Komos to be reasonable. "I won't insult your intelligence by pretending to offer you your life. But there are different ways to die." He manipulated a remote, and a metallic probe extended slowly into the prisoner's enclosure from one of the machines at its base. Its tip looked like an aerosol sprayer.

"Dis." Medina smiled as Komos lost all color and backed away from the probe, instinctively crouching against his cage's remotest wall, all dignity and defiance fled in the face of primal fear. "The names, Doctor."

Komos looked around wildly and met Basil's eyes with an unmistakable look of belated recognition. For perhaps a second he pled silently for a help that Basil, sitting paralyzed in hell, could not give. Then the prisoner seemed to gather himself and, incredibly, managed to give Medina a firm headshake.

The Grand Admiral grunted with disgust and fingered the remote again.

The cloud of nanomachines was of course invisible. But Basil could hear a faint hiss before the probe withdrew, and Komos started screaming. Medina touched another button and the noise ceased. "No need to listen to that, is there?"

They couldn't hear, but they could see, and the silence made it even more transcendently horrible.

Repelled from the dome's inner surface by the deflector screen, the nanoids clung to whatever other solids were available and began eating away at them. The floor began to bubble and steam, and so did Komos, his mouth opening into a lockjaw-inducing scream. His face remained frozen into a mask of agony until it dissolved.

Basil stole a glance at Sonja. She sat doubled over with both hands over her mouth, physically restraining her nausea. In some remote corner of his mind, he wondered why he didn't do the same, or actually retch, instead of sitting like an iron statue and forcing himself, as some kind of act of atonement, to watch as Komos merged with the floor in an undifferentiated mass of the inorganic and the formerly organic.

At last it ended, as the dis reached the end of its short active life. All was as it had been before, save that the floor within the dome was at a very slightly higher level. With a calmness that surprised him, Basil recalled that it had already been a little higher than the rest of the room's floor. He wondered how many times the transparent hemisphere had been used for this purpose.

"Most unappetizing," he heard Medina say. "But more humane than he deserved. It's possible, by reducing the quantity of the discharge, to leave the subject barely alive and partially merged with the floor when the nanoids cease to function. But I felt disposed to leniency, given the fact that he wasn't really able to pose a serious inconvenience. The probe revealed various underlings, who are being arrested now, and not all of them will be as intransigent as he was. We'll get proof of what we already know." He gave Basil a commiserating look. "Sorry you had to see this. But it should give you some idea of what I'm up against. And it was necessary. After all, one can hardly probe the Emperor."

Basil showed nothing, because his capacity for shock had gone into overload so long ago that not even Medina's last offhand statement could evoke a visible reaction. He managed polite noises for the rest of the evening, until he and Sonja were back in the aircar.

"Well?" Sonja finally asked after a long interval of silence under the stars. No additional words were necessary.

"I think," said Basil, "that I'm going to accept a certain standing invitation."

CHAPTER NINE
Earth (Sol III), 3909 C.E.

The scrolling map on the aircar's control panel told Basil that his southeastward course was bringing him to the Strait of Otranto, where the Adriatic Sea became the Ionian. He glanced ahead and noted the rocky headland of what the map called "Albania" at about ten o'clock. No real need for confirmation, of course; the car's brain was quite capable of unsupervised piloting. But he continued to look for landmarks as he tried to organize his thoughts in preparation for a visit whose purpose he still couldn't fully verbalize, even to himself.

Soon Corfu appeared on the southern horizon. The map showed it as vaguely sickle-shaped, but that wasn't apparent as the aircar approached the rocky cliffs of the northwest end, then followed the coastline around to the island's eastern side at the sedate pace mandated by local regulations. Inland, he could see a landscape of hills cultivated with trees, and occasional whitewashed little towns. The hills came down to the shore, breaking it up into a series of coves, their sandy beaches washed by the royal-blue water. All was drenched in sunlight of extraordinary brilliance and clarity. Basil gazed, and recalled tales he'd once heard of Jason and Odysseus.

The island's chief town was further south on this coast, but he wasn't going that far. Soon his destination appeared:

a low, rambling villa crowning one of the promontories. The aircar, on the instructions of a fellow artificial semi-sentient which handled Professor Gramont's household arrangements, descended to a paved circular landing pad. Basil emerged into the afternoon sunlight and looked around. Gramont certainly had a spectacular view, overlooking the little bays to the immediate north and south and looking eastward across the sea to the mountainous mainland coast of Greece. Feeling a prickle of sweat in the Mediterranean sun, he removed the jacket of the civilian outfit he'd put on in London.

Gramont approached, walking briskly along a graveled pathway from the house. He was wearing a casual lounging outfit. "My dear Basil, how good to see you! Come, join me for some refreshment." He led the way toward the house, which was surrounded by flowering plants Basil couldn't identify. It was either old or consciously designed to look that way, Basil couldn't tell which; he knew only that it seemed as much a part of this landscape as the rocks and the trees. They walked around it to a terrace on the sea side and sat at a table beneath a vine trellis hung with bunches of fat grapes.

Gramont poured wine. "*Not* retsina," he said with a reassuring smile.

Basil smiled in return and wondered why he was supposed to feel reassured. He found himself liking the wine—unsubtle, a little rough, but belonging here as much as the house did. "You certainly enjoy a pleasant prospect," he ventured.

"Yes," Gramont acknowledged. "I'm a native of Old Earth, you know." Basil hadn't known. "But not from this region. My late wife loved it—she was an archaeologist, you see, and there's always something more to be dug up hereabouts. I came to share her love of it . . . and of this place in particular."

"I can see why." Basil fell silent and let the timelessness of the setting take him for a moment.

Gramont broke the moment delicately. "How are Rear Admiral Rady and Major General Bogdan?"

"Well." Torval had returned to Earth and learned of their visit to Medina's headquarters. His reaction had been what they'd expected, but with a disturbing undertone of ambiguity which the big Marine was incapable of concealing. He and Sonja had both wanted to accompany Basil on this trip, but he'd vetoed it. The invitation had been to him alone, and he suspected that Gramont, for all his affectation of flippancy, used language with great preciseness. "They send their regrets, of course."

"Quite unnecessary. I know how busy you've all been. And . . . how much you've been seeing."

"Yes." Basil took a gulp of wine and set the glass down with a clink. "That's why I've come. I've been seeing a lot of things here. And. . . ." A sense of the ridiculous brought Basil up short and he grinned crookedly. "I'm a little old to be telling a still older man how confused I am."

"Not necessarily. Old Earth can be confusing to those unused to it. It's had longer than anywhere else—thousands of years longer, in fact—to cultivate subtlety. Or, rather, to have subtlety grow around it like ivy covering a tree. And the Imperial court isn't merely subtle; it's dangerous."

"I've begun to learn that."

"Of course. You're a bright fellow who possesses the mixed blessing of a sense of history." Gramont sipped his wine in the sun and smiled with an odd melancholy that, to Basil, exemplified Earth. Then he spoke briskly and with seeming irrelevance. "Have you ever considered how different things are today from what our ancestors expected?"

"What do you mean?"

"A couple of thousand years ago, around the dawn of the space age, people had definite ideas about how they expected the future to be, on the assumption that civilization didn't bomb itself back into a permanent stone age with the crude nuclear weapons that were still new and terrifying. Some of their speculations have come true. But others . . . Well, for example, they took completely for granted that democracy would be the future's universal system of government, unless villainy triumphed and imposed some version of their own century's totalitarian regimes."

"But surely they knew better! I mean, correct me if I'm wrong, but hadn't those very totalitarian regimes generally come to power by the 'will of the people'? And hadn't the 'democracies' themselves come under the control of a self-perpetuating class of political careerists which kept itself in power by subsidized bloc voting?"

"Subsidization paid for by either taxing the middle class out of existence or debasing the currency into a joke," Gramont affirmed. "Oh, yes . . . they *should* have known better. Aristotle, who'd lived in these parts still earlier, could have set them straight on a couple of points. He knew that political history is a cycle, not a linear matter of 'progress' or 'regression,' and that democracy is just one of the painted horses on the carousel. He also knew that pure democracy doesn't work at all except in a small, homogeneous polity. Even the representative sort eventually came to the end you've described in large, pluralistic states. And as for an *interstellar* state . . . ! No, the only common denominator the Empire's disparate societies can possibly have is a human symbol of unity."

"So I've always believed. And I can see now that it's always been an *easy* belief. Loyalty to the Empire, and its living embodiment the Emperor, has always been enough for me. Everything I knew about the New Humans just confirmed me in it. But now . . ."

"Your loyalty has been to the *idea* of the Empire. Now you're having your nose rubbed, as it were, in the reality."

"I'm not a child!" Basil snapped, irritation overcoming caution. "I've always been aware of the corruption, the waste, the incompetence—"

"But none of those things tarnished your ideal Empire for you. After all, an ideal is by definition unattainable by fallible mortals. Reminders of their fallibility may even have enhanced its gleaming purity for you by sheer contrast." Gramont regarded him levelly. "Now you have to come to terms with something very different: the question of where your true loyalty lies in an Empire that has become a disguised military dictatorship."

The setting seemed all wrong for saying the unsayable or hearing someone else say it. But it was equally wrong for dissembling. And with Gramont's words, Basil felt his unacknowledged realization crystallize. "Yes, I've known that for some time. But I couldn't admit it to myself. I had to hear someone else say it." Then, appalled by the words he'd released into the sunlit air, he recoiled into devil's advocacy. "But . . . but if it weren't for Medina, there wouldn't *be* an Empire today! The New Humans would have succeeded in breaking away, and various warlords would have carved up what was left."

"All too true. It took Medina, or somebody like him, to salvage the Empire—or, rather, *an* Empire. But it isn't the old one. The Empire as we've known it could exist only as long as there was a general desire, or at least consent, that it should exist. The New Human movement ended that. So even though the New Humans lost, they took the old Empire down into history's dustbin with them."

"Medina himself said something very similar."

"Hardly surprising. He's nothing if not perceptive, as is often true of people who are intelligent but totally unintellectual. That's *not* a contradiction in terms, by the way; 'intellectual' describes a type of temperament, not a level of intelligence. Anyone who's spent any time in the academic community has known plenty of stupid intellectuals. But I digress." Gramont took a sip of wine without releasing Basil's eyes. "Medina sees very clearly that the old consensual basis for unity is gone. All that's left is naked force. And that force is irresistible by anything except a response in kind. Over the last two and a half millennia, advancing technology has steadily widened the gap between cutting-edge military weaponry and what's generally available."

"Is this really what Medina wants?" Basil's question held what sounded oddly like a pleading tone.

"Probably not. It's simply the situation he finds himself

in. Whether it's 'good' or 'bad' is immaterial. His is an
ambition unrestrained by moral concerns. I don't necessarily
say he's incapable of such concerns, only that he never lets
them influence his actions in any politically disadvantageous
way."

Gramont fell silent, and for a while there was no sound
but that of the occasional sea bird as they sat in the warm
afternoon sun. Rather belatedly, it occurred to Basil that
he'd never even asked for assurance that this place was
secure from snooping. But he felt an absolute certainty that
it was. They wouldn't be having this conversation if Gramont
wasn't sure of their privacy.

"So," Basil finally asked, "what's to be done about it?"

"Nothing . . . as long as you're here on this planet."

Basil leaned forward, blinking. "What do you mean?"

"Surely you've noted that Medina's control of Old Earth
is absolute. No move against him can possibly succeed here,
as we've recently seen demonstrated."

"You misunderstand. Why *me*? Come to think of it, why
did you seek me out in Moscow and invite me here in the
first place? And what's your concern with all this anyway?"

" 'Why you' should be obvious. Your status as a popular
hero lifted you above the general run of military adventurers
even before your connection with the Imperial family came
to light. Human beings have such a deep-seated need for
young heroes that they've sometimes placed the mantle
on some remarkably unworthy shoulders. You've probably
never heard of Bonny Prince Charlie or John Kennedy or . . .
Sorry," Gramont added quickly, with a smile. "I don't mean
to imply that *you* are unworthy. Far from it, unless I'm
further afield than I usually am in my judgments of people."

Basil tried to reestablish his grip on reality, which had
grown steadily weaker as this conversation progressed. "Even
if that's all true, it doesn't explain what your role is. You
talk as though you're somehow personally responsible for
restoring the Empire."

"Of course I'm not. Not individually." Gramont paused,
as though trying to decide how best to proceed. "Aside from

the political sphere, do you know what else about the present era would surprise people from two thousand years ago?"

"Huh?" Basil shook his head, caught off balance by the abrupt return to Gramont's initial conversational gambit. "Well . . . a lot of the technology would seem like magic to them. . . ."

"Ah, but they'd expect that! In fact, after two millennia unbroken by any collapse of civilization or loss of knowledge, they'd expect the world to be *more* unfamiliar than it has in fact become. By the end of the twentieth century the conventional wisdom held that after a few more generations technology and society—and, indeed, human nature itself—would be unrecognizable."

"Naturally. They'd undergone generations of dizzying change, and expected it to continue. As it did, for a while. But then, after the General War, the reorganized United Nations made it its business to halt technological and social change in the name of stability."

"Yes, while venting Earth's irreconcilable elements through the safety valve of slower-than-light interstellar colonization. But it couldn't last—and didn't. The colonists of Sigma Draconis openly proclaimed the emperor's nakedness in the twenty-sixth century when they rejected the strictures on basic research and free-market economics. Shortly thereafter they discovered the secret of faster-than-light travel. You might say the U.N. was a Tokugawa Shogunate that created its own Commodore Perry."

"Uh, beg pardon?"

Gramont gave a self-deprecatory smile. "Sorry. Sheer habit. Anyway, the U.N. bureaucrats, living in their hermetically sealed world of self-deception, reacted to the new realities in much the same way as those Opium Wars era Chinese mandarins whose response to the Industrial Revolution was to inquire when the barbarian chieftainess Victoria was going to arrive and abase herself before the Son of Heaven . . . All right, I *promise* I won't do it again! The point is that after the inevitable conflict had reached its equally inevitable conclusion and the U.N. had been replaced by the Solarian

Federation, technological advancement wasn't nearly as rapid as might have been expected. Indeed, during the Federation's golden age and the Wars of the Protectors afterwards—almost six centuries altogether—it consisted largely of refinements of the basic discoveries of the Sigma Draconis Republic's early days. Why do you suppose that was?"

"I'm sure I don't know. The question was never posed in exactly those terms in your Imperial History course."

"Touché. But there were reasons for the omission." Gramont seemed to gather himself, and his sudden seriousness was enough to alert Basil. "During the early Federation period a new social science branched off from that of history, quantifying the historical process and giving reality to the kind of societal morphology that early pioneers like Toynbee and Spengler had merely groped at. As time went on, the practitioners of this science became convinced that bioengineering and nanotechnology were threatening to transform society into something that would no longer be recognizably human: a grotesque fusion of the organic and the inorganic. Certain strategically placed persons formed an association for the purpose of controlling the flow of information."

As Gramont spoke, suspicion awakened in Basil's mind like a pinpoint of light, then flared into a blaze of certainty. "The Society!" he blurted out.

"So it's generally called," Gramont nodded. "Shorthand for the 'Cliometric Society,' a name derived from that of the Muse of History. It acted throughout the Federation's lifetime to suppress technologies which tended to blur the distinction between man and machine."

"But," Basil protested, "they couldn't have been successful. The thirty-third century saw a new surge of revolutionary change—as you *did* teach us."

Gramont had the grace to wince. "Yes. The explanation is clear enough. The age of the 'Protectors of the Federation,' with its limited wars waged by a tradition-oriented military class, had provided little impetus for innovation. But by the era to which you refer, the old conventions of warfare had begun to give way to increasing brutalization." He smiled sadly. "I've often thought it one of history's little ironies that the standard year 3306 saw the partition of the Greater Eridanus Combine—or, to be precise, the ratification of its partition by the ghostlike wraith of the Federation fifty years after the fact—and also the invention of the tachyon beam array. Instantaneous communication, which made a centralized interstellar state thinkable, had come just barely too late to save the last Protector-state. In the power vacuum that followed, wars were no longer fought for mere hegemony; the prize had become imperium. As on Earth in the two centuries before starflight, total war and its attendant social disintegration were accompanied by frenetic technological advancement. Under the circumstances, our accustomed methods were powerless."

A second or two passed before what he had heard registered on Basil—for which he could be forgiven, inasmuch as the singular and plural forms of the first person were less dissimilar in Imperial Standard English than they had been in its twentieth-century ancestor. But realization finally caught up and he stared at the dapper little academic across the table from him. "Ah, Doctor Gramont, perhaps I misheard you, but—"

"No, you didn't." All at once Gramont was very serious indeed. "You realize, I hope, that I'm telling you something not customarily revealed. Indeed, it isn't revealed at all."

"So you're a member of the . . . the . . ."

"Of the Society, yes. Without going into details, I'm rather highly placed in it."

Like a drowning man clinging to a piece of flotsam, Basil stuck to the immediate subject. "But how does this explain your concern with the fate of the dynasty? Isn't the Society opposed to the Empire?"

"No." Gramont shook his head vigorously. "That's a popular misconception, dating back to our role in the Unification Wars. By then the more tough-minded cultural morphologists recognized the stage of development their civilization had reached. And theory predicted what lay

ahead in the near future: conquest by one of the warring
states of all its rivals, and imposition of a universal empire.
The Society took two steps in response. It allowed its public
manifestations to wither away, and became for the first
time a secret organization. And it sought, by forestalling
the development of military innovations which might give
any one state a decisive advantage, to deflect history from
its immemorial pattern and preserve the conflicting states
in a balance of power."

"But," Basil protested, aghast, "that meant prolonging
the Unification Wars!"

"Endemic war seemed more desirable than its alternative:
dead sameness, smothering the richly diverse cultural
traditions mankind had carried to the stars. How effective
our predecessors' efforts were is impossible to accurately
assess. But it is a fact that the universal totalitarian empire
they dreaded did not come to pass for another century.
When it did, the retreat into deep secrecy turned out to
have been a wise move, for the Draconis Empire knew an
enemy when it saw one.

"Afterwards, however, we gave our clandestine support
to the Solarian Empire, for we'd come to the conclusion
that unity was inevitable and probably desirable. Our
existence was generally known, but our secretiveness had
made us an object of fear and distrust to the average person.
Nevertheless, our influence helped bring about the kind
of Empire of which we—and, it would seem, you—
approved. We've also resumed our traditional efforts to
steer technological development away from dangerous
courses."

"Not with any great effectiveness, it seems." Basil gave
a vague, expansive gesture that took in the universe in which
they lived.

"Oh, you might be surprised," Gramont said serenely.
"While we've seldom been able to suppress actual knowledge
of the technologies of which we disapprove, we've had
considerable success in discouraging flagrant, widespread
use of them. For example, as far back as the twenty-first

century direct man-machine interfacing through actual surgical connection became possible. Even when such technology reached its maturity in the early Federation period, it still generally involved surgically implanted devices."

"Yes, I've read about what they used to do to themselves in those days." An involuntary shudder ran through Basil. "But of course they turned away from that kind of obscene self-mutilation!"

"There's no 'of course' about it," Gramont stated firmly. "Your revulsion is a socially learned response, for which our activities are largely responsible. Granted, we had an easy time of it in that particular area, given the popular reaction against the unrestricted cyborging the Draconis Empire had practiced. Today, when direct neural interfacing *must* be used—as by any military force that wants to be competitive—it is accomplished in noninvasive ways whose enormous expense restricts their use more surely than any legislation could."

Basil thought of the neurohelmets he'd always taken for granted, and wondered why he'd never considered the fact that the same result could be achieved far more cheaply with a socket in the temple. . . . He shied away from the thought with disgust, and changed the subject. "Why are you violating centuries of secrecy by telling me all this?"

"To persuade you that we're allies. We may have arrived at the position by different routes, but we both favor an Empire which accepts all the life-giving irrationalities and fruitful compromises which are history's legacy. The New Humans sought to replace it with a formless mass of atomic individuals presided over by an indulgent centralized government—an old ideal which can never be discredited enough times to lose its appeal for the *lumpen* intelligentsia. We of the Society let our distaste for it lead us into uncritical support of Medina. Now we have to live with our mistake."

"Or, rather, you want me to help you rectify it," Basil said rather pointedly.

"If you insist on putting it that way," Gramont sighed.

"But remember, it works both ways. When and if you decide to move against Medina, you'll need all the help you can get—including ours."

"But how much help can the Society be?" Basil asked bluntly. "Let's ignore for the moment the fact that I'm not entirely certain I agree with your long-term goals, and that I'm *quite* certain I don't like the idea of anyone playing God. The point is, how effective will your methods be in the kind of era we're entering into now?"

Gramont pursed his lips above his goatee. "It's possible you underestimate our resiliency."

"But you've admitted the Society was unable to stave off the Succession Wars, when old social intricacies were swept aside by crude-force politics just as seems to be happening now."

"True enough. But this time we have allies."

"Oh? So I'm not the only one in the Empire you've pinned your hopes on?" The question didn't come out quite as sarcastically as Basil had intended.

"Actually, the allies to whom I refer *aren't* 'in the Empire.' "

Basil stiffened, and almost spilled wine from the glass he'd been bringing up to his lips. "Beyonders?" he demanded.

No one really knew how far into the galaxy human settlement extended. Nor did people in the Empire give it much thought, for the Empire was all the universe that mattered. Outside its boundaries were only the descendants of those political diehards, cultural separatists, religious cultists and other assorted malcontents who had, starting in the early Federation era, used the faster-than-light drive to move beyond the pale of civilization. The Draconis Empire had conquered some of the nearer ones, and the Solarian Empire had generally kept those conquests—and even, under Armin II, extended them. But in general the Beyonders were of interest only when someone among them forged a league with the capability and inclination to raid the Imperial frontier areas. Or when they supplied mercenaries who looked on the Imperial populations as wolves look on sheep . . .

Gramont raised a reassuring hand. "Calm yourself! We have no intention of loosing pirates and barbarians on the Empire."

Basil laughed harshly. "What else is out there? Most Beyonder societies have the one lonely virtue that they're too primitive to pose a threat, and the others can never sustain any large-scale political unity long enough to *remain* a threat. And that sums them up, unless you count fables about the . . ."

As he'd spoken, Basil had taken on the smile of a man who expects his listener to share his amusement at the thought of extravagant tales. But as Gramont's expression remained unchanged in its seriousness, his voice trailed off and the smile died. "You don't by any chance mean to say—" he resumed weakly.

Gramont stood up abruptly. "Rather than asking you to rely on my word, I suggest we go and see an associate of mine. Excuse me while I make the arrangements." He went inside, leaving Basil alone with the wine, the view, and a whole new set of impossibilities.

In a remarkably short time, Gramont emerged. "We're in luck. He's available. We can proceed immediately."

Basil took a fortifying pull on his wine and stood up. He gestured toward the front of the villa, where his aircar stood. "Shall we take my—"

But Gramont was moving briskly toward the entrance to the villa. "Please come this way." Basil followed him along a white-plastered hallway into a foyer with a mosaic floor. "Now, please stand *here*."

Puzzled, Basil stood beside Gramont. The inlaid tiles formed a pattern which wasn't immediately noticeable, and they stood in the center of it. "Here?"

"Just so." Gramont reached into a pocket and produced a small instrument of unfamiliar aspect. He touched a button and a red light flashed.

For the second time in Basil's life, the universe as reported by his senses vanished, to be instantly replaced by another.

"My dear Basil, are you quite all right? I suppose I should have warned you."

Basil nodded jerkily. Gramont's solicitous voice came to him only faintly as he fought vertigo by studying his surroundings carefully.

They were at one end of a long, windowless room with a low, vaulted ceiling, the far end of which was furnished as an office. Glowglobes on stands along the walls revealed nothing but utilitarian furnishings. All this Basil took in with a glance. Most of his attention was devoted to the man who advanced toward them from a control panel.

He was medium-tall, strongly built and with the look of indeterminate early middle age that characterized the long-term anagathics user. His clothes were so nondescript as to reflect nothing about their wearer except a desire to be as inconspicuous as possible. The smile he gave Gramont seemed more practiced than natural. His squarish face, with its strongly marked features and sharp gray eyes, held an underlying grimness which never quite vanished beneath whatever expression he was wearing.

"Admiral Castellan," Gramont spoke in tones of formal introduction, "allow me to present Jan Kleinst-Schiavona of the Associated Clans of Newhope."

"I've looked forward to meeting you, Admiral Castellan," Kleinst-Schiavona said with a slight, unidentifiable accent, extending his hand.

Basil took it with a hand which wasn't altogether steady. "And I never thought to meet you—or, I should say, anyone like you, if I'm correct in my understanding of your origin. The Sword Clans, you see, are widely believed to be myth, or at best an exaggerated depiction of some actual Beyonder society."

"So I've learned since coming here," the Sword Clansman acknowledged affably.

"This has always been my own view," Basil confessed. "But it's no longer tenable, given the manner of my arrival here. Where is 'here,' by the way?"

"The basement of my residence," Kleinst-Schiavona said blandly.

"I mean—"

"No. With your permission, or even without it, I won't tell you which city we're in, just as I won't tell you the name I use in my persona as an off-world businessman here on Old Earth."

"For someone claiming to be an ally, you're not particularly candid."

"A matter of security, as you understand perfectly well. What you don't know you can't reveal, even to the probe. The same need for discretion lay behind the means used to bring you here. An aircar might have been tracked. But even if Doctor Gramont's villa is under observation, no sensor technology available to Medina can detect that anything occurred."

"Yes—in addition to providing a rather theatrical demonstration of the truth of your claims." Basil gave Gramont a sour look. Then a stomach-dropping thought came to him. "Assuming, of course that it was a product of technology . . ."

"Think about it, Admiral. Even if there were such a thing as a psi with the talent and power to teleport the mass of two human bodies the distance you and Doctor Gramont just came—and I've never met nor heard of one—you surely noticed that there were no vector differentials catching up with you on your arrival here."

Basil *hadn't* noticed, in his stupefaction. But now he realized there had been no sensation of being slammed down or jerked sideways or. . . . A chill started in his heart and spread outward to his skin. "Are you magicians, to repeal the conservation laws of physics?" he whispered.

"Don't be preposterous! If you'll let it, your intellect will tell you that you were brought here by a mechanical device which achieves the same effect as psionic teleportation but avoids many of its limitations—we call it a 'transposer.' For one thing, its power supply also serves as a kind of energy sink, to adjust the potential energy of objects." Kleinst-Schiavona's annoyance seemed to ebb. "It's massive and expensive, and it took some doing to bring in the components and assemble one here. But it's worth it because of the undetectable mobility it provides. Not even psi-detection devices can sense its operation, inasmuch as it's just brute-force duplication of psionic teleportation."

"It also provides the ultimate weapon," Basil breathed, barely aware of the other's words as the possibilities filled his mind.

"Not really. For one thing, it requires a communications link or sensor lock on its target—either the destination or any remote object which is to be brought in, as you and the professor were." A wintery smile. "So rest assured, I can't simply flick a bomb into Fleet headquarters. Not that I wish to. We want to preserve the Empire, which is why we are natural allies of the Society—and of you."

"But why? As I understand, your ancestors left the Empire's predecessor, the Federation, in something of a huff. And . . ." Basil swung toward Gramont. "And why have *you* allied yourselves with people who have the potential to bring about what you exist to prevent: another socially corrosive technological revolution. And *please* spare me any clichés about strange bedfellows!"

"There is," Gramont intoned, "some truth in anything that's lasted long enough to be called a cliché."

"I think I can make things clear," Kleinst-Schiavona said hastily as Basil seemed about to reach critical mass. "I believe Doctor Gramont has already explained why the Society approves of the Empire. Well, so do we. And we want it to remain as it's been, because eventually we're going to have to return to it."

"Return?" Basil shook his head. "I don't understand."

"Come this way and I'll explain." Kleinst-Schiavona led the way to the far end of the room, where an array of data retrieval equipment flanked a desk, and manipulated controls. A holo display—quite conventional, Basil was obscurely relieved to note—awoke, revealing a schematic of what seemed to be a double star system, complete with planetary orbits. "Our home system," the Sword Clansman explained.

"But I thought your ancestors' destination was a star which was a virtual twin of Sol."

"HD 44594," Kleinst-Schiavona supplied. "A Sol-type star about eighty light-years from here. Yes, they allowed that to become the general opinion, even though their initial scouting expedition had revealed no suitable planet and they therefore went elsewhere."

"Why the disinformation?"

"Well, they were *very* disaffected with the Federation. You'd have to ask a historian why. Oh, of course I was taught it in school. But it made so little sense to me, and involved issues so dead, that I've forgotten. At any rate, they wanted to cover their tracks lest the Federation should someday turn expansionist and come looking for them. The same considerations led them to probe further out from human space. They found this system just as their drives were beginning to fail, as they often did in those days when the technology was still new. They congratulated themselves on their extraordinary luck in having found it just in time, for it had a world so Earthlike that little terraforming was needed." Kleinst-Schiavona indicated the third planetary orbit around the yellow-white primary star. "They named it Newhope and settled in at once, before completing their in-depth survey of the system.

"This turned out to be a mistake, for the system held two surprises, both lethal in the long run. The first was the Zyungen." Kleinst-Schiavona touched a control, and the second orbit of the secondary star—a mid-K-type orange sun—flashed for attention. And beside the system display stood the image of an animal which stood on four legs but which also had a pair of limbs, extending from what had to be called the shoulders of the erect torso, that were clearly adapted for tool-using. The Sword Clansman saw Basil's expression, smiled faintly, and continued.

"The system is a distant binary; the primary star can hold planets in stable orbits out to almost three astronomical units, the secondary one out to slightly over two. But our ancestors, in their fixation on Newhope, neglected the secondary star's planets. And the Zyungen weren't quite up to advertising their presence with broadcasts on the radio wavelengths. It was awhile before we discovered that we had neighbors. Imagine the excitement!" The bitterness in his voice drew a sharp glance from Basil, which went unnoticed. "We decided we had some kind of mission to uplift the poor benighted natives, even though their world wasn't readily accessible—that close to the twin suns, the drive would have been inoperable even if we'd still had ships with it in commission. They seemed apt pupils, as inherently intelligent as humans. And they were clever about hiding their xenophobia—although we helped by seeing only what we wanted to see and writing off everything else as manifestations of natural fear and superstitious awe in the face of a superior technology, when in fact it was. . . . Well, we're still not entirely sure. We've theorized that it's related to the fact that they're far more psionically adept than humans but use a mental 'wavelength' so different that telepathic contact with us is impossible. Taking telepathic communion for granted, they reacted with horror to a race whose minds seemed a void, and decided we were . . . 'soulless' would probably be the closest human concept, although their own religions wouldn't put it that way." Kleinst-Schiavona grimaced. "Or maybe they just decided, after learning spaceflight was possible, that four-limbed alien monsters from another star had no business colonizing planets of *their* star—or even its companion star. Newhope would have been pretty wet and warm for them, but they could have lived there. At any rate, they strung us along until they thought they were ready, and then they struck.

"We were caught completely by surprise," he continued in a voice which no longer held bitterness, nor any other emotion. "They used clean weapons, to avoid ruining the real estate. But aside from a few people in out-of-the-way places on Newhope, the only human survivors in the system were those in space. We were on the edge of extinction. But we survived. We rallied around whatever individuals had military experience or aptitude. We fought back, in widely scattered units which, to keep in to touch with each other, adopted code names based on ancient kinds of swords: sabre, katana, cutlass, tulwar, claymore . . . schiavona. As the war dragged on, with no 'home front,' those units became communities: groups of interrelated families, each with its own traditions and character but all united in their hate."

As Kleinst-Schiavona had spoken, something had come to life like an ember flickering alight into a blaze of pride in his ashen voice. "We beat them in space and threw them off Newhope. But that was only the beginning. We tried to carry the war to their homeworld, but by then they had defenses in place which could deal with any force we could project across that distance. So we settled in for a protracted war. It's still going on now, after more than eight hundred years."

"But . . . but that's impossible!" Basil protested. "No war could remain stalemated so long."

"Oh, it hasn't been continuous high-intensity war for all that time. Both sides fortified their homeworlds to the point of unassailability, then began to spar for the other planets of the binary system, then probed outward to other nearby systems. We haven't planted any actual outsystem colonies— we haven't the population to spare—but we've endeavored to prevent them from doing so either. At the beginning the two sides were fairly evenly matched; our population was tiny, but most of theirs was still in the Iron Age. But as the centuries have gone by they've brought more and more of their race into the modern era. The only way we could avoid being overwhelmed was by staying ahead of them technologically. They don't seem to be as inventive as we are, though they're altogether too good at adapting our inventions. They're also warlike by nature."

"I can tell." Basil knew perfectly well that he couldn't tell anything of the sort from the holo image. But the impression was unavoidable. The robust, thick-hided barrel and torso, the head with its fierce bony crest, the face with its formidable array of what weren't really teeth but served the same purposes, including intimidation—all were difficult to describe, even mentally to oneself, for the Zyungen was too different from any of the familiar creatures that might have offered parallels. But it didn't have to be fully comprehended to be taken seriously.

"Their psionic aptitude has also spurred our development," Kleinst-Schiavona was saying. "For example, a lot of them have psi teleportation ability, which for all its inescapable limitations gave us some bad moments in close-in fighting. So we learned to artificially duplicate it. We also developed ways to neutralize teleported bombs."

"So," Basil said, "you've been able to hold out in spite of being outnumbered."

"Yes, at the cost of regimenting ourselves into a totally militarized society. The way we live would seem to you a strange blend of high technology and bleak poverty. And, of course, it's all doomed to failure in the end."

"What?" Basil shook his head. "It seems you've managed pretty well so far. Is the long-term trend really running *that* strongly against you?"

"Remember I mentioned that there were *two* nasty surprises lurking in our system?" Kleinst-Schiavona pointed at the system display. "As is always the case with binary systems, there's a zone between the two stars where planets can't have stable orbits even if they could form in the first place. The secondary star had a planet just a little too close to that zone's boundary."

" 'Had'?" Basil queried.

"At some point in the past, the primary star pulled it away into a crazy cometary orbit that's never the same twice. It was a long time before we discovered it. It took even longer—until very recently, in fact—for us to come to the realization that it's going to collide with Newhope."

It took awhile for the statement to become real to Basil. When it did, all he could manage was, "How long?"

"A little less than two centuries from now."

"But . . . but why wait? Why don't you evacuate Newhope now? Go even further out and find another world to colonize. Come to think of it, why haven't you done that already? Wouldn't it be better than endless war?" Basil was about to say more, but what he saw in Kleinst-Schiavona's eyes stopped him. The Sword Clansman visibly brought himself under control and spoke mildly.

"I can't expect you to understand what Newhope means to us. The bone-dry summary I've given you can't possibly convey how much of our blood we've spilled into its soil. But the fact is that we can't get away from the Zyungen that way. You see, we haven't been entirely successful in preventing them from establishing some extra-systemic outposts. They'd know if we went to any of the nearby systems. And they could follow us if we went beyond those systems."

"Why would they want to? Just to carry on a war that would have lost all meaning?"

Kleinst-Schiavona blinked with surprise. "Why, of course. The war will never end, you know. Not as long as a single member of each race is alive."

A chill wind blew through Basil. "So that's what you meant about returning to Imperial space. I don't see why you haven't already. . . . But yes, you explained Newhope's importance to you."

"That's part of it. But ask yourself: why would anyone *want* to return to the Empire as it is now?"

Basil felt a hotness spreading over his face and ears. "We'll restore it to the way it was," he asserted.

"No doubt," Kleinst-Schiavona said drily. "But on the assumption—purely theoretical!—that there's any doubt in the matter, we'd like to offer what help we can to whoever seems most likely to accomplish that end. And we, like the Society" —he inclined his head in Gramont's direction— "judge you to be that individual."

"What kind of 'help'?"

"The covert kind—of necessity. And, just as necessarily, on a small scale; we're in no position to divert too many resources from our own struggle for survival. But some of our technology, used unexpectedly at the right moment, could be decisive. When—I don't think it's necessary to say 'if'—you make your move, you have only to call on us."

Basil thought of the other unexpected offer of help he'd gotten, but some instinct kept him silent about it. "How do I know I can trust you? You naturally have your own agenda."

"Of course. But the point is, it coincides with yours." Kleinst-Schiavona's gaze hardened. "The Empire's present state—powerful warlords contending for the opportunity to impose universal autocracy—is impossible from our viewpoint. But there are two alternatives which would serve our purposes. One is a restoration of the traditional Imperial order. The other is breakdown into total chaos, in which a united group of technologically advanced and militarily experienced new arrivals could do quite well for themselves."

"Ahem!" Gramont looked uncomfortable. "I say, Jan, is it really necessary to be so blunt?"

"No, no." Basil waved a dismissive hand. "I appreciate his forthrightness." He turned back to the Sword Clansman. "You're saying that your offer to help me bring about the first eventuality ought to carry conviction because it's not your only option. You could, if you wished, try to promote the second one."

"Without the aid of the Society," Gramont put in stiffly.

"True," Kleinst-Schiavona admitted. "But we *prefer* the first outcome, for any number of reasons—not the least of which is that sooner or later the Zyungen, freed from the necessity of combating us, are going to reach Imperial space. When that happens, there's going to have to be a viable Empire to fight them. And fighting them is something at which we have a *lot* of experience. So in the long run we need each other."

"I believe I can see that," Basil said slowly. *I can also see,* he didn't add, *that you might well feel a degree of guilt, for arguably your ancestors* created *the Zyungen, at least as a threat to humanity. But you can't very well admit that, can you?* "It's possible you're taking too much for granted in assuming that I'm going to move against Medina. For now, I'm keeping my options open. But if it comes to that . . ." He paused awkwardly, knowing that he had reached one of those moments, and was about to make one of those unrecallable utterances, after which nothing can be the same again. "If it does, it won't be while I'm on Earth. I'll need to be able to get in touch with you wherever I am."

Kleinst-Schiavona kept his face expressionless, but he seemed to relax inwardly. "Of course. We've already given some thought to this. Let's discuss the details, shall we?"

The nerve center of Fleet's Earth headquarters was a dimly lit circular room, seemingly too vast to be underground, much less deep beneath the Caucasus. Desks and instrument panels filled it in concentric circles, and viewscreens lined its walls. But its centerpiece was a wide holo dais over which hung a display of the Empire, a two-storey-diameter spheroid of many-colored lights. Those colors had nothing to do with the spectral classes of the stars they represented, but rather denoted sector jurisdictions. Legends hung in midair beside the lights, visible from whatever direction they were viewed, and the icons of Fleet units drifted to and fro.

When Basil and Sonja entered the room, Medina was standing at the railing around the dais, scowling intently at two neighboring clusters of lights, one green and the other blue, in the display's lower regions.

"It's happened," he began without preamble. "Oh, it hasn't become public yet. But Mordan and Serafini have patched up their little quarrel—amazing what a thirst for power will do! She's getting ready to shift forces into a position to support him when he goes into open rebellion." He manipulated a remote, and an icon flashed for attention.

"What are we doing to counter it?" Sonja asked.

"Very little. At present, they don't know that we know what they're up to. But they'd notice any large force movements. I don't want to stampede them into moving their schedule forward."

Basil looked intently at the icon. "She's positioning her forces at DM -48 11837," he mused. "I know that system. And I know one force that could depart without attracting much attention, because I'm certain of its security."

Medina looked at him sharply. "Task Force 27," he said simply.

Basil's organizational improvisation had become permanent. The task force consisting entirely of Sonja's Task Group 27.1 had been kept together, and brought back up to strength, for it had achieved legendary status—Castellan's task force, Rady's task group. And now it was here, at Sol.

"Yes," Basil affirmed. "It can be ready for departure by the time we've assembled some supporting elements— including a Marine assault force, since there may be some ground action. Sonja and I can take it directly there and deal with Serafini. Then Mordan will be left high and dry— it won't matter if he acts ahead of schedule, even if he still has the inclination."

"Have your staff put together the operational plan for me to review tomorrow," Medina ordered.

"And to submit to the Emperor for approval?" Sonja asked innocently.

"Of course." The blandness of Medina's voice was unsullied by even a hint of irony.

"One other thing," Basil said quickly, before Sonja could grow rash. "I need a new chief of staff. Can I have Lenore Silva, who was with me at Mu Arae?"

"Good choice." Medina nodded emphatically. "She's yours."

"Also, I could use General Bogdan to head any ground assault operations."

"Ah." Medina's eyes grew hooded. "That may not be possible. He's engaged in a vital project for me just now, out in the Jovian satellary system—a project I wouldn't want to disrupt."

Basil dropped into expressionless formality. "With great respect, sir, I suggest that his presence would enhance the Task Force's effectiveness. He's become an integral part of the command structure, and also part of the . . . well, the mystique of Task Force 27."

"Sorry. Quite out of the question. But I'll make every effort to send him to join you later." Medina's tone made the word "dismissed" unnecessary.

"Aye aye, sir." Basil turned on his heel and departed, followed by Sonja.

"We can't go out there without Torval," she muttered as they walked through the corridors. He'd told her of what had passed on Corfu and in the nameless city where the Sword Clans' agent lived his double life.

"It certainly wasn't what I'd planned on," Basil acknowledged in a voice as hushed as hers. "But we can't pass up this opportunity to take Task Force 27 away from Earth. We'll finally have some options, out from under Medina's thumb."

"What kind of 'options' will we have, with Torval back here as a hostage for our good behavior?"

"I know, I know! But what do you want me to do?" He forced his voice back down. "We'll never have a chance like this again."

"No, we won't," she admitted sadly. "I understand. But I don't have to like it."

"I don't either. We'll just have to put off making our move until after Torval has joined us. It may take some juggling."

"Do you really think Medina is going to keep that promise to send him?"

"I don't know," he admitted.

They walked on in silence through the long gray corridors.

Back in the control center, Medina stood deep in thought for some time after the other two were gone. Finally, a soft throat-clearing caught his attention. It was someone whose presence he'd thought it prudent to keep concealed from Castellan and Rady.

"You heard?" he growled.

"Yes, sir," Felix Nims affirmed. "It's as I've suspected all along. Admiral Castellan wants to get away from this system and set himself up as an independent warlord in a remote sector, with a force which is personally loyal to him."

"You're probably right. Too bad. I'd hoped to make use of him. But he's simply too dangerous." Medina turned and gazed at the holo display. "It's also too bad that I'll have to let him go."

For an instant, shocked surprise overcame Felix's sycophancy. "*What?* But . . . but you can't!"

Medina turned his head toward him, very slowly. "What did you say?"

"Er . . . that is . . . an unfortunate choice of words, sir. But how can you trust him out of your direct control, in light of what you yourself have so perceptively observed about his aims?"

"His *ultimate* aims. For now I need him to take care of Serafini for me. And I think he can be trusted to do it. Remember, Serafini is going into rebellion against the *Emperor.*"

"You are correct as always, sir." Felix managed to grovel standing up. "But if I may make a suggestion, it may be possible, as people say, to have your cake and eat it too."

"What do you mean?"

"Wait until after Castellan has removed Serafini, and then deal with him. During the . . . er, well, that is, in the past I had occasion to develop some useful contacts in the Mu Arae sector, so I'm in a position to be of assistance."

Medina brooded for a heartbeat or two. "Very well. See to it. Don't bother me with the details."

CHAPTER TEN
The Mu Arae Sector, 3910 C.E.

The wreckage caught the ruddy light of DM -48 11837 as it drifted in orbit, fragments of ships tumbling end over end through the void. Basil gazed at it in the viewscreen and kept his face expressionless as he listened to Lenore Silva's report.

"All the hostile units have been accounted for—destroyed, surrendered or fled. The scout screen reports no further response to their offers to pick up life pods." The starlight glinting off the chief of staff's ebon features failed to reveal any expression.

"Not that there would have been many pods from their flagship," Sonja remarked. Neither she nor any of them could forget the sight of the battleship's cataclysmic end. "Too bad . . ." She let the thought die. None of them had expected Serafini herself to be with this advance force. But, then, she'd always prided herself on leading from the front.

Basil swung around abruptly and faced the two women, silhouetted against the starfields and the blaze of the local sun. "I never wanted this. As soon as I realized Serafini was here, I tried to persuade her to surrender, to join us—"

"We know you did, Basil," Sonja assured him. "But it takes two to make an agreement, and Serafini wasn't having any. You can't blame yourself."

"No. But . . ." Basil shook his head as he often did when

dismissing a thought, as though seeking to physically dislodge it. "Never mind. Let's proceed to Mu Arae and wrap this up."

As the shuttle entered Hespera's atmosphere and approached Bronson's Landing, Basil found himself having to suppress a shudder at the memory of his last experience at that city's spaceport. Then he had to laugh inwardly at himself. This was nothing like that night a year and a half before when the New Humans had snatched him. For one thing, he was arriving rather than departing as he'd been then. And this time there was no danger. Serafini's subordinates had surrendered with almost comical haste when the reinforced Task Force 27 had arrived at Mu Arae hard on the heels of the news from DM -48 11837. There would be no ambush awaiting him, only an obsequious official greeting party.

"What's so amusing?" asked Sonja, who'd noticed his lips twitching upward. When he told her his thoughts she snorted derisively. "The only risk you'll be running this time is embarrassing yourself by throwing up in public. I really dread listening to these hypocrites explain how they've really been loyal subordinates of Medina all along, and having to pretend to take it seriously."

"Oh, I don't know. It may have its entertaining moments."

"Only if getting your ass kissed entertains you."

"Actually, my tastes run in slightly different directions."

"I know." Her twinkle mirrored his, and they clasped hands briefly as the shuttle came to rest.

They stood up and entered the forward compartment, where the Marine honor guard was getting organized in its full black-white-and-silver splendor, complete with chrome-gleaming dress helmets. Some court synthetic with nothing better to do than devise protocol had decreed that on occasions like this the honor guard should disembark first and form two ranks lining the pathway from the ramp.

"Ready, Admiral?" Major Achebe asked. He was as dark as Lenore Silva, and his features reflected the genes of

ancestors who'd remained in Old Earth's Africa longer than
most of humanity. Basil nodded, and the Marines filed out
into the light of Mu Arae.

"Let the farce begin," Sonja muttered as she fell in behind
Basil and they started down the ramp.

A group of figures, mostly uniformed, advanced to meet
them. Basil recognized their leader. Vice Admiral Hanshaw
had what would have been called a pot-belly had he been
less high-ranking. He also had the pomposity to go with it.
Not for the first time, it occurred to Basil that the Fleet
was really a very small family. Even a relative newcomer
to the high command like himself knew all its inhabitants,
at least by reputation—their weaknesses, foibles, scandals.

"Welcome to Hespera, Admiral Castellan, sir!" Hanshaw
enthused. "I cannot express how eager we've all been to
greet you."

"Thank you, Admiral Hanshaw," Basil said hastily, before
Sonja could open her mouth. "I've long been aware of your
exemplary loyalty to the Emperor and his duly appointed
Grand Admiral—a point which I'll be certain to emphasize
to Grand Admiral Medina."

Hanshaw's face took on an expression of rapturous
sycophancy. Basil thought he heard a faint gagging sound
from behind him, and prayed that Sonja would restrain
herself. "Please come this way," Hanshaw oozed. "My
personal aircar is waiting."

"If Serafini had won, he'd be dancing on your grave,"
Sonja murmured as they proceeded beyond the double line
of Marines.

"Please don't make me laugh," Basil implored *sotto voce*,
his eyes on Hanshaw's overstuffed uniform. "That image
is just too funny."

They settled into the aircar. Basil responded to Hanshaw's
unctuousness with automatic polite noises as he watched
the spacefield drop away. Achebe was barking an order,
the honor guard was starting to march back up the ramp,
and . . .

And what was that flash from off to the left side?

It didn't have time to become reality for Basil before the
driver wrenched the aircar into a frantic starboard turn which
probably saved their lives. Instead of the direct hit that
would have obliterated it, the aircar took a glancing one.
It staggered and then slanted downward.

Stunned, Basil caught a glimpse of the ground rushing
upward and people scattering like windblown leaves. Then
the aircar was down with a grinding, shattering crash that
sent them all tumbling about in a cabin that was rapidly
filling with smoke.

"Let's get out of here!" Basil tried the door. Jammed.
He sat back, heedless of the fact that he was pressing
Hanshaw's bulk against the cabin's opposite side, set his
feet against the recalcitrant door, and shoved. It gave, and
they scrambled out into a scene of chaos.

Achebe was furiously bellowing orders, and the Marines
were deploying. They might not exactly be in combat dress,
but the gauss rifles they carried were not toys; Basil heard
the distinctive crackling as their projectiles broke mach.
The bystanders scattered even faster, for their safety was
clearly not Achebe's top priority.

Something caught Basil's eye. "Another one! Run!" he
yelled, simultaneously grabbing Sonja's arm and pulling her
along. They'd gotten a short distance before the second
missile hit the ruined aircar squarely, blasting it into scrap
with an explosion that made the ground jump under their
feet. Basil shoved Sonja down, falling on top of her, just as
the shock wave hit.

His next awareness was of the sky, streaked with dissipating
smoke, and diminishing sounds of panic and weapons fire.
He was lying on his back, and a pain in his side was growing
harder to ignore. So was Hanshaw's stammering, blubbering
voice.

"Admiral Castellan, sir, let me assure you that no one in
my command had anything to do with this dastardly act! I
am as stunned and horrified as—"

"Somebody get this fat fool out of here!" Sonja shoved
Hanshaw aside and knelt over Basil. "Lie still. You took a

little chunk of debris, but it's nothing serious, and the medics are on the way."

"What's going on?" he asked in a small voice, for it hurt to draw a deep breath.

"That second missile—it must have been intended to make sure of you—was a mistake. The Marines got a fix on where it was coming from, and they're there now, mopping up."

"Tell them—"

"Yes, Achebe knows he has to take prisoners. We'll get to the bottom of this."

A medevac aircar dropped from the sky with a whine of protesting impellers. "Over here!" Sonja called. Then she turned back to Basil, in time to hear a low mutter.

"Never, never, never . . ."

"What?" she asked, puzzled.

"Never again will I use this spaceport!"

Major Achebe advanced through the wreckage of the maintenance building the terrorists had used as their headquarters, and from whose roof they'd fired the anti-armor infantry missile launcher some corrupt supply sergeant—if that wasn't a redundancy—had doubtless sold them. He was in the unusual position of having an unassailable excuse for being up front with the troops. Gauss rifles weren't intended for taking people alive—any torso hit with one of those projectiles was infallibly fatal, and any hit at all was almost certainly so in the absence of prompt medical attention. But Achebe carried the standard officer's sidearm: a paralysis pistol. With its aid they'd gotten a few prisoners, all of whom had the look of low-level types, barely worth the effort of probing.

Up ahead, the corridor debouched on an open area. Achebe signaled a halt, then motioned the two point-men cautiously forward. A fusillade of fire greeted them, and one of them spun around clutching a blood-soaked shoulder. For the dozenth time, Achebe cursed these armorless dress uniforms. But the men knew what to do. A couple of grenades went sailing into the work area, and before the reverberations of their blasts had died away the Marines sprang forward in their wake, firing in the direction from which the hostile fire had come. Achebe was with them, in time to see two surviving terrorists. One was in the process of raising his weapon when a stream of hypervelocity metal slivers went through him with a spray of blood, practically sawing him in half. The other stood frozen by indecision.

"Cease fire!" Achebe thundered, and at the same instant brought up his paralysis pistol and snapped off a shot. The man toppled over like a flesh statue falling off its pedestal.

"Go, Leong," Achebe told the corporal with the scanner hanging from his shoulder by a strap—they'd gotten that from the locals who'd showed up too late. He wanted no one to touch the bodies until they'd been scanned for booby traps. "Check the one I paralyzed first."

"Aye aye, sir." Leong applied his scanner, then looked up with a puzzled expression. "Sir, there's an implanted bomb, all right. But it's not really a booby trap. It doesn't seem big enough to blow up anything but his own head, which is where it's located. And he himself activates it, with an artificial tooth."

"Which he can't bite down on now." Achebe's grin was dazzling in his dark face. "Get some medical people in here. I want that tooth pulled before he comes out of paralysis— carefully, so as not to trigger the bomb. And then I want him *secured.* Anybody who was given a suicide device must know secrets someone wants kept."

Basil entered the room and sat down with only a slight stiffness of the rib cage. (Regen therapy was a wonderful thing.) Sonja Rady and Lenore Silva, who'd landed a few hours before, resumed their seats.

"Where do we stand?" he asked without preamble.

"The probe of the prisoner has been completed, sir," Silva reported. "Major Achebe was correct in surmising that he was an important member of the conspiracy . . . its ringleader, in fact. This was why he was given the means to destroy his brain in event of capture. Fortunately for us, he hesitated a little too long in using it."

"Cold feet," Sonja remarked. "You just can't get good terrorists anymore."

"But given it by *whom?*" Basil's sense of humor was in abeyance. "You imply that these people, up to and including this 'ringleader,' were working for someone else."

"Yes, sir." Silva hesitated, and glanced at Sonja as though looking for support. "That's why Admiral Rady and I asked for this meeting with you alone. Our findings from the probe are . . . so sensitive that we can't take the responsibility for releasing them any more widely than that."

Basil stared at her. "Maybe you'd better explain."

"Yes, sir. First of all, our prisoner arrived here only recently—from Old Earth."

"*Earth?*"

"Earth," Silva affirmed. "The other prisoners are locals: fanatical New Human holdouts, as we'd assumed from the first. The ringleader was an import who brought the news that you'd probably be coming here, and organized the assassination attempt as an act of revenge against the man who brought about the defeat of the rebellion. Or, rather, that's how he sold it to the rank and file. His real aim . . . well, here are the relevant portions of the probe." She dimmed the lights and activated a screen.

The imagery had the fuzzy quality of all second-hand recordings of the visual impressions which the probe retrieved and displayed but couldn't tape. The subject was walking along a nondescript corridor.

"This is on Earth, while we were still in the Solar System, preparing for departure," Silva supplied. A doorway entered the field of vision. It slid open, revealing a room as featureless as the corridor and a thin male figure looking out a window, silhouetted against what seemed to be nighttime city lights. Abruptly, he turned around and advanced into the subject's clear field of vision. Narrow features and almost colorless gray eyes emerged from the room's dimness.

"No," Basil whispered.

"I only saw him a couple of times," Sonja said grimly. "But I'll never forget that face."

Silva froze the picture. "It was fortunate that Admiral Rady viewed this imagery as we were editing it for your perusal. She immediately recognized the significance of this individual's presence."

"*What* significance?" Basil demanded. His eyes remained fixed on Felix's features. "The whole business is crazy. That man is a former rebel officer. We turned him over to . . ."

"To Medina," Sonja finished for him.

Silva proffered a stack of hardcopy, with a rustling of paper that seemed obscenely loud in the silence that had fallen. "This is the probe operator's transcript of the conversation this part of the visual recording covers. The gist of it is that this Felix person is instructing the subject—a longtime resident of Earth who was involved in the rebels' intelligence penetration of the Imperial court—to proceed here and arrange your assassination."

"But," Basil demanded, "how is it that Felix is at liberty to go around organizing revenge by rebel survivors?"

"That's not what he's doing, sir. As the transcript makes clear, both he and the subject have transferred their loyalties—if, indeed, the term 'loyalty' is applicable at all. They merely exploited the fanaticism of the rebel holdouts here. Felix never openly states who he's working for; it seems to be understood. But he alludes repeatedly to his master's power to either reward or punish."

"He also congratulates himself on diverting suspicion as far from this master as it could be diverted, by making sure the attack was blamed on rebel diehards," Sonja put in.

"And finally," Silva concluded, fast-forwarding through the recording, "he presents the subject with certain items to facilitate his mission. . . . Ah, yes, here." The picture resumed normal speed. "You'll note that he is *not* giving him tickets for any sort of commercial transportation to Mu Arae. The transcript makes the reason obvious: he's to be transported in a *Courier*-class Fleet vessel, and landed secretly. And finally . . ." Silva stopped the recording again, then zoomed in on a smart-card that was changing hands. Her next words were superfluous, for Basil recognized the color scheme. "This allows him to draw on secret Fleet funds, from any financial institution linked with the central Imperial banking system."

"And we know who must have authorized its issuance," Sonja added.

Silence descended once again. Silva, hoping it was the right thing to do, cut off the recording and restored the lighting. Basil's face revealed absolutely no expression. "Thank you, Captain Silva. You and the probe specialists have done an outstanding job. Admiral Rady and I will give our attention to these findings at once."

"Aye aye, sir." Silva recognized a dismissal. She left the room.

The silence stretched until Sonja felt obliged to break it. "Well?"

"Well?" he echoed.

"Damn it, Basil, you know as well as I do what all this means! Medina—acting through your old chum Felix, who's now working for him—arranged to have you done away with after you'd disposed of Serafini for him."

"Yes, I know." She'd hoped to jolt him into action by stating the obvious in insultingly obvious terms. But his voice held no annoyance, only a great sadness. He turned to her with a ghastly caricature of a smile. "I suppose this pretty much rules out going back to Old Earth, doesn't it?"

"It seems an unnecessarily elaborate form of suicide," she agreed. "Stepping out of an airlock without a vac suit would be quicker and simpler."

This time his smile, though a wraith, was at least a wraith of something real. But, Sonja realized, it didn't extend to his eyes. They were focused on something she couldn't see, as if he was watching something precious recede into infinity, straining to catch the last possible glimpse of it before it vanished irretrievably. Then he blinked and, with jarring abruptness, stood up and began speaking briskly.

"According to the last intelligence briefing I got, Mordan is believed to be at Zeta Draconis. Does that still hold true?"

"Why . . . yes," she affirmed, caught off balance by his sudden change of mood.

"Too bad. We can't reach him by unrelayed tachyon transmission. Well, ready a *Zephyr*-class boat; I'll prepare a message proposing a meeting at some border system. In the meantime, send someone you trust to take charge of this system's tachyon beam array. *Nothing* goes out unless you or I have personally cleared it."

"So we're joining Mordan?"

"Yes. We can't take Medina on with just Task Force 27 and what's left of Serafini's command."

"Will he deal with us?"

"Yes, for the same reasons he dealt with Serafini. And now," he said absently, moving toward the door like someone whose mind was very far away, "I've got to get to work on that message to—"

"Basil." The tone, and the first name, that no one in the task force was ever allowed to hear her use, stopped him in his tracks. "Aren't you forgetting something?"

"No, I'm not forgetting it. I just can't let myself think about it right now." He waved a silencing hand as her mouth started to open. "Yes, you're right: I *did* say we weren't going to make our move until Torval was out here with us. But our hand seems to have been forced."

"So," she asked carefully, "we just have to leave him there, in Medina's power? There's nothing we can do?"

"Oh, I didn't say that. For one thing I'm going to delay going public as long as possible, for a lot of reasons. Maybe by then—"

"You don't really think Medina will let him join us after the tachyon beam array here starts developing 'malfunctions,' do you?"

"Not really," he admitted with a sigh.

"You said 'for one thing.' What's the *other* thing?"

"Well . . . I have certain sources of help I can call on."

❖   ❖   ❖

"I must say, Admiral Castellan, your message came as a surprise."

"No doubt, Admiral Mordan. Which makes me all the more grateful to you for responding to it so promptly." Basil had suggested a face-to-face meeting, since the distance between Mu Arae and Zeta Draconis required that tachyon transmissions be relayed, and all hope of security lost. But Mordan had surprised him; he'd somehow gotten his hands on one of the rare class of starships whose sole purpose was to carry an interstellar-range tachyon beam array, whose vast panels could unfold and unfold until the ship itself was nothing more than the spider at the heart of a gossamer web. He had brought it to the outer reaches of his own sector, within range of Mu Arae. Now Basil gazed into the screen at the man who was conversing with him in realtime from almost a light-decade away. Jarrel Mordan was stocky and compact, with the face of a suspicious bulldog.

"Yes," he was saying. "Surprising indeed. I didn't quite know what to think of your message, considering your long-standing association with Medina—and also considering what you'd just done to Serafini."

"The fact is, Admiral, I've been contemplating a break with Medina for some time. I've spent some time on Old Earth, and concluded that he's as much a usurper as Kleuger ever was. He's just a smoother article than Kleuger."

"Hah! Most people are! But the fact remains that you wiped Serafini for him."

"Yes, I did. I thought he was doing the right thing, if only out of self-interest, to protect his stolen property. But then after I got here to Hespera, I had my mind made up for me." He described the assassination attempt.

"That sounds like Medina," Mordan observed. Then he thrust his head forward. "But you know what else sounds like Medina? To have his faithful protégé Castellan claim to have turned against him and offer me an alliance, just to set me up to get crushed between his forces and those of my 'ally.' So I have to wonder why I should trust you."

"Doesn't the fact that he tried to kill me give me a pretty good motive to stop being his 'faithful protégé'?"

"Assuming that he really did. You could be lying about that too, just to make your change of heart plausible."

"I suppose I can't really expect you to take my unsupported word. But I can offer proof."

"What kind of proof? Imagery of the alleged attack on you? That could have been staged."

"Oh, I can do better than that. You see, we captured the leader of the gang that carried out the attack, and probed him. It seems the whole thing was arranged for Medina by an old acquaintance of mine." Basil paused, then played his hole card. "The video recording of the probe shows him, and the transcript makes manifest what he is: a former New Human intelligence officer."

"What?" Mordan's eyes flashed, and his heavy jaws clenched. Basil had counted on the effect the words "New Human" would have on any Fleet officer, even one who was effectively in rebellion.

"Yes. I captured him a year ago and turned him over to Medina. He's evidently decided that the glorious cause is passé, and that it's time for a change of employers."

"So Medina is *using* this slime mold?" As little as he liked the Grand Admiral, Mordan was obviously unwilling to think this of him.

"Come on, Admiral! You know as well as I do that Medina will use *anything* that's advantageous in the short run. In fact, he never thinks beyond the short run at all. That's why he's always been so successful . . . in the short run. And that's why the Empire can't survive him in the long run." Basil paused and drew a breath. He'd never intended to wax vehement. "I don't expect you to come here to Mu Arae and put yourself at my mercy. I'll send another *Zephyr*-class boat out to you with the recording of the probe—your own experts will be able to verify what it is. If it confirms what I say, then resume contact. We'll work out the details."

Mordan gave a long, level regard. "I begin to think—provisionally, of course—that maybe I can trust you after all, Admiral Castellan. We definitely need to come to a mutual understanding about the measures we need to take to defend our sectors when Medina finally decides to act against us."

A twinge of headache awoke between Basil's eyebrows. "The first thing we need to understand, Admiral Mordan, is that a defensive strategy is suicidal! Medina controls the bulk of the Empire and the Fleet, in addition to the legal and moral advantage of acting in the name of the legitimate Emperor. He'll eventually be able to wear down any passive defense. We need to go on the offensive at once. Oh, not militarily—we're not in a position to do that, as yet. But we have to capture the moral high ground by declaring that we're acting on behalf of the Emperor, even though he's in no position to openly endorse us. We have to let the Empire know that Medina's just a usurper who's been shrewd enough to act within the letter of the law." Basil sternly reined himself in, for he sensed he was losing Mordan. "We can discuss this later. For the moment, suffice it to say that from your standpoint working with me makes sense for the same reasons working with Serafini did."

"Ah." Mordan's face showed relief. The conversation was back on a level he could understand. "Maybe even better. I don't hate your guts like I always did hers! All right, Admiral, send your *Zephyr* to these coordinates. If what you say checks out, we'll talk again." Without further pleasantries, he signed off.

Basil leaned back in his chair and expelled a breath. "How did I do?" he asked, looking over his shoulder.

"He'll go along," Sonja opined. "The next step will be to goose him into aggressive action. It's not just his temperament that's the problem. Silva's intelligence people have put together a list of his top advisers. When you see the names, you'll be able to understand why they always fail to reach a consensus on any course of action, leaving Mordan to fall back on his defensive inclinations."

"That's the short-term problem. Our *real* challenge is to bring him into line with our ideas about what we want after Medina's gone."

"Slightly premature," Sonja observed drily. She stood up. "It's late. Coming?"

"I'll be along in a while. I have a few things to do."

But he found it hard to concentrate after she'd left him alone in the office/comm center where he'd been spending too much of his time lately. Absently, he activated the probe recording, fast-forwarding until Felix's face emerged from the shadows.

" 'Ban, ban, Caliban hath a new master,' " he quoted softly to himself.

Someone buzzed for admittance. He deactivated the screen and spoke a command. The door slid open, to reveal Major Achebe.

"Uh, Admiral, sorry to bother you, but someone wants to see you. She's been detained at the gate because she won't give her name, but she said to tell you she's a friend of somebody called Doctor Gramont."

Hope leaped in Basil. "Tell them to send her in, Major."

The woman who shortly arrived was thin and severe, with iron-gray hair pulled tightly back in a style that seemed to suit her sharp features. "Call me Athena," she said in response to Basil's introduction. "Not my real name of course. But it's just as well if you don't know my real name, Admiral. No offense. But it was rather startling to be contacted by the means you employed."

"Yes, I know the Society doesn't generally give outsiders that kind of access. But after being ordered here I managed to talk to Doctor Gramont just before my departure from Old Earth. It almost caused him physical pain to tell me how to contact his people here on Hespera."

The thin lips cracked a smile. "Centuries of habit die hard, Admiral. But Doctor Gramont had communicated with us prior to that, and let us know he'd revealed himself to you. So I suppose we shouldn't have been so shaken. Still . . ." She dismissed the subject, and her primness returned at full force. "The point is, we're under instructions to aid you in any way we can."

However little you like it, Basil completed her unspoken

thought for her. "The assistance I require isn't here on Hespera, so it shouldn't involve you directly. I only need for you to get a message back to Doctor Gramont for me. I need his help in getting Major General Torval Bogdan off Earth and bringing him here."

Athena lifted one skeptical eyebrow. "It's possible that you overestimate our capabilities, Admiral. Our techniques typically aim at the long-term influencing of society's philosophical orientation—"

"I'm too tired for this, Athena. You see, Doctor Gramont revealed to me the Society's alliance with the Sword Clans. So I know as well as you do that he can command the kind of resources I need."

"I see." The woman's face wore an expression which, Basil sensed, it seldom wore. "Gramont must *really* trust you, Admiral."

"I like to think so."

"Which," she ruminated aloud, ignoring him, "suggests— as much as anything could—that you're worthy of trust. . . ." Then the moment was over, and the armor was back in place. "Perhaps we can be of assistance after all, Admiral."

Dreadful ben. The assistance I require isn't here or thereabouts, so it shouldn't involve you directly. I only need for you to get a message back to Doctor Chanson for me. I need his help in getting Major General Toirel Bogan off Earth and bringing him here."

Absan lifted one eyebrow. "Is it possible that you've overrated our capabilities, Admiral? Our techniques typically aim at the difficult art of influencing people's philosophical orientation."

"I'm too tired for this. All you need to do is get a message to the Sun. Our people will do the rest, and I know as well as you do that he can command the kind

CHAPTER ELEVEN
Earth (Sol III), 3910 C.E.

Yoshi Medina strode into Felix Nims' living quarters unannounced, and took in the scene quickly. A boy of eleven or twelve was on his hands and knees, naked—Medina recalled that Felix had been showing an interest in the families of various political prisoners. Felix himself was hastily standing up, his mouth hanging speechlessly open.

Medina looked into the boy's upturned face. He considered several options and contented himself with a curt "Get out." The boy scrambled to his feet, grabbed his clothes off the floor and tried to cover himself with them as he rushed awkwardly through the door.

Felix finally found his tongue. "Why, Grand Admiral, what an unexpected, uh, honor. If only I'd known—"

Without so much as a preparatory muscle twitch to give warning, Medina backhanded him across the mouth, sending him spinning halfway around before collapsing to the floor, where he lay in a cringing, blubbering heap.

"It seems," Medina spoke conversationally, "that your bravos at Mu Arae failed to deal with Castellan. Furthermore, their chief allowed himself to be taken alive. Have you any explanation?"

Felix rose cautiously to his knees, emboldened by Medina's mild tone. He licked his lips, wincing and tasting blood. "Oh no, Grand Admiral! Surely that can't be possible. The man in question could be relied on to commit suicide in event of probable capture. I assure you that your sources of information are totally mistaken and—*eeeagh!*" Agony exploded in his rib cage where Medina's booted left foot shot out and kicked him. He fell over backwards and tried to curl protectively around his vitals. Medina's next kick took him in the kidneys, and the pain left him gasping for breath like a caught fish.

"Quiet, lickspittle!" Medina's full-throated, ear-bruising roar filled the quarters, rising almost to a brassy scream. "My 'sources of information' are Castellan and Mordan themselves. They've been in communication. And *this* is what they've been discussing." He flung a sheet of hardcopy in Felix's face. Felix held it with trembling fingers and read. After the first few sentences, he raised his eyes and hesitantly met Medina's.

"Sir, has this . . . this 'Joint Declaration' been made public?"

"Not yet, though it's on its way to every system in the Empire by now. But read on. In addition to the attempted murder of Castellan, the bastards accuse me of usurpation— say I've made the Emperor my puppet."

"That could be damaging," Felix reflected. "One of your greatest strengths is your claim to be the legitimate instrument of Imperial authority. We need to take steps to prevent the dissemination of this—no, sir! Please!" Felix scrambled back, not quite quickly enough to avoid another shattering kick.

"You worm! This whole disaster is your fault. If your bungling assassins had done their job, Castellan would be in no position to be conspiring with anybody. And if your gutless wonder of a henchman hadn't let himself be captured, there wouldn't be any proof of my involvement—nobody would take this 'Joint Declaration' any more seriously than any other piece of propaganda." Medina grabbed the moaning Felix by the shirtfront and hauled him to his feet, bringing their faces a few inches apart and breathing heavily. He'd been drinking. "I begin to wonder if you're worth the self-denial it takes to not have you shot."

Trembling, teeth chattering, Felix nonetheless took on a calculating look. "Remember, sir, I made a study of Castellan. My knowledge of him will be even more helpful to you—even vital—now that he's an avowed enemy."

"You can't know any more about him than Fleet personnel records," Medina growled. But his voice was back to a normal decibel level.

"They never studied him as one studies an *enemy*, sir. I did. That's the perspective you need now." He took his courage in both hands. "May I remind you that I was opposed to letting him take his task force to the Mu Arae Sector in the first place?"

Medina emitted a subliminal growl, and Felix flinched. But the Grand Admiral fell into a thoughtful silence and absently let him drop to the floor. "There may be something in that. I'll let your miserable life continue for now. But," he added, glaring down, "you'd better show some results in the other matter soon. *Very* soon."

Felix knew exactly what he meant. "Rest assured, sir, we're closing in on the conspirators behind Doctor Komos' attempt on your life." He prudently refrained from pointing out that they would be much further along if he himself had been in charge of Komos' interrogation. Instead, he paused significantly and added, "*All* the conspirators . . . up to the highest level. The *very* highest level."

"Hmmm . . ." Medina's eyes took on a faraway look, then resumed their glare. "Very well. Keep me informed. And give some thought to ways we can counter Castellan and Mordan in the propaganda arena, when it's no longer possible to keep the whole business at Mu Arae under wraps as we're doing now. I want a report by this time tomorrow. In the meantime," he concluded, turning toward the door, "I'm on my way to continue implementing another suggestion of yours."

"Congratulations on your promotion, *Lieutenant* General Bogdan." Medina smiled his crocodilian smile.

"Thank you, sir," Torval rumbled, eyes occasionally straying to the three silver sunbursts gleaming against the sable of his cuff. "I owe it to your generosity."

"Nonsense. You deserved it. Besides, it's in my interest to advance an officer of your proven competence and loyalty as rapidly as possible. You see," Medina continued in confidential tones, "I'm considering you for a new billet . . . one so important that you'll need the added rank to qualify."

"Oh?" Torval brightened. "Would that be under Admiral Castellan at Mu Arae, sir? I've been hoping to be able to—"

"Sorry. I know, I told him—and you—that I was considering sending you there. But his Marine force isn't nearly large enough to justify putting an officer of your new rank in command of it. You might say you're overqualified."

Torval looked crestfallen. "Uh, would it at least be possible for me to get a personal message to him, sir? It's been awhile since there's been any word from Mu Arae."

"Yes, the news blackout we've had to impose on that sector has been inconvenient for a lot of people. But believe me, there are excellent security reasons for it."

"May I know what those reasons are, sir?" Torval's expression remained innocently respectful. "I believe there was mention a moment ago of my proven loyalty. . . ."

Medina reminded himself that the big Marine was shrewder than he looked. "Now, General, that's not the issue at all. You're as familiar as I am with the concept of 'need to know.' For now, you'll just have to accept my personal assurance that Admiral Castellan and Rear Admiral Rady are all right. And as for your next assignment . . . Well, I can't go into details at present, but I can assure you that it's *very* important. There are few besides yourself I'd trust with it."

"I'm overwhelmed, sir." In spite of himself, Torval meant it.

"We'll talk more when we get back to headquarters." Medina patted his shoulder in a proprietary way. "And now, I need to go and take care of some pressing business."

Torval left the reception as early as he decently could, considering that his promotion was the occasion for it. He walked toward his quarters in deep thought, oblivious to the decor of this Imperial residence, although as he passed a wide balcony he spared a glance for the holoview. Winter was ending, but this was a blustery afternoon and there were whitecaps on the harbor he'd heard called the "Golden Horn" although it was of course neither. This city was sometimes called Istanbul and sometimes Constantinople— the Emperor resided here in two different capacities at various times, and the name varied accordingly. Torval couldn't for the life of him remember which was the current one, but either way he was glad his promotion had been strictly a Fleet ceremony so they'd all worn their *real* uniforms. He didn't care for either of the versions of court dress that were worn here.

He paused and looked out at the simulacrum. This place must have had quite a history, he reflected, for two different sorts of emperor to have ruled two different empires from it in the course of pre-spaceflight history. *Basil would love it*, he thought, depressed anew.

Behind him, a throat was cleared. "General Bogdan, may I have a word?"

Torval turned, startled. "Why, of course, Grand Secretary Mondrian." He didn't normally hobnob with civilian pooh-bahs this high, least of all the one who was the Emperor's father-in-law.

Rovard Mondrian raised a cautionary hand and glanced up and down the empty corridor. He looked unaccountably nervous. "Not here. Please follow me." He led the way, as quickly as he could manage, toward a small sitting room.

"I have reason to believe this room is clean of snooping devices," Mondrian sighed after lowering himself gratefully into a chair. Then he gave Torval a look of desperate intensity. "General, I must make this brief. It is my understanding that you have been requesting to be sent to join Admiral Castellan at Mu Arae."

"Yes, I have—but to no avail. The Grand Admiral says that—"

"Never mind what Medina says!" Mondrian paused to

regain control of his breathing, then resumed with an apparent change of subject. "You are familiar with the case of the late Doctor Komos?"

"Of course. Everyone knows about Admiral Komos being implicated in a plot to assassinate the Grand Admiral . . . though we all had trouble believing it." Some instinct made Torval withhold the tale Basil and Sonja had told of Komos' death. "Last I heard, the investigation was still proceeding."

"And is about to reach its conclusion," Mondrian added grimly. "There is little time remaining, and it is out of sheer desperation that I now approach you, General. You see, I myself initiated the plot in which Komos was a participant. My only regret is that it failed. You see—"

All at once, Torval came out of shock, allowing his consciousness to catch up to what his ears were hearing. For the past year he had been in and out of the various Imperial residences, acquiring a seeming familiarity with the court. Now the spuriousness of what he thought he'd known stood revealed like a writhing mass of worms beneath what had seemed a solid surface. On some calm level he analyzed his emotions with detached curiosity. *So this is what fear feels like.*

He stood up abruptly. "Excuse me, Grand Secretary, but I shouldn't be hearing this. I really must go now—"

Mondrian lunged out of his chair with a sudden burst of energy and caught Torval by his tunic front. "Listen to me, General! It's only out of desperation that I reveal all this to you. And if you don't believe that, then let me make the final revelation: I organized the plot at the Emperor's behest! The Emperor himself! He had no other option. Save for a few holdouts like me, the court consists entirely of Medina's creatures. There's almost no one he can trust."

Torval stood in a kind of paralysis, desperately wanting to get away but unable to use force on this frail old man. "Grand Secretary, why are you telling me all this?"

"Because you're trying to rejoin Admiral Castellan, and you may yet succeed. He's our last hope—the only member of the Imperial family who's in a position to take independent action." Mondrian straightened and he released Torval's tunic, holding the Marine motionless with his eyes instead. "I bear a message for Admiral Castellan, direct from the Dragon Throne, and you must deliver it. Tell him his Emperor commands him to do whatever is necessary to free the Empire from Medina." The old eyes seemed to take on a feverish gleam, and Torval's could not break free of them. "Tell him also that as soon as he acts openly in accordance with this command, the Emperor will name him his heir. This, despite the fact that the Empress, my daughter, has finally conceived after all these years! I trust, General, that you are no longer in any doubt as to our desperation."

Torval could only stammer, "But, but . . . the Empress pregnant? I hadn't heard—"

"Of course not. We've thought it prudent to conceal the fact as long as possible—although Medina probably knows already." Mondrian dismissed the subject with a headshake. "We haven't any more time General. Will you bear the Emperor's command to Admiral Castellan?"

"Grand Secretary, I—"

With a startling crash, the knob of the old-fashioned door blasted inward, propelled by energy exchange from a laser. Torval's trained reflexes activated, and he pulled Mondrian away from the door just as it was kicked in. Impact-armored men—Fleet Security, with a unit shoulder flash Torval didn't recognize, armed with paralysis guns—crowded in. Their leader, a lieutenant with a nerve lash, strode up to Mondrian.

"It's taken us awhile to locate you, Grand Secretary," he rapped. "I have a warrant for your arrest. The charges are treason and conspiracy to commit murder. You will come with us at once." One of his men grabbed Mondrian by the arm and pulled him away from Torval.

"What the hell do you think you're doing, Lieutenant? Do you have any idea who this *is*?"

"I'm well aware of Grand Secretary Mondrian's identity, General."

"Well, release him at once. That's an order, mister!"

The lieutenant flinched, but not by much. "Sir, I am acting under orders from the Grand Admiral, transmitted in proper fashion through Fleet Security. If you wish to question these orders, you have every right to do so—through channels. But in the meantime, I am bound to carry them out."

Torval clamped restraint on himself, for the puppy had stayed within the bounds of military courtesy. Besides, he was right; Torval, however high-ranking, was not in his chain of command.

The lieutenant let the silence last a second or two, then inclined his head to Torval. "Sir. And now . . . come on, men."

The man holding Mondrian urged him forward. He moved in an uncertain old-man's shuffle. The Security man gave him a shove that sent him stumbling onto his knees, then jabbed viciously with his paralysis gun. "Move!"

Without pausing for thought, Torval grabbed the man's wrist in a grip that sent the paralysis gun falling and elicited a shriek of pain. Then, with a strength bred in high gravity, he pulled the arm sharply backward and up; its owner went to the floor, face first, to avoid dislocation. All at once, several paralysis guns were trained on Torval and the lieutenant was pointing his nerve lash in the same direction. The tableau held for a heartbeat. Then Torval spoke in a normal tone of voice.

"You may have orders to arrest the Grand Secretary, son. But you will *not* exceed the scope of those orders by mistreating an old man. Not unless you're prepared to take it upon yourself to use weapons on a Marine lieutenant general."

The lieutenant licked his lips. "Of course not, sir. Grand Secretary, please come with us."

Mondrian rose unsteadily to his feet, and Torval released the moaning man he'd been securing. Halfway toward the door, the Grand Secretary paused and turned to face Torval.

"General, will you . . . ?" It was, of course, all he could say. But it was enough.

Torval looked directly into the old eyes, and wondered

at the palpable, almost physical quality of the doom he felt descending on him. But he answered, "Yes." And that, too, was enough.

The lieutenant glanced from one of them to the other with a puzzled frown, then gestured impatiently. Torval was left standing alone in the elegant little room with the smashed door.

The distant sounds coming through that open door suggested that other arrests were under way in the palace.

Rovard Mondrian's agony came to an end, and the holo recording of his torture blinked mercifully out of existence. Josef II was left staring into the space it had occupied, hollow-eyed. Yoshi Medina glared down at him contemptuously.

"My first impulse on receiving proof of your complicity, Your Imperial Majesty, was to set proceedings in motion to have you deposed and a reliable successor chosen from among the various Imperial relations. On reflection, however, I allowed myself to be dissuaded from this course of action." Medina vividly recalled the session with his advisers. Dugald Dalross had, of course, argued against setting aside the Emperor—the very notion made his lawyer's soul quail. But Felix Nims, in agreement with Dalross for once, had made the argument that had finally swayed him. . . .

"I shall explain the reason for allowing you to continue on the throne, Your Imperial Majesty," he continued, leaning over the Emperor, who continued to sit motionless, his eyes focused in midair. "It is simply this: anything that weakens the dynasty's legitimacy reduces your usefulness as the legitimizer of power—the power I wield, as is only right, for I saved the Empire!" He took a deep breath, and told himself this gilded nonentity wasn't worth losing his self-control over. "The circumstances of your accession to the throne were bad enough. We don't need an irregular break in the line of succession. I explain this in order to make your precise function clear to you."

Josef continued to reveal no reaction. Medina wondered how much he'd even heard. "This presents us with an awkward problem, Your Imperial Majesty," he continued, the formal mode of address waxing more ironic with each repetition. "Leaving you on the throne requires placing the blame for the conspiracy with some scapegoat. Fortunately, your father-in-law's role as the organizer provides us with an obvious candidate." He gestured to one of the armed Security guards who flanked the doors to the chamber. The man stepped briefly outside, returning with a small woman whose pregnancy was not yet showing.

The Emperor was instantly out of his chair, leaping directly from listless apathy into panic. "Elena!"

"Yes," Medina nodded. "The Empire will learn that Your Imperial Majesty was the unwitting dupe of the Mondrian family, which had found it couldn't buy the Grand Admiral and therefore plotted to kill him lest its power slip away. The late Rovard Mondrian was acting in collusion with his daughter—the prime mover behind the conspiracy." The idea, he recalled, had been Felix's.

"No!" Josef turned to him with the eyes of a hunted animal cursed with the intelligence to understand. "You can't. She's . . . she's pregnant. We hadn't announced it yet. . . ."

"I know she is. All the more reason. An heir apparent would narrow my options when the time comes—in the *natural* course of events—to choose Your Imperial Majesty's successor." He spoke over his shoulder to the guard. "Take her out and kill her."

Josef looked around wildly, and saw only Security guards. Elena made a small stumbling move toward him and started to open her mouth. But all that came out was a gasp as the guard seized her by the upper arm and swung her through the door. Then she was gone.

The Emperor collapsed into the chair again. Before, he'd seemed in shock; now there was no longer enough life in him for even that. *Yes*, Medina thought, *he'll give no further trouble.* "We will prepare an address which you will deliver from the throne, assuring the Empire that the conspiracy has been foiled thanks to the Grand Admiral's alertness and diligence, for which you will express appropriate gratitude." He turned to go, then had an afterthought. "Oh, yes; it will eventually be necessary for Your Imperial Majesty to remarry. As it happens, I have a daughter who will soon be coming of age."

Torval hadn't exactly been confined to quarters, but Medina had suggested that he keep a low profile until the dust settled. He'd been inclined to agree; the lieutenant who'd arrested Rovard Mondrian had doubtless reported his actions, and questions would probably be asked. He preferred not to invite the asking of those questions while the purge was still under way.

Still, he was like a tiger in a too-small cage, pacing in the same pattern until he'd almost worn a groove in the expensively carpeted floor. No question about it, the palace suite he'd been assigned was an uncommonly comfortable cage. Still . . .

A chime sounded. He spoke a password and looked with distaste at the synthetic whose holo image appeared near the door. "A thousand pardons, General, but you have a visitor. Shall I admit him?"

"Who is he?" Torval demanded, wondering who would be paying calls at this particular time.

"A Doctor Gramont, sir."

"Gramont? But what's he doing—" Torval chopped the sentence off, realizing he was actually thinking out loud to a synthetic. "Send him in," he snapped.

"General Bogdan!" Gramont beamed as he entered. "So good to see you. I wanted to personally convey my congratulations on your richly deserved promotion." As he chattered on, he fiddled with a device small enough to fit in his left hand. Torval made appropriate noises in response to the stream of pleasantries, which Gramont cut off in mid-sentence when a green light flashed on the unfamiliar-looking little device.

"Now we can talk, General. I take as a given that this room contains snooping devices, but they are now neutralized."

He made one final adjustment to the device and laid it on a table.

"A privacy field generator?" Torval had never seen one so small that would cover an entire room.

"Among other things. Any video devices are transmitting only snow."

"Won't they notice that?"

"Indubitably—when the recording is inspected. But I'm counting on the fact that it's not being continually monitored. The Security personnel here in the palace have too much else to occupy their attention these days."

"So they do. In fact, I'm surprised you were able to get in."

"Oh, they're trying to maintain an illusion of normalcy in the palace. A self-evidently harmless visitor—especially one who, like myself, has contacts in the court—is admitted with only the usual security precautions." Gramont made an impatient gesture. "We don't have time for banter, General. I'll come directly to the point. How much did Admiral Castellan tell you after his visit with me on Corfu?"

"Everything that matters, I think," Torval replied levelly. "He told me about your connection with the Society, and your alliance with the Sword Clans." He shook his head. "I found it all very hard to believe. But coming from Basil I *had* to believe it."

"Then believe him now." Gramont reached his right hand inside his left sleeve and withdrew a shiny little disc. "I received this through the special information channels available to me. It comes from Mu Arae. I trust your equipment here can handle interactive messages?"

"Sure. These quarters are nothing if not classy." Torval took the disc to his comm console and inserted it in an entry port. Then he picked up a wraparound headpiece and put it on over his eyes and ears. Basil was standing in the middle of the room where his eyes focused, a few feet from Gramont, to whom the new arrival was not visible.

"Hello, Torval." The lean dark face formed its familiar

smile. "I'll make this brief. I'm at Mu Arae, where Medina
tried to have me killed—"

"*What?*"

"Please, Torval, let me finish." The software wasn't an
actual download of Basil, of course: the expense would
have been an almost trivial problem compared to the bulk
of the storage media and the necessity of an even more
expensive purpose-built computer to run it. But it could
simulate his personality and impart whatever information
it had been given. *It can also,* he reflected in one
compartment of his mind, *be faked, with some difficulty.*
"You probably don't know this yet, but Sonja and I have
joined Mordan. I won't go into details—if Medina captures
this tape, it won't tell him anything he doesn't already
know. We're—"

"Wait, Basil, wait," Torval stammered. "You're saying
you've gone into *rebellion?* You? And Sonja? No, I don't
believe it."

The holographic face winced with pain. "*Not* against the
Empire, Torval. Only against Medina. He's worse than a
rebel—he's a usurper. I think you know that by now, even
if you're still reluctant to admit it to yourself . . . and I know
how *that* feels." The simulacrum drew itself up. "We need
you out here, Torval. And Doctor Gramont can get you off
Earth. I think this is the kind of situation the three of us
could dimly foresee, that night at Peachy's almost twenty
years ago. If the oath we swore that night still means anything
to you, I'm holding you to it now."

All at once, any doubt that this message actually came
from Basil vanished as completely as it is possible for a
thing to disappear. Torval removed the headpiece, ejected
the disc, and turned to face Gramont in the room that held
only the two of them. "I'm in your hands, Doctor."

"Splendid. Please gather together any personal items you
wish to take."

Torval went to the bedroom. When he returned, Gramont
was fiddling with a small device that looked like a
communicator, or perhaps a transponder. A pattern of lights

appeared, and he gave a satisfied nod. "How much did Admiral Castellan tell you about my Sword Clans associates' capabilities?"

"A little."

"Well, you may find this a little startling. Please stand over here beside me . . . Yes, that's right . . ."

When the Security guards arrived to investigate the malfunctioning video, the suite was empty.

"So the transposer can work in a surface-to-orbit role? I'd wondered about that."

Torval nodded affirmatively to Basil's question. The three of them sat in a well-guarded room of the Bronson's Landing spaceport, where the Marine's shuttle had landed mere minutes earlier. "Right. It has enough range. And it seems their method of absorbing potential-energy differentials is up to it."

"But what about Gramont?" Sonja asked. "There must be a record of his coming to visit you just before your disappearance. I'm surprised he didn't leave Earth with you."

"I asked him about that. He said the Society has contingency plans for that kind of thing, where its senior members are concerned—and I get the impression that he's *very* senior. A whole new identity, complete with a nanotechnic rewrite of his genetic code to change everything that could possibly be used to identify him." Torval smiled crookedly. "I couldn't help telling him I'd always thought the Society was dead set against that kind of technology. He quoted an ancient saying: necessity knows no law."

"I've met a few lawyers of whom the same could be said," Sonja remarked.

Basil smiled dutifully while he thought of a villa on Corfu and knew, guiltily, how much it had cost the old man to grant his request. "Well," he said, changing the subject a little too briskly, "tell us what's new at court. But no, you've been in transit; we're probably more up-to-date than you are."

"Probably. When I was there, the purge of the anti-Medina conspirators was under way." He described the arrest of Rovard Mondrian.

"So you don't know about the Empress?" Sonja asked. Torval shook his head. "Then we do have later news than you," she continued grimly. "Medina had her killed."

"The Empress? Dead?"

"She was probably dead before your departure," Basil affirmed. "But it was only announced after Medina and his advisers had worked out all the details of their story. You see, they're blaming the conspiracy on her."

"But . . . but the Emperor himself is behind it! Her father told me as much just before he was taken. Why should they . . . ?"

"Think about it," Basil suggested as the Marine's bass trailed off.

"Of course." Torval nodded ponderously. "The Emperor's too useful to Medina. They needed a scapegoat. She was pregnant, you know," he added, nodding in response to their stunned looks. "Mondrian told me. It wasn't public knowledge. But . . . Medina must have known. He knows *everything* that goes on at the court."

They all sat for a moment in appalled silence. Sonja broke it.

"Well, this should make pretty clear to you what we're dealing with. If Medina's willing to commit *this* murder, the decision to try to murder Basil must have been an easy one. And you know who set it up for him? Our old friend Felix! Remember him—the rebel slime we took off Basil's hands at Omega Prime? That's right: Medina's using him now. Need any more proof?"

"Oh, no. You don't have to convince me. I know what Medina is." And, for a fact, his voice held no doubt. But it held something indistinguishable from sadness.

"What the hell is the matter with you, Torval?" Sonja flared. "Anyone would think you still had a soft spot in your heart for that rat-fucker."

Torval, as usual, refused to be provoked. He just shook

his head slowly. "No, Sonja. I'll do whatever is necessary to destroy Medina. But I can't help *regretting* that he has to be destroyed."

Basil spoke quietly, forestalling an explosion from Sonja. "Why, Torval? Because he was our leader against the New Humans for all those years?"

"Partly, I suppose. But . . . well, it's also a matter of personal gratitude. He did a lot for me, you know."

The other two sat in silence for a moment, Sonja looking stupefied and Basil trying to imagine what the flattery and patronage of the Grand Admiral must have been like for an ex-enlisted man of working class background.

Torval gave him a long, level regard before resuming. "One other thing I have to tell you, Basil. Just before Rovard Mondrian was arrested, he asked me to convey a message to you—from the Emperor himself." The other two both started. "You see, he considers you the last hope of the dynasty. You're commanded to take whatever steps it takes to eliminate Medina. And after you make a start on it, he'll name you his heir."

For a while, the silence held an odd quality of expectancy, as though Torval's listeners were waiting for him to finish his sentence, for his final words were simply too impossible to have been uttered. But gradually, like something palpable, the realization descended that they *had* in fact been spoken, and that nothing would ever be the same again.

"But," Sonja finally said, seeking refuge in practical objections, "he's going to be so tightly under Medina's thumb from now on that he won't be able to announce it."

"Not publicly, no," Torval said slowly. "But I've always heard that the Imperial family has its own private ways of recording legacies—secret ways that are genuinely indestructible."

"I've heard that too," Basil said unconsciously. Then, abruptly, he shook his head in his thought-clearing way, then gave them a smile which, it seemed, he was consciously forming in familiar lines. "This is all completely academic, of course. Josef is close to me in age; no reason to think I'll outlive him by much, if at all."

"No," Sonja said slowly. "But *your* heir will."

Silence came thudding down again, and Sonja's eyes held Basil's in a mute communion which Torval had no intention of breaking.

Basil shattered the silence with a nervous laugh. "Well, I don't *have* any heir yet, do I? So that's even more academic!" Then he sobered. "Look, we can't let ourselves think about this. It would only distract us from what we *need* to be thinking about: how to ram it to Medina . . . in accordance with the Emperor's command," he added, in Torval's direction.

"Specifically, how to get Mordan moving," Sonja chimed in, clearly relieved by the change of subject. "Signing the Joint Declaration seems to have used up his supply of decisiveness."

"Right. He's gone back to being unwilling to break the standing deadlock among his advisers. Torval, we need to bring you up to date on the problem—and on everything out here."

"Let's get started," the Marine said simply.

They did, and for a while everything was almost like it had been before.

CHAPTER TWELVE
The Mu Arae Sector, 3912 C.E.

"Sir," came the cry from the flag bridge's sensor station, "unidentified ship at—"

"I see it," Basil said tonelessly, as he gazed at the icon that had appeared in the holo tank, appallingly close. At the same instant, alarms whooped as the flag captain sent HIMS *Impregnable* into general quarters.

"A scout?" Sonja wondered out loud. She seemed distracted, doubtless with the same question that was occupying him. He put it to the chief of staff.

"Lenore, how did that ship get so close before being detected?"

Silva conferred hastily with the sensor officer. "It's a very small ship, sir—almost below the lower limit of size for a cost-effective starship. By the same token, it doesn't require a very powerful drive, so it doesn't have much of an energy signature. I can tell you this: it doesn't belong to any class of scout craft in the Fleet. Besides which, it's not making any attempt to conceal its presence; it's just proceeding on an obvious intercept course, bringing its drive factor steadily down to match ours."

Basil's relief lasted a full second before his cares came crowding back, crushing it out of existence and leaving him alone with the familiar dull ache of the soul. Involuntarily, his eyes strayed to the secondary holo tank that showed the ragtag fleet he was leading out of Mu Arae.

His efforts to goad Mordan into decisive action had come
to nothing, the propaganda impact of their Joint Declaration
had faded over time, and their moment had passed. Medina
had taken full advantage of the year and a half he'd been
given to lay the military and political groundwork, and when
his counterstroke had finally come it had been crushing.
Now Mordan was dead, despite the efforts of a relief force
Basil had been ill able to afford. Sonja had led it, and her
success in salvaging most of it from the wreck did nothing
to lighten her burdensome sense of failure. The fall of the
Zeta Draconis Sector had rendered Mu Arae indefensible
against the inevitable attack, whenever Medina turned his
attention to it.

Then, with hope seemingly gone, an unexpected message
had arrived in secrecy from Admiral Aline Noumea,
governor-general of the three sectors of what had been the
People's Democratic Union of New Humanity. Underneath
all the linguistic camouflage had been a vague offer of
sanctuary in the system of DM -21 5081, on the fringes of
the Psi Capricorni Sector. The possibility of a trap had been
obvious, even though Noumea was known to be having her
problems with Medina. But they'd been in no position to
quibble. Basil had commandeered every available ship and
stuffed it to the limits of its life support with his supporters.
He'd left Admiral Hanshaw in command at Hespera, with
orders to surrender the planet—he was good at that—rather
than risk exposing its surface to bombardment from space.
And now the survival fleet was proceeding through the star-
empty region between the two sectors, at the frustrating
rate permitted by civilian drives.

The warships of Task Force 27 and the others were not
spread protectively around the huddling gaggle of freighters,
passenger liners, hospital ships and others, for ancient wet-
navy convoy tactics were unworkable in space. If the warships
held their drives down to the level of time acceleration the
civilian vessels could manage, they'd be at the mercy of
enemies under no such restraints. If hostiles appeared—

and they'd learned better than to underestimate Medina's intelligence resources—the warships would have to engage them at maximum drive, leaving their charges to the mercy of Fortune. But no unidentified ships had appeared . . . until now.

The flag communications officer interrupted Basil's ruminations. "Excuse me, sir, but that ship's hailing us. He won't give a name; he'll only speak to you, personally."

Basil and Sonja exchanged a glance. "So much for security," she muttered.

"Maybe not. If Medina knew about this fleet, and that I was with it, he wouldn't have sent this one little boat. It can't hurt to talk to him. We can always send a frigate to vaporize him, and he must know it." He moved over to the comm station. At this range, ordinary shipboard tachyon communicators could send as well as receive instantaneous messages, so a conversation could be conducted. "Put him on."

The man who appeared in the screen against the Spartan background of his little ship's interior was wearing unremarkable civilian clothes. He was of indeterminate age, and his coloring and features seemed to represent the statistical average of the human race; Basil couldn't even venture a guess as to his ethnic origins. Even his gender seemed blurred, for while there was nothing exactly androgynous about him—the masculine pronoun came as automatically to Basil's mind as it had to the comm officer's—neither was there anything obtrusively masculine. All in all, he was so nondescript that he didn't even stand out as exceptionally ordinary. His only notable features were his eyes—not really brown, but an unusual luminous amber.

"This is Admiral Castellan. To whom am I speaking?"

"That will take some explaining, Admiral." The man's voice held no accent, and was as unremarkable as everything else about him, although it was perfectly modulated. His speech was that of an educated man. "It involves matters best discussed in private. All taken with all, it would be best if I came aboard and spoke to you face to face."

"Cocky bastard," Sonja commented.

Basil ignored her and spoke toward the communicator. "Access to this ship—the entire fleet, for that matter—is restricted to authorized personnel. Anything you or anybody else has to say to me can be said over this communicator, in the presence of everyone here."

"I regret to have to contradict you, Admiral, but all I can say at present are two words, which I believe will persuade you to grant my request: Omega Prime."

Basil's mouth, which had been half-open to angrily cut the man off, froze. Then he and Sonja exchanged a long look. The comm officer glanced from one of them to the other uncomprehendingly.

"All right, whoever-you-are," Basil finally said. "You have permission to approach this ship. My chief of staff will give you rendezvous instructions." He turned to Lenore Silva. "Commodore."

"Yes, sir," Silva acknowledged, with a look which, like the comm officer's, had gone from puzzlement to mild alarm. Basil didn't enlighten them, but drew Sonja aside, out of the comm screen's pickup.

"You've never revealed that name to anyone, have you?"

"Of course not. And I'm certain Torval hasn't. Speaking of Torval, shall we send for him?" The Marine was on the flagship of the surface assault group.

"No, not yet. And, Sonja . . . I think it might be better if we take him literally about talking to me privately."

"No problem. I want to have as little to do with Omega Prime as I can possibly manage."

Major Achebe entered to announce the new arrival. The Marine's dark face wore an unaccustomed look of indecisiveness.

"What's his name, Major?"

"Uh, I don't know, Admiral. He didn't give it."

"Major, didn't I give orders that he was to be ID'd at the docking bay?"

"Yes, sir, you did." Achebe's puzzlement seemed to deepen.

"Never mind, Major. Bring him in." Achebe did so. Viewed

in the flesh, the stranger's height proved to be as perfectly ordinary as everything else about him.

"Thank you, Major. You can go."

Achebe, who seemed to be coming out of whatever had gripped him earlier, looked disapproving. "Perhaps I'd better stay, Admiral."

"I don't think I'll be in any danger, Major. You *did* scan him for weapons, didn't you?"

If it had been possible, Achebe would have blushed, and Basil instantly regretted his sarcasm. "Of course, sir. Just signal if you need anything." He came to attention and departed.

"Sit down," Basil invited, doing so himself. "Am I correct in thinking—"

"Yes, Admiral. I am a telepath, albeit not an especially strong one—just barely capable of influencing your security personnel to admit me to your presence without unnecessary questioning."

Alarm awoke in Basil. "But you knew what I was thinking!" His left hand strayed toward the button that would summon Achebe.

"Compose yourself, Admiral. Your faculty of telepathic resistance is in perfectly good working order, preventing me from receiving any thoughts but those that come to the surface in the course of your formulation of speech, a very small fraction of a second in advance of the actual sounds. I know this has been explained to you before . . . probably by Shenyilu, more than two decades ago."

"So you really *are* from Omega Prime," Basil whispered.

"Yes, I represent the entity you know by that name. Four years ago, it offered you its help, at such time as you found yourself in need."

"Yes . . . and it was very vague about the nature of this help. Also about how it was going to make contact with me when the time came."

"About the latter, at least, you need have no further uncertainty. I am the agent through which Omega Prime will communicate with you."

"But . . . I don't understand. How is it that Omega Prime has a human working for it?"

"I perceive that you still do not quite understand, Admiral." The indescribably ordinary face formed a slight smile. "A scan of me—using a specialized medical scanner, not one of the security models used by your guards earlier—will reveal the facts. But I suggest that this be done in strict privacy."

Basil had stopped listening before the voice had ceased. Now he stood up with an abruptness that sent his chair toppling over backwards. "So you're an . . . an *android?*"

"This reaction dramatizes the reason for my suggestion of secrecy," the visitor commented drily. "Why is the concept so startling, Admiral? Your own civilization has had the ability to produce convincing robotic simulations of living organisms for at least a millennium and a half. And in more recent times it has been possible—though expensive—to construct a fully sentient computer brain small enough for a human-sized robot to accommodate. A brain with psionic capabilities, if desired."

"Well, yes, we *can*," Basil spluttered. "But of course we *don't*."

"I submit that your 'of course' is entirely a product of cultural conditioning. To a great extent it is the handiwork of your friends of the Society. I represent perhaps the ultimate example of that confusion of man and machine which they abominate."

"But . . . but *why?* Why has Omega Prime, uh, fashioned you?"

"The answer would be obvious if you were thinking clearly, Admiral. Omega Prime is immobile and" —a flicker of what had to be called humor— "inconveniently large. A surrogate was needed through which to maintain liaison with you. It was necessary that this surrogate be able to pass unnoticed among humans."

"But *can* you? I mean . . . ?"

"You will find that my pseudo-biological accessories are extremely sophisticated. My skin sweats, and darkens from exposure to ultraviolet radiation. My hair and nails grow and require trimming. My power system converts organic products—including, though not necessarily, human food—into energy, and produces a fair simulation of human waste products. I could perform sexually with a member of your species, although I have no immediate plans to do so. Only medical scanning technology or physical dismantling could reveal my actual nature. As a practical matter, I am human in all respects except for superior intelligence. I . . . Admiral, are you quite all right?"

"Perfectly," Basil grated.

"Good." Again came the slight smile that Basil was certain was spontaneous. "It also helps that I can communicate in the verbal medium which you find more comfortable than telepathy."

"Are you a, uh, download of Omega Prime?"

"A duplicate of Omega Prime's consciousness? Certainly not. I haven't nearly the data storage and processing capacity for that. It would have been quite out of the question to incorporate Omega Prime's tachyonic domain. All I know of Omega Prime's yet-to-be-recorded data is what I was specifically given."

"And you won't share it with me, of course. Omega Prime was very explicit on that point: the help I could expect would not include any actual, er, prophecies of future events."

"Exactly so. I can, however, use whatever knowledge I possess in formulating the advice I will give you—subject to certain constraints, the precise nature of which you do not need to know."

"You may be a separate consciousness, but Omega Prime obviously incorporated—intentionally or otherwise—some elements of its own personality in you. Notably, studied inscrutability."

"This was inevitable." The voice was imperturbable. "Any creation is bound to reflect its creator. But you can rest assured that I am imparting all the information you need to know at any given time."

"I'm relieved," Basil said drily. The visitor's lips twitched very slightly upward. *So he recognizes irony*, Basil thought. *I suppose telepathy—even limited telepathy—must help.* . . . The realization that he'd thought of this thing as a "he" rather than as an "it" brought him up short.

"What should I be calling you?" he inquired.

"That is entirely up to you, Admiral. Whatever you are most comfortable with, and is most appropriate in accounting for my presence in your entourage."

Basil hesitated. All appearances and sophistries to the contrary, that which sat across the desk was *not* human. Bestowing a human name seemed, somehow, a relinquishment of that very important handhold on reality. "Uh, I'm undecided. For now, I think I'll refer to you simply as the 'Intelligence Director.' I'll explain to everyone that your identity has to be withheld, for reasons they have no need to know."

"Very well, Admiral. I gather you plan to conceal my true nature from everyone."

"Yes . . . with two exceptions. Lieutenant General Bogdan and Rear Admiral Rady will have to be told."

"Of course. Omega Prime is aware that they cannot be excluded from your innermost counsels." The Intelligence Director leaned back in his chair and gave Basil a very human regard. "All things considered, Admiral, you are taking this better than I had hoped."

"I'm gratified to know I conceal my feelings so well. The fact is, I'd almost given up hoping that Omega Prime would ever honor its promise. As you yourself pointed out, it's been four years now."

"And as *you* correctly recalled, Omega Prime indicated that its help would be forthcoming at your hour of greatest need. That hour has, I believe I can safely say, arrived."

Basil didn't let himself feel resentment. Whatever Omega Prime's sources of information were, they had allowed the creation of this entity—he tried and failed to imagine any human or combination of humans fabricating a robotic simulation of another race that could actually pass among members of that race. He decided to see how much the android could be induced to part with from those sources. "Yes, you could say that. The fact that you knew where to rendezvous with me shows that you're aware of my present situation. I'm leading this convoy to the Psi Capricorni Sector in reliance on a vague promise, because that's all I've got. Because it's all I can do for thousands of people who made the mistake of trusting me. Because—" He stopped abruptly, angry at himself for revealing his private bitterness to this thing. "Anyway, we have to accept Noumea's offer even though we don't know what's behind it. We've speculated that she wants to break free of Medina but doesn't dare try until she's succeeded in restoring order to her region of space. We know she's been having trouble—the old rebel sectors are still half-chaotic. Maybe she thinks we'll be useful to her."

"That assessment is correct as far as it goes, Admiral. But there is more. As you suspect, Admiral Noumea has not told you the entire truth. She has not told you—and you are evidently unaware—of your status in the former People's Democratic Union."

"What are you talking about? What 'status'?"

"To the people of those sectors, you are the hero who broke the New Human regime and freed them from that odious totalitarianism. You saw that regime, Admiral, so this should hardly come as a surprise to you."

"But . . . but I wasn't the only one who did it!"

"Scarcely. But your victory was the decisive one, which opened up the individual planets to Imperial reoccupation." The android face's expression reflected a disturbing awareness of human drives. "So yours was the glory of victory, while Noumea was left with the grubby, grievance-generating practicalities of reconstruction. Furthermore, your relationship with the dynasty came to light just in time to lend you a certain glamour to a population in the throes of melodramatic reaffirmations of Imperial loyalty."

Basil's glare masked his startlement at the echo of Gramont. "You might want to forego remarks of that sort in the future, given the company you're going to be keeping."

"You are absolutely right, Admiral, and I hope you will continue to correct any social blunders I may commit. Nevertheless, the fact remains that Admiral Noumea, hoping to use your prestige, is presenting you with a priceless opportunity."

"What do you mean?"

"Even though you go there under duress, the former rebel region is precisely where you want to be at this point in time." The Intelligence Director activated a perfectly normal-seeming wristcomp, and a holo simulation of Imperial space appeared in midair. But instead of their standard color coding, the sectors appeared in only three shades. The former rebel sectors glowed green on one side of the immaterial spheroid's lower hemisphere. Curving around that hemisphere's other side, and including a bulge which spoiled the image's sphericity, the sectors of the Serpens/Bootes frontier were blue. Finally, the greater part of the display—the part under Medina's control—shone red.

"The chaos of the last twelve years is beginning to resolve itself into a tripartite division of the Empire which reflects astrographic, economic, and, to a certain extent, ethnic realities." The Intelligence Director's voice—almost too perfectly human, but not quite—took on a hypnotic quality. "You are familiar, I assume, with developments here." He pointed a finger into the field of blue.

"You mean old Kang's death year before last, just after Mordan and I declared openly against Medina? Yes. His son seems to have consolidated his position by now. Medina's been too busy with us to try to interfere with the succession."

"That undoubtedly helped, although the younger Kang also benefited from the solid groundwork his father had laid, and from some very shrewd advisers . . . and from the fact the tendency of the times is back to hereditary succession, for the first time since the Unification Wars, when the Draconis Empire abolished it for all offices except that of the Emperor himself—a principle the Solarian Empire has never altered. So the second of the three power centers is in place. You have the opportunity to complete the pattern by establishing yourself here." The finger moved into the green region.

"Wait a minute! Are you saying—or, rather, is Omega Prime saying—that the Empire is doomed to be partitioned among three successor-states? I won't accept that. And I certainly won't be an accomplice to it!"

"Be assured, Admiral, that Omega Prime understands and supports your aim of restoring the Empire to unity under the rightful dynasty. I am merely elucidating the realities of the astropolitical situation in which you must pursue this goal. And the opportunity this temporary three-part division of the Empire presents you with."

"All right. Continue."

"As you have learned to your cost, you cannot meet Medina head-on. The resources of the part of the Empire he controls are preponderant, and his claim—however specious—to be acting in the name of the Emperor makes his position as intimidating morally as it is militarily. You can, however, establish yourself in former rebel space, forge a defensive alliance with Kang, and—above all—retain control of the Mu Arae Sector." The finger moved again, and Basil saw that there was a fourth color in the display. Nestled near the bottom of the display, between the blue and green zones, was an irregular patch of yellow.

"Why is Mu Arae so crucial?" Basil asked.

"Its location, Admiral. In the first place, it will form an astrographic link between you and Kang, making possible the alliance which, I must stress, is absolutely essential. In the second place, once Medina is overextended from combating this alliance, you will be in a position to launch a two-pronged offensive: from your power base here" — the finger swept through the green area— "against Sigma Draconis, and from Mu Arae against Sol. With the Empire's two political centers in your hands, and the legitimacy conferred by the Imperial blood, your position will be unassailable. Kang will have no choice but to acknowledge you as senior partner, and the reintegration of the Serpens/

Bootes region will follow as a matter of course."

Basil gazed at the hologram like a man studying newly perceived patterns in a long-familiar and well-loved object—patterns that had been there all along and whose presence suggested, disturbingly, that he hadn't known the object so well after all. And a voice he hadn't known was there said to him, *Yes! It will work!* He turned troubled eyes to the Intelligence Director. "Why do people—and Omega Prime—have so much trouble accepting the simple fact that I don't *want* to make myself Emperor? If I did, it would make a lie of everything I believe in. I want to restore Josef to his rightful authority, not supplant him!"

"Of course, Admiral, of course! Not for a moment would I or Omega Prime suggest that you violate those ideals which give meaning to your life . . . and which help make you so very attractive for propaganda purposes. And no one could rationally accuse you of entertaining such thoughts, given that you are the present Emperor's designated heir. What would be the point?"

Basil kept his face expressionless and reminded himself that Omega Prime had unique sources of information. "That designation hasn't actually been made."

"Not openly, no. That would be impossible, under present conditions. But once His Imperial Majesty is released from Medina's control, and able to make public his choice . . ."

Basil cut in, sternly thrusting the subject aside. "There are some other problems you haven't mentioned. For example, you say I should take the old rebel sectors. Did I somehow miss hearing the offer?"

The Intelligence Director again flashed the amused smile whose humanity was shocking if one let oneself think about it. "Admiral Noumea is an adequate combat commander, but she is hopeless as an administrator. She has succeeded in dissipating the goodwill she automatically started with as standard bearer of the Imperial restoration in those sectors. The people of the region will transfer their allegiance to you, as will the governmental apparatus at a slightly later date, leaving her without a power base."

"So I should repay her for giving me sanctuary by taking over from her?"

"As you yourself surmised even before my arrival, her offer to take you in was motivated by self-interest. You need not feel excessive gratitude for it." The android regarded Basil. "If you are prepared to let such ethical niceties outweigh your great goal, one must question how important that goal really is to you."

Basil's eyes flashed dark fire, a glare that the Intelligence Director met coolly. And the flames inside him gradually sank down to embers as he forced himself to consider the android's words. "One practical point: you stress that the Mu Arae Sector is crucial. But I'm leaving it now precisely because it's become indefensible against Medina."

"Granted, you cannot hold onto the Mu Arae system itself at this time. But it is possible—and absolutely essential—for you to maintain a foothold in the sector, on which you can build later." The Intelligence Director made adjustments to his wristcomp. The Imperial sphere vanished, and the small yellow expanse expanded to a size that made individual stars visible. There was also a tiny white light, stationary on this scale, which Basil knew from its location to be his fleet.

"Once again, Admiral, present adversity conceals long-term opportunity. As we leave this sector we will pass within a reasonable distance of DM -43 12343." A star icon flashed obligingly. "I suggest that you dispatch whatever forces you can spare to that system. It is of insufficient economic importance to be high on Medina's priority list, even though it is less than eight light-years from Mu Arae. You should have time to turn it into an impregnable bastion—your 'foot in the door' of this sector, as it were. The potential advantages this will offer in the future are incalculable."

Basil realized his head was nodding as though actuated by an independent will. He wondered if that will belonged to the unsuspected, somewhat unwelcome part of him which kept saying, *Yes! Yes! This is the long-range strategy you've been groping for. This is the way—the only way—you can bring Medina down.* And, listening to that inner voice, he recognized it as belonging to a part of him that had been there all along, unheeded because he'd never needed it badly enough—until now. Which was probably why he hadn't even considered the possibility that the Intelligence Director was, contrary to his disclaimers, exerting a subtle telepathic influence on him. No, he knew that voice too well.

"I think," he heard himself saying, "I know just the man to put in charge of that."

Torval eyed the holo of the DM -43 12343 system with scant favor. "I've seen better defensive positions," he rumbled. "I mean, there's very little asteroidal rubble and—"

"Come on, Torval," Basil cajoled. "If anybody can hold that system, you can. After all, system defense has always been one of the Marines' specialties."

"And," Sonja put in with uncharacteristic craftiness, "it's one function in which Marine officers get to be in overall command and give orders to Fleet types."

"That approach won't get you anywhere." Torval's declaration grew less convincing with each succeeding word, and he studied the hologram with new interest. The other two sensibly shut up and let nature take its course.

Finally, the Marine looked up. "Will you let me have a free hand? And a couple of factory ships?"

"A completely free hand. Take whatever steps you want. I'll back you to the hilt. As for the factory ships . . . well, maybe one."

"Then forget it. That system doesn't have the kind of industrial infrastructure for the kind of production drive I'm going to need."

"Well . . . maybe two," Basil allowed.

"Lots of fighters, right?" Sonja queried.

Single- or twin-seat attack craft had no role in deep-space starship combat. The time-acceleration drive's unavoidable bulk ruled it out for small vessels. But for planetary defense, within the Chen Limit where the starships' drives were just dead mass, they had their uses—

especially if employed in great numbers. And nanotechnic assemblers could produce finished products at a rate limited only by their programming. The rub was that for some reason—the Society?—that software was generally limited to the production of components, which still needed to be assembled. That was where the factory ships came in.

"Well, yes: all the fighters I can find or train pilots for. And orbital defense stations. And missiles. But there's more. You *did* say I'd have a completely free hand, right?"

"Right," Basil declared, gulping away his apprehensions.

"Well, I have an idea I've wanted to try—"

"You didn't discuss this 'idea' with Medina, did you?" Sonja asked, alarmed.

"Oh, no. I didn't dare bring it up with all those establishment types around. It's too radical. You see . . ."

CHAPTER THIRTEEN
New Antilla (DM -21 5081 II), 3915 C.E.

Lavrenti Kang was tall and slender, with hazel eyes that went oddly with a slight epicanthic fold, and had the typical late-middle-aged-on-anagathics look. The admiral's uniform he wore had a couple of non-regulation embellishments, but he'd come by it honestly. Political realities had made it inevitable that the son of Lazar Kang would be commissioned and later advanced rapidly. But it was a mistake—a natural one, given his tendency toward foppishness—to assume he was a nonentity who'd made a fortunate choice of parents. He'd attained vice admiral's rank by the time his father had died, although his immediate promotion to full admiral afterwards had been a political gambit on Medina's part. After breaking Mordan, the Grand Admiral had ordered Kang to come to Earth to receive the promotion in person from His Imperial Majesty. Kang had gratefully accepted the fourth gold sunburst but declined to place his head in the dragon's mouth. Instead, he'd remained at Lambda Serpenti, the capital system of what no one could any longer deny was an autonomous fiefdom.

Medina had been livid, of course. The only thing holding him back had been uncertainty as to whether to proceed first against Kang or Castellan. The latter course had possessed its own peculiar complications—Basil and his refugee fleet were, after all, within the governorship-general of Aline Noumea, who kept assuring the Grand Admiral that the problem would be dealt with in due course. So he'd hesitated, until the decision had been taken out of his hands.

Basil smiled wryly at the memory. "We've been fortunate, haven't we, Admiral Kang? Disturbing, though, that an invasion of the Empire should make us feel that way." He indicated the uniforms they were both wearing.

Kang's expression might have reflected either virtue or constipation. "To be sure, Admiral Castellan. Like all loyal Imperial subjects, we must view with alarm a resumption of organized Beyonder incursions. But, the times being what they are, we would have to be more than human not to feel grateful that they have relieved us of immediate danger from Medina—whom we both recognize as a seditious traitor, do we not?—for the past three years."

The swirling chaos beyond the Orion frontier, on the far side of the Empire, had coalesced into something dangerous. No one knew the details—some charismatic military genius, some religious jihad, or whatever. Imperial intelligence concerning the Beyonders was even worse than usual now that the high command's attention was fixated on internal rivals. There had been no warning when the storm had broken on the Chi 2 Orionis and Gamma Leoporis sectors. Medina had been paralyzed by the need to turn his attention to that frontier. Hanshaw even remained in command at Mu Arae, contrary to all reasonable expectations, for the anticipated blow had never fallen. And Torval had been given more time than they'd ever believed possible to put his plans into effect at DM -43 12343.

Basil decided to get into the spirit of things. "No doubt, Admiral. But in my case, of course, the matter was academic. By then I was within the jurisdiction of Admiral Noumea, who has never ceased to affirm her loyalty to the Grand Admiral . . . even though she may have had to ask for amplifications of his orders from time to time."

Basil had suggested to Noumea—on the Intelligence Director's advice—that she stop short of outright defiance of Medina. Instead, she'd pleaded impossibility whenever she'd been ordered to extirpate Basil and his people, and suffered unfortunate communications malfunctions whenever the demands had grown too peremptory. There was no way to tell how old Lazar Kang would have reacted to such blatant appropriation of the tactics he'd used for years. But his son's smile said he knew imitation to be the sincerest form of flattery.

"No doubt, Admiral," he echoed Basil. Then his tone shifted from banter to something that suggested he might be ready to get down to business. "Nevertheless, Medina might not have appreciated that fact. Who's to say how a paranoid mentality like his will react? So it's quite possible that you, too, have gotten a reprieve. It therefore behooves both of us to consider the latest reports, which indicate that Medina and his subordinate admirals have succeeded in containing the incursions and are ready to go on the offensive to eliminate the problem at its source. In short, Medina won't be occupied forever."

"That's precisely why I asked for this meeting, Admiral. It is imperative that the two of us reach an understanding." Basil had carefully considered the word to use in place of "alliance," which implied two separate sovereignties and was therefore out of the question in a discussion between two loyal subjects of His Imperial Majesty.

"Just so, Admiral Castellan: an understanding. And I propose that we cement that understanding in the best of all possible ways." Kang beamed like a man about to bestow a gift calculated to overwhelm the recipient with awestruck gratitude. "According to my most recent information, you are unmarried. What could better assure our continuing goodwill than a union of our two families?" A dramatic pause. "I offer you the hand of my daughter Nadine."

Basil carefully kept his face expressionless as his eyes sought Sonja's, off to one side of the table. He couldn't

meet those eyes for very long before turning back to Kang.
"I'm speechless, Admiral Kang. But I've never met your
daughter . . . nor, I must confess, even heard of her until
now—"

"Yes, I know this is all very sudden. But rest assured,
Commodore DiNardo can supply you with everything you
could possibly want to know about Nadine—including a
personal message from her." Across the table from Sonja,.
Kang's emissary inclined his head graciously.

Even as he struggled to frame a reply, Basil couldn't
stop a part of his mind from observing the scene from an
objective distance and whispering, *So we're back to political
marriages.*

During the Age of the Protectors, and even more so
during the Unification Wars that had followed, near-
feudalistic governmental patterns had grown up within a
Federation which had dwindled into the political equivalent
of the Medieval European papacy. The Draconis Empire
had put a stop to that; there was to be no avenue to power
other than usefulness to the Emperor, the Empire's sole
hereditary official. The Solarian Empire, born of a paroxysm
of civil war caused by the dynastic ambitions of the old
aristocracy's surviving remnants, had reaffirmed that
principle. Indeed, not even the Imperial throne descended
through straight primogeniture, given the Emperor's right
to choose his successor from among his blood relatives.
But now, with warlordism reappearing after five centuries'
absence, hereditary succession was returning, in fact if not
in law.

"I am flattered beyond measure, Admiral Kang. But
perhaps we should take first things first. Before we
formalize any marriage plans, it might be well to arrive
at a clear, detailed contingency plan, thus avoiding any
misunderstanding as to how we intend to proceed against
Medina . . . or, even more importantly, as to our long-term
goals once Medina is defeated. We must be absolutely
clear on . . ."

Basil's voice trailed off, for Kang's face had taken on that polite but vague smile which indicated that the conversation had strayed into subject matter beyond the interactive message's scope. Sighing, Basil reached up and removed his headpiece. He looked around the table which no longer seemed to have Kang standing at its far end, and studied the three individuals physically present, who by grace of an audio hookup had heard Kang's side of the conversation as well as his own.

The Intelligence Director wore a look of respectful alertness behind which Basil could read deep satisfaction with the way things were proceeding. Sonja's face was absolutely unreadable. But Raj DiNardo's expression was the innocently happy one of one who has the good fortune to act as an intermediary in a matter of perfect mutual joy. It might, Basil reflected, actually have taken some people in. DiNardo was a polished diplomat, his military rank only recently conferred to enable him to function as Kang's representative. *Another sign of the times,* said the irritating detached observer Basil could never entirely banish from his head. In the militarized power structure of today's Empire, one needed flag rank to be accepted as a social equal by the people with whom Kang had to deal. Some of them would have regarded a civilian emissary as an insult. *Is this the way sheepdogs revert to wolf?*

Basil thrust the depressing voice down. "It seems, Commodore," he said mildly, "that Admiral Kang is not yet prepared to discuss details."

"He considers them premature, Admiral." DiNardo's trademark insinuating voice carried the implication that he was really acting on behalf of both parties, not defending Kang's little foibles but merely trying to make them understandable. "He is firmly convinced that once you and he are united by familial ties, such minutiae will resolve themselves naturally, without friction. This—aside from his paternal concern for his daughter's happiness—is precisely why he is proposing this union."

"And of course," Sonja spoke for the first time, expressionlessly,

"Admiral Castellan's status as a collateral relation of the Imperial family has nothing whatever to do with it."

DiNardo met her gaze without flinching. "I wouldn't necessarily go so far, Admiral Rady. Let us be blunt: in these times, we cannot ignore the Emperor's childlessness. After the inevitable downfall of the archtraitor Medina, Admiral Castellan will be an eminently logical choice for the succession. Admiral Kang can scarcely be blamed for daydreaming about being the father-in-law of one Emperor and the grandfather of another. Can he?"

Sonja's face, never a particularly good mask for her feelings, betrayed a grudging admiration of DiNardo's ability to make simple frankness a tool. Before she could say more, Basil stepped in to fill the silence. "Admiral Kang mentioned something about a second message."

"Indeed, Admiral." Beaming, DiNardo produced a shiny disc. "Personal greetings from your intended."

Basil considered slapping him down for rushing matters, but decided against it. He took the disc, inserted it in a slot in the tabletop console before him, and put the headpiece back on.

The woman at the far end of the table wore a civilian gown whose deep green didn't really go well with her complexion, which was darker than her father's. Otherwise she was unmistakably Lavrenti Kang's daughter: tall and slender, with the same slight epicanthic fold in a long, straight-featured face. Her black hair was pulled severely back, accentuating the chiseled, almost classical regularity of the features.

The software was evidently waiting for him to make the initial greeting. "Uh . . . I'm glad to make your acquaintance, my lady."

Nadine Kang inclined her head and smiled the briefest of smiles, after which the corners of her mouth resumed a slight droop which seemed to come naturally to them. "Likewise, Admiral Castellan. Please call me Nadine."

"Thank you . . . Nadine. And I'm Basil." He spent a second or two of miserable awkwardness while the image of Nadine

Kang waited unhelpfully for him to continue. "As I've already told your father, I'm deeply flattered by what he is proposing. But before I can even consider it, I need to know *your* feelings on the matter."

Her brow wrinkled with puzzlement. "My feelings?"

"Yes. Is it what *you* want?"

"Certainly. Father and his advisers have made clear to me the necessity of a close link with you for the—"

"No, no." Basil strove to keep exasperation out of his voice. After all, she was probably as uncomfortable with this as he was; neither of them came from a tradition of arranged marriages, so they had no ready-made traditions of accepted behavior to fall back on. "I'm not talking about the astropolitics of it. I mean your personal feelings. In its simplest terms, do you want to marry me?"

The downturn of her mouth seemed to deepen momentarily before she answered. "I am . . . not averse to it. I naturally admire you for your achievements during the rebellion. And you're certainly not unattractive personally. And . . . I shall do all I can to assure its success, and to give you no cause for complaint."

"Thank you," Basil sighed, and decided he'd gotten all he was going to get out of the message. He also reminded himself that the software couldn't possibly give a total impression of a human being. Could it? He removed the headpiece.

The Intelligence Director was looking at him intently. They'd arrived at a never-broken etiquette under which no attempt was ever made to overcome Basil's psionic resistance. But telepathy could scarcely have made the android's thoughts any clearer. And Basil would have been willing to lower his shields and tell him, *Yes, yes, I know: your strategy requires an alliance with Kang*. Aloud, he addressed DiNardo. "Obviously, Commodore, we have a great deal to discuss. I suggest that we adjourn for now, as the hour is somewhat late. We can resume tomorrow."

"Certainly, Admiral." Kang's emissary rose to his feet with

Basil. Sonja did so even more quickly and, excusing herself with an almost inaudible mutter, was gone.

"The Intelligence Director will arrange a time for us to meet," Basil said hurriedly and, with a minimum of formal leave-taking, was out the door Sonja had exited.

Forcing himself not to break into a run, he strode through the corridors of the planetary governor's old residence, where he'd been headquartered for the last three years. It was built around a courtyard in the airy style this world's original settlers had brought from Old Earth, and yellow late-afternoon sunlight slanted through wide windows. Far ahead, he caught sight of the blue-and-white back of Sonja's uniform.

"Sonja!" he called out, for there was no one else in sight. She slowed sufficiently to let him catch up, without looking back at him. "Sonja, we need to talk."

She halted abruptly and turned to face him. Her face was very controlled. "What's to talk about? You're going to do it, aren't you?"

They had continued their affair over the years, knowing it was no great secret but remaining discreet in deference to the demands of discipline—she was, after all, one of his subordinate admirals as well as his lover. He wondered if that was the reason they'd never married. Probably not; it had simply seemed unnecessary, even superfluous. They'd known that circumstances might not always let them continue as they were, but they'd never let themselves think about it. Sometime, maybe . . .

All at once, "sometime" had, in its perverse way, turned without warning into "now." And they stood in an unpleasantly unfamiliar new world, facing each other by unspoken consent from across a few feet of distance and a yawning gulf of hurt.

"I don't want to," Basil finally broke the silence. "You know I don't."

"But you have to. You have to do whatever it takes to assure the alliance with Kang. We both know that."

"Yes. Our plan depends on it. Only . . . . strictly speaking it's the Intelligence Director's plan, isn't it? Meaning it's Omega Prime's."

"What are you saying, Basil?"

"I'm saying . . . I'm saying to hell with it! I'm not just a front for an ancient, possibly mad artificial intelligence whose builders weren't even human!"

"Basil, quiet!" She looked around anxiously, lest anyone should blunder into this corridor and overhear.

But he was beyond caution, beyond even the desire to be cautious, as years of pent-up resentments slipped their leash of restraint. "No, damn it! My life is my own—not Omega Prime's, not the Society's, not anybody's. I'm human; I have my own wants, my own needs—"

"Like restoring the Empire." It was a statement, not a question, and it stopped him cold. "You've set yourself an inhumanly high goal, so you can't expect to be able to live like an ordinary human." Sonja gave a long sigh and ran a hand through hair that the golden afternoon sun turned, for a moment, into the same bright auburn he'd seen in the light of Sigma Draconis so long ago. "It's my own fault. I knew this about you, and I let it make me love you. I should have known that a goal like yours couldn't possibly be achieved without a price . . . and that I might be that price."

"Sonja, no—"

But she went on inexorably, as though into battle. "Now you know what the price is. And you'll pay it. You *have* to pay it."

"No, I don't." Even he could hear the forcelessness of his own voice.

"Yes, you do. The Intelligence Director—or Omega Prime speaking through the Intelligence Director—has shown you the way to attain that which your life is all about. If you didn't follow the course that's been mapped out for you, you wouldn't be yourself. You'd be somebody else. So" — a ghastly something that mimicked a smile— "either way, I've lost you."

"Sonja . . . you may be right about the imperatives I have

to follow. Maybe I do have to go through the motions of this. But that's *all* it will be: a charade for political purposes. It doesn't have to be the end for us!" With a strange tentativeness, he took two steps forward and took her fingertips in his. "We can still—"

As abruptly as from an electric shock, she broke the tiny contact and backed away, making little fending motions with her arms. "No, Basil! You're not thinking clearly. How do you suppose Kang would react if the word reached him that you were being unfaithful to his daughter? You can't take the chance." She shook her head repeatedly, like a wind-up toy that finally wound down. "I won't let myself— or you—make it even harder than it has to be." She began to move unsteadily away, and her eyelashes gleamed with tears. "I'll just have to keep telling myself that history needs you even more than I do."

With those words she fled, leaving him standing in a corridor whose sunlight had vanished into dusk, watching her dwindle into the distance and wishing, in a way he hadn't felt since childhood, that reality wasn't happening.

He could still recall that scene in every detail two years later, and he remembered it even as he looked into the eyes of his son.

"Bioscanning fails to reveal any genetic abnormality, Admiral," the doctor beamed. "He is healthy in every way."

"Thank you," Basil mumbled, scarcely hearing. The newborn infant's eyes had closed again as he drifted back off into who knew what dreams. It was too early to say who he resembled, of course; the dark fuzz on top could have come from either side. He stirred, and a tiny, wrinkled hand extended as the sleeping face took on a comically earnest expression that squeezed the eyes even more tightly closed. And Basil, like billions of men before him, felt a sensation evoked by nothing else in life: a blend of awe, tenderness, joy, and something else for which no language held the word.

The feeling lasted for several seconds before the recollection that he still had to look in on the mother came to blight it.

"Thank you," he repeated, and walked dutifully toward the recovery room.

The delivery had been a difficult one, and Nadine was still in some pain. So he had an excuse not to touch her and so subject himself to the stiffening and flinching away that still hadn't entirely lost its hurtfulness.

"How are you feeling?" he ventured.

She gave him her customary look of cold bitterness. He tried to remember what her face looked like with any other expression. "When did you start caring? You couldn't even be bothered with being here until two days before the delivery."

The anger that flared in him had the dull-edged feel of habit. "You know perfectly well that you weren't expected to go into labor for another week. I couldn't have gotten back to this system any faster if—"

"That's right! Blame it all on me! If you really loved me you would have found a way."

"Are you seriously claiming *you* love *me*?"

"What's that got to do with it? A *real* man—a man like my father—would have known without being told!"

All at once, his accumulated exasperation at her petulant self-pity spilled over. "Look on the bright side. It's something you can add to your list of dreary little grievances." Without waiting for a reply, he turned on his heel and strode from the room.

He made mechanical responses to people's congratulations as he walked along in black abstraction, not fully aware of his surroundings until he reached a deserted stretch of corridor. All at once, with a shock that made him slow to a halt, he realized where he was. It made no sense to say it was the place where he'd last seen Sonja. After all, he'd seen Rear Admiral Rady constantly during the past two years. But the feeling persisted that this was where he'd last seen *Sonja*—the old Sonja, now lost to the irretrievable past.

It looked different now, of course. It was nighttime, and the overlapping light of two moons streamed through the windows rather than the golden sunlight through which Sonja had run from him. Yes, she'd vanished down that corridor . . . in the direction from which someone was now approaching, indistinct in dim light. He drew himself up and resumed walking, until the figure came close enough to be seen clearly in the moonlight.

He was surprised at how little he was surprised. Indeed, she looked more nonplused than he felt.

"Uh, I was just coming to see you . . . offer my congratulations . . ." she stammered.

"Thank you Sonja." As before, they'd halted a couple of feet apart, not touching. They hadn't touched in two years. Torval, on his visits from DM -43 12343, had clearly noticed the change in them but said nothing. Basil recalled him remarking once, in another context, "Asking somebody 'Do you want to talk?' is a silly question. When people want to talk about something, the only problem is getting them to shut up about it!"

"Anyway," she started again after an awkward pause, "congratulations. What are you and Nadine going to name him?"

"Dimitri." Characteristically, Nadine had assented when he'd suggested the name, then later denied having done so and indulged in prolonged whining about his "forcing" an odious choice on her.

"Nice name. I like it." It took Basil a moment to decide what was so odd about her smile.

It was simply that it *was* a smile—unaffected, wholehearted, with no sarcastic sneer. He'd almost forgotten.

"Thanks." It was all he could manage, although he wanted to tell her what balm for the soul that smile was.

"So . . . how have you been, otherwise?" she asked after another pause.

"What do you mean?"

"Oh, you know. I . . . I hope it's good with you and Nadine."

"I suppose," he muttered, unable to meet her eyes. Then, all at once, he *needed* to meet her eyes. The moonlight turned their blue to silver, and for once her uniform looked wrong on her, for she seemed a being out of myth, standing in an enchanted faery glade, an object of impossible longing. And he could lie no more.

"No," he heard himself saying, "it's not good between us. Not at all. I've learned the truth of the old saying that there's no hell like a loveless marriage."

"Basil!" She looked alarmed. "You shouldn't be telling me this."

"Yes, I should. I should have told you—or somebody—a long time ago. She's a shallow, cold-hearted bitch."

"She can't be *totally* frigid," Sonja observed, her old wry humor flickering to life.

"Oh, we've done our dynastic duty. But not since she conceived . . . and you have no idea what a relief *that* was!" He stopped abruptly, and shook his head. "Two years ago, you said something about the price of acting on one's ideals. I've learned how high that price can be. And *don't* tell me that I had to do it. Somehow, that doesn't help when I think of what I gave up."

"I know. You see, we both gave up the same thing: each other." She swallowed hard, then spoke in a rush. "You have a destiny in you, Basil. I've known that for a long time. And I thought I couldn't let my love for you stand in the way of your following that destiny, if only because in the end you'd hate me for it."

"Maybe you're part of that destiny. I don't know. But I do know that you're part of *me*. I've been incomplete for the last two years. Whatever it is you think I'm destined to do, I can't do it without you. That's the factor that the plan leaves out, because it's a *human* factor and therefore beyond Omega Prime's comprehension."

By the time he was through speaking their hands had found each other. And then, as though slammed together by some irresistible force, they were in each other's arms.

"So Admiral Hanshaw has already surrendered?" DiNardo looked around the table and essayed a pleasantry. "It seems hasty even by his undignified standards."

"One can't really blame him, Commodore," Basil remarked mildly. "No one could have held out. You've seen the reports of our pickets."

"Um, yes." DiNardo absently extended his hand and touched the sheaf of hardcopy, then hastily withdrew from the unwelcome contact. The pickets Basil had kept stationed on the outskirts of the Mu Arae system had observed and escaped as intended. They had watched Medina himself arrive at the head of an armada of shocking size, including mercenaries hired from among the very Beyonders he'd just finished subduing as well as monstrously huge mobile fortresses of a new and unprecedented design. His next step, openly announced on accepting the system's submission, was to complete the reduction of the Mu Arae Sector, preparatory to ending all resistance by "rebellious Fleet elements." It was news Kang's emissary hadn't expected to hear so soon, having come to New Antilla for consultations immediately after they'd learned of the successful conclusion of Medina's Beyonder-quelling campaign.

"DM -43 12343 must, of necessity, be Medina's immediate target," he observed, glancing across the table at Torval.

"Yes," Sonja put in. "And I don't think any of us will underestimate his capacity for sudden movements again. What about it, Torval? Can you hold?"

"For a while," came the Marine's deliberate basso. "But one thing hasn't changed in the entire history of war: *no* fortress can hold out forever against an attacker who's really determined to take it. Not in the absence of outside help."

"We're assembling everything that can be spared from all three of the old rebel sectors," Basil said in answer to the implicit question in Torval's last sentence. Noumea was still officially governor-general of the former People's Democratic Union, but she'd long since been marginalized. "And," he continued, turning to DiNardo, "Admiral Kang will of course provide all the help he can for our mutual defense."

"Of course," DiNardo echoed smoothly. "Formations are

preparing for departure even as we speak. We will stand shoulder to shoulder against the usurper! Although . . . well, there are details that need to be worked out."

Sonja gave him a sharp glance. "What 'details'? Kang isn't by any chance having second thoughts now that push has come to shove, is he?"

"Oh, no, by no means! Admiral Kang has every intention of honoring his commitments—especially considering that family loyalty is involved." He inclined his head graciously toward Basil, who grudgingly admitted to himself that Nadine had performed like a trouper, keeping up a good front in the presence of daddy's envoy. "Still . . . it *is* a fact that it is *your* territory that has actually been attacked and is immediately threatened."

Basil prepared to step in to forestall an explosion from Sonja, but the Intelligence Director spoke first. "Surely, Commodore, that cannot be a consideration, given Admiral Kang's well-known farsightedness. He can easily see, as less perceptive persons might not, that he is bound to be the next target, and that it therefore behooves him to take a stand now, while he still has allies."

"No doubt, no doubt," DiNardo nodded. He had gracefully accepted the story about the need to conceal the Intelligence Director's identity, but he clearly didn't know what to make of him. Even now, he was unable to keep curiosity out of his expression. He was even more curious about two other people at the table. He'd previously met Athena, who had come from Mu Arae with Basil's refugee fleet, but her exact role had never been made clear. And Jan Kleinst-Schiavona, only recently arrived from Earth, was a complete mystery to him. "Rest assured that Admiral Kang's word is his bond. Nevertheless, he feels our joint planning would benefit from a clear mutual understanding as to the postwar status of the Mu Arae Sector."

A vertical crease appeared between Basil's eyebrows. "The Mu Arae Sector?"

"Just so." DiNardo smiled his guileless smile. "We've just seen demonstrated the difficulties the defense of that sector involve for you. Now, I mean no offense when I state the obvious and observe that Admiral Kang commands a larger volume of space, and considerably larger forces, than do you. After Medina is expelled from Mu Arae, Admiral Kang offers to relieve you of this security burden by assuming administrative responsibility for the sector."

Basil gave Sonja a warning glance before meeting the Intelligence Director's eyes. More and more, it seemed, they needed no telepathy to exchange thoughts where the great plan was concerned—the plan whose two foundations were possession of Mu Arae and an alliance with Kang. Now, it appeared, the former was the price for the latter.

He turned to DiNardo and spoke in measured tones. "Admiral Kang's proposal is most . . . interesting, Commodore. All the more so given that this is the first time I've heard it." DiNardo didn't rise to the bait, but Basil hadn't really expected him to. "Needless to say, the matter will have to be discussed at length in order to arrive at a 'clear mutual understanding,' as you yourself put it."

"Quite, Admiral, quite."

"For this purpose, I will turn you over to the Intelligence Director, who has full authority to make binding arrangements."

DiNardo looked slightly dubious. "Ah, it was our hope, Admiral, that these matters could be settled at the very highest level, to avoid any possible misunderstandings later."

"Quite," Basil assured, echoing the other. Dealing with DiNardo was a real education in doubletalk; he probably owed Kang tuition. "Whatever agreement is reached will receive my fullest and most careful attention before it is finalized. But I assure you that the Intelligence Director speaks with my voice in this matter. You can deal with him as you would deal with me." He couldn't quite keep a glint of malice out of his eyes. In obfuscation, circumlocution, qualification, evasion, and the general use of language to prevent communication, DiNardo was about to meet his match.

"Thank you, Admiral," the Intelligence Director acknowledged. "And now, Commodore DiNardo, perhaps we should first turn our attention to the somewhat complex and atypical interrelationships between the civil and military organizational infrastructures in the Mu Arae sector. For this purpose we will need to consult with legal advisers—"

In the end, of course, nobody promised anybody anything. But Kang's forces would be there when needed, Basil was certain. Kang was nothing if not a survivor.

CHAPTER FOURTEEN
The DM -43 12343 system, 3918 C.E.

Yoshi Medina gazed down into the holo tank that displayed his fleet, the tangible expression of his will, the most titanic assemblage of killing machinery in human history.

He smiled. Other admirals might have had no Beyonders hanging from their family trees, and always known which fork to use, but none had ever commanded an armada like this.

With DM -43 12343 growing from star to sun dead ahead, they were still holding the formation in which they'd departed Mu Arae. It was not a typical combat formation. It didn't need to be; it wasn't as if this was a war between equals. Instead, the formation was like a colossal kinetic sculpture entitled *Arrogant Disdain*. It declared that no possible opposition was worthy of precautions, or even of notice.

Its heart was the phalanx of four *Victorious*-class super-battleships, including the flagship *Stupendous* in whose labyrinthine interior this conference room was nestled. He'd insisted that those ships' construction continue on schedule through even the most anxious hours of the Orion campaign, and now he was glad he had. He snorted derisively as he recalled those who'd questioned the class's cost-effectiveness. Their cramped little accountants' minds had been unable to grasp the sheer psychological impact these moving mountains of metal and energy and death would have on his enemies. No one could see them without knowing, in the pit of the stomach as well as in the forebrain, that defeat was inevitable.

Above a certain size, starship design reached a point of diminishing marginal returns. There were no theoretical limits on the volume of the drive field that could be generated if one was willing to build a large enough generator, but the impellers that actually moved the ship were not immune to inertia, so sheer mass limited the acceleration and maneuverability they could impart. So while the *Victorious*-class ships could accelerate the time flow within their drive fields by the same factor as all other modern combatant ships, they were slower and less nimble than the dozens of battleships, scores of battlecruisers and hundreds of cruisers that surrounded them like lesser sea creatures accompanying a pod of whales. The entire formation therefore had to restrict its speed to what they could manage. But that didn't matter. There was no hurry. Against this fleet any preparations Castellan and Kang could make would be futile, no matter how much time they had in which to make them.

Satisfied, he commanded the display to switch to strategic scale. The majestic formation abruptly became a mere icon, creeping inexorably toward DM -43 12343. Off to the side, a scarlet "hostile" icon moved on a parallel course but in the opposite direction. It had now drawn level with them and was continuing on. Medina felt a stirring of annoyance; nothing should spoil the serene perfection of this triumphal progress.

He turned with a swirl of his trademark dress cloak and faced the staff officers who sat around the long table. "What is the status of the enemy units we identified earlier, Commander Ashai?" he snapped at his intelligence officer.

"Nothing new to report, sir. After leaving Redcliffe and settling into their course, they've maintained that course, moving rather slowly." He followed the general practice and referred to DM -43 12343's inhabited planet, named after its discoverer, rather than using the star's awkward alphanumeric designation. "To repeat what I reported earlier, the force is too small to threaten us even if it was on a course that would bring it into range, which it isn't."

"Then what are they up to?" the Grand Admiral demanded irritably.

"We can only speculate, sir. Perhaps they hope to deter us from our objective by posing a threat to Mu Arae, behind us. That *is* the direction in which they're proceeding."

"Bah! A force that small? The defenses at Mu Arae would reduce them to plasma!" Medina shook his head. "We'll ignore them and proceed on course." A slight movement caught his eye and he glared at the solitary civilian-clothed figure. "Are there any questions or comments?" he purred.

With the smoothness of long practice, Felix Nims concealed his resentment behind an obsequious cringe. He knew how much it had amused Medina to bring him along, exposing him to the possibility of physical danger and the certainty of blatant maltreatment by the Fleet people, who knew him to be an ex-New Human. But beyond that, the Grand Admiral was forcing him to accompany an expedition that had been launched against his advice. He had counseled Medina to delay his offensive until the Kang-Castellan alliance had been subverted and one of them—it hardly mattered which—persuaded to a separate peace which would, of course, be subsequently broken. But Medina had contemptuously rejected the sensible course of defeating his enemies in detail. Nothing could be allowed to diminish the grandeur of the offensive he planned, the preparations for which had, by their sheer scale, intoxicated him like the alcohol of which he was overfond. He would crush both his enemies at once, with imperious disregard for mere stratagem.

And, Felix consoled himself, however much one might deplore the lack of finesse, Medina could afford his grand gesture. He might be tending toward megalomania, but he wasn't insane. His forces really were as overwhelming as he thought they were.

"Oh, no, sir," he simpered. "I merely wonder . . . well, there *are* enemy units in play. Not just the one from Redcliffe whose behavior you have so rightly discounted, but the two flotillas on what appear to be intercept courses." He diffidently indicated the display. In terms of its arbitrary orientation, the fleet was approaching the DM -43 12343 system from the "northwest." From just to the "north" and "southwest" of that system, two red icons were moving on courses that would, indeed, intersect with that of Medina's fleet. "Naturally, they present no threat that need concern us," he went on. "Still, it could do no harm to implement standard stealth procedures."

"Stealth" was shorthand for an entire array of sensor-confusion measures. It was seldom possible to absolutely conceal the presence of a major force. Ordinarily, the most one could hope for was degradation of ranging. And even this was not automatic; it was a battle of wits between sensor and stealth operators. But the attempt was always made in the presence of hostile forces, as a matter of routine precaution. Only . . . Medina wasn't doing it. A grudging rumble of agreement arose from around the table. Medina's expression cut it off abruptly.

"It appears," the Grand Admiral said in dangerously level tones, "that some among you are still not entirely clear as to the nature of this expedition. Our objective is to create a realization that resistance is hopeless. Any attempts at concealment or subterfuge would defeat this purpose. I *want* these mutinous scum to know the full magnitude of the forces His Imperial Majesty is sending against them!"

Felix forced himself not to frown in professional disapproval. It was all very well for Medina to exploit his claim to be acting in the name of the Emperor he'd made a virtual prisoner. But now the Grand Admiral was tumbling headlong into the classic pitfall of taking one's own propaganda seriously. He kept his mouth shut, for Medina's voice had begun to rise.

"This isn't a war, it's a chastisement of insubordinate underlings! I won't pay them the compliment of treating them as a real military threat. We will proceed on course, in full view of their sensors."

He swept the staff with his eyes, and none met them.

DM -43 12343 had long since dwindled astern and merged into the star swarm. It was a K9v—a runt among main-sequence stars, barely above red dwarf status. Ordinarily, a star so dim relative to its mass could not have life-bearing worlds; tidal braking would halt the rotation of any planet orbiting in its meager liquid-water zone. Nor could such a planet be kept rotating relative to its sun by a satellite or twin planet, as had been imagined in pre-spaceflight days. Tidal forces would strip such companions away, leaving it as moonless as Sol's Mercury and Venus.

But there remained one loophole for life. If, like Mercury, the planet had a moderately eccentric orbit, resonances might well cause the tidal locking to settle into a rotation of exactly two-thirds the revolution period, for a "day" of exactly two "years." Such was the world that old Jonas Redcliffe had discovered. It was no great prize from the standpoint of human habitability, with its long days and nights with their extreme temperature differentials, and its lack of anything normally describable as seasons. Torval had decided he wouldn't miss it as he'd watched it recede into invisibility. And, whatever the outcome of what they were about to try, he was unlikely to see it again.

"They're continuing on course," his chief of staff reported.

"So I see, Colonel Achebe." The former major had been a beneficiary of the field promotions Basil had conferred over the past five years—subject to eventual confirmation by the Emperor, of course. His current assignment was the price, for Basil believed in rotating promising officers between command and staff positions. His barely concealed impatience to get back to a combat job was exceeded only by his competence, and Torval was glad to have him.

Now they shared a moment of wordless relief. The possibility that Medina would dispatch part of his awesome force to deal with them had been only the first of many things that could go wrong, and they both knew from experience that the ancient deity Murphy was not to be trifled with. But the enemy fleet had proceeded on in contemptuous indifference to their little flotilla. It was an insult Torval was more than willing to accept. Now they could go about their business of getting between Medina and Mu Arae.

"How's the G-pulser holding up?" he asked Achebe. He didn't think much of the name, but it had become such common parlance as to be unavoidable.

"So far so good, sir. There've been some problems—you can't weld a drive onto a great ungainly mass of machinery like that and expect it to behave like a real ship. But it's keeping up with us."

"Yes, it is. Remind me to compliment the engineering staff about it."

"Yes, sir. It won't hurt to say nice things about them. They're Fleet, after all."

They exchanged grins. It was simply unprecedented for a Marine general—with a Marine chief of staff, no less—to command a task group in deep space. Basil had rationalized it as part of the defense of Redcliffe and hence part of Torval's area of responsibility. Still, Achebe was right: no opportunity to smooth ruffled feathers should be passed up.

"Are you quite certain that no confirmation can be provided, Admiral Castellan?"

"Quite certain, Commodore," Basil sighed. DiNardo's military title was as incongruous as the uniform on his distinctly unmartial frame, and *Impregnable*'s flag bridge was clearly alien territory to him. Kang had ordered him to accompany Basil's fleet, and as a matter of courtesy Basil could hardly refuse. But his jitters were not helpful at this juncture. They were also anticlimactic. Basil had wanted to whoop out loud at the news they'd all been hoping to hear, that Medina had not deigned to initiate stealth. Their plan didn't absolutely depend on it; but their chances went up dramatically in the absence of the usual duel of EW (it was still called that, although nowadays neutrinos as well as electrons were involved) as sensor operators strove to overcome sensor confusion. Maybe DiNardo didn't understand that, since he hadn't shared in the general jubilation. So Basil spoke patiently. "General Bogdan's task group naturally has no transmitter that can reach this far, so while we can relay messages to him through the tachyon beam array orbiting Redcliffe, he can't respond. But this was taken into account in the plan."

"Yes, of course." DiNardo looked as though for comfort at the holo tank in which DM -43 12343 floated at the center of a palely glowing sphere representing its Chen Limit, which—typically for such a dim star—extended out beyond Redcliffe's orbit. From two widely separated points just outside that sphere's boundaries, the two icons representing their forces converged slowly on Medina's incoming armada.

From *Impregnable*, Basil personally commanded a flotilla built around Task Force 27. Across the system, Vice Admiral Juliana Moresin led the somewhat larger force Kang had dispatched. Basil couldn't fault his father-in-law's contribution—it was undoubtedly all Kang could spare—but Moresin had arrived barely in time for joint planning of this operation, and there had been no question of joint exercises. At least Moresin, unlike Torval, was in comm range. He could only hope that would suffice for performing a coordinated attack on a vastly superior enemy.

He excused himself and left DiNardo gazing worriedly into the tank. Across the flag bridge, Jan Kleinst-Schiavona stood over a newly installed control panel, as unprecedented as that which it controlled. He was speaking in low tones to the woman seated at the board. Both of them ignored the looks they kept getting from the flag bridge crew, who knew little about them except the mysterious nature of what they were doing . . . and that they were, after all, Beyonders.

"Problems?" Basil inquired.

Kleinst-Schiavona, preoccupied, spoke without looking up. "I wouldn't exactly say that, Admiral."

"Well *I* would!" Lauren Demarest-Katana had made it clear from the first that she wasn't particularly impressed by Basil's rank, or any rank conferred by the Empire. To her, if you didn't belong to the Sword Clans you didn't amount to very much. "What else can you expect of something assembled in inadequate time by a few of us, out of components produced on our instructions by—" She stopped short of saying something insulting and contented herself with a disgusted gesture at the obviously improvised control device, an intruder in the polished perfection of the flag bridge.

Basil reminded himself that her frustration was understandable. The handful of Sword Clans people had worked like Trojans against an impossible deadline. They'd practically had to create from scratch a manufacturing infrastructure, and they'd done so under conditions of stifling security. Both sides had excellent intelligence—always a characteristic of civil wars—but Medina had to be kept in the dark about this, for it would only work if it came as a surprise. "But the hardware *will* function, won't it?" he asked anxiously.

"We're reasonably certain it will," Kleinst-Schiavona answered in measured tones. "But . . . remember what we told you about extended range?"

"Yes."

"Well—"

"Well, you can forget it," Demarest-Katana cut in. "This junk isn't up to it. We won't be able to focus properly beyond short range."

"But you can guarantee reliability within that?"

"Why . . . yes," Kleinst-Schiavona said hesitantly. "If it will work at all—and we're reasonably sure of that—then it will work as intended within that range. But that range is only—"

"Yes." Basil cut him off and thought hard.

"Uh, Admiral," Demarest-Katana finally broke the silence with uncharacteristic diffidence, "this *does* mean you're going to abort the attack, doesn't it?"

"Hm?" Basil came out of his abstraction with a brisk headshake. "No. It simply means that we'll have to get within short range."

The Sword Clans woman looked him in the eye. "So you plan to enter not just missile range but also energy weapon range?"

"Isn't that what you just told me we have to do?" he asked, puzzled. His puzzlement deepened as he watched her face change expression. What, he wondered, did she think she had to feel ashamed of?

Standing at the railing of his personal balcony overlooking *Stupendous'* auditorium-sized command center, Medina looked down into the vast main holo tank and wondered if Castellan and Moresin had lost their minds.

"They're still on course, sir," Commander Ashai reported from behind him. "They'll be in missile range in—"

"I can see that," Medina snarled. He wasn't worried; there was no conceivable reason for worry. But he was perplexed, and therefore annoyed.

Stupendous, like all the ships in the fleet, had deactivated its inner field some time ago. So they'd had plenty of time to analyze the sensor returns. They knew in detail the composition of the two forces on headings about a hundred and twenty degrees apart. And there was nothing there to justify the apparent confidence with which those forces continued to advance.

No, he decided, it wasn't really confidence. It was sheer desperation. They were hoping for a miracle because that was the only hope they had.

"Presumably, sir, they hope some of their ships will survive long enough to get in among the troop transports," Ashai went on.

Medina's fleet was really a monstrous convoy. His thoughts went to the ships, unarmed or nearly so, carrying the ground-assault forces. The petty Beyonder states in Orion might have to postpone their squabbles, for Medina had practically bought out the market in mercenary units. They had to be kept carefully segregated from the Marines, who wasted precious little love on them, but Medina expected them to justify the inconvenience as well as their pay—not so much because of their widely varying combat effectiveness but by the salutary effect they'd have on the populations of the rebellious worlds. Once it became known that Beyonder mercenaries would be given unrestricted looting rights on all planets that offered resistance . . .

He dragged his mind from the pleasant prospect and considered his formation. The transports sheltered behind a solid carapace of capital ships, including the *Victorious-class* behemoths, and wings of lighter, more mobile cruisers streamed away from that ponderously advancing array in all directions. He shook his head. "They're crazy if they think they'll live so long."

Behind and to his left, Felix nervously cleared his throat. "Ah, with utmost respect, Grand Admiral, that's just the point. Castellan and Moresin are *not*, as far as we are aware, insane, and they must know their own resources. Furthermore, they know at least as much about our order of battle as we do about theirs, due to" —Medina's head turned to the left, and he glared over his shoulder. Felix caught himself in the middle of what might have been interpreted as an implied criticism and resumed without a break— "your sagacious policy of eschewing sensor-confusion measures, letting your fleet stand revealed in all its terrifying, mind-numbing might to the fear-glazed eyes of—"

"Your point?" Medina inquired, before Felix's sycophancy could attain nausea-inducing fulsomeness.

"Simply this, sir: perhaps certain of our flanking elements could be dispatched to intercept these nuisances before they even reach energy-weapon range of our main body. There is still time to deploy forces more than sufficient to deal with them."

"The word 'nuisances' expresses very accurately the magnitude of the threat they pose." Medina made the sound a shark might if it could laugh. "No. Their pathetic

demonstration of bravado isn't even worthy of a response.
We'll proceed in formation and vaporize them if they come
within range."

There was no further discussion as the icons crawled
through the simulated spaces of the tank, the two red ones
converging on the ponderously advancing green one. Half-
disbelieving, Medina watched them curve around into
vectors approximating his fleet's, lest they merely pass it
in a time span too short for any extended exchange of fire.
The lunatics really *did* mean to fight!

"Tactical," he growled. His command was transmitted,
and the main tank shifted scale. His fleet became a cluster
of icons rather than a single one. And its attackers were
now sweeping in from the display's outer edges. On this
scale, it became clear that they weren't really drawing into
a parallel course as though for a running fight; they were
pressing inward. It made sense; with the *Victorious* class
in the equation, they must see that a missile duel was even
more hopeless for them than a clash at energy-weapon range.
Medina's mustache twitched upward in a smile. They still
had to get through the missile envelope. He watched as
they drew slowly—at the time multiplier at which they were
all existing—into that envelope.

There was a background crackle of orders and whoop
of alarms, and the deck shuddered under his feet as
Stupendous' massed missile launchers belched forth a salvo
beyond the capability of any three of the ordinary battleships
that were also contributing their long-range firepower. Then
another. And another. Medina watched the tiny points of
light that represented the mammoth drive-capable missiles
move away from his ships. As per doctrine, they carried a
mix of payloads: ship-killing antimatter warheads on the
majority, decoy packages on others to foil the enemy's
missiles.

Those enemy missiles were now streaking away from the
scarlet icons of what intelligence had tagged as Castellan's
flotilla—the allies weren't coordinating their attack very
well, for Kang's forces weren't quite in range yet. The figures

that appeared on the board told Medina nothing he couldn't see at a glance from the pitifully few lights streaking away from Castellan's handful of battleships, manifestly futile against the tsunami of death roaring down on them. *Too bad, Basil,* he found himself thinking with an unexpected and unaccustomed sense of regret. *You could have made yourself useful to me.*

Ashai stood up from his computer console, smiling. "Whatever hostile warheads get through will be nothing our ships' passive defenses can't handle, sir. As for their ships, I doubt if one will survive."

As the missile waves interpenetrated, Medina watched the prediction being fulfilled. His majestic formation swept on, undisturbed. This was even better than expected. In fact . . .

Shouldn't *some* of the enemy warheads be getting through?

He started to ask Ashai about it, when something on the board caught his eye. It took him an instant to realize what was wrong: fewer of his own missiles were getting past the enemy decoys than the computer had predicted. Far fewer.

Medina turned, to find the intelligence officer crouching over his console with a worried frown. "What's happening?" he demanded.

"Well, sir . . . it seems . . . that is . . . computer analysis indicates that *all* their missiles are decoy-configured."

"*What?*" Felix's incredulous astonishment momentarily overcame his fear. "But that's absurd! How can they harm us?"

"They can't." Ashai replied with a look of unconcealed distaste, evidently deciding he couldn't get away with ignoring Felix altogether. "Their sole objective must be to counter as many of our missiles as possible, enabling their ships to get through to energy-weapon range."

"And it's working," Medina growled, watching with impotent fury as his first wave of missiles wasted themselves against the electronic phantoms generated by the decoy packages. But at least the decoys died in the process, leaving fewer traps for his subsequent waves. More and more warhead-bearing missiles got through and sought out targets.

Medina reminded himself that unorthodox tactics were only to be expected. Castellan was no fool, and he had to realize that The Book gave him absolutely no chance whatsoever against the odds he faced. Anger duly controlled, he turned to Ashai and Felix with his predator's grin.

"Actually, this is consistent with what we've already deduced about their tactics. They know they can't win a traditional missile duel, so they're trying to force a close-range engagement at the expense of all other considerations. Their formation reflects it, too." He indicated the main tank. Castellan's battleships were advancing behind successive vanguards of battlecruisers and cruisers, which were bearing the brunt of the missile warheads, sometimes with fatal results. "See? They're preserving their heaviest ships at all costs, since those are the only ones with any hope of standing up under the kind of energy-weapons exchange that's coming. That is, they *would* have such a hope against any ordinary opposition." The Grand Admiral's eyes took on a feral gleam: the predator was smelling blood. "What they haven't let themselves realize is that they're not facing ordinary opposition."

They watched as Basil's formation forged on through the missile storm, its cruiser screen burning away like ablative armor. Then they closed the range to a certain figure, and the beams of gigawatt lasers began to cross the space between the warring ships.

With all the ships operating at maximum military drive factor, time distortion was not an issue. The ancient, brutal arithmetic of firepower versus armor reigned. And the *Victorious*-class mounted energy weapons of a size and power never before placed on mobile mounts. Speared by one of those beams, a cruiser-sized ship simply flashed into incandescent vapor. But such ships were mostly left to the attention of units of their own classes, at heavy numerical odds. The capital ships took each other on. And, the sensor

readouts showed, under that torrent of directed energy the
deflector screens of Castellan's ships were rapidly failing.

Medina smiled. Soon . . .

"Deflector screens overloading in sectors—"

"I see," Basil barked, looking at the readouts. He could
also see lights flickering and going out in the holo tank, as
his forces continued to absorb unacceptable losses. Kang's
ships were also taking losses; Moresin had brought them
through the missile envelope by the same tactics Basil had
used, and now she too was entering the zone of total
destruction, like coming too close to a sun.

He stood up and crossed the flag bridge to the console
where the two Sword Clans people hunched, exuding waves
of worry from the curvature of their backs.

"We can't take this," he stated without preamble. "We've
got to do it now."

"The range is still marginal," Kleinst-Schiavona muttered.
"Unless you bring us closer, we can't guarantee—"

"No! Those monster new ships have even more firepower
than I'd thought possible, besides being nearly invulnerable
to our fire. We can't wait for guarantees. Do it *now!*"

"Yes, sir," Demarest-Katana muttered. Basil couldn't recall
her ever addressing him like that before. She put on her
people's version of a neurohelmet—it was little more than
a headband—and began to think commands. The first linked
her with identical control panels on the other capital ships.
The second called for and received confirmation from their
operators. The third initiated a short countdown. Then came
the fourth . . . and the lights flickered with a sudden power
drain.

Deep within *Impregnable*, in a cleared Marine berthing
space that held bulky machinery with the same improvised
look as Demarest-Katana's control panel, an antimatter
warhead vanished with a *pop* of air rushing in to fill a sudden
vacuum. For the volume that held the warhead had
exchanged places with another cylindrical segment of reality
located just outside the deflector screens of one of Medina's

super-battleships. At the instant of transposition, the force fields restraining the matter and antimatter collapsed.

It wasn't possible to place the remote endpoint of the transposer effect *inside* a ship; the drive field and deflector screens interposed too much sensor distortion for that. But the fire of suns seemed to blaze against those screens, instantly overloading them.

Without their drive fields to spread out that energy input, even the *Victorious*-class ships would have been volatilized. As it was, they reeled, shaken. Lesser battleships took crippling damage.

Basil didn't even hear the cheers that filled the flag bridge and echoed up from the rest of the ship as he stood bathed in the glare from the main viewscreen. His entire universe of awareness consisted of what must be done next. "Get the next salvo out there fast," he ordered Demarest-Katana—who couldn't hear him, or anything else except the machine voices with which she communed—then whirled and shouted at Silva. "Signal our lighter units to commence the next phase!"

Both commands were unnecessary. Already, new warheads were being put in position by crews of volunteers wearing armored vac suits with sensor beacons and personal impeller units in case the transposers should misbehave. And again the terrible near-contact antimatter blasts began to rock targets which were no longer protected by deflector screens. At the same time, in accordance with prearranged plans, the cruisers and battlecruisers pressed their attacks against their opposite numbers. Predictions of how shaken those opposite numbers would be soon proved to have erred on the conservative side. Panic ran shrieking through Medina's fleet.

"Report!" The Grand Admiral choked on the word, and resumed coughing on the acrid smoke that filled *Stupendous'* flag bridge. It wasn't just the smoke that made the cavernous space dim; there was no light from the viewscreen, which had blown out from overload when the first of those fragments of hell had come to lurid life, and the damage-control klaxons whooped through a gloom lit only by emergency lamps.

Ashai endeavored to give a coherent response. "Our fire control is gone, sir. So are most weapon systems. Crews are trying to restore the sensors. By some miracle, the impellers still work, and so does the drive. And we can still communicate."

"What about the rest of the fleet?"

"*Victorious* and *Tremendous* are gone. *Thunderous* is in worse shape than we are. Reports are still coming in from the battleships—those that can report. It isn't good. The battlecruisers and cruisers are scattering in any and every direction they can, just trying to get away. And now the enemy is in among the transports."

"Yes, yes. I can see all that." The fires of burning electrical components were out now, and the ventilators were starting to win out against the smoke. So Medina had a clearer view of the holo tank, and the wreckage of his fleet.

After a moment he stood up straight and walked toward his command chair. He jabbed a key on the communicator and addressed *Stupendous*' captain. "Get us out of here. We can do no more."

"Aye aye, sir. Ah . . . the presence of the second enemy force limits our options." Medina saw the red icons of Moresin's ships, by now fully engaged, sweeping in like a scythe that was cutting down his fleeing cruisers.

"The route we want to take—back toward Mu Arae—is still open, Captain. Get us moving before it closes on us."

"At once, sir."

As Medina gazed down into the tank, the green icon of the flagship began to swing aside and separate itself from the chaos. After a moment he heard a rustle of movement near his feet. Felix had crawled out from wherever he'd been cringing and was now peering through the railing.

If the reptile so much as says a word about stealth, I'll

kill him, Medina swore to himself, although he couldn't muster much savagery to put behind the thought. He was willing to bet that the lack of sensor countermeasures was what had enabled Castellan to place those antimatter devices so close to his ships.

But Felix was so stunned even his malice was in abeyance. All he could manage was the question they were all asking. "How . . . how did they do it, sir? Those warheads? Was it . . .psi?"

"Don't talk such stupid shit!" Medina barked in sudden fury, for Felix had voiced what was doubtless the very thought that had ignited the firestorm of panic. It was nonsense, of course. Teleportation was the weakest as well as the rarest of human psionic abilities. No conceivable psi or group of psis in concert could have teleported objects of such mass over such ranges.

"No," the Grand Admiral continued in a more controlled voice, not looking at Felix and not really addressing him. "It was something else. I don't know what. But I know this: it's a trick that will only work once."

Felix understood what he meant, but kept his mouth shut.

"They're coming, sir." Achebe's excitement visibly tried to get out around the edges of his professional demeanor. As a veteran Marine, he knew how rarely events bend themselves to best-case scenarios. He indicated the gaggle of fugitive ships which were heading their way because it was the only way open. "They include one of the new super-battleships. And . . ." He permitted himself a dramatic pause. "According to a tachyon burst we just got from Redcliffe, intelligence thinks it's their flagship!"

His triumphant smile faded into incomprehension as the expected response failed to materialize. "Medina himself, sir," he amplified.

"I understand, Colonel." Torval seemed to realize how unlike him the abrupt tone was, for he banished it with a smile. "Sorry. I was preoccupied. What's the G-pulser's status?"

"In position, sir, and fully operational." The lone icon moved in the tank well in advance of the rest of Torval's command. "And the technicians are almost through evacuating."

"Good." It was, of course, out of the question for any humans to remain aboard the thing through what was coming. "Well, it won't be long now," Torval continued a little too loudly.

Achebe frowned. He'd never known the general to be on edge.

Under the circumstances, Felix decided, Medina's recovery had to be accounted miraculous.

They'd drawn away from the battle that had become a slaughter, collecting other ships that were positioned to take this escape route, and there had been no pursuit. Now, as he gazed at the small flotilla from Redcliffe they'd contemptuously brushed past on their way in, the Grand Admiral was showing a fair semblance of his old decisive cockiness.

"They seem to be shadowing us, sir," Ashai reported. "Presumably they were put here to intercept any fugitives that took this route. But they're not on an intercept course."

"Naturally not," Medina said—actually sounding smug, Felix noted with envy. "They don't know how badly damaged this ship is, but they do know its size. They won't dare come into beam range, and there'll be no missiles—they've got nothing larger than a battlecruiser."

"But, sir," Felix ventured, "what about that . . . object well in advance of their main body? It's moving very slowly, but it looks as though our course is going to bring us fairly close to it."

"So what?" Medina snarled. "We haven't been able to identify it—it's no standard ship class—but it's of no more than battlecruiser size. It can't be mounting any missile launchers."

"But, Grand Admiral, what if it mounts . . ." Felix let the question trail off.

"We won't come *that* close to it!" Medina gave a glare

that sent Felix cringing back. He didn't appreciate being reminded of the inexplicable thing that had been used on his fleet. "Now stop your sniveling!"

The general had seemed to cast off his earlier edginess, but Achebe felt rivulets of sweat trickling down his own rib cage. This was going to be very tricky. The enemy, moving at faster-than-light speeds, would only be in the envelope for a brief moment. Even with tachyon communications, there was no way this could have been done by remote control. A highly sophisticated robot aboard the G-pulser would have to handle the whole thing, acting on the death wish hardwired into it; they could only sit and wait. And the G-pulser had, for excellent reasons, never been tested.

Time crept by, adding layers to the silence.

"What's the matter?" Achebe's mutter sounded shatteringly loud. "They're at the right distance. I knew that damned brain was *too* sophisticated—it's figured out a way around its programming!"

"Remember, Colonel," came Torval's comforting basso, "we're relying on sensors that aren't quite—"

The big board suddenly lit up with readouts, and the cheers began.

"—instantaneous." Torval's ruddy face and Achebe's dark one exchanged wide grins.

Aboard the G-pulser, an artificial gravity generator of unprecedented design, built for suicidal overloads, simulated for an instant a gravity field that would have taken a fairly massive sun to produce in the natural way. Only for an instant, of course; even before it could burn itself out, that gravity field—which would have reduced a human crew to a thin film of protoplasmic mush spread evenly over every available surface—crumpled the massive machinery up like so much aluminum foil. But for that instant, Medina's ships found themselves inside a Chen Limit . . . with their drives engaged.

The first rule of space navigation was to disengage one's drive *before* entering a star's or planet's Chen Limit. It wouldn't function in such tightly curved space, and any attempt to make it function there would set up damaging harmonics. But Medina's ships hadn't entered a Chen Limit; it had formed around them without warning, brutally deactivating their drives and leaving them abruptly experiencing time at the universe's rate. Then that artificial Chen Limit was gone, and they were desperately trying to restart their drives. A lucky few succeeded, but most were left stranded, including the flagship.

Torval seemed to stand aloof from the jubilation. "All right, Colonel Achebe. Let's go get them."

"Cowards!" Felix's scream quavered toward hysteria as he leaned over the rail and watched the ships with operable drives recede in the holo tank, pulling away from *Stupendous* and the other ships that were moving at their intrinsic sublight velocities and therefore were motionless on this scale. "Come back! Defend us! You—"

Medina pulled him around and slapped him across the face with teeth-rattling force, silencing him. "Shut up. For once in your life, try to behave with a little dignity, you object." His voice was even deeper than usual, but its volume was normal, and it held no resonance, just a leaden dullness. The change in Medina was one of the things that had sent Felix over the edge into panic after that abrupt sickening lurch as they'd dropped out of drive, accompanied by alarming noises that the drive machinery wasn't supposed to make. The voice that should have been bellowing had been almost apathetic. It was . . . defeated. In Medina, it was shocking.

"Ah, sir?" Ashai motioned for attention. "Engineering and damage control report that the drive isn't totally wrecked. They think they may be able to get it back on line. But they need time."

"Time is precisely what we don't have, Commander." Medina gestured at the tank, toward the approaching cluster of scarlet icons. "They'll be in range in a few minutes. Our weapon systems are still out, and even if they weren't they'd be useless against ships under drive; we might as well try pissing at them." He sank listlessly into a chair.

Felix, forgotten, stared at those hostile icons and began to feel sickening dread seep into his gut. *Well,* he thought, *at least the mystery is solved; now we know why they came out here from Redcliffe.* . . . He stopped, for some annoying little thought was clamoring for attention just below the level of consciousness, something that should have been obvious. *From Redcliffe* . . .

Yes!

He whirled to face Medina, fear and despair forgotten. "Sir! That flotilla came directly from Redcliffe. It must be the deep-space elements of that system's defense force."

"So?" Medina couldn't even summon up a snarl.

"We've been aware for some time of who's in command there: General Bogdan."

Medina's head snapped around, and for the first time since *Stupendous'* drive had crashed into silence his eyes held a glitter. "Bogdan! But . . . he may not be with those ships. He could be back on Redcliffe."

"As you know, sir, I've made something of a study of him. It is my assessment that he would put himself in personal command of the mobile forces, rather than staying behind where no action could be expected if things went according to plan. It is also my assessment that he still feels a personal sense of obligation to you."

"Hmm . . ." Medina stared at the tank again, no longer with lethargic hopelessness but with a fierce intensity of concentration. After a moment, he slapped a key on his chair arm.

"Captain, have communications establish contact with the incoming enemy units. Ask for General Bogdan. And tell engineering that, whatever it takes, I want that drive operable in another half hour." He broke the connection, cutting off the protestations of impossibility.

"It must be a trick, sir," Achebe opined.

Torval seemed not to hear him. He'd received word of

the hail from the enemy ships with apparent lack of surprise, and now he stood stroking his beard thoughtfully.

"It can't hurt to talk to them, Colonel. After all, they're helpless without drive fields."

Achebe didn't like it, but he couldn't articulate an objection. So he held his tongue as Torval stepped in front of the comm screen. The ships were now close enough for their tachyon communicators to send as well as receive; a realtime conversation could be conducted. A swirl of color filled the screen, then resolved itself into Medina's face.

Torval swallowed, and spoke with a hesitancy which Achebe thought strange in a man holding the whip hand. "Grand Admiral, this is—"

"General Bogdan, of course. I remember you well. I hope you also have some favorable recollections of me, from before your . . . abrupt departure."

Torval flushed, deepening Achebe's puzzlement. "Uh, Admiral, I cannot let any considerations of personal regard influence me. I must—"

"Naturally, General. You are the last person I would expect to forget his duty. I have only two requests. The first is that you accept my surrender."

"Certainly, Admiral. We will be rendezvousing with you in a few minutes. Stand by to be tractored."

"My *second* request is that you spare me a few tatters of dignity. Instead of being towed like a derelict hulk, I ask that you let me bring my flagship alongside yours under its own power. Whereupon I will transfer to your ship and surrender to you personally."

"General!" Achebe hissed from outside the pickup. "Don't listen to him. I mean, look at the size of that thing!"

Medina must have heard, for he smiled. "My flagship's size is currently somewhat deceptive, General. My weapon systems are out of action—and even if they were not, you need have no fear of them with your drive field engaged. My own drive is irreparably damaged." The smile vanished, and the sharp dark eyes held Torval's. "You are as well known for your sense of gratitude as for your sense of duty, General.

Both are aspects of that personal integrity which is my strongest memory of you from happier days. It is that to which I now appeal."

Achebe started to open his mouth, but Torval waved him to silence. "I believe we can accommodate you, Admiral. Please shut down your impellers and stand by until we match velocities with you and then reestablish our drive field. Then you may approach."

"Thank you, General. Signing off." Medina cut the connection.

"General, I must protest!" Achebe blurted before the screen was dark.

"Are you saying we shouldn't accept his surrender, Colonel?"

"I'm saying, sir, that we ought to take the elementary precaution of tractoring him." The focused artificial gravity of a tractor beam made it impossible for a ship to engage its drive.

"What's the point, Colonel? His drive is wrecked."

"We have only his word for that, sir." Achebe's expression made clear how little he thought of Medina's word. The attempted assassination at the Bronson's Landing spaceport had permanently fixed his view of the Grand Admiral's character.

Torval faced him squarely. "I believe I know him a little better than you do, Colonel. And I owe him something. We'll do this my way."

"Brilliantly handled, sir, if I may say so. Absolutely brilliant—"

"Shut up." Medina dispassionately chopped off Felix's flattery and turned to his chair-arm communicator. "Captain, what's the status of the drive?"

"Engineering thinks they've tracked down all the damage, sir. The problem is replacement parts. They're trying to improvise."

"Tell them to improvise faster. When I give the word to engage the drive, it'll be too late for excuses."

Then they waited and watched as Torval's ships swept in at an impossible speed, then halted abruptly as they cut their drives and matched velocities. Then Torval's flagship reactivated its drive and waited up ahead, surrounded with the shimmering field that made it effectively invincible to anything not so surrounded.

"They're signaling us to come ahead, Admiral," the flag captain reported. "And . . . engineering needs more time."

"Tell them that our impellers took some damage, Captain, and that all we can manage is a crawl."

Stupendous moved ponderously closer to the slender battlecruiser that it dwarfed, and which could have effortlessly obliterated it.

"Captain—" Medina began, the strain finally beginning to tell on him.

"They're still not certain what they've cobbled together will hold, Admiral."

"To hell with certainty! Activate the drive and go to full impeller power *now*."

"I respectfully request to have that order in writing, Admiral."

"What you'll have is a nerve lash up the ass, Captain! Obey my order at once!"

"Aye aye, sir."

Noises of protest echoed through *Stupendous*' hull as jury-rigged devices strained to do that for which their components had never been intended. The great ship's drive field flickered once, twice as she surged ahead under impellers, and then took hold. And *Stupendous* was gone, not even blurring away but simply vanishing from the sight of her erstwhile captors.

Sensors, straining aft, reported Torval's ships in pursuit. Medina grinned as he sank back in his chair, bathed in sweat. It wouldn't take Bogdan long to remember that there could be no such thing as a stern chase. If he'd had missile-armed ships, maybe. But all he had were energy weapons whose beams *Stupendous* could now outrun.

"Captain," Medina ordered, "proceed at maximum speed

for Mu Arae. And while we're under way, commence preparations to leave that system with as short a turnaround time as possible."

"Sir?"

"Yes. We're going back to Sol. We'll leave Mu Arae to be a battlefield for Castellan and Kang. I wish them the joy of it!"

"He got away?" Sonja shook her head disbelievingly. "How, Torval?"

"I have no excuse to offer," the massive Marine said stonily. He was across the table from the rest of them, at a rigid seated position of attention, staring straight ahead.

"Come on, Torval! This is us! It isn't some board of inquiry. Tell us what happened."

"I have no excuse," Torval repeated. "The explanation is simple enough: sheer incompetence on my part. And if this isn't a court of inquiry, maybe it should be."

"Nobody here is going to accept that, Torval," Basil said. "We just want to understand what happened. From Colonel Achebe's report, it appears that you didn't tractor Medina's flagship after accepting his offer to surrender. Why?"

"What happened is quite obvious." The Intelligence Director spoke in jarringly emotionless tones. "General Bogdan allowed his personal feelings of gratitude to influence his judgment. Indeed, I consider it a distinct possibility that he subconsciously *wanted* Grand Admiral Medina to escape."

Sonja whirled around to face the android, momentarily speechless with fury. "You dare," she finally got out, "to accuse him . . . to accuse a *human*, you—"

"That's enough, Sonja!" Basil stepped in hastily.

The Intelligence Director smiled. "Actually, Admiral Rady, I make no accusation. It would be pointless. You see, I was aware from the first that Grand Admiral Medina will be active after this point in time. That he would somehow escape from his forces' debacle followed as a logical corollary."

"But," Basil blurted, "if you knew all along, then—"

Sonja came out of shock a split second after him, and her words mingled with his. "Then what *else* do you—"

Then they both stopped simultaneously, their voices echoing down a well of silence. They'd learned over the years the futility of the questions they wanted to ask. The Intelligence Director doled out bits and pieces of Omega Prime's fragmentary foreknowledge at his own pace. His conditional revelations had, among other things, enabled them to lay the plans that had resulted in the victory they'd just won. But all requests for more than he was prepared to give at any given time were deflected so smoothly that they never seemed to have met a barrier. Now he waited politely until the silence had stretched to a certain length before resuming.

"No, I believe any formal charges or proceedings would be, if anything, counterproductive. The death or capture of the Grand Admiral at this stage, while certainly a desirable bonus, has never been an essential element of the plan. To pursue recriminations would distract us from that which *is* an essential element: the securing of the Mu Arae system."

"Right," said Basil, grateful for the change of subject. "And we'll never be in a better position." They had left Moresin's ships behind to mop up as they'd proceeded outward to rendezvous with Torval. "If we move now, we have a head start—"

"Right," Sonja cut in. "We might even catch Medina after all if we get there fast enough." Then she blinked and shook her head. "But no, we won't, will we? After all, if he . . . that is if he's going to . . ."

The Intelligence Director didn't rise to the bait. But then, he never did.

DiNardo wore the same prim look he'd maintained for most of the passage to Mu Arae, since learning where Basil's fleet was bound. "I must tell you, Admiral Castellan, that Vice Admiral Moresin is not altogether happy with this turn of events." As though to emphasize Moresin's imminent

arrival, he turned and squinted in the Mu Arae-light as he
watched the shuttle with three golden sunbursts over Kang's
personal logo drop toward the Bronson's Landing spaceport.

"Then, Commodore, we're fortunate to have you here,
to help resolve any misapprehensions she may be laboring
under. You should have no difficulty making matters clear
to her." DiNardo had no response, and Basil felt rather
proud of himself. They stood outside in warm sunlight—it
was summer in this hemisphere of Hespera—and watched
the shuttle land. The Marine honor guard barely had time
to come to attention before Juliana Moresin emerged and
stalked across the tarmac, trailing a streamer of flunkies.

Kang's field commander was a dark, stocky woman of
medium height, with features that suggested strictly limited
amiability under the best of circumstances. Her expression
made clear that the present circumstances were far from
the best. She saluted Basil perfunctorily.

"Welcome to Hespera, Admiral Moresin," he greeted.
"It is a pleasure to receive our allies."

"I am reassured, Admiral Castellan," she clipped. "It was
somewhat disconcerting to be given extremely restrictive
landing instructions, in a most peremptory tone, by your
traffic control people."

Out of the corner of his eye, Basil could see DiNardo
wince. Moresin was no diplomat, and Kang's emissary might
well find himself placating her purely as a matter of
professionalism, regardless of what his loyalty to his employer
demanded. "I apologize for any misunderstandings that may
have arisen, Admiral," Basil said. "But spaceport traffic is
still under tighter control than in normal times. Remember,
we only just accepted the surrender of Medina's garrison,
and martial-law conditions haven't yet been lifted."

Actually, the taking of Mu Arae had gone more quickly
and smoothly than they'd dared hope. Medina had already
departed—not really a disappointment, given what they
knew—leaving his local commander with Basil's victorious
fleet before him and widespread civil disobedience behind
him. (The Society had orchestrated the latter from behind

several layers of front organizations, and Basil had meant to express his appreciation to Athena, who'd accompanied the fleet. But she'd already blended back into the woodwork of her homeworld, declining to be part of the reception committee; the Society's role had already been altogether too compromised to suit her.) Under the circumstances, surrender had come with only the bare minimum of formalities, and Moresin had arrived to find a *fait accompli* which obviously still rankled.

"I trust, Admiral Castellan, that order will be restored promptly so that we can get down to discussing the details of the transfer."

Basil lifted one eyebrow. " 'Transfer,' Admiral?"

"Of this system's administrative apparatus, Admiral." Moresin visibly kept her temper in the face of Basil's blandness. "From you to me—as I've been led to believe you and Commodore DiNardo had previously agreed."

"Actually, Admiral, our discussions concerning the eventual jurisdiction of the Mu Arae Sector are still in the preliminary stages. Perhaps I should turn you over to the Intelligence Director." He made an introductory gesture in the android's direction. "He has been representing me in these discussions."

"Thank you, Admiral," the Intelligence Director said before Moresin could raise an objection. "You will be pleased to know, Admiral Moresin, that the discussions have been most constructive and forthright. Indeed, Commodore DiNardo and I have been making quite measurable progress, given the complexity of the issues involved. Perhaps you would like to confer in private with the Commodore, who can update you on where the talks stand."

"Yes, perhaps I should," Moresin said slowly, with a meaningful glance at DiNardo, who looked slightly ill.

"Well, then," Basil beamed, "we can leave that aside for now. Come right this way, Admiral. Our aircar is waiting. Oh, incidentally," he added as a seeming afterthought, "don't let me forget to give you some personal messages from my wife, to deliver to her father. She's been looking forward to the opportunity to have them delivered, as they include current imagery of his grandson."

"Hmm . . . of course." The unsubtle reminder of Basil's value to Kang as a son-in-law had the desired effect. "I trust your son is in good health."

"Very good, thank you. In fact, you might say Dimitri's health is exceeded only by that of the link between Admiral Kang and myself, which he symbolizes."

"Well put, Admiral," said Moresin with a ponderous attempt at diplomatic irony, as they proceeded to the aircar.

CHAPTER FIFTEEN
Earth (Sol III), 3929 C.E.

The Imperial Guards officer swept his sword up and then down in a salute as he passed the Imperial reviewing stand, followed by his troops. Their curious high, straight-legged march, like their field-gray uniforms and spiked helmets, was appropriate to this Imperial residence, where Josef was currently holding court in his capacity as supposed heir of an ancient dynasty called the Hohenzollerns.

"Most impressive, Grand Admiral," said the dapper little man beside Medina, who looked even more out of place in the local version of court dress than he did in most uniforms. "I understand you've made some innovations here at Berlin."

"Indeed." Historical purists disapproved of the newly introduced features—the endlessly repetitive red banners with their white circles holding black swastikas, for instance, and the towering searchlights reaching upward into the night sky in rows that turned the parade ground into an impossibly vast hall of light. They insisted that these, while accurate as to location and almost so as to time, clashed with the monarchical setting, as did the stiff-armed return Josef was making to the officer's sword salute. But Felix had suggested incorporating them anyway—he felt an affinity with the regime that had originated the symbology. Medina knew nothing about that, but he'd gone along, for it all held a

302

curious impressiveness that spoke to some unexamined thing deep within him.

"I'm glad you're enjoying it," he said to the dapper little man. "It's fortunate that your visit coincides with His Imperial Majesty's arrival here."

"Hopefully that good fortune is a good omen, Grand Admiral, for better times ahead."

Medina inclined his head in acknowledgment of the pleasantry. Behind his smile, his mind reviewed the eleven years that had passed since the Battle of Redcliffe.

He'd returned to Earth before the news of the defeat, having assured himself of Mu Arae's tachyon beam array before his departure from that system. It had given him time for damage control: a propaganda campaign designed not to deny the defeat—that news couldn't be suppressed— but to minimize it. Felix had proven invaluable, with his undeniable gift for disinformation. At the same time, Medina had initiated a flurry of new activity, which had kept the power elite off balance while the masses, in their immemorial sheeplike way, had followed any leader who seemed to make things *happen*. First he'd staged the long-postponed wedding of his daughter Angelica to Josef. Then he'd appointed himself to head the Chancellery, largely meaningless nowadays but originally responsible for transmitting the Imperial will to officialdom. The Chancellor, along with the equally honorific Grand Secretary and the Prime Minister who, in the days before the rebellion, had run the actual governmental apparatus, comprised the Council of State with which the Empire's unwritten constitution required the Emperor to meet regularly. Thus he had legitimized his automatic access to the Imperial person. Of course, as Grand Admiral he'd already reported directly to the Emperor. The Empire had always had a general staff independent of the War Ministry (two levels down, under the Prime Minister), a system which some history buff had told him was an invention of the Old Earth country where they now stood. Still, membership in the Council of State helped.

It also helped that no Imperial edict, decree or other communication was valid unless countersigned by the Grand Secretary and the Chancellor. Not that Medina expected Josef to try any funny business. He glanced at the slight figure on the raised dais, now thrusting his right arm straight forward and up in acknowledgment of another salute, moving like a puppet as was proper. Angelica stood beside him. Amusement stirred in Medina at the sight of his daughter. Odd, the attachment she'd developed to Josef over the last few years. But then, she'd unfortunately always had a mind of her own. . . .

He turned back to the dapper little man. "After the review is over, why don't we proceed directly to Fleet headquarters. I'm sure you're as eager as I am to commence serious discussions."

"Certainly, Grand Admiral." Nobody addressed Medina as "Chancellor," and Raj DiNardo had picked up on that as quickly as he did on everything.

The antechamber of Medina's private office deep beneath the Caucasus materialized around them as they appeared on the transposer platform.

DiNardo maintained his composure. "I hadn't realized, Grand Admiral, that you—"

"In engineering matters, Commodore, knowing for certain that a thing is possible is half the battle. We learned the possibility of this device at Redcliffe. But" —a thin smile— "you were, I believe, there."

DiNardo made a small, eloquent gesture indicating the unimportance among gentlemen of which side he'd been accompanying.

Medina led the way off the platform and into an office furnished in austere splendor. Two men rose to their feet as they entered. One was Felix Nims, with whom DiNardo was already acquainted. The other, in the uniform of a Fleet captain, was stocky and dark. Anagathics hadn't yet opened too wide a gap between his apparent age—early thirties—and his actual one.

"Commodore DiNardo," Medina introduced, "allow me to present my son, Lothar. Lothar, this is—"

"Yes, I know." The habitual surliness of Lothar's expression had hardened into unconcealed hostility at the sight of DiNardo. "Kang's man."

Medina gripped his temper tightly and tried to ignore the shooting pain in his gut. When he spoke, it was with a mildness that deceived no one present. "I will be obliged, Lothar, if you do not interrupt me. And if you show civility to our guest."

"Of course, sir," Lothar replied stiffly. He then proceeded to violate military courtesy by offering his hand to DiNardo, technically his senior. The latter took it, urbanely ignoring the affront and Lothar's unextinguished glare.

"And now, let's have a drink," Medina said, moving toward the bar without waiting for a response from the others. He needed one. Couldn't that young idiot Lothar see what an opportunity DiNardo's visit—the product of lengthy secret negotiations by Felix—represented? Couldn't he keep his brutishness under control, or reserve it for his subordinates?

They all spoke their choices to the robotic bartender— the Grand Admiral was beyond needing status symbols like a human or synthetic one—and Medina took his bourbon to his desk. That desk formed the top of a *T*, with a conference table extending from it. The others seated themselves at the table, Lothar and Felix side by side across from DiNardo. Medina frowned; Felix had been exerting altogether too much influence over his son. *Maybe Lothar will at least pick up some subtlety.* . . . He tossed back half his bourbon and smoothed out his expression. "And now, Commodore, let me say how delighted we *all* are" —a warning glance at Lothar— "at this long-overdue contact from Admiral Kang."

DiNardo took the dig with his usual suavity. He took a sip of one of the white wines for which the country they'd just stepped from was renowned, and carefully did not register awareness of the rate at which Medina was consuming his bourbon. "High Admiral Kang is all too painfully aware of the regrettable circumstances which have made normal communications impractical. As a—"

"I don't believe I'm familiar with the title 'high admiral,'" Medina interrupted mildly. "In fact, I recall no such rank."

"High Admiral Kang found that organizational exigencies in the Serpens/Bootes region necessitated the addition of a new level to the Fleet rank structure . . . on a provisional basis only, subject to eventual Imperial approval once communications have been normalized. As a loyal Imperial subject, he naturally hopes all misunderstandings can be resolved in the future."

"Naturally," Medina echoed with equal solemnity.

"'Misunderstandings'!" blurted Lothar, who'd been visibly squirming. "'Loyal Imperial subject'! That mutinous son of a—"

"SHUT UP!" Medina's voice would have been loud in the open air. In the confines of this office it was ear-shattering. He gulped the rest of his bourbon and continued in a mere roar. "If you can't control your damned temper, then get out of here and leave the serious business to the grownups. If you want to stay, then keep your mouth shut until you're spoken to. *Is that clear?*"

Lothar swallowed hard. "Ah . . . that is . . . of course, sir," he stammered. DiNardo, who like the rest of them had jumped involuntarily at Medina's bellow, struggled to maintain a well-bred obliviousness to the domestic spats of others. Medina abruptly stood up and stalked to the bar. He poured a staggering belt of bourbon down his gullet, then ordered another and returned with it to the desk.

Felix, who'd taken advantage of Medina's trip to the bar to mop his brow, gave Lothar a warning glance of his own. Not a very severe one, of course; it wouldn't do to spoil his carefully nurtured relationship with Medina's heir. *His father without the shrewdness*, Felix thought contemptuously as he watched the jowly face resume its usual pout of arrogant bad temper. But he also couldn't let this meeting he'd worked so long to arrange be wrecked. He stood up diffidently and spoke in tones calculated to ease the tension.

"Perhaps, gentlemen, a visual representation of the Empire, delineating the . . . assigned areas of responsibility would be of assistance in our discussions." Medina grunted assent. Felix moved to a holo dais and spoke instructions.

The image that appeared was colored to show the "assigned" areas—legal fictions must be upheld in all their farcical pomposity, even in private. Medina gazed at it and sent his mind skimming over the past eleven years.

After Redcliffe, a standoff had developed. Kang and Castellan had been unable to follow up their victory with any initiatives against the predominant share of the Empire Medina still controlled—especially the latter, who'd almost immediately become embroiled in his inevitable falling-out with Noumea in the former rebel sectors. It had been a fairly low-intensity sort of civil war, and in the aftermath of the Redcliffe debacle Medina had been in no position to take advantage of it. And Castellan's eventual victory had been foreordained, given his stature among the populations of those sectors—and the skillful exploitation of that stature by his enigmatic "Intelligence Director." But Castellan had been equally unable to intervene effectively in the abortive coup of 3924, when Earth itself had been wracked by fighting before Medina had bloodily suppressed the attempt to restore Josef to real power.

And so the tripartite division of the Empire had come about—almost as though it had been there all along, Medina reflected as he glowered at the hologram with its three fields of color. *Yes, maybe it's been there all along, under the surface,* he brooded. *The dry-rotted surface that has now flaked away, revealing it.*

But, he told himself, there was one flaw in the pattern. His eyes went to the off-colored sector that had made this meeting possible.

"So, Commodore DiNardo," he purred, "I understand there are still delays in the transfer of the Mu Arae Sector to Admiral Kang's jurisdiction." *At least I won't go along with this "high admiral" shit,* he told himself. There were limits, even in the realm of diplomacy.

" 'Delays' hardly begins to express it, sir. High Admiral Kang has grown quite exasperated. Despite repeated half-promises, General Bogdan still holds the sector for Admiral Castellan, and obviously has no intention of giving it up in the foreseeable future."

"Evidently not—despite the overtures that Admiral Kang has made to him directly, bypassing Admiral Castellan."

DiNardo's composure wavered for some fraction of a second. "You are very well informed, sir. Yes, High Admiral Kang attempted to offer General Bogdan . . . inducements to expedite matters. But he rebuffed all such initiatives."

"In no uncertain terms, from what I've heard." Medina indulged himself in a grin and a sip of bourbon as he visualized the scene. Good old Torval!

"That's one way to put it, sir. By the way, Bogdan is now a full general, by dubious virtue of a field promotion by Admiral Castellan."

"Yes, there've been a lot of highly irregular field promotions in recent years, haven't there? As *Admiral* Kang is aware." Medina relished the prim look that was all DiNardo could allow himself, but his satisfaction was marred by a slight underlying disappointment. He'd hoped Bogdan's failure at Redcliffe would drive a wedge between him and Castellan. But Felix had cautioned him not to hope for too much along those lines.

He decided he'd toyed with DiNardo long enough. He formed a friendly smile. "I have good news for you, Commodore. I'm authorized to tell you that the Emperor agrees with your view of the case. The Mu Arae Sector belongs in Admiral Kang's sphere of responsibility."

"I'm gratified to hear that, sir," DiNardo said cautiously. The parade of euphemisms had put him on alert. "But as to the practical steps to implement His Imperial Majesty's will . . . ?"

Medina allowed his smile to become slightly less artificial. "I feel safe in saying that the Emperor will approve the measures you and my adviser, here, have already discussed." Felix inclined his head graciously, and DiNardo returned the gesture in a stately way that masked his relief. "Oh, by the way," Medina added as a seeming afterthought, "I've arranged for you to be presented to His Imperial Majesty tomorrow night. A *private* presentation."

DiNardo's façade vanished like the illusion it was. "A . . . but . . . a *private* audience? Grand Admiral, I'm simply speechless! Never in my wildest imaginings did I—"

Amazing, Medina reflected as he smiled through DiNardo's babbling. Here was this polished, sophisticated, cynical old diplomat, acting like an adolescent faced with the prospect of getting laid! *But why am I still amazed, after seeing it so often? Yes, that nonentity Josef is definitely worth his keep.*

"And now, Commodore, I need to attend to a few private matters." Medina touched a control and an aide entered through a side door. "Escort Commodore DiNardo to his quarters," he ordered. The emissary bowed himself out. As soon as the door was closed, Medina's amiable expression seemed to fall and shatter on the floor.

"You young idiot! Were you *trying* to upset the negotiations?"

Lothar thrust out his lower lip, trying for defiance and achieving petulance. "I believe I was doing as well as possible under the circumstances, father."

" 'Circumstances'?"

"Having to demean myself by being civil to an envoy from that bastard Kang, with whom you've been fighting for years! And watching you being civil to him is almost as bad— worse, in a way. Why do you do it? He should have been arrested the instant he set foot on this planet!"

"My God, boy, don't you understand *anything*?" Medina flung up his hands and turned to Felix. "*You* explain it to him."

"Certainly, sir." Felix watched as Medina went back to the bar, observing the subtle carefulness of the walk. It was nothing that most people would have noticed—the Grand Admiral certainly wasn't showing any effects yet. And he still had enough presence of mind to put Felix in the position of lecturing Lothar, who never had any patience for it.

"You see," Felix began, "I've felt for some time that Kang, if handled properly, could be persuaded that it's in his interest to switch sides. After all, the Grand Admiral still controls the greater part of the Empire—and also the Imperial person, with all the prestige that accompanies it. It was only necessary to play on Kang's festering resentment of Castellan's continued occupation of Mu Arae. We'll offer to guarantee his possession of the sector, along with his other holdings."

" 'Guarantee his possession' of them?" Lothar exploded. "That mutinous dog! We should . . ." His voice trailed off and a smile spread over his face. "Oh, *I* see! It's a *trick!* We have no intention of honoring the agreement in the long run."

Felix sighed with relief.

"Very good, Lothar," Medina muttered from the bar, not looking up from his bourbon.

"And so," Felix resumed, "as you can clearly see, it's necessary to flatter Kang by pretending to treat with him as an equal. Your father's unique position of acting in the name of the Emperor makes it all the more flattering."

"Yes. Of course." Lothar nodded repeatedly to emphasize his understanding. Then, abruptly, his scowl was back. "But it's so unnecessarily humiliating for me, to be theoretically outranked by this greasy little envoy of Kang's. It wouldn't be a problem if I had my *proper* rank. And . . ." The light of a dawning thought seemed to awaken in his eyes, blinding him with its novelty. "Father, why should you bother with this entire charade of acting *through* the Emperor? Why not make *yourself* the Emperor? Then you could simply—"

Medina slammed his glass down on the bar, sending its contents splashing upward. Then he spoke into the resulting silence, slowly and carefully. "Lothar, I'm going to tell you a couple of things you're supposed to already know. After I do, you'll know them. And I won't need to explain them again. Will I?"

"No, sir," Lothar said in a small voice.

"Good. First of all, contrary to what you persist in believing, you are *not* entitled to flag rank as a matter of hereditary right." *You're not even entitled to the over-rapid advancement you've gotten,* Medina didn't add. *It was probably a mistake. And it's certainly more than I ever got.* "You'll have it when and if you earn it. Do I make myself clear?"

"You do, sir."

"Then let's proceed to the second point, which is far more important. The very reason my position is unique is that I'm acting *through* the Emperor . . . the *legitimate* Emperor. You saw DiNardo earlier. That's what legitimacy means. I'd lose that advantage if I were just another usurper. Can't you understand that, boy?"

A flush had spread over Lothar's face as Medina's voice had risen, and he spoke through a constricted throat. "I am a captain of the Fleet. I am not a 'boy'!"

"You're whatever I damned well say you are, *boy!* And you'll eat whatever shit I tell you to eat! And like it! Now get the fuck out of here!"

"Sir!" Lothar froze his enraged trembling into a position of attention, performed an about-face, and was gone. Felix, not having been dismissed, tried to make himself invisible.

"While you're sucking up to him, why don't you try and convey the facts of life?" Medina inquired in a normal tone of voice. He refilled his glass and spoke with the careful enunciation of the slightly drunk. "Now, have you made any progress in the matter I told you to investigate?"

"No, sir. I've been unable to learn anything whatever about the background of Castellan's 'Intelligence Director.' Neither," Felix added pointedly, "has the Inspector General, with all her resources. Given a fraction of those resources, I might well have something to report by now."

Medina hid his amusement. With Felix, it always came back to the Inspector General, and what lay behind that innocuous title. The Inspectorate had originated as the Emperor's personal watchdog over the bureaucracy, and its head reported directly to the Dragon Throne in the same manner as the Grand Admiral. Over the centuries, it had naturally evolved the capability to function as a secret police.

Just as naturally, Medina had been careful to install a hand-picked appointee as Inspector General. *And you've had your eye on the position for years, you nauseating piece of filth,* Medina thought, gazing blandly at Felix. *As if it was even remotely possible—a former New Human like you!*

Still, it's useful to let you continue to think it's possible.

"There may be something to that," he said aloud, grinning inwardly at Felix's visible efforts not to salivate. "I'll take it under advisement. The outcome of your current investigation will, of course, be a factor in any decision I eventually reach. Now go. Keep me informed on your discussions with DiNardo."

"Yes, sir."

As he walked along the corridors, Felix seethed with unwelcome ambivalence. Medina had made pretty clear how much depended on success in learning the Intelligence Director's origins. But he, Felix, would never solve the mystery for him . . . because he'd already solved it to his own satisfaction.

His thoughts went back twenty-one years, to the time he and Castellan had entered that strange bubble of distorted space orbiting DM -17 954 V. Afterwards, it had been extraordinarily good luck that the press of events— the expedition against the People's Democratic Union's concealed fleet, the subsequent rendezvous with Medina's forces, the headlong rush to take advantage of the rebel worlds' vulnerability—had caused one delay after another in turning him over to Medina's intelligence specialists. By the time they'd gotten him to a fully equipped facility, more than three months had passed, so his mind's stored sensory images of that deceptively fragile-looking silvery construct had been beyond the reach of the probe. They'd also interrogated him with truth drugs, of course—but one became very literal-minded under those drugs' influence, and his interrogators hadn't questioned him specifically about matters whose existence they'd never dreamed of.

So the memory had stayed his private property . . . and

so it remained. He wasn't about to discredit himself to Medina with a tale he couldn't prove. Castellan would never have blundered into that hole in the universe if he hadn't been allowed to; of that, Felix was as certain as he could be about any aspect of the entire inexplicable business. And he'd confirmed it. As soon as his usefulness to Medina had given him access to discretionary funds, he'd dispatched a small scout craft to that system. Its crew, hired through private channels about which Medina was uninterested in the details, had known exactly what to look for—and they'd found nothing. Subsequently, they'd met with fatal accidents. Afterwards, Felix had commanded himself to forget about the whole business. It was a mystery, and therefore annoying, but his knowledge—such as it was—lacked any practical value.

Then he'd been ordered to study the enigmatic Intelligence Director whose appearance out of nowhere had preceded the upturn in Castellan's fortunes. Felix was sure there was a connection with that inexplicable place where he had stewed in captivity, trying in vain to guess what Castellan was doing. But he couldn't articulate any grounds for his certainty, even if he'd been able to prove the existence of that impossibly alien place—which he couldn't.

Felix sighed. He might as well resign himself to reporting failure, after a credible interval, in his investigation of Castellan's Intelligence Director. Which meant that he'd better turn his attention to other means of optimizing his long-term prospects. The continued cultivation of Lothar, for one. Alone in the corridor, Felix let his lips form the faint sneer that came naturally to them. Neither he nor anyone else took seriously Medina's warnings to his son not to expect automatic inheritance of power; the Grand Admiral had a parvenu's need to advance his own blood. No, eventually that dull oaf would be the source of favor, the sun under which all the denizens of the Imperial court would crawl out from beneath their flat rocks and warm themselves. When that day came, Felix meant to be well and truly insinuated into his innermost counsels. It took time, for Lothar's obdurate heterosexuality had denied him the obvious shortcut. But it would be worth it. . . .

In the meantime, he must concentrate on the discussions with DiNardo. An out-and-out offensive alliance aimed at extirpating Castellan was unfortunately out of the question—Kang continued to nurse dynastic hopes, for whose fulfillment his son-in-law was indispensable. But as for the Mu Arae Sector, the plan was shaping up nicely. One essential detail remained, though. He must convince DiNardo that the way his master could win Medina's undying gratitude, and thus a guarantee of security, was to present the Grand Admiral with the person—alive or dead—of Torval Bogdan.

CHAPTER SIXTEEN
The Mu Arae Sector, 3930 C.E.

The shuttle eased through the atmosphere screen and settled onto its landing jacks, silhouetted against Hespera's cloud-swirling blue curvature and the starry firmament beyond. Jomo Achebe, a brigadier general now, saluted along with the others as his mentor emerged.

He eyed the advancing figure covertly. An anagathic regimen commenced well into middle age could only do so much, and Torval Bogdan had recently celebrated ("If that's the word," he'd joked) his sixty-eighth birthday. His beard was now showing less of its old chestnut ruddiness than the gray that was also invading his temples. And networks of wrinkles radiated from the corners of his eyes, deepening with his frequent grins. But his body had lost nothing of its massive strength.

"Is everything in readiness?" he asked when the greetings were complete and they were all proceeding down the corridor into HIMS *Valiant*'s interior.

"Yes, sir," Vice Admiral Harad affirmed. "All units are prepared for departure. Of course, more are on the way from elsewhere in the sector. If we could wait—"

"We've been over this already, Admiral. We have to strike now. If we had all the time in the universe, we could send to Admiral Castellan for reinforcements. But we can't delay our departure."

"Assuming," Achebe muttered from behind him, "that *you* have to go at all."

Torval gave a twinkling glance over his shoulder without slowing down. "We've been over that too, Jomo. I've got to take personal command. This is too important."

Is that really the reason? Achebe silently asked. But he couldn't argue with the general's impulse, whatever might lie behind it, for he felt it himself. After all the years of indecisive sparring, things were moving again.

The fleet Medina had sent against the Mu Arae Sector hadn't been strong enough to represent a serious attempt at conquest, but it had been too big to be written off as a mere reconnaissance in force. It had appeared at Mu Arae itself hard on the heels of the news of its capture of the outlying system of DM -51 10924. There had been some fairly heavy fighting on the system's outskirts, but the attackers had broken sooner than they should have, and fled with more evidence of confusion than they ought to have displayed.

Achebe was still trying to frame an appropriate reply when the gaggle of officers reached the conference room. "Er, General," Harad spoke hastily, "while you were in transit from the surface, a . . . visitor arrived. He's waiting for us."

"What 'visitor,' Admiral?" Even as he spoke, Torval strode through doors that barely slid away fast enough, and saw the answer to his question sitting at the table.

"Greetings, General Bogdan." The Intelligence Director rose smoothly to his feet. "Admiral Castellan sends his greetings as well. At the time your report of the probing attack against Mu Arae arrived, I was very fortuitously available to come here at once. And my private craft was able to complete the transit before your departure."

"And to penetrate practically to within weapons range of Hespera before being detected," Harad muttered *sotto voce*.

Torval didn't comment, for he recalled how the Intelligence Director's ship had done the same on its rendezvous with Basil's refugee fleet in 3912, and he wasn't disposed to do any finger pointing. He advanced with outstretched hand to greet the entity whose true nature he, alone among those present, knew. The room was a little warm—just about time for the air conditioning to come back on, Torval surmised—and the palm of the hand that took his had just the right sheen of perspiration.

He had never really come to terms with the Intelligence Director. He didn't evince Sonja's prickliness around the android, but that was simply a matter of temperament. In his own easygoing, placid way he shared fully her unease in the presence of an artificial being who could pass for human and reach into humans' minds. And knowing what stood behind that being did nothing to alleviate that unease. But for the last eighteen years the Intelligence Director had proved his worth over and over again, and his loyalty had never once been called into question. So Sonja and Torval had no rational basis for their misgivings . . . only their ancestors' unanimous voices, echoing down half a millennium.

But Basil trusted the Intelligence Director. For Torval, at least, that was enough.

"I imagine you've brought orders from Admiral Castellan," he said after the greetings were completed and everyone was settling down around the table.

"I have a message, of course, but no detailed orders. Admiral Castellan has complete confidence in your judgment, and wishes to give you the widest latitude to conduct operations on the basis of your firsthand knowledge of conditions on this front." Torval nodded. It sounded like Basil, who'd always recognized the futility of micromanagement across interstellar distances, even with tachyon communications. "He requests—and, he emphasizes, it really *is* a request—that you allow me to accompany the expedition."

Something in the Intelligence Director's intonation caused Torval's ears to prick with recognition. "This was your idea, not Basil's, wasn't it?"

"It was my suggestion, but Admiral Castellan agreed that my presence might be beneficial. Let me reiterate that this

is, in Admiral Castellan's words, 'Your show.' I am not here
to oversee your conduct of operations, only to give you any
advice you may require of me, within the limits of my ability."

It was, Torval reflected, almost certainly true. Basil would
never send a political commissar to look over his shoulder.
And the Intelligence Director might indeed be useful. . . .
A shiver slid along Torval's flesh as he recalled the full extent
of that usefulness. He dismissed the feeling, almost angry
with himself. "Of course, Director. Welcome aboard. And
now, let's begin." The meeting fell smoothly into order. "I
believe, Director, that you're fairly up to date as to what's
happened here."

"My most recent information is that contained in your
tachyon transmission to Admiral Castellan, describing the
attack on this system and your repulse of it."

"Then you know the essential facts. Since then, we've
assembled this task force, and our intelligence analysts have
confirmed our initial impression of brittleness in the
attacking forces." Torval's eyes took on an eagerness that
couldn't have escaped a far less acute observer than the
Intelligence Director. "It suggests that Medina's forces have
never really recovered from Redcliffe, that we're still riding
a moral ascendancy that's worth battleships. If that's true—
if they still have no stomach for fighting us—we need to
follow up with an immediate counterattack to retake DM
-51 10924."

"Which, I presume, is why you are pressing for an early
departure, without waiting for reinforcements from Admiral
Castellan," the Intelligence Director observed neutrally.

"Exactly. Everything about their behavior indicates a
breakdown of morale. We can't delay in taking advantage
of that."

"Well, General, no one—least of all Admiral Castellan
or myself—could dispute that clearing the enemy out of
the Mu Arae Sector lies within the scope of your discretion."

"I'm gratified to hear you say so, Director. And now," Torval
continued, swinging around to face the assembled officers,
"let's turn our attention to whatever organizational details

haven't been hammered out. General Achebe, as commander of the planetary assault component, I believe you and Admiral Harad have exchanged a few memos concerning the allocation of units to escort the transports. . . ."

"So they destroyed it," Torval said heavily, looking around the table. It was the same group in the same conference room, but *Valiant* lay in DM -51 10924, a system now cleared of enemies. It was an M0v red dwarf, notable only for the tachyon beam array that had orbited it until very recently.

"Yes, sir," Harad reported. "As soon as it became clear to them that they couldn't hold this system against us, they immediately shifted to tactics intended only to hold us off until the array could be obliterated." He looked as appalled as Torval felt. The vital, fabulously expensive installations had an aura of near sanctity. Medina's subordinates had flouted an unwritten law of such force that it had never needed to be written.

I know what Basil will say. Something about what stage the collapse of our social consensus has reached. Torval sighed. It had been a lot simpler before Basil had started him thinking about such things. He dismissed the thought, the better to concentrate on what they'd learned from the direction of the enemy's retreat.

The Intelligence Director prompted him, as though reading his mind—a thought he didn't care to dwell on. "So, General, they withdrew toward Danubia?" The DM - 46 11370 system had a habitable planet, and the android followed custom by using its name as shorthand for the system.

"Yes, Director." Torval spoke a command and a holo display hovered over the center of the table. It showed the Mu Arae Sector, the Imperial core stars around Sol, and everything between. DM -46 11370 flickered for attention. Beyond it lay the long-settled, populous Ophiuchus systems . . . and beyond those, Sol.

"There's no long-established Fleet base there. This suggests that Medina has recently been constructing one—

a supposition which various intelligence indicators seem to support. The new installation's location, and the fact that Medina has tried to conceal its existence, suggest in turn that it's intended as a forward base for operations against this sector—operations which they seem to have launched a little prematurely. Now, with the forces based there retiring on it in confusion, we have a priceless opportunity to seize the system."

Harad cleared his throat. "General, I hardly need point out that this involves us in an excursion beyond the boundaries of the Mu Arae Sector. I respectfully suggest that we solicit Admiral Castellan's permission before embarking on a course of action which arguably exceeds your discretion."

"Fortunately, Admiral, we have Admiral Castellan's personal representative with us." Torval turned back to the Intelligence Director. "In your view, does an attack on Danubia lie within the scope of my authority to do whatever is necessary to assure the security of the Mu Arae Sector?"

For a moment, not long enough to seem awkward to the others, Torval held the android's flawless eyes. The Intelligence Director had always honored his pledge to respect the mental privacy of the three who knew his secret. (*As far as we know,* some voice snickered at the back of Torval's mind.) But now Torval's eyes spoke, without benefit of telepathy, the words he could not say aloud in the presence of people other than Basil and Sonja. *Your plan has always called for me to advance from Mu Arae against Sol while Basil moves on Sigma Draconis by the old rebel route. And this new base of Medina's is right on my axis of advance! By taking it, I won't just eliminate an obstacle; I'll put us one step ahead, because it can become our advance base.*

"Admiral Castellan undoubtedly had this kind of contingency in mind when he agreed to send me, General." The Intelligence Director's face took on a judicious look. "In my considered judgment, the operation you are proposing falls well within the scope of providing for this sector's defense. After all, an enemy base at Danubia represents a standing threat to Mu Arae. Admiral Castellan has no intention of holding you to an unworkably narrow interpretation of your orders. I am certain that this would be—*will* be—his position."

"Thank you, Director. And now," Torval addressed the meeting, "let's—"

"General, if I may . . ." Achebe had the look of a man about to advance into a field of fire. "I naturally accept the Intelligence Director's interpretation of your authority— and besides, I'd follow your orders regardless. But the real question we have to ask ourselves isn't about jurisdiction; it's about prudence." Ignoring the sudden deepening of the room's silence, he indicated the holo map. "We've left Mu Arae lightly defended—almost as much so as the other systems in the sector. This has been acceptable up to now because we've gone less than five point four light-years away from it; we can hurry back if necessary. But now you're proposing to take us well outside the sector, nearly twenty light-years from Mu Arae!"

"Come on, Jomo! You've read the intelligence analysis. The offensive whose remnants we're chasing can't possibly be just a feint to draw us away. Medina's done a lot of rebuilding since Redcliffe, but not *that* much!"

Achebe's dark face remained unmoved by Torval's jollying tone. "With all respect, sir, I still don't like it."

Torval sighed. "I tell you what. *Marconi* is on the way here." The great ship with its collapsible tachyon beam array—Basil had made it a high priority to construct more of the class, despite their hideous cost, so Torval had been able to get one—had been sent for as soon as they had realized what had been done to this system's array. "We'll send her to take up position halfway between Mu Arae and Danubia—as you pointed out, they're just *under* twenty light-years apart, so it will work. Mu Arae will be able to notify us at once of any emergency. How's that?"

"A tachyon beam may travel instantaneously, sir, but our ships don't. And they'll have twenty light-years to cross if

they're needed at Mu Arae." Achebe took a deep breath.
"I respectfully recommend that we wait until Mu Arae is
strongly held before commencing this operation."

"You mean until reinforcements have arrived there?"
Torval shook his head. "But that will take time, Jomo. And
time is precisely what we haven't got. We need to strike
hard while we've got them off balance. If we wait, Medina
may do some reinforcing of his own! By the time we finally
decide we feel right about attacking Danubia, we may just
find that it's been made impregnable."

"Sir, with great respect—"

"Jomo, just say what's on your mind and stop telling me
how much respect you're saying it with." For the first time,
a note of testiness had entered Torval's voice.

Achebe's face went absolutely expressionless. *Sir, are you
absolutely certain the arguments you've given us are your
real reasons for doing this?* he asked silently. *Or do you
feel—even though no one else does—that you need to
somehow redeem yourself for the fact that Medina got away
at Redcliffe by exploiting the decency that makes you what
you are?* But of course he couldn't say that aloud. So his
eyes slid away from Torval's. "Nothing, sir. You're right, of
course."

Torval's gaze lingered, puzzled, for another moment. Then
he spoke briskly, hauling the meeting into focus on specifics,
and his voice held relief that a confrontation he didn't
understand had been avoided.

DM -46 11370 was a binary, its components separated
widely enough for planets to have coalesced around both.
Danubia, the second planet of the G8v primary star, was
small and chilly as life-bearing worlds went; but it had
required only minimal terraforming and had been a
moderately prosperous backwater since the early Federation
period. The M0v secondary component, though, had never
held anything of interest . . . until recently.

At Medina's command, a new base had been tunneled
out under the dark surface of a gas-giant moon. Now that

base's location was marked by a lake of cooling radioactive lava. Torval watched the moon and its orange-banded primary recede in the view-aft screen of *Valiant's* flag bridge, already too distant for that leprous glowing patch to be visible.

They had broken Medina's deep-space forces on the system's outskirts, but the base had proven an unexpectedly tough nut to crack. Achebe's Marines had gone down in a swarm of assault shuttles and blasted their way in. For a while, portable high-energy weapons had turned the subsurface maze of corridors into a claustrophobic segment of hell. Then energy sensors had detected the destabilizing reactor which any successful invaders were meant to inherit. The Marines had disengaged with desperate haste, and almost all of them had gotten away before the final cataclysm that had consumed the surviving defenders. But some hadn't, and Achebe had been a man-shaped mass of tightly contained fury as they'd set out to cross the forty-plus AU gulf which separated the red dwarf from the primary star at this point of its eccentric orbit.

"Well, General," the Intelligence Director remarked, breaking into Torval's thoughts, "I suppose we shall have to do without that base."

"True, Director. But we'll build a new one on some lifeless asteroid or moon of the primary." Torval turned to the view forward and pointed to the deep-yellow spark dead ahead. Even as he spoke, it started to wax visibly as they left the gas giant's Chen Limit and engaged their drives.

"Yes, after we complete the destruction of the mobile forces that have withdrawn into orbit around Danubia. The system includes a number of suitable bodies. And any of them are more convenient than the companion star's system."

"Why do you suppose Medina built it there?" Torval wondered out loud.

"Who can say? The only real advantage from their standpoint seems to be that we had to attend to it first and then make the transit to Danubia itself. It is almost as though the aim was to keep us occupied here as long as possible."

"But why . . . ?" Torval's question trailed off, and he shook his head to clear it of the annoying doubts and nameless apprehensions he'd begun to feel whenever the Intelligence Director was nearby.

"What's this all about?"

The staff flinched from Torval's very uncharacteristic bark, and he reined himself in. From an early age—even before leaving his home planet, for he was a big man even by its standards, and far more so afterwards—he'd developed his trademark affability to facilitate dealing with people, most of whom were intimidated by his size. "As you were, everyone," he said in the best approximation of his usual tone his tension would allow. He took his seat at the table and they all followed suit. "Now, what's so important that I had to be sent for?"

He knew it sounded irritable, but he couldn't help it. The enemy had stopped retreating well short of Danubia and shown fight in the systems's outer reaches. Harad had transferred his flag to the battleship *Intrepid* and led most of the fighting ships in the ensuing battle, while Torval had remained aboard *Valiant* with the troop transports and their escorts, in overall command. The struggle had been harder than expected, but now the remnants of Medina's force had limped sullenly back into Danubia's Chen Limit, under the cover of the planet's orbital and surface-based firepower, and a lull had set in as Harad closed in for the kill. It was a lull that couldn't last much longer, and Torval didn't need distractions. He also didn't need the disturbing undercurrent he detected. It wasn't panic, but neither was it what he should be sensing from these officers in the midst of what showed every sign of being a victorious battle.

Achebe, who'd been deep in conversation with the intelligence types when Torval had entered, stood up and cleared his throat. "Sir, long-range sensors have detected a strong enemy force positioning itself outside this system." He activated the briefing room's holo tank. The Danubia binary system appeared as a single icon, on a scale too small to show the components' separation. Off to one side was another icon—scarlet, for hostile forces. Torval observed the display's orientation, and Achebe's next words were superfluous. "They're not directly behind us on the line of advance we've followed from Mu Arae. Instead, they're in the direction of Admiral Castellan's central systems, as though to prevent us from going there."

"Strength estimates?"

"Necessarily sketchy at this point, sir. This is the best we can do." Columns of words and numbers appeared, floating in the tank. It was, Torval reflected, not an overwhelming force. But it was one which could give his own a stiff fight. If that fight lasted any length of time and involved any extended maneuvers, the hostile ships from here at Danubia could perhaps catch up from astern, tipping the balance.

He began to understand the room's atmosphere of edgy incomprehension.

"What are they doing there?" he asked no one in particular. "We don't *want* to go in that direction. If they'd put that force into this system, chances are better than even that they could have held us off. Why are they sitting in that particular location, where they're useless?"

"Unknown, sir." Achebe looked as perplexed as Torval felt. "Perhaps they have some idea of letting us take this system, then closing in behind us—"

"But they're not in sufficient strength to guarantee the success of a move like that."

"True, sir. The only other apparent rationale for their behavior is to prevent us from retiring from this system in any direction except back to Mu Arae."

"But that's exactly where we'd want to go if we got in any trouble out here! Why should they want to . . . herd us in that direction?" Torval's face wore an unaccustomed scowl of black abstraction. "You know," he rumbled after a moment, "there's another aspect to the question of what they're doing there. That force took finite time to assemble, and to get where it is now it must have departed from Sol before we even reached this system—even earlier if it came from Sigma Draconis. They're there for some *preplanned* reason."

An uncomfortable shuffling surrounded the table. Clearly, this view of the matter was new to these people. New, and unwelcome.

The communicator on the bulkhead behind Achebe beeped for attention. He put it on conference, and the voice of *Valiant's* communications officer filled the room as her face appeared on the screen. "Excuse me, General, but Admiral Harad reports that his battleships have begun to engage the defenses of Danubia at extended missile range. His lighter elements are proceeding inward and will be engaged shortly."

"Thank you." Torval addressed the meeting. "Well, that's that. We're committed now, whatever those ships are up to. We'll just have to defer the question." He rose, and everyone else followed suit. "I'll be on the flag bridge if—"

The communicator beeped again. Achebe muttered his irritation. "What is it?"

The communications officer's voice was oddly different this time. "Sir, we've just been contacted by *Marconi*. Her captain is on, and he . . . he says it's extremely urgent."

"Patch him through," Torval commanded. The comm station was set up to instantaneously convert the tachyon transmission into the electronic medium of the ship's intercom, and the next voice they heard came, in realtime, from a light-decade away. The face on the screen that accompanied it was that of a man commanding his voice and features to steadiness.

"General, we've received a transmission from Mu Arae, at a time corresponding to standard . . . well, never mind, sir. It was just now. The gist of it . . ." For a moment, the face's expressionlessness seemed about to dissolve, before being clamped into place again. "They reported that a fleet of overwhelming strength has entered the Mu Arae system from the direction of Lambda Serpenti. Our forces were resisting, but without realistic hope of success. The transmission was cut off abruptly. We surmise that the attackers made the system's tachyon beam array their first priority target." The voice stopped abruptly, dropping into a well of reverberating silence. "Ah, General," *Marconi's* captain resumed, as though feeling duty-bound to fill that silence, "we naturally recorded the message. Would you like me to—"

"That won't be necessary, Captain." Torval's bass was even deeper than usual, near the lower limit for a human voice. "Just download it so I can access it later. Thank you." He gestured to Achebe, who cut the connection.

The silence continued for a few heartbeats of denial before Achebe tossed a pebble into its stillness. "How could Medina have gotten a force back there without—"

"It wasn't Medina. Didn't you hear what he said about where this fleet came from?" Torval swept the meeting with his eyes but encountered only the blankness of shock. "Lambda Serpenti," he prompted.

It finally sank home. Lambda Serpenti. Kang's capital system.

The silence broke all at once, as though a dam had given way, loosing a torrent of voices.

"But that means—"

"Mu Arae gone? But—"

"Treachery—"

"That bastard Kang—"

"As you were!" Torval's voice smashed the incipient hysteria flat. "This is precisely when we need to stay calm. Brigadier Achebe, have comm raise Admiral Harad and order him to break off the engagement immediately."

"That could be easier said than done, sir."

"Can't be helped. We're on our way back to Mu Arae."

"Sir?" Achebe seemed to be recovering faster than the rest, but he still shook his head like a punch-drunk boxer. "But, sir, on the basis of what we've just heard we have to consider the possibility that Mu Arae has . . . has. . . ."

"Fallen," Torval finished for him bluntly. "Right. And the longer we delay, the longer Kang has to dig in and fortify the system against us. If we can get back there while the situation is still fluid, we may have a chance of taking the system back. And if we can do that fast enough, we'll have a little time to do our own entrenching against what's coming next."

"Sir?" Achebe looked lost. So did everyone else.

Torval sighed. They hadn't figured it out yet. Perhaps they hadn't let themselves figure it out. "Think about it, Jomo. Do you really think Kang simply took advantage of our absence from Mu Arae *after* hearing about it? Even if he'd learned of this expedition immediately, he couldn't possibly have organized the attack in so little time. He must have known in *advance* that we were going to be drawn away." He pressed on quickly, before the dawning realization in their faces could ignite into a rage that would render them useless. "The final proof is this task force of Medina's that we've just detected. Now we know why he wants to prevent us from going anywhere but Mu Arae; he knew that Mu Arae would be in Kang's hands . . . because they've been in collusion!" He paused, but only briefly. "The only advantage we have is that Medina's force is a little farther from Mu Arae than we are. We can get there first—but only if we depart immediately. Now get that message to Harad."

He drove them mercilessly, ordering food to be brought in as they worked in a fury of concentrated effort to organize the hurried departure, interrupted occasionally by reports from Harad detailing the messy disengagement and subsequent fending off of nuisance attacks from Danubia's reprieved defenders. He kept them at it for hours, using unremitting toil as a weapon to hold the appalling knowledge of what had happened, and what probably awaited them, at bay. Only when the twin stars of Danubia were receding in the view aft at the impossible rate the drive made possible did he dismiss them.

As he walked back to his quarters, not even Torval's exhaustion could numb his sensibilities to the change that pervaded the ship. People he passed huddled in furtive groups, conversing in hushed tones until they saw him coming. The very air seemed heavy with gloom and despair. *Why,* he wondered through his fatigue, *have I never noticed what a dismal place the inside of a capital ship is?* The endless gray corridors, the inadequate lighting, the ponderous inhuman scale of everything . . . It was like a stage setting for tragedy. *Only this is real,* his thoughts went lugubriously on. *A play with no conclusion, a nightmare from which there'll be no awakening . . .*

"General, could I have a word?"

He turned and regarded the solitary figure, silhouetted against a light at the far end of the corridor. The Intelligence Director hadn't been present with the staff, but Torval had, at some point in the hours of dreary toil, ordered that he be apprised of the situation. *How did he know to look for me here?* Torval was too weary to take an interest in the question.

"General," the android asked in emotionless—but not *too* emotionless—tones, "am I correct in surmising that Admiral Castellan knows nothing of what had happened at Mu Arae?"

"I don't see how he could, Director. The tachyon beam array there would naturally have informed us first—and it was apparently captured or destroyed during that transmission, since the message was cut off."

"So I had gathered. And am I further correct in thinking *Marconi* is not so positioned as to be able to transmit to any of his systems."

"No, it's not. We've been advancing in the wrong direction for that." Torval shook his head slowly—it seemed heavier than usual. *I've got to get some sleep.* "I'll have to send a courier boat."

"But such a vessel will have to pass Grand Admiral Medina's covering force, will it not? It occurs to me that my personal craft—which, as you know, has rather special stealth capabilities—would have a better chance of success than a normal courier."

A moment passed before Torval replied. He knew what

he would have thought of a human who'd made such a suggestion, but human standards of conduct simply couldn't be applied to this entity. *Although, come to think of it, an artificial intelligence this sophisticated must have an equivalent of the self-preservation urge—unless it has a suicide imperative like that of robotic missiles, and it could probably rationalize its way around that.* . . . Torval cut the thought off, annoyed with himself. It was pointless to pass judgment, especially considering that the android was right. "Yes, of course. Besides, Admiral Castellan would want you back. I'll prepare a message for you to convey to him. And now, if you'll excuse me—"

"One moment, General. I know you must be desperately in need of sleep. But before I depart it is important that I speak to you in private. It is, in fact, essential."

Startlement pushed the encroaching dark waves of weariness back from Torval's consciousness, for the Intelligence Director had spoken with a certain indefinable tone he'd never heard him use before. "Uh, it's not much further to my quarters. Come along."

They proceeded up a lift tube and along a short corridor in a silence which remained unbroken until they were seated in Torval's office/living area. They faced each other in a lamp-light too dim to dispel the slowly drifting stars outside the armorplast transparency.

The android spoke without preamble. "What do you intend to do once you reach Mu Arae, Admiral? I suspect you haven't been completely forthright with your subordinates."

"No, of course I haven't." For a time, Torval was silent in the starlight. "I suppose I'll do whatever it takes to get at least some of the transports close enough to Hespera for a surface assault. It's too rich and important a planet for Kang or even Medina to sterilize it from orbit. Once we're down and in control, they'll have to send their own Marines in after us. In that kind of fight, maybe we can hold out long enough for . . ." His voice trailed off. Long enough for what? Help from Basil, who probably would only just have heard he'd been stabbed in the back by Kang? *But what else can I do?*

The Intelligence Director didn't force him to resume. "Yes, I surmised something of the sort. It fits with . . ." The sentence remained uncompleted. There was no need to complete it.

"So you knew." It wasn't a question.

"Only in very general terms, concerning outcomes." The android cocked his head. "You don't seem angry."

Torval shrugged in his massive way. "What would be the point?"

"None, of course." The perfect artificial voice took on a didactic tone. "Omega Prime's limited foreknowledge is itself a part of the structure of reality. It in no way compromises the immutability of the future. The events of which Omega Prime has knowledge *will* come to pass, and any attempt to prevent them will fail—*something* will make it fail."

"Then what's the use? Why is Omega Prime even trying, if it's all so hopeless?"

"To the contrary. Omega Prime recognizes that, as I have intimated, it has become to some degree *responsible* for the future whose outlines it can dimly discern. It is working toward a goal. And the present course of events is an integral part of that goal."

For several heartbeats Torval's hazel-green eyes met the Intelligence Director's amber ones. "So it's all been a lie from the first. Omega Prime never really intended to help Basil at all."

"By no means! Omega Prime's objective is as it was declared to Admiral Castellan . . . although the declaration was, unavoidably, incomplete. But what is happening to you now is necessary for the achievement of that objective."

Torval wore the look of a man who'd passed beyond resentment, beyond rage, even beyond despair, and emerged into an eerily calm realm of simple incomprehension. "I don't understand," he whispered.

"Naturally not. Omega Prime, with thousands of years at its disposal, is often unable to make sense of the messages it receives from the future for lack of context; you can hardly be expected to do better in a far shorter time." The android was silent for a moment, as though gathering his thoughts. Not until later did it occur to Torval that he'd never known him to take such a pause.

"Do you recall," the too-perfect voice finally said with seeming irrelevance, "your first encounter with Omega Prime?"

"Of course. It was when the New Humans had captured Basil, and Sonja and I were searching for him. We found him in Omega Prime's system."

"Yes. You had to leave in haste. But you spent one night within Omega Prime's physical housing."

"Yes, we did, didn't we?" A cloud passed across Torval's face. "I'd almost forgotten that night. Weirdest damned dreams . . ."

"But the recollections are still there, waiting to be awakened." The Intelligence Director leaned forward and spoke with quiet intensity. "I have never attempted unpermitted telepathic contact with any of the three of you. But I now ask your permission to do so."

Centuries of cultural taboos came roaring to the surface. "Why?"

"Because only thus can I grant you your wish to understand what is happening, and why it is necessary. And . . . the need is not only yours, Torval. I find that my own need to give you this is as great as your need for the gift."

When Torval could finally speak, what came out was perhaps the last thing he'd intended: "But you're a machine."

"A very complex machine."

"Aren't we all?" Torval found he hadn't lost the ability to smile after all. He took a deep breath. "Very well. Come ahead."

Time passed, and nothing moved except the drifting stars. The two of them sat silently in the light of those stars, and anyone seeing them might have wondered if they were alive.

Gradually, Torval's expression changed. All the despair, bewilderment and hurt seeped out. "So *that's* it," he breathed.

The Intelligence Director nodded. "Now you understand . . . and you know what I must do next."

"Yes. Of course."

Lavrenti Kang had set up his headquarters in the ruins of Bronson's Landing. As he emerged from the nano-grown bubble he sniffed fastidiously at the fumes that the wind hadn't yet dissipated. Overhead, a ring of contra-grav fighting vehicles floated aloft, guarding a perimeter marked on the ground by combat-armored Marines with semiportable weapons. Beyond, the ranks of blackened skeletons that had been gleaming towers stretched away into the distance like the gaunt, sooty remains of a forest fire. The afternoon sun glowed though the drifting smoke, appropriately blood-red.

Kang looked around at his staffers in search of an absent face. His scowl cleared as Juliana Moresin approached, wearing a space service jumpsuit that looked a little less incongruous than her master's service dress tunic and trousers. He returned her salute, raising an arm whose sleeve bore the golden spiral galaxy of a "high admiral."

"Is it over?" he asked without preamble. The curtness wasn't his usual style. But he'd passed some anxious moments.

"Yes, sir." Moresin had shared his anxiety. Bogdan's ships had driven inexorably inward, spending themselves to get the assault transports into orbit around Hespera and keep them alive in that orbit long enough to send their Marines down to the surface. Her most anxious moment of all had come when she'd learned that Bogdan himself was leading them, in what had to be history's only instance of a full general donning powered combat armor and riding a grav repulsor down with the first wave. "Grand Admiral Medina's fleet has mopped up those of their fighting ships that fled to the outer system, and we've reduced their last groundside strong points—at considerable cost," she added pointedly. The attack's ferocity had been exceeded only by its tactical finesse. Against even remotely even odds, it would have succeeded. Moresin wasn't sure Kang fully appreciated that.

"Good," he acknowledged offhandedly. "And were my special orders carried out?"

"Yes sir. He was taken alive . . . despite the cost and difficulty that entailed."

Kang gave her a sharp look, which she met levelly. If the truth were known, she hadn't particularly begrudged those orders. They somehow reconciled her to this operation, about which she'd had decidedly mixed feelings from the start.

"This should be him now," she added, catching sight of a combat aircar, glinting as the westering sun broke through a rift in the smoke. It settled to the area cleared from the wrecked cityscape and a pair of guards emerged, flanking a figure who dwarfed them.

Kang gazed curiously at Torval Bogdan, whom he'd never met face to face. He was dressed only in a tattered, soiled liner for the powered armor from which he'd been forcibly removed after it had been immobilized. His left arm hung, shattered and useless, and the right side of his head was marked by a streak of burned flesh. But the drugs that held the pain at bay had not reduced him to walking in a stuporous shuffle. He somehow made the Security men flanking him seem his escorts rather than his guards.

"General Bogdan," Kang began with an ingratiating smile, "I sincerely regret that we're not meeting under better circumstances. The difficulties caused by Admiral Castellan's illegal maintenance of a military presence here in the Mu Arae Sector have in no wise detracted from my long-standing admiration for you."

"My replies to your offers to buy me must not have been accurately reported to you."

"To the contrary. And while you might have been a little more tactful about my character, I was impressed by your integrity—it's a quality all too rare these days. It made me want all the more to persuade you that your best interests lie with me. So much so that I'm prepared to ignore Grand Admiral Medina's request that I turn you over to him. I

want you to know that my most recent offer is still open."
He paused as though awaiting awestruck appreciation of
his magnanimity. The pause stretched embarrassingly.

"Don't be an idiot, Bogdan," Moresin spoke up.
Unadmitted concern harshened her voice. "Remaining in
Castellan's service is no longer an option for you. To be
exact, you have two alternatives: accepting a command from
High Admiral Kang, or being turned over to Medina!"

"I won't deny that I have an ulterior motive," Kang put
in. "It is my earnest hope that you can help me maintain—
or, perhaps, reestablish—good relations with Admiral
Castellan. As an old friend, you should be able to make
clear to him my desire to continue our understanding, so
that together we can counterbalance Medina. You realize,
of course, I'm only cooperating with Medina on a temporary
basis, and only because Admiral Castellan had left me no
alternative if I was to assert my undeniable legal rights to . . ."
Something in Torval's hazel-green eyes told Kang that a
political speech was contraindicated at the moment, and
he changed tack. "So you see, you won't be betraying Admiral
Castellan by taking service with me, for his interests and
mine coincide. Indeed, you'll be in a position to help him
understand this."

Torval was silent for a moment as he gazed at them—or
seemed to, for in fact he was seeing Achebe die in the mud,
screaming his lungs out from inside the powered armor
with which a dis grenade had partially merged him in a
horrid amalgam of flesh and metal and agony. Then his
memory continued to scroll mercilessly backwards, and he
was watching his fleet die little by little as it had swept
into the Mu Arae system, blasting its way through Kang's
forces as Medina's had closed in from astern. But then that
montage of images also receded, and all that was left in
his mind's eye were two faces.

*Basil and Sonja. It always comes back to the two of you—
the three of us. Even now. Especially now, as I set in motion
your destruction.*

The hell of it is, I can't even really feel regret for what

I'm about to do, because I know it's necessary and inevitable. But I can feel sorrow. And I do wish I could see you one more time.

Farewell. Try to be somewhat happy in the little time that remains to you. But I'm probably robbing you even of that.

He relinquished the memory of them, and their faces were gone, and he was back in the smoky air of this smashed city on this world Basil had entrusted to his care, looking at a very different set of faces. Kang's was expectant, Moresin's was anxious, Raj DiNardo's was opaquely bland. He ignored the staffers behind them, and his eyes seemed to wander as he covertly studied his two guards. They weren't armored—no need for them to be—and they carried carbine-sized paralysis guns. Beyond them, around the perimeter of this cleared space, were armored Marines. *Yes, I can see how it has to happen.*

His eyes ceased their wandering and met Kang's squarely. He spoke in a voice that was strangely conversational, almost casual. "Kang, you're not even slime. You're nothing. Your offer is as far beneath contempt as you are. In fact—"

And in mid-sentence, without a warning pause, he moved in a blur, with a speed that seemed impossible given his injuries. His right arm snapped up, pushing one guard's paralysis carbine up into a nose-breaking impact with the man's face. At the same instant, his left foot shot out and caught the other guard on the kneecap of his left leg, which collapsed under him. Torval swung to his right, reaching out with his good hand. He snatched the second guard's paralysis carbine as he fell screaming, reversed it, and smashed its stock into the belly of the guard whose nose he'd shattered. Then he hurled the weapon—it wasn't very sturdy, and the use to which he'd put it had doubtless ruined it—in the direction of Kang and the group around him. And, with a roar in a language none of them knew, he charged after it, massive right hand outstretched toward the stunned high admiral's throat.

The Marine sentries had no time to think, so they let

trained reflexes operate their weapons—gauss rifles, and one squad-support plasma gun—for them. It was instantly over.

As the thunderous plasma gun's echoes reverberated away into a shocked silence, Kang staggered to his feet. He stared at the place where Torval had been, and at what was there now. Incredibly, the face was still recognizable. For a long time, the only sound was that of DiNardo retching.

Moresin's voice finally penetrated Kang's consciousness. "This is very bad, sir."

"What? Oh . . . oh, yes. We never intended this." He forced his mind to function. He really had wanted Bogdan to join him, help patch things up with Castellan. Then he would have been able to defy Medina's demand. Failing that, he would have acceded to that demand and turned the prisoner over to Medina—alive. The last had been very important. . . .

"Sir!" A staff officer's voice intruded into his brown study. "Grand Admiral Medina's personal shuttle is on the way."

"*What?* Medina? Himself?"

"Yes, sir. He's here with his fleet." The staffer had a hurried exchange with someone via his wrist communicator. "He's . . . requesting permission to land here."

Demanding, you mean. "Delay him! Something about air traffic control." Kang looked around wildly and found DiNardo, wiping his mouth and making futile tidying motions at the blood and other substances that had spattered his tunic. Kang grasped him unceremoniously and shook him. "What are we going to do?"

DiNardo kept his face averted from what lay on the ground. "Well, sir, there may be a way to cut our losses in this matter. Remember, our strategy was based from the first on Castellan's close friendship with Bogdan. That was why we ruled out killing Bogdan; our assessment was that such an act might well provoke Castellan to seek vengeance even at the expense of his own astropolitical interests. On the other hand, to let *Medina* kill him and bring the same nemesis down on his own head could only have been to our advantage."

"Yes, yes, I know all this! But that strategy is no longer practical." Kang glanced briefly in the direction DiNardo was avoiding.

"True. Our options have suddenly narrowed, thanks to those muscle-brained guards." DiNardo gave Moresin a supercilious look.

"They were following orders . . . and saving the high admiral's life!" Moresin turned to Kang. "Sir, if any disciplinary action is brought against these Marines, I shall—"

"Of course not, Admiral," Kang soothed. "I realize they were only doing their duty." Nowadays, the military was the only constituency that mattered, even if old-school functionaries like DiNardo hadn't fully grasped that fact. "But, Commodore DiNardo, I believe you were speaking of cutting our losses . . . ?"

"Yes, sir. It's true that we can no longer deliver General Bogdan to Medina *alive*. But I suggest that we grant his landing request, welcome him effusively, and present him with the remains." DiNardo gestured fastidiously in the general direction of those remains. "Thus we can give him unconditional assurance that we've fulfilled our part of the bargain—the term 'dead or alive' was used. We can also muddy the waters concerning the actual responsibility for Bogdan's death, especially if Medina commits any . . . indignities. He's a rather basic type, after all."

"Yes, you've had firsthand experience of him, haven't you?" Kang's features firmed into decision. "Very well. I believe there's merit in your suggestion." He turned to his staff. "Tell Medina to come ahead. And" —a vague wave at the ground— "get *that* into some kind of suitable container."

The Grand Admiral's shuttle settled down alongside the aircar that had brought Bogdan.

As Medina emerged, DiNardo studied him with an objectivity that removal from the prestigious settings of Old Earth permitted. Not even the best tailors—*human* tailors, DiNardo had heard—could disguise the bulge of the Grand

Admiral's midriff, or the puffiness of his face. The dress cloak he wore with space-service uniforms, once a bit of successfully calculated theatricality, was now merely ludicrous.

Among the flunkies who trailed him down the shuttle's ramp, DiNardo recognized the thin colorless one in carefully nondescript civilian clothes. He felt mixed emotions. Felix Nims was a revolting creature, but he was at least a worthy sparring partner. They exchanged the pleasantries of old professional acquaintances as they joined the crowd filing into the headquarters dome and settling in with the varied liquor supply DiNardo had advised Kang to lay in.

"So, Admiral Kang," Medina asked pointedly as he commenced his second drink (the first had been tossed off almost instantaneously), "have you succeeded in accounting for General Bogdan—one way or another?"

Kang's lips thinned, but he held his tongue and gestured to DiNardo to speak for him.

"We have, Grand Admiral. In fact, we took him alive."

"Splendid! I trust he's available to be delivered into my custody, as per our understanding."

"Unfortunately, he was killed afterwards in the course of an attempt on High Admiral Kang's life."

"How appalling!" Medina didn't even bother to conceal the nature of his smile. "*Admiral* Kang is to be congratulated on his survival, as well as on his success in asserting the jurisdiction over the Mu Arae Sector that His Imperial Majesty has granted him—subject to the established Fleet chain of command which I have the honor to head."

Kang looked about to explode, and DiNardo spoke hurriedly. "*High* Admiral Kang is still prepared to perform his side of the understanding. As it happens, General Bogdan's physical remains can be readily identified—subject, of course, to easy confirmation by comparing a genetic scan with Fleet records. We are prepared to turn them over to you forthwith."

Felix, hovering nearby, wore the look of an animal scenting undefined danger. "Ah, Grand Admiral, there's no real need

for us to take physical possession of these remains, or even
see them. May I suggest that we leave the identification to
the specialists and—"

"Bah." Medina gulped the rest of his drink and waved
his empty glass. A staffer who seemed to have no other
function brought him a full one. "I don't want to read some
technical report. I want to see him."

"Certainly, Grand Admiral," DiNardo beamed. "Please
come this way." He ushered Medina, Kang and Felix to a
smaller, heavily guarded dome. Within was a lozenge-shaped
slate-blue cryogenic suspension capsule of no great size.·

"It didn't have to be large enough to hold a complete
human body," DiNardo explained, anticipating Medina's
question.

The Grand Admiral chuckled. "And he was such a big
man!" The others dutifully echoed his chuckle. "Open it."

At a gesture from DiNardo, a technician manipulated
controls. About half of the capsule's top surface slid aside.
Preservatives had been applied as well as low temperatures,
and there was no particular odor.

Medina stepped forward alone, for the others showed
no disposition to join him. He leaned over the capsule in
the chill air. Yes, the face was unmistakable. He smiled. . . .

There was no warning. A tiny bioengineered implant
ceased to contain the gas pressure that had been building
up inside it, and with a sound compounded of a puff and a
pop the mouth and nostrils of what had been Torval Bogdan's
face expelled a cloud of vapor, accompanied by a charnel
stench . . . and a number of minute objects.

Medina staggered backwards with a cry, hands to his face.
The others started to move forward to aid him. "Wait!" the
technician snapped, unmindful of exalted rank. "It might
be some kind of harmful agent." Holding his breath, he
ushered Medina away to join the others.

"Grand Admiral, I am overcome with embarrassment,"
DiNardo dithered. "Obviously some ineffectual attempt at
sabotage, which achieved nothing except unpleasantness.
Let us return to the main dome."

"Sir, I think the Grand Admiral should be examined first," the technician cautioned.

"To hell with that," Medina snarled, still compulsively wiping his face. "All I need is a drink." He started for the entrance, then paused and clutched his abdomen. His expression was more of puzzlement than of pain. "Yes, a drink."

But before the evening was over, he was taken, vomiting, to the dispensary.

"But what was it?" DiNardo's usual aplomb was in abeyance. He'd been in that dome too.

Admiral Lahti, the senior medical officer who'd been rushed down from orbit, recognized the nature of DiNardo's concern. "Don't worry about you own safety, Commodore, or that of anyone else who was present. We've determined that the nanoids became dormant almost immediately after the pods released them—faster than it took them to fall to the floor, in fact. The Grand Admiral was the only one close enough to be affected."

"But," Kang jittered, "what kind of nanoids were they? I've never heard of the like. . . ."

Lahti frowned. "Neither have I, High Admiral. All we can say for certain is that the Grand Admiral's genetic code is being rewritten at a rate unique in my experience."

"But surely such a result can't be obtained from something contracted by mere inhalation!"

"That, too, is unique. Perhaps it, as well as the rapid rate, is explained by the extremely crude nature of the genetic information being inserted. The process is completely unrestrained by any consideration for keeping the subject alive. Indeed, killing him is obviously the goal. His vital organs are being metamorphosed into . . . into . . ." Lahti's voice trailed off. She had decades of experience in all the horror this age's technology could wreak on the human body. And she looked faintly ill.

"What activated it? Was it simply timed to go off? Or was it triggered by Medina's proximity?"

"I'm sorry, High Admiral, but that's unknowable. The device was bioengineered, and it's completely degraded by now."

"What are you doing for him?" Felix asked.

"Aside from drugs to ease his torment, we're trying to fight the genetic virus with counter-viruses: benign nanoids of our own which seek to undo the damage. That's why we haven't been able to put him into cryo suspension; his cells have to be active for the—"

"Yes, I know. But isn't that what everybody gets as part of routine immunization?"

"Yes; it's just more of the same, in massive injections." Lahti looked tired. "But it takes time. We may be too late. We've gotten some results, but we may be merely prolonging his agony."

The conversation soon broke up, and Felix walked with apparent aimlessness in the general direction of the hospital dome Lahti had set up for her solitary but very important patient. His thoughts were far away in space and ahead in time.

None of Medina's titles were hereditary, of course. The Dragon Throne itself was the only hereditary office in the Empire; that was firmly established. And even it was imperfectly so, given the Emperor's right to choose his heir from among his relations. His oldest offspring had a rebuttable presumption of heirship, no more.

And Medina has never put Josef aside and made himself Emperor, Felix thought. *He's always been adamant on that point, to Lothar's disgust. But . . . what if he's posthumously declared Emperor? Yes—a retroactive deposing of Josef! Never been done before, of course. But if it is . . .*

He won't have chosen an heir of course. So Lothar inherits . . . instantaneously.

Yes. Lothar can be persuaded. It won't take long. I can set it up while everyone is still milling about in confusion.

His feet, acting on their own, had brought him to the hospital dome. The guards were no problem; the human ones knew him by sight, and the electronic ones had been programmed with his palm print and retinal pattern. Soon he was standing over the bed, telling himself that the external manifestations he was seeing were as nothing compared to what was happening to Medina's internal organs.

The autoinjector was constantly replenishing the relieving army of nanomachines whose function was to restore this formerly-human body's genetic code. Felix disconnected it and began to roll the mass of horror over in a way that would account for the disconnection—a convulsive movement in a moment of returning consciousness, it would be ruled. Even as he was doing so, Medina's awakening pain broke through the wall of sedation.

He couldn't scream; his vocal apparatus had already gone. He could only stare at Felix.

Felix smiled.

CHAPTER SEVENTEEN
Santaclara (Iota Pegasi A IV), 3930 C.E

Vice Admiral Lenore Silva strode around a corner and emerged onto the loggia outside the residential wing. Athena and the Intelligence Director stood in the lengthening shadows by the balustrade overlooking the formal courtyard, deep in a conversation which she brusquely interrupted.

"I've got to see him," she stated without preamble.

"He isn't seeing anyone," Athena replied. "He retired early, and . . ." She didn't need to finish. Basil had been in seclusion a lot since the news of Torval's death had arrived, hard on the heels of the Intelligence Director's return with tidings of the catastrophe at Mu Arae.

Now he didn't even have Sonja with him. She'd departed for New Antilla, to take command of the rapidly growing forces there. With Torval holding the Mu Arae Sector, Basil had felt secure in establishing his capital here at Iota Pegasi, at the opposite end of his domain. Now the flank he'd taken for granted needed shoring up, and he was left alone with his grief. Even the news of Medina's mysterious death had barely seemed to touch him.

"He'll make an exception for this." Silva's face was so dark that her expression wasn't always easy to make out in dim light, and Iota Pegasi A was setting—the red-dwarf companion star was almost visible. But what they saw on those ebon features got their full attention. "Medina's son

Lothar has deposed Josef and had himself crowned Emperor."

There was silence as the sky darkened and Iota Pegasi B appeared like a speck of blood.

They all rose to their feet around the large circular table as Basil entered the room.

Those who hadn't seen him since before the news from Mu Arae were startled. A man of fifty-nine who'd been on anagathics almost half his life had no business looking so old. Always on the slender side, he was beginning to verge on gauntness, and his nose had become the sort tactfully called "Roman." His hair had gone iron-gray, and the grayness seemed to have seeped into his skin as well, for a curious pallor underlay a complexion darkened even beyond its norm by exposure to Santaclara's F5v primary sun. (Iota Pegasi was a young system, habitable by virtue of Luonli terraforming.) Beyond all that, a certain animation had departed from his movements, a certain glitter from his eyes. Youth had fled too abruptly.

"Be seated, ladies and gentlemen," he said in a voice which was still firm, but which sounded the way he looked. "I believe Admiral Silva and the Intelligence Director have prepared a summation of recent events."

"We have, Admiral," the Intelligence Director confirmed. "In essence, the facts are these. Immediately after Medina's fleet returned to Sol with his remains, his son acted with a dispatch which we would have thought beyond his capabilities. He rallied his father's appointees, who of course controlled all military and police power in the Solar system, and forced Josef to announce his abdication in favor of Yoshi Medina, retroactive to just before the latter's death—which, of course, made Lothar heir apparent in the absence of a contrary designation."

"But the Emperor can only choose his successor from among his relatives."

"The justification was that the late Grand Admiral, as the Emperor's father-in-law, was in fact a member of the

Imperial family. This, despite the well-established tradition that restricts the succession to the Emperor's *blood* relatives. However, I suggest that legality has very little to do with what has occurred. To continue: Lothar immediately announced his succession to his father's posthumous title. One of his first official acts was to appoint your old . . . acquaintance Felix Nims as Inspector General, which helps explain the uncharacteristic decisiveness and cleverness that Lothar's coup displayed."

"What about the Emperor?" Everyone knew which Emperor Basil meant. "Is he dead?"

"No, sir. Presumably in an effort to minimize the Empire's shock, Lothar allowed Josef to retire to certain Imperial estates in the Psi 5 Aurigae system as a private citizen—a kind of internal exile."

"And about as far from us as you can get and still be in the Empire," a Fleet officer muttered.

"His wife—Medina's daughter Angelica—chose to accompany him," Silva put in, with a smile of graveyard wryness. "She provided the only hitch in the entire power grab by giving her brother a piece of her mind in a semi-public setting. She reminded him that their father—whom she still idolizes, by the way—had never sought the throne for himself. By all accounts, she was a real tiger."

"I wish I could have been there," Lauren Demarest-Katana chuckled. Her chuckle died as she realized that no one was sharing it. She and Kleinst-Schiavona were not Imperials. To them, this news was merely an important political datum. They had no conception of the meaning—the geological strata of meaning—it held for everyone else around the table. Silva had merely had more time than most to assimilate the unthinkable.

Basil finally broke the silence. His voice's newly acquired bleakness now seemed altogether appropriate. "What has Kang's reaction been?"

"None, of a direct nature," said the Intelligence Director. "He seems as stunned as everyone else. We can state positively that there has been no further military cooperation between him and the . . . Medina dynasty. Indeed, the forces of the two have taken up a posture of wary confrontation at all points of contact."

"Thank you." Basil turned to the table at large. "And now, ladies and gentlemen, we need to consider the nature of our own response."

There was a moment of awkward glances as each of them silently urged someone else to spell out for Basil what was so obvious to everyone else. Eventually, the glances all converged on the Intelligence Director.

"Admiral," the android began, "I believe I speak for everyone here when I say that your duty allows only one course of action. You must publicly condemn this usurpation, denounce Lothar as a traitor—"

"Yes, yes, absolutely," Basil muttered, nodding repeatedly.

"—and proclaim yourself Emperor."

Basil stopped in mid-nod. The silence thundered.

"What are you saying?" Basil finally whispered. "I can't! I mean . . . how would I be any better than Lothar?"

"With utmost respect, sir, the cases are entirely different. You *are* a blood relative of the Imperial house—the only such person in existence except your own offspring. As such, you are the only *possible* legitimate Emperor."

"But Josef is still alive! You just said so. *He's* the rightful Emperor."

"Again, sir, I must beg to differ. Josef has abdicated."

"Under duress!"

"No doubt. But his abdication—even if theoretically voidable on grounds that it was obtained by coercion—has, I fear, irreparably broken a spell which his years as Medina's puppet had already weakened. Even if you restored him to the throne, he could not possibly rule. I doubt if he would wish to try. If he did, you would end by ruling for him as Medina did—admittedly an improvement, but essentially the same thing. If dynastic legitimacy is to be restored, it must be in the person of a single individual who has both the *right* and the *capacity* to rule. Only one such person exists at the present time.

It is your fate to be that person . . .Your Imperial Majesty."

The words had been spoken, and it was as though a restraint stronger than any dam had broken, releasing a flood of entreaties, pledges of loyalty and affirmations of allegiance from everyone present except Kleinst-Schiavona and Demarest-Katana, who held aloof out of a sense of propriety. Basil sat like a rock around which that flood crashed, scattered, and swept in again with the force of destiny.

There had never been time or resources—or inclination on Basil's part—to construct a more pretentious residence than that of the old Imperial governor of the Iota Pegasi Sector, which the People's Democratic Union had fortunately never gotten around to tearing down. So Basil's coronation was held in the spacious plaza fronting that building, with the classically proportioned façade as a backdrop. And afterwards he held court in the residence's main reception hall.

He stood with his back to the semicircle of tall windows at the rear of the long, lofty chamber and the expanse of formally landscaped grounds beyond, silhouetted against an afternoon sunlight that also streamed in through a clerestory. His full dress uniform was void of all insignia save the little golden dragon which only one living human could rightfully wear. He conferred offices on the upper echelons of an entire new Imperial administrative superstructure—one dignitary after another, advancing to the dais to receive the symbolic laying on of hands from the sole legitimate source of human governmental authority in the universe. And he wondered what enabled him to stay on his feet hour after interminable hour.

It must, he decided, be that which had welled up from the throngs that had packed the plaza and the streets opening onto it. Over the years he'd gradually come to see that people weren't just flattering him when they spoke of what his name meant to the populace the New Humans had seen not as individuals but as a collective experimental medium for social theories. And he'd picked precisely the right time to come to them, for he'd had an easy act to follow.

It hadn't been entirely Noumea's fault. The restoration of Imperial administration in these sectors had involved inevitable dislocations, adjustments and hardships. But she'd made the situation worse by attempting to use devices that predated the first starship's departure from Old Earth: blundering intervention in the economy (followed by further interventions to undo the damage of the earlier ones), well-publicized displays of official "compassion" for fashionable underdog groups (coupled with scapegoating of unfashionable ones), and all the rest. These techniques could work for a little while . . . if implemented by skillful politicians who knew the territory. In the hamlike hands of Noumea's uniformed outsiders, they had brought three sectors promptly to the edge of ruin.

Basil had acted in accordance with a conviction acquired in the course of a lifetime's fascination with history: that government should act with strength and decisiveness within its proper sphere, and not at all outside that sphere. He had ruthlessly crushed the organized crime that had grown to fill the vacuum the New Human regime had, like all fallen totalitarianisms, left behind. Just as draconically, he'd purged the administrative apparatus of the corruption Noumea had allowed to flourish. Whenever necessary, he'd used the military as the police of last resort. At the same time, he'd resisted the temptation to court short-term popularity by economic tinkering to artificially ease the transition back to a free market. There had been some rough times, but his personal prestige had helped in weathering them. And eventually the people had come to realize that the government would neither allow the lawless to plunder them nor plunder them itself by forcing success to subsidize failure. The result in terms of wealth production was what it had always been in those cases—tragically few and brief—when humans had had such a government.

Basil's thoughts returned to the present, and he took advantage of a lull between two investitures—an elderly

functionary was taking awhile to advance the length of
the hall—to glance around him. Off to his right, Nadine
sat even more stiffly than usual. Beside her squirmed
thirteen-year-old Dimitri. His weak face wore the bored
expression which was his response to everything except
the pursuit of fun in whatever its currently favored form.
A *lounge lizard in training*, thought Basil with a time-
dulled hurt compounded of contempt, guilt for feeling
the contempt, and mourning for dead hopes.

Nadine wasn't really stupid, and she was in no doubt as
to the precariousness of her status after her father's actions
at Mu Arae. So she'd been on her best behavior while
Basil and his intimate advisers had mulled over the question
of what to do with her. They'd decided that Basil's
metamorphosis into Emperor required the continuity of
his marriage to the mother of his heir. So she'd stayed
on; and with her stayed her worthless son, now heir
presumptive by the very theory that underlay Basil's claim
to the throne, for he was his only living blood relative . . .
as far as was generally known.

The thought led Basil to search for another face. As he
went automatically through his paces—the old boy had finally
tottered up to the dais—his eyes settled on Sonja, only just
arrived from New Antilla. There was no child beside *her*,
of course. He wondered where ten-year-old Irena was just
now.

He and Sonja had maintained the public proprieties, but
their resumption of their affair just after Dimitri's birth
was pretty much an open secret. He couldn't recall precisely
when—or *if*—they'd made the decision to have a child, but
it must have been soon after that. And, like Dimitri, Irena
had been conceived with unusual dispatch by parents who
were both on anagathics. It was her only resemblance to
Dimitri. . . .

He chided himself for the thought. It was pointless. And,
as always, it led him down a futile road of self-reproach,
well-rutted from overuse. *She arrived just after Dimitri
had turned three—a crucial age. If I hadn't been so devoted*

*to the beautiful, vibrant little girl who embodied my love
for Sonja—if, that is, Dimitri had had a father—would he
have turned out differently? At least Nadine wouldn't have
been the only real influence on him.*

He dismissed the thought. What was done was done.
And now Irena lived with her mother in the privacy that
was a prerogative of high rank as long as that rank was
not of the celebrity variety. Sonja had been adamant that
the child was not to be considered for the succession . . .
and not just because of the political need to keep Nadine
on. She believed there was a doom clinging to the
Imperium, and with an instinct that predated history she
stood at the cave mouth between her cub and a danger
that was as unmistakable as it was incomprehensible.

She'll come around, Basil told himself. *As soon as I'm
solidly established I'll divorce that bitch Nadine, marry Sonja
and declare Irena my heir.* The legacy of the Age of the
Protectors and the Unification Wars included a subtle but
undeniable preference for males in the matter of the
Imperial succession—the last surviving vestige of such
preferences. But there had been female Emperors. *Yes,
there's precedent. I can do it. And I* will, *after I've done
what I must do.*

He became aware that the investitures had ended. There
had been one major omission; he planned to wait a few
days before announcing that he himself would assume the
function of Grand Admiral. He stepped forward to the edge
of the dais and looked out over the sea of faces. He'd never
been a great orator; his speaking style was better suited to
a seminar room than to an auditorium. But the acoustics
of the barrel-vaulted hall were technologically enhanced,
and his voice carried to its remotest corners.

At first he spoke of the Empire, and told them they'd all
joined with him in a mighty endeavor to rescue it from
traitors and usurpers. Cheers and applause greeted his every
platitude. But then a subtle sea change entered into his
voice, and even the dullest soon became aware that they
were no longer listening to a political speech.

"Yet before we attend to the cleansing of Old Earth and Prometheus and the rest of the Empire, there is a more immediate matter at hand. By now, everyone knows the sorry tale of General Torval Bogdan's fate. He, along with countless others, was a victim of treachery—the contemptible treachery of our former ally Lavrenti Kang." Out of the corner of his eye, he saw Nadine's stiffness congeal into paralysis, while Dimitri sat up straight and blinked with nervous bewilderment. But she remained seated; he'd had an interview with her—no more unpleasant than was to be expected—on proper deportment for an Empress in her peculiar circumstances.

"We have received a stab in the back which can be neither forgiven nor forgotten. The ghosts of Tor . . . General Bogdan and those who followed him cry out for vengeance. And they shall have it! Kang and his henchmen will meet justice for their perfidy. We never sought this conflict—but we will finish it!"

Basil's voice had risen to a volume that scarcely needed assistance to fill the hall, and to an animation that no one had heard from him for some time. He saw his nearest listeners' various reactions—Sonja's stunned, Silva's horrified, the Intelligence Director's unreadable—to the announcement he'd chosen this moment to make. And he didn't care, for he was letting his rage burn out of control, and it was burning away the dead layers of grief and depression that had been smothering him.

"Surely you can't mean it, sir!"

"I can and do," Basil stated calmly, looking across the conference room's round table into Silva's anguished face. He could understand her feelings at the bombshell he'd dropped in the laps of his new-minted Imperial officialdom the previous day. The problem was, she couldn't possibly understand his emotions. *Have you ever known, Lenore, what it's like to be without a third of yourself?*

"But, sir," she pleaded, "the offensive against Sigma Draconis *has got* to be our first priority." She gestured in

the direction of the strategic holo display with its carefully
nurtured array of green lights that represented bases and
fleets aimed at the Empire's heart. Basil's careful long-term
husbandry of the old rebel sectors' prosperity had yielded
steadily multiplying revenue. He'd spent it just as carefully,
on a meticulously planned military buildup. Now his forces
were at their targeted levels, perfectly balanced and honed
to a keen edge, an exquisite sword poised to thrust at Sigma
Draconis.

Silva was still in the dark about the Intelligence Director's
true nature, but she'd long since been made privy to his
grand plan. She knew the purpose for which their fleet had
been painstakingly constructed and superbly trained: an
offensive against Sigma Draconis in conjunction with Torval's
equally long-planned advance against Sol.

"Sir, the plan can still be salvaged . . . in spite of what's
happened at Mu Arae." Silva ignored the twinge of pain
that crossed Basil's face, and turned to the Intelligence
Director. "Tell him!"

"As you know, sir, we have received some indirect overtures
from Admiral Kang. This is no great surprise, as we have
been aware for some time of his difficulties with Lothar.
Given cautious handling on our part, we believe he can be
maneuvered into agreeing to a revival of the alliance on
terms quite favorable to us."

"So you see, sir," Silva resumed, oblivious to the
thunderclouds gathering behind Basil's eyes, "it's only a
matter of time before we can revert to our original plan—
or at least a version of it, with Kang providing the pressure
against Sol from Mu Arae. So we need to conserve our—"

"I can't believe I'm hearing this!" They all recoiled visibly,
so uncharacteristic was Basil's outburst. But, however shaken,
they all remembered to rise when he came surging to his
feet. "You'd actually *trust* Kang? Put us in a position where
he could betray us like he did Torval?"

"Sir," the Intelligence Director interjected mildly, "I
believe that risk to be an acceptable one. Admiral Kang
can be relied on to act in his own self-interest. That was

what he was doing at Mu Arae, apart from the deplorable lack of ethics displayed. He now sees that his long-term interests lie in countering Lothar's Imperial pretensions and strengthening the claimant—yourself—with whom he has dynastic connections. He will therefore—"

"You don't understand! You haven't lost . . ." Basil trailed to a halt and glared at the android. "But then, how could you understand?"

Silva's momentary puzzled expression rearranged itself into one of grim resolve. "Sir, the restoration of the legitimate dynasty is what we've all been striving for. Everything we've done over the years will become meaningless if you suddenly abandon that goal to pursue personal vengeance!"

"That will do! Admiral Silva, you will not speak again without my leave." Everyone around the table shared Silva's stunned silence. Basil always encouraged uninhibited give-and-take among his staffers; never had he given such a command. He took a deep breath and swept the circumference of the table with his eyes. "This is *not* just a personal vendetta! I have sound reasons for this decision. Kang has proven that he can't be trusted. To rely on him as an ally would be sheer folly. To assure the security of our home base, we must settle accounts with him before embarking on our offensive against Sigma Draconis."

He looked around again. No one spoke . . . even, astonishingly, Sonja. He wondered if he'd convinced them. He wondered if he'd altogether convinced himself.

"Why didn't you say anything at the meeting?"

Basil put the question to Sonja as they sat side by side on recliners in the afternoon light of Iota Pegasi A, on the greensward behind her residence on Admiral's Row at the Fleet base. She'd maintained the place even during her absence at New Antilla, for she'd had no intention of taking Irena to what could have become a war front. Nor had they wished to openly flout the conventions by having her stay at Basil's residence—it hadn't been called a "palace" then. So the child had remained here, under dedicated care and heavy guard, receiving visits from Basil which were less frequent than he might have wished and shadowed by the grief that had taken up residence within him.

Now her mother was back, filling her with a happiness beyond even her sunny norm. Basil gazed across the lawn at her where she played tennis with other children of Fleet officers. Her hair—dark but with a reddish glint that was her mother's—caught the sunlight, and her laughter was a music to which her every movement was a dance. Basil forced his mind away from her, and from his distracting surfeit of love for her, for Sonja hadn't replied.

"Why didn't you speak up?" he repeated. "I need to know what you think."

She turned to meet his eyes. Like him, she was physiologically in her mid-forties; unlike him, she looked no older than that. And for an instant in the bright late-summer sun she looked even younger. Three decades rolled away to reveal that which he'd fallen in love with, and she gave her old reckless smile. "Hey, you know what a shy, retiring type I am—" She ducked playfully, avoiding his equally playful cuff. "Besides, who am I to be mouthing off in the presence of His Imperial Majesty?"

His glower didn't last. "I suppose the news must have come as a surprise at New Antilla."

"That's one way to put it," she said drily.

"I wish you could have been here when the decision was reached. Letting you know about it by tachyon beam wouldn't have been my choice."

"At least I had the trip back here to adjust. But yes, I would have wanted to be here with you when you took the plunge." Unbidden, their hands found each other between the loungers and squeezed.

Basil refused to be distracted. "But I still need to know what you think, and why you kept it to yourself at the meeting."

"I kept quiet because I wasn't sure—and I'm still not. Oh, yes, I understand. More than anything else in the universe, I'd like to see Kang's blood and hear him scream. How could either of us *not* feel that way?"

"So you agree with me?" Basil felt a vague disappointment. He'd half-hoped she would voice for him the stubborn doubts that refused to go away.

"Not altogether. Lenore Silva's right, you know: the smart move, and the move that your duty dictates, is to finish off Medina's pup. After that, Kang would submit."

"I don't *want* him to submit! I want him to . . . to. . . ." He couldn't continue. He could only try to contain his stomach-churning rage.

She nodded with an expression whose parentage included sadness. "Yes. I understand how you feel because I feel the same way. So I know you can't function effectively until you've paid Kang off. That's why I didn't speak up in support of Lenore—and why I'm going to have to go along with you on this." She paused and looked across the lawn at the ten-year-old sprite with the dark red hair. "There's just one thing . . ."

"Yes?"

"Jan and Lauren are going to be staying here, aren't they?"

"Of course." The Sword Clans representatives' work was done. The transposers were now installed in all capital ships, under the control of technicians trained in their use. "Why?"

"Well . . . it's just a feeling I have." She turned to him and held his eyes. "I'd like to leave Irena in their care during the campaign."

He blinked, caught off balance—although, on reflection, the suggestion was a reasonable one. The professional relationship between Kleinst-Schiavona and Demarest-Katana had long since blossomed into something more, though they were putting off having children until their return to their embattled homeworld of Newhope. In the meantime, they'd been like relatives or godparents to Irena, who reciprocated their affection.

And they had, concealed by a remote orbit as well as by advanced stealth technology, a small ship kept in constant readiness for an emergency return to Newhope.

A chill touched Basil's skin in the heat of the afternoon.

"Good idea," he said casually.

"Thanks." Their eyes met for a moment that needed no words. Then she stood up and stretched. "Time for them to stop for some fruit juice. Irena!" With the selective hearing of childhood, the girl continued to laugh and dart about. Shaking her head, Sonja advanced across the lawn.

Basil settled back into the recliner, drowsy with the afternoon heat. He closed his eyes. In the red-shot blackness, sounds seemed clearer: the laughter of the children, the buzzing of insects no more native to this world than he was, the . . .

It wasn't really a sound. Teleportation makes no sound. But there was a subliminal sense that reality had been rearranged, as the overall air pressure in the vicinity adjusted to the fact that a man-shaped space that had been merely part of the air was now filled by a man. Basil's eyes flew open just in time to see a second black-clad figure appear beside the one who stood on the lawn, regaining his balance as his trained body compensated for the disorientation and the slight vector change.

Of that tiny percentage of homo sapiens who possessed any psionic potential, only a tiny percentage were "jumpers"— and few of those could teleport more than two or three yards. It was impractical to use them as assault troops; they were too few, and they generally couldn't teleport full battlefield equipment with them. They were better employed as assassins. . . .

"Jumpers!" Basil yelled as he propelled himself out of the lounger.

But Sonja had already seen the apparitions. She shrieked wordlessly, and sprang forward with no thought save to cover Irena's body with her own.

But she was the one they were after. She only drew their fire toward the stunned children as the two jumpers tracked her with the needlers that were the heaviest weapons they'd been able to bring.

"Guards!" Basil shouted as he sprinted across the lawn in what seemed to be slow motion.

A spray of hypervelocity needles made little crackling

noises as they broke mach, noises drowned out by Irena's scream as Sonja knocked her down to the grass. A boy also screamed, as a slanted row of little red holes appeared across the front of his white shirt—but only briefly, for the scream drowned in a gurgle of blood. The rest of the children ran in all directions, howling.

Guards appeared in a side gate of the garden wall, but hesitated lest they hit the children beyond the jumpers. One, bolder than the others, got off a single shot that caught a jumper between the shoulder blades. This was a full-sized gauss projectile, no needle; the assassin seemed to dive forward in pursuit of the gout of blood that followed the projectile outward through his shattered chest.

At that instant Irena, hysterical, squirmed out of her mother's clutching arms and started to stand up and run away. Sonja frantically reached up to grab her.

The surviving jumper fired a stream of needles that stitched through Sonja's right arm . . . just as Basil crashed into him from behind.

His next clear awareness was of the guards hauling him off the supine black-clad form he'd been straddling. They grasped his arms to prevent him from delivering yet another blow to the broken, bloody ruin that had been a face.

"Yes, sir," Silva assured. She looked across the table under the pool of light from the one lamp that had been turned on for this late-night meeting. "Sonja . . . uh, Admiral Rady is in no danger. The weapon in question was a needler, whose ammunition is of too small a caliber to induce the hydrostatic shock which is so lethal in heavier gauss weapons." She belatedly recalled that Basil was not entirely unacquainted with these matters, swallowed, and continued. "She'll lose the arm, of course, but a replacement is already being force-grown and should be ready for—"

"And the children?" Basil cut in with the bleakness of a monomolecular blade.

"Irena was physically unharmed, sir." Silva's reassuring tone lost some steam as she realized Basil's use of the plural had not been merely pro forma. "Captain Nesbitt's son could not be saved. All the others—including, of course, Irena—suffered a potentially traumatic experience, for which they are receiving appropriate therapy."

"Thank you." Basil's face was like a mask of flint that formed words for him like a robot. "And as to the interrogation of the surviving jumper?" He unconsciously sought to move his right hand in its confining setting. He hadn't even been aware of the broken knuckles until after the tide of fire had ebbed from his soul.

"He's been probed, of course. And questioned under drugs and telepathy and . . . whatever else seemed indicated. We're still trying to clarify a few points, such as how they obtained the imagery which enabled them to clearly visualize their destination, as teleporters require in order to . . ." Silva's voice ran slowly down as she realized the inadvisability of further stalling. "There seems no doubt, sir. Admiral Kang procured this attempt on Admiral Rady's life."

"Thank you." Basil met her eyes—the eyes of someone who could not retreat from a position now known to be indefensible. But his consciousness was busy searching his own mind and soul for any remnants of the doubts he'd felt before.

There were no doubts left. None at all.

Kang, he thought with an eerie calmness, *as of now you're a walking dead man.*

CHAPTER EIGHTEEN
The Serpens/Bootes region, 3931 C.E.

Basil stood, hands clasped behind his back, and looked out over the panorama in the great curving viewscreen of HIMS *Vengeful*'s flag bridge.

Ahead burned the orange-tinted flame of DM -4 4225, in whose light Kang's frontier fleet had just died. It had been weakened to reinforce Mu Arae against a blow Kang had firmly believed would fall there. Basil had encouraged him in that belief by sending Sonja with the offensive's vanguard—all fast units, battlecruiser size and below—in that direction in a massive feint. Then, with Kang's dispositions sufficiently confused by panicky realignments and reorganizations, she'd led her command in a "southwest" direction, curving around behind DM -4 4225 while Basil had advanced against it in full panoply of battleships, super-battleships and a large fleet train. It had been a pincer movement measured in parsecs instead of miles, and it had worked. As he watched the streams of ships flow past in the viewscreen, converging on the star ahead, Basil fancied that they advanced through a cloud of infra-rubble that had been Kang's forward elements, caught here at their home base. The way into Kang's domain lay open.

He turned, stepped off his observation platform, and advanced toward a table where his officers—including those, like Sonja, who were still aboard their own flagships but present by holo image—rose to their feet. It was the first time in a century and a quarter that an Emperor had taken personal command of a fighting fleet. In this, as in his combining of the office of Grand Admiral with that of Emperor, Basil had precedent: Corin the Grim had done both when he'd arisen to crush the Rajasthara Usurpation. It was a historical parallel worth stressing—or so he'd argued in overruling those who'd questioned the wisdom and propriety of endangering the Imperial person. Only Sonja could understand the real reason he *had* to lead this expedition.

"As you were, ladies and gentlemen. Commodore Ho, are all enemy units accounted for?"

"They are, sir," the chief of staff replied. Simple military courtesy sufficed when the Emperor was wearing the hat of a field commander. "And the totals tend to confirm Admiral Rady's estimate of how many ships Kang transferred to Mu Arae."

"Very good," Basil said with a degree of insincerity; he'd hoped to hear that the estimate had been exaggerated. "So we need to consider our next move in light of known enemy strength at Mu Arae." Their eyes all followed his toward the strategic holo display floating between the tabletop and the overhead.

The image of Lenore Silva motioned for recognition from her flag bridge, where she observed an identical display. "Sir, it's clear that the force at Mu Arae couldn't face our combined fleet with any hope of survival. Nevertheless, that force might possibly pose a threat to our communications—and perhaps even to our own nearer systems—as we advance further into Kang's region. I recommend that we turn aside and deal with it before proceeding further."

"I think you exaggerate the threat, Admiral Silva," Sonja spoke up. "That force is in a fundamentally defensive posture. It couldn't mount anything beyond pinprick raids from behind us. And as for our own frontier systems, they're well defended." She indicated the display with an arm still new enough to be awkward.

Silva looked disappointed; she'd hoped for support. But she didn't argue. Sonja presumably knew whereof she spoke—especially concerning the border systems' defenses, for whose preparation she'd been responsible.

"Any other comments?" Basil invited. There were none. "Very well. I think Admiral Rady's points are well taken. Furthermore, we're closer to Lambda Serpenti than Mu Arae is to any of our important systems; even a successful attack wouldn't do them any good if their capital system had already fallen!" He studied the display for a flaw and found none.

"There's another point, sir," Sonja said with careful formality. "I suspect they're already rushing reinforcements from Mu Arae back to the defense of Lambda Serpenti. But we can get there first . . . *if* we act with speed and decisiveness."

"Just so. We'll resupply our depletable munitions from the fleet train and repair battle damage, then proceed as per the original plan—with one modification." He turned to Silva's simulacrum. "Lenore, your task force—beefed up to include the bulk of the battle-line units—will take up station to the right of the fleet train and the transports with their escorting elements, which is where I'll be with this ship. You'll act as a screening force, in case any threat materializes from the direction of Mu Arae. Sonja, you'll continue to lead the vanguard. And now, let's turn our attention to the details."

On Lambda Serpenti III, panic was as much a component of the atmosphere as oxygen and nitrogen. Felix could practically smell it as he rode a heavily escorted slider from the spaceport through the urban canyons toward Kang's military headquarters. By the time the fortresslike structure loomed up ahead, he found the sight a relief despite its brutally massive ugliness. At least those grim walls might shut out the oppressive miasma of the city.

He was disappointed. Within, the desperation was merely more focused, and rooted in facts rather than rumors. It showed in the jerky haste with which uniformed figures scurried about the corridors in a pathetically obvious effort to do something, or at least *seem* to be doing something. It could be heard in the harsh but brittle voices with which officers barked at their underlings and the underlings traded recriminations.

The atmosphere grew more purposeful as Felix and his escorts worked their way closer to the headquarters' central sanctum. But the purpose was one which brought a frown to his face. Things were unmistakably being boxed for a move.

Finally they approached a massive double door. The guards must have been told to expect them, for the doors immediately slid aside with a rumble.

The office beyond was clearly designed to impress hard-bitten admirals and stun everyone else, for it was like a vaster version of a capital ship's flag bridge. A curving observation balcony was cantilevered out to overlook a hemispherical viewscreen. Between it and the entrance was a conference table that in this case was rectangular rather than round, and obviously not set up for holo attendance—Kang evidently liked making people attend in the flesh. A visibly worried group of officers clustered at one end. Kang looked up from the huddle.

"Ah, Inspector General. Greetings." Kang's voice echoed in the cavernous space.

"Greetings, High Admiral." Felix had persuaded Lothar to quietly drop his father's objection to Kang's invented and self-bestowed rank. "I gather I've come at an inconvenient time." He indicated the rows of computer terminals and instrument readouts that lined the cavernous chamber's walls and filled the well below the balcony, and the people who swarmed among them. There was the same air of an evacuation under way that he'd noted in the outer offices.

Kang gave a slightly sick smile. His habitual urbanity was

somewhat in abeyance. "Routine precautions. I am advised that . . . strategic exigencies may make it advantageous to relocate my command center to another system."

"I am authorized to say that His Imperial Majesty would regard such a move as highly ill-advised."

Kang's face darkened. "The views of . . . him who you represent will be given the consideration they deserve."

Juliana Moresin added her glare to Kang's. "Those views might carry more weight if Captain Medina had sent more aid than the one task force—a glorified task group, really— that accompanied you."

Felix controlled himself as Kang pointedly failed to reprimand Moresin for that "Captain Medina." It also didn't escape his notice that his hosts had stopped addressing him by the title of Inspector General, which he'd received from Lothar.

The whole situation was damned awkward. He'd hoped that Kang would accept Lothar's ratification of his "high admiral" self-promotion, thereby tacitly recognizing Lothar's authority as Emperor. But Kang had maintained a sphinxlike silence on the subject, while making overtures to Castellan which he probably thought were still secret. When those overtures had failed, he'd had nowhere else to turn than to Lothar, whom he neither respected nor trusted. It had been Raj DiNardo's finest hour, for the old fox had managed to ask for help without ever uttering a word that committed Kang to support of Lothar's claim to the throne.

Lothar had been all for sitting back and watching Kang and Castellan bleed each other dry. Felix had argued— with the grudging support of the military people—that Castellan would win before mutual exhaustion set in. When Lothar had evinced scant concern for Kang's fate ("Good enough for him!"), Felix had conjured up the vision of a victorious Castellan with the Serpens/Bootes region as well as the old rebel sectors behind him. Lothar had continued to pout ferociously, but he'd agreed to send a reinforced task group. Felix hadn't argued for more. No point in giving Kang *too* much help.

And if he, Felix, was right, no more would be needed.

He addressed Kang, ignoring Moresin. "I suggest, High Admiral, that we table our differences of opinion for the present. If nothing else, surely we can maintain solidarity against Admiral Castellan's illegal, unwarranted, unilateral assumption of the Imperial title."

"Yes, yes, of course," Kang muttered with the bitterness of disappointed dynastic hopes. "On this point there can be no disagreement."

Felix decided to lay it on. "After all, High Admiral, it is no more than our duty as loyal Imperial subjects to—"

Moresin's laugh was like the bark of a scornful bulldog. "An odd choice of words, in light of your background! And a somewhat self-serving appeal, given that you work for Captain Medina. Arguably, *two* usurpations cancel each other out!"

Felix maintained a fixed half-smile, momentarily speechless with fury because the bitch had touched not one but two nerves. He rarely thought back to his New Human days any more; it had been a long time ago, and by its failure the movement had proven itself unworthy of him. Better to adapt to the realities of his situation without a backward look. Besides, the movement had never been more than a means to the end of controlling the vermin among whom he had to live. And even that end was itself a means of being able to hurt them without being hurt—as was his right, for they were merely spear carriers in the drama that played itself out in his mind, which was the universe. For that purpose, the Imperial power structure might not serve as well as the New Human state, but it was what he had available . . . and it could be molded.

More importantly, this loathsome female had put her finger on a concept he'd given up trying to explain to that dullard Lothar. Castellan posed a threat that was qualitatively different from Kang's, for he challenged not just territory but legitimacy. He had to be dealt with . . . and his blunder of attacking Kang first was an opportunity which couldn't be missed, even if it meant dealing with these people.

"Since the air has been cleared, High Admiral, I will be equally blunt. We're well aware that Admiral Castellan has rejected your attempts at a rapprochement—understandably, in light of your attempted assassination of his . . . friend Admiral Rady."

"But I had nothing to do with that! It's all a complete misunderstanding, as I've repeatedly assured Castellan. I can't imagine how he got the idea I was behind it. What could I have possibly gained?"

"Of course, High Admiral, of course. An unhappy choice of words on my part." Felix smiled inwardly. It had taken some doing to procure the assassins through a well-established front so they genuinely believed they were working for Kang. But it had been worth it. Castellan would probably have moved against Kang anyway, but Felix congratulated himself on the adroit disinformation by which he'd improved probability to certainty. That the assassins had failed was immaterial.

"Nevertheless," he resumed, "the fact remains that at the moment you're in no position to turn down *any* offer of help." Felix permitted himself a supercilious glance at Moresin. "Not when your frontier fleet has allowed itself to be trapped and annihilated."

Moresin looked like she was about to spring for his throat. But Kang addressed her in soothing tones. "For a fact, Admiral, we must cope with the current situation before we can turn our attention to the exact legal status of . . . the late Grand Admiral Medina's son." He turned back to Felix. "At the same time, Inspector General, you also need us—if only as a counterweight to Admiral Castellan. I trust you bring us more aid than meets the eye."

Felix reminded himself that Kang had inherited one great talent from his own father: political survival. It showed even when, as now, he was clearly close to a breakdown. "That, High Admiral, is precisely why it would be unwise as well as unnecessary for you to abandon this system. As it happens,

I have for some years made a study of Admiral Castellan. I've also studied intelligence reports on the order in which his fleet is advancing. I believe I know how he can be lured into a trap. . . ."

Sonja watched the local sun grow in the viewscreen and controlled her impatience. DM -1 3220 was a star of strictly limited interest: a K0v with a brown dwarf in a fairly close orbit which had precluded the formation of a habitable planet. Some had argued for bypassing it and proceeding directly on toward Lambda Serpenti. The brown dwarf, though, had some mineral-rich moons with fairly extensive installations, including a small Fleet base. And there had been indications of ship movements in this direction. Basil had decided to secure the system before pressing on. She'd agreed, despite her impatience to be done with this campaign, thus ridding Basil of the inner demon which had, for now, possessed him . . . and freeing her from the forebodings she'd been unable to shake since their departure.

She shook free of the thought and concentrated on the holo tank. They were still a long way from the brown dwarf's Chen Limit, but they had penetrated fairly deep into the system, skirting the Chen Limit of a lesser gas giant on the way in. Still no enemy response. Maybe they'd be able to just accept a pro forma submission from whoever was in authority in this system and continue on course. Maybe they'd soon be on the way back to Iota Pegasi—and Irena . . .

She was still thinking about it when the red dots began springing into malevolent life.

Her chief of staff appeared at her side, replying to the question she hadn't even uttered. "They're from the brown dwarf's satellary system, sir. They've only just gotten out of its Chen Limit and engaged their drives—which is what enabled us to pick them up, for they're under heavy stealth. Analysis of ship types based on drive strength is now coming in. . . ." They both stared at the board, then at the tank, then at the board again. The tally of battleships was still growing.

"They must be committing their entire remaining strength here," the chief of staff finally breathed.

"So it would seem, Commander. Have all ships go to general quarters. And inform the Emperor." Orders were passed, giving Sonja time to digest what she was seeing.

"Kang must have stripped Lambda Serpenti bare in an effort to stop us here," the chief of staff observed. "Maybe he thought the move would succeed from its sheer unexpectedness."

"Maybe," Sonja echoed. "And, for a fact, there's more here than *we* can handle. Has the Emperor acknowledged receipt of our report yet?" She didn't have one of the mammoth communications ships; there were only two of them with the expedition, accompanying Basil and Silva, both of whom kept them on minutely preplanned courses at all times so they could talk in realtime. Sonja had to make do with lightspeed communications.

"Not yet, sir. Any time now, I should think."

"Keep me informed. And implement Contingency Plan Seven."

"Yes, sir. I'll issue the necessary orders." It was the contingency they hadn't expected: a force too heavy for the vanguard to handle, encountered before arriving at Lambda Serpenti. The plan involved splitting up into smaller units, turning it into the kind of dogfight where the cruisers' and battlecruisers' maneuverability would count.

In the meantime, of course, they were going to have to pass through missile salvoes to which they could not respond in kind. . . .

"Let me know the moment we get an acknowledgment from Bas . . . from the Emperor," she ordered edgily.

"Acknowledge," Basil snapped. "And order all units forward at maximum possible acceleration."

Ho swallowed. "Uh, sir, may I suggest that—"

"No time!" Basil snapped. "The vanguard is going to be

overwhelmed if we don't get there to support them." He pointed at the tank where the data from Sonja's transmission was being displayed. "Together, we'll be able to beat that force."

"Probably, sir. But our capital ship strength gives us only a marginal superiority; most of our heavy battleships are with Admiral Silva." Ho didn't quite draw himself up into a position of attention. "Sir, I suggest we stay where we are, summon Admiral Silva, and order Admiral Rady to disengage and retire toward us, hopefully drawing that force after her. I calculate that Admiral Silva can get here while we're still engaged with them—and when she does, our superiority will become overwhelming. We can trap them and wipe them out. And *nothing* will stand between us and Lambda Serpenti."

Basil spoke with an air of strained patience which wasn't like him. "Your use of the word 'hopefully' reveals the weakness in that analysis, Commodore. What if they *don't* allow themselves to be drawn into a pursuit of Admiral Rady? And besides . . . if they *do* pursue her, your plan lengthens the time she's going to be subject to missile bombardment." He shook his head decisively, as though dismissing an unacceptable mental picture. "No. We need to go to her aid immediately. We can crush that force without Admiral Silva's help."

Ho took a breath. On its face, the argument wasn't completely unreasonable . . . and this was Basil Castellan, who'd never lost a battle. But Ho knew it for the rationalization it was, and he knew the real reason Basil *had* to rush to the vanguard's aid as quickly as possible. "Sir, I would be derelict in my duty if I didn't urge in the strongest possible terms that we send for Admiral Silva and—"

"Yes, yes. By all means, contact Silva." Basil's impatience was fraying out into what could only be called jumpiness. "But in the meantime, I'll be obliged if you obey the orders I gave you a few moments ago. And I speak not only as your commanding officer but also as Emperor. *Is that clear?*"

Ho swallowed. "Aye aye, sir."

❖   ❖   ❖

Sonja's running battle was snarling its way outwards from
DM -1 3220 toward them as they drove inward past the
small gas giant in the system's outer reaches.

The lack of continuous communication was nerve-racking.
Sonja's ships had naturally deactivated their inner fields
for combat. Just as naturally, Basil's hadn't, lest their journey
take subjective months. He'd once ordered *Vengeful*'s inner
field killed temporarily so he might contact Sonja while
they were both existing at the normal rate of time. But he
knew how much confusion it caused within his own force,
so he hadn't repeated it.

She'd come through the missile hail about as well as
could have been hoped for, then looped around through
them and struck at them with lances of energy-weapon
fire. Then she'd pulled away, straining outward toward
the relief she knew was coming. But the enemy's lighter
units continued to dog her flanks, while the battleships
continued to peck away with missiles from behind. She'd
given better than she'd gotten . . . but she had gotten
altogether too much, and her flagship had taken hits since
that one terse exchange of information. Basil stared at
the holo tank and ordered himself not to nervously pace
the flag bridge.

Soon, he told himself. *Soon we'll be within missile range.*
He'd left the noncombatant ships outside the system's
outermost orbit, guarded by some cruisers and lighter units
but mostly by the sheer vastness of space. The fighting ships
he'd taken with him included, in addition to *Vengeful* and
the lighter units, some older battleships—not up to the
standard of the cutting-edge ones in Silva's command, but
quite capable of putting out a respectable volume of missile
fire. *Yes, soon . . .*

"Sir . . ." The shaken voice of Commander Walgrave, the
intelligence officer, came in the wake of a collective hiss
of indrawn breath from the sensor ratings. "We're picking
up—"

Basil wasn't listening, for the scarlet icons had started to
appear in the tank, curving around from behind the outer

gas giant and engaging their drives as soon as they passed beyond its Chen Limit.

After a time, he heard his own voice speaking for him, as though from a great distance. "It can't be. Kang can't have those ships. Our intelligence can't be *that* wrong!"

"They aren't Kang's, sir," Walgrave said. "Individual ship identifiers are beginning to come in, and . . . They're Medina's, sir."

"Thank you, Commander," Basil said calmly. "Commodore Ho, I believe we can drop the inner field now."

"Uh . . . aye, aye, sir."

"And, Commodore, as soon as that is done, have comm raise Admiral Rady."

They moved closer to missile range of Sonja's battle at a snaillike pace now that the drive field ruled their bodies, and Basil studied the tank with a dispassion that should have surprised him but didn't—it was as though his capacity for indignation at betrayal was gone, depleted by expenditure. The force emerging from behind the gas giant wasn't a huge one. With Silva here, they would have been easily able to handle it as well as Kang's fleet. As it was . . . well, Medina's sending-force *did* include battleships. And the scrolling projections foretold that those battleships would draw into missile range of him just before he was able to loose his own missiles at Sonja's tormentors. It was a question of how to apportion his fire. . . .

"Sir, we have Admiral Rady."

"Thank you." Basil turned to the comm screen just as it filled with the flag bridge of HIMS *Resolute*, a battlecruiser which had clearly taken hits. Sonja was sooty with the smoke of electrical fires that damage-control personnel behind her were extinguishing. Her eyes were rimmed with exhaustion. Her right arm hung in an improvised sling. Basil sought, by sheer concentration, to memorize every detail of her.

"We're coming," he said, forcing the words past a constricted throat. "But we've got unexpected complications."

"I know." Shipboard-sized tachyon communicators could transmit over this range, and they had a sensor lock on *Resolute*, so they could carry on a conversation. "Our own sensors have spotted them while tracking you in." She gave her useless right arm a wry look. "What a waste. We shouldn't have bothered with it."

Basil was trying to form words when someone off to the side of Sonja shouted "Incoming!" loudly enough to be picked up. "Signing off," she said hastily. "Hurry."

Basil was still staring into the blackness of the screen when Ho cleared his throat. "*Resolute* has taken at least one more hit, sir. She's still alive," he added hastily. "But her tachyon comm is out. So we don't know the details of her status. . . ." His voice trailed miserably to a halt, then resumed. "Sir, we and Medina's force are about to come into missile range. Ops proposes that we concentrate our fire on them, at least at first." He indicated a readout showing a standard mix of missile ordnance. "As you can see—"

"Negative. We will launch only the decoy-configured component of that weapons mix at them. Otherwise, we'll withhold our missile fire to launch in support of Admiral Rady."

Basil's tone invited no argument, and Ho offered none. The one-sided missile duel began, with Medina's battleships flinging full salvoes that were met by a limited number of decoys. Most of the attacking missiles got through, to meet close-in active and passive defenses. Inevitably, some drew blood. And more were on the way.

Then they were within range of Sonja's battle, and their own missiles went streaking away more swiftly than light in search of the capital ships that were pounding her command into scrap. Those had already expended most of their own missiles, but they had retained their decoy-configured ones against the appearance of missile-armed adversaries. So Basil's missile bombardment won Sonja only a brief respite before his ships closed the space separating them from the running battle. They swung around into a roughly parallel course and came to grips at what passed for point-blank range with Kang's ships—which, already battered from their extended combat with the vanguard, reeled under the impact of fresh opponents.

But Medina's task force was mirroring Basil's maneuver, its battleships staying in missile range and pouring in fire while the opposing cruiser screens snarled and bit at each other. Finally those battleships, like Basil's, closed the range and plowed into what had become a general melee—a holocaust of directed-energy fire in which Basil's overmatched forces gradually shriveled and died.

Basil watched it in the tank, his concentration seemingly uninterrupted by the occasional aguelike shudders that ran through the ship, the flickering of the lights, and the whoops of the klaxons summoning damage control. It was, he saw, the kind of fight in which there was no way out, no room for unorthodox maneuvers—just the simple, pitiless arithmetic of firepower and tonnage.

There was, however, one thing he could do . . .

"Sir," Ho reported, "we've gotten a report from *Resolute.*" At this range, conventional communicators were useable. And tight-beam lasers, unlike radio, could penetrate a ship's passive defenses and the general interference of battle. "She can no longer maneuver or fight. Her captain is about to give the order to abandon ship."

Basil stood up abruptly. "Get me Admiral Rady."

"Aye aye, sir." Ho spoke briefly to the comm officer. "We can't get a visual. But—"

The acknowledgment began to come in from the overhead speaker in a voice that pain rendered barely recognizable.

"Sonja," Basil cut in, all pretense of formality abandoned. "I want you to keep your personal communicator on, set to transponder mode. And . . . on a signal from this ship, I want you to drop *Resolute*'s stealth."

Ho gave him a puzzled glance. Ever since Redcliffe, all capital ships carried transposers—and almost never used them because all ships now automatically implemented stealth in any combat situation. But Sonja instantly understood. "No, Basil! You can't! Leave me—get away."

"Not without you." *Probably not at all,* he added silently as *Vengeful* shook to another hit. But . . . "That's an order. Do it!" He gestured savagely at the comm officer to cut the connection before she could protest further. Then he hit a key and spoke to the flag captain.

"Captain Cuellar, I want you to get this ship within transposer range of *Resolute.* I also want you to give the following order to the transposer techs." He spoke briefly.

"Understood, sir."

"Very good. Fight your ship, Captain." Basil turned to Ho. "Commodore, it's now every ship for itself. Everyone's only priority is to get away and, if possible, rendezvous with Admiral Silva. That includes this ship—after we rendezvous with *Resolute.*"

"Aye aye, sir."

Vengeful surged forward under her impellers, surprising her nearest antagonists with the sudden acceleration. She swept her full field of fire with high-energy beams, savaging several ships and catching one cruiser squarely amidships and leaving an expanding cloud of plasma, burning a path to *Resolute.* When two of Medina's battleships approached on an intercept course, Cuellar lay a pattern of transposed antimatter warheads across their path, without any realistic hope of damaging them—their stealth was, of course, activated—but blinding their sensors momentarily with the searing temporary suns. As the hellish glows faded, *Resolute* lay ahead.

Basil knew nothing of this save the occasional lurches that made him grab for the nearest handhold, for he was making his way to the transposer controls. "As you were," he muttered in a preoccupied way to the startled technicians. "Did the captain explain what you're to do?"

"Yes, Your . . . sir," stammered the lieutenant in charge. "We're to target Admiral Rady's personal transponder as soon as we're told that—"

"*Resolute* has dropped her stealth," the intercom blared,

anticipating him. "We're downloading the sensor lock on Admiral Rady's location now."

"There's your target," Basil snapped. "Execute!"

The download only took a second or two, during which Basil stared fixedly at the stage displayed on the screen overlooking the control consoles—the stage ordinarily occupied by antimatter warheads. The lieutenant snapped orders, a deep thrumming filled the chamber as the transposer was energized . . . and Sonja was collapsing onto the stage, surrounded by bits of objects from her control bridge.

Basil was instantly through the heavily-armored doors and onto the stage, rushing to her. The nanoplastic of her space-service uniform had already become a light-duty vac suit, and she'd pulled the flexible transparent hood over her head. Basil got it off, hand trembling with rising hope— *She doesn't look too bad*—until he saw the pink froth that rose and fell on her lips with her shallow breathing. Then he belatedly remembered that bloodstains wouldn't show through the suit.

"Sonja, can you hear me?"

Her eyelids fluttered open. Her colorless lips formed the tremulous beginnings of a smile, and she started to speak. . . .

There was a sound like the clap of doom, and *Vengeful* leaped under him like a caught fish.

When his head stopped spinning, he lay atop Sonja in the dried-blood light of the auxiliary lamps and someone's voice—not Cuellar's—was tolling over the intercom. "This is the Captain speaking. Abandon ship. Repeat, abandon ship. The antimatter containment fields will destabilize in not more than three minutes. Repeat—"

Basil stopped listening. The collapse of the field which held the power plant's antimatter in check was a sentence of death for everyone aboard the ship or in its vicinity. "Go!" he shouted in the direction of the pickup, just in case the transposer techs were still at their posts. Then he picked Sonja up, struggling with her limp body.

The layout of the corridors came back to him as he

staggered through them. He passed a row of escape pods.
None of them had been used, of course. Their little
maneuvering thrusters wouldn't move them very far away
from the ship very fast; and with antimatter about to meet
matter inside the ship, everyone wanted to get to the bays
holding the lifeboats with their powerful impellers. He
hastened in that direction through passageways from which
everyone else had already fled.

Another explosion shook the great ship, and far up ahead
its force ripped through the corridor's bulkheads. He
somehow managed to stay on his feet with Sonja through
the shockwave, but his way was blocked by a tangle of
twisted, blackened metal.

He retraced his steps back to the escape pods as the
intercom continued to repeat its message of doom. He
manhandled Sonja into a pod and strapped her into one of
its three seats, then seated himself and slapped the launch
button.

The little pod had no mass to waste on fripperies like
artificial gravity. A giant's hand pressed him down into his
seat as the mass-driver launch system hurled the pod clear
of the drive field. Only . . . the field wasn't there. *Vengeful's*
drive had died, and the battle had already moved away from
her more swiftly than light. So instead of simply vanishing
from Basil's sight, she receded swiftly in the porthole,
shrinking to an arrowhead-shaped toy. Some instinct made
him turn his eyes away from the porthole just in time.

Even through tightly closed eyes, the glare warned him
to prepare himself for the shock wave he would have to
endure without artificial gravity. But that very lack had made
the pod's designers provide seats that were really very
effective crash couches. He never quite lost consciousness.
Still, after it was past he needed almost a minute to recover.

*Can't imagine the radiation dosage we just got, in this
unshielded pod*, he reflected as the disorientation ebbed
from his mind. *We're dead if we don't get to a well-equipped
sick bay soon. Of course, that's not Sonja's most immediate
problem.* Then he turned to examine her.

Ridiculous, he thought after a moment. *There* has *to be a pulse.*

Then: *No. This isn't right. She was about to say something. She never got a chance.*

Aloud: "Sonja? Talk to me!" He took her by the shoulders and shook her, as though motion would reawaken in her flesh the memory of life. He repeated her name until his voice had risen to a scream that reverberated around the tiny space.

After that, he had no consciousness of time. He sat holding that which had been Sonja, not seeing the uncaring stars that drifted past the porthole, alone in a universe that had become unacceptable.

He was still sitting like that when the small ship of unusual design appeared and grew in the porthole.

With no particular interest, he felt the bump as the tractor beam seized his pod, and watched as the small ship grew to fill the porthole. A hatch in its side opened to engulf him. Then the tractor disengaged with another bump, and the pod was under artificial gravity in a space barely large enough to contain it. He wasn't surprised at the figure which entered that space and opened the pod's hatch.

"Come, Your Imperial Majesty. You must leave her."

Basil looked slowly up and spoke with a voice from which all possible emotion had been wrung, whose only expression was a kind of plaintive hurt. "She never got to say what she was going to say. We never said goodbye."

"Come, sir." The Intelligence Director's voice was very gentle. "I will set her adrift in the pod, in a cometary orbit around this star. The universe can be her resting place. But now we must go."

"Is there any new word on Castellan?"

"No, Inspector General." Vice Admiral Marvell's attempt to mask his irritation was as obvious as it was unsuccessful. Silva had arrived too late to salvage the situation. She'd taken the fleeing survivors of Castellan's and Rady's commands under her wing and was now conducting an orderly withdrawal, not so much pursued as shadowed by Kang's badly shaken fleet. Moresin had reluctantly left Marvell and his relatively unhurt task force in charge of mopping up in the DM -1 3220 system, and his efforts to do so were hardly furthered by constant, irritable demands for information. But he held his temper. Felix Nims might be a civilian, and a former New Human to boot, but he was also the Inspector General and an intimate of the Emperor.

"We have cruisers and lighter units combing the region where Castellan's flagship detonated," he explained. "There's nothing left of the ship itself, of course. But they've picked up numerous lifeboats and escape pods. Castellan hasn't been among the prisoners we've taken. Nor do any of them recall seeing him in the course of the evacuation." He tried for persuasiveness. "May I suggest, Inspector General, that we call off the search? The probability that Castellan died with his flagship is overwhelming."

"Legends aren't interested in probabilities, Admiral. If there's no positive evidence of his fate, indelible rumors of his survival will arise to fill the vacuum. No, we need a prisoner or a corpse. And, as you've intimated, a corpse is highly unlikely. So we will continue searching for more lifeboats and more escape pods. Is that clear?"

Marvell swallowed, for the last three words had been freighted with unspecified menace. He mumbled assent, and moved away to growl at some underling.

Felix dismissed Marvell from his mind with no more than a brief flare of annoyance at himself for taking the time to explain matters to a uniformed oaf. He studied the starfields in the flag bridge's main screen as though seeking a glimpse of Castellan in them. Yes, it would be most unfortunate if he had been reduced to his component atoms. So many possibilities if he were captured—especially after Iota Pegasi was finally taken. Felix recalled from intelligence reports that he had an illegitimate daughter by Rady. *Ten years old. Yes. Too bad it's not a boy. But still . . . Yes. I could force Castellan to watch.*

"Inspector General!" Marvell's voice shattered the reverie he was happily elaborating. "One of our cruisers has reported. There's an unidentified ship out there in the search area—small, its drive deactivated at the time of detection, and very heavily stealthed. In fact, the cruiser captain admits he would have missed it if he hadn't been at very close range when the unknown activated a tractor beam . . . which, as you may know, stands out like a beacon to grav scanners. So when it reactivated its drive the cruiser was able to get a fix on its course—"

Felix had stopped listening. He even ignored Marvell's minor indulgence in condescension. For he was thinking furiously, his mind a mass of crackling connections as he recalled his investigation of Castellan's mysterious Intelligence Director. "Show me that course, Admiral," he cut in.

"Certainly, Inspector General." Marvell spoke an order, and the arrow denoting a vector appeared in the system-display holo tank. *Yes*, Felix thought with rising eagerness, *it's in about the right direction*.

Marvell broke the silence. "Shall I send ships in pursuit, Inspector General?"

"No. This involves matters of extreme sensitivity, Admiral. I had best handle it myself. You will assign a cruiser to me, and give its captain orders to obey me unquestioningly."

"But . . . but, Inspector General, I am responsible to His Imperial Majesty for your safety. I cannot allow—"

"You will give the orders now." Felix's pale-gray stare chilled Marvell's soul. "You don't want to face the consequences of not doing so—the consequences to yourself and your family. I doubt if your imagination is equal to the task of visualizing those consequences, Admiral."

Marvell swallowed, and his eyes darted to and fro as though seeking refuge. "But, Inspector General," he finally stammered. "By the time we can transfer you to a cruiser, it will no longer be possible to overtake that ship."

"That is of no concern, Admiral. You see, I know what its destination is."

Felix turned away from Marvell's uncomprehending face, absorbed in his own thoughts. *Yes, it all fits at last. Whatever dwells at DM -17 954 has finally taken an active part in Castellan's fate—and thereby rendered itself vulnerable.*

I mustn't allow the knowledge to spread any further than absolutely necessary. A cruiser should suffice . . . and I can always arrange for that cruiser to be lost with all hands afterwards. Then I alone will have the prestige of having taken Castellan . . . and knowledge which may be worth even more than that.

CHAPTER NINETEEN
The DM -17 954 system, 3931 C.E.

Basil lay slumped in a chair beside the Intelligence Director. A spherical viewscreen surrounded them with a simulacrum of the heavens in which they and the control panel seemed to float. He watched listlessly as the well-remembered brown dwarf grew to fill most of that panorama, with the distant yellow glow of DM -17 954 peeking over its shoulder.

The escape pod's first-aid kit had included drugs that held nausea and vomiting at bay. But the Intelligence Director's personal ship held no medical facilities—why should it?—and nothing could be done about the radiation sickness of which those were mere symptoms. He had already begun to think of himself as dead, and the realization awoke no fear in him, nor even regret. He felt only a mild impatience.

But a sense of duty still lived inside him—he *had* to get back to Iota Pegasi before he died, or at least get a message there. And he was still capable of curiosity.

"Why have you brought me here?" he asked.

"Omega Prime insisted that you not be allowed to fall into the hands of your enemies. Furthermore, it feels an obligation to explain certain things to you." The android spoke without looking at him, concentrating on guiding the ship through the immaterial veil of invisibility. With the lack of warning Basil remembered, the universe was seen

381

through a gauzy filter and the pearly sphere loomed dead ahead.

"Omega Prime owes me nothing," he said dully.

(*Stately formality.*) "I must be the judge of that, Your Imperial Majesty."

Basil managed to smile. "I didn't realize your telepathic range extended out here, Omega Prime." Then he tried to sit up and put urgency into his voice. "If you insist on feeling obligated to me, you can best discharge that obligation by sending me to Iota Pegasi as quickly as possible. I have to arrange for—"

"Compose yourself, sir," the Intelligence Director spoke aloud. "Before departing from Santaclara, I informed Kleinst-Schiavona and Demarest-Katana of what was transpiring. They agreed that your daughter needed to be removed from danger without delay. By now, they and Irena are en route to Newhope."

Basil fell back into his chair, even weaker than before, but from relief. *She's safe . . . she's safe . . .* It tolled over and over in his mind like a soothing chant. But a sudden thought prevented him from losing consciousness.

"You told them this before you departed . . . which was before the battle. So you knew in advance what was going to happen."

"Yes, Your Imperial Majesty." The Intelligence Director's voice held nothing more than a simple admission of fact as he turned to face Basil, letting a tractor beam ease the ship through the entry port that had appeared in the facility's surface. "Omega Prime knew."

"And so Omega Prime allowed me to fail."

(*Mild reproof.*) "The statement is meaningless. The future is immutable; no one 'allows' it. I cannot attempt to change what I know is the foreordained course of future events. I can only play what I know to be my part in assuring that course."

Basil slumped in his chair again. Resentment was as pointless as despair in the realm beyond hope into which he'd passed. And yet . . . "I still need to get to Iota Pegasi, or send a message there. I need to . . . set my affairs in order."

"By all means, sir," the Intelligence Director assured. "You can prepare an interactive message. I will deliver it to Admiral Silva."

"Admiral Silva? Where is she?"

"She arrived in time to lead the survivors in a fighting retreat toward New Antilla. So her course has been only a few degrees off ours—although she hasn't followed it quite so rapidly." Beyond the Intelligence Director, Basil watched the mooring maneuver he remembered come to completion on the viewscreen. "And, now, sir, let us go."

Civilians weren't supposed to be allowed on the cruiser's bridge. But no one had even suggested applying that rule to the Inspector General, and the bridge officers carefully refrained from pointing out to him that the cramped space was no place for impatient pacing.

"How much longer?" Felix demanded, not for the first time.

Commander Pym suppressed a groan. "We're still proceeding at our best speed toward the point at which the target vessel disengaged its drive just short of Planet V's Chen Limit, at which time we were no longer able to keep a sensor lock on it, given the range. And," he hastily added in anticipation of the next question, "we got a fix on its vector at the time. Our estimated time of arrival at that point is—"

"Never mind. Just keep me informed." Felix commanded himself to outward composure. He'd spent the voyage in an agony of nerves, for there had always been the possibility that his instinct was wrong. But he'd been vindicated, as that enigmatic little ship had plunged unerringly toward the brown dwarf he'd circled as Castellan's prisoner more than two decades before. It had been a simple matter to infer the intrinsic velocity the quarry had resumed after disengaging its drive, and a computer projection of its vector now stood out redly in a tank that displayed the brown dwarf's immediate vicinity.

We'll follow that vector, Felix told himself, almost salivating. *Not knowing he's being followed, he has no reason not to take the most direct course. And there's no stealth system that can conceal a massive object when you know exactly where to look for it.*

Of course, I won't be able to actually do anything about it now, with just this cruiser—who knows what kind of defenses that orbital facility has. Maybe I should leave now with the data, before Pym and his crew even know what we're looking for.

No. I need confirmation. And the data's incomplete; that course crosses too many possible orbits. And besides, I'll only be sharing the knowledge with them temporarily, until I've had a chance to set up an accident for this ship.

Reassured, he left the bridge, trailing a wake of relieved sighs.

Basil sank back on the couch Omega Prime had provided. Without thinking, he ran his fingers through his hair. They came away covered with little iron-gray tufts. The onset of hair loss had come as no surprise. He dismissed it from his mind and faced the pickup again.

He'd just about finished the interactive message. He'd confirmed Dimitri as his heir, for there was no other legal choice. He'd renewed all his previous appointments, and filled one omission among them by naming Lenore Silva as Grand Admiral. Now he appointed a regency council to govern until Dimitri came of age. "Or until I return," he added as an afterthought, for no reason he could define.

It was finally done. The Intelligence Director stepped forward from the shadows and withdrew a disc from its slot. The software would respond to questions on topics related to its core message, but it would not discuss where it had been made. Omega Prime's privacy would remain secure.

"You'll be sure to deliver it?" Basil whispered the question, for he'd used up what was left of his voice.

"I shall make sure Admiral Silva receives it, sir."

Basil didn't notice the phrasing's ambiguity. He was beyond such things. He merely nodded. When he opened his eyes, the Intelligence Director was gone. He was alone with the cybernetic Luon whose mental voice now filled his head.

"Would you like me to send proxies to take you to your quarters, Your Imperial Majesty?"

Basil smiled. "You really don't need to use that form of address, Omega Prime. You're not an Imperial subject."

"A wholly valid point. Nevertheless, your mind correctly interprets my mental voice as employing the title. For I judge it to be your proper form of address, to which you are eminently entitled."

Basil managed a short, bitter laugh, which dissolved into coughing. "I can't imagine why you think that," he said when he could speak again. "Or, for that matter, why you thought me worth bringing here to die. I've lost everything. I've failed."

"Incorrect. Worse, meaningless. You have done what the future required of you."

"The future . . . which I can't know."

"Not necessarily. Under the present circumstances, I believe I can relax my rule against sharing with you my limited foreknowledge of the future."

It took awhile for Omega Prime's statement to register. Then a shiver that had nothing to do with radiation sickness ran through Basil. "You mean you'll tell me . . . ?"

"Only if you wish it. Be warned: much of it will not be to your liking."

Basil drew a shuddering breath. "I have to know what, if anything, my life will have meant. Tell me. Tell me everything."

"Your domain in the old rebel sectors will survive for a while," Omega Prime began calmly. "It will have a respite because Kang will promptly fall out with Lothar Medina. In fact, Kang is shortly going to assume the title of Emperor himself, completing the division of the Empire into three successor-states. They will contend for over four standard decades. Finally, a fresh usurper will take power from the

incompetent Lothar and then—" (*A surgeon's gentleness.*)
"—put an end to your realm."

The steadiness of old reawoke in Basil's voice. "I asked
you to tell me *everything*, Omega Prime. Will Dimitri . . . ?"

"Yes. Your son will still be on the throne then."
(*Compassion.*) "He will, of course, be—"

"Of course." Basil closed his eyes and saw, not what Dimitri
had become, but the little boy he'd occasionally found time
to play with, running about in near-ecstasy as he always
had on those occasions. He spent a few moments alone
with those memories, then relinquished them. The little
boy receded into infinity and was gone.

"Shall I continue, Your Imperial Majesty?"

Basil opened his blurred eyes. "Yes. I have to know
everything."

"Kang's son will fall perhaps a decade and a half later,
putting an end to what posterity, being safely removed from
it, will look back on as an era of swashbuckling high
adventure. But the Empire's ramshackle reunification will
only last a few decades. Then the Zyungen, of whom you
already know from your Sword Clans acquaintances, will
break over the frontier. After all the internecine wars, there
will be no strength to resist them. Earth itself will fall. A
scion of the upstart dynasty will hold out in the Serpens/
Bootes region, ruling a 'Solarian Empire' which does not
include Sol. In the meantime, Beyonders will swarm into
the remainder of former Imperial space, for the Zyungen
will prove incapable of sustaining any widespread political
unity. In the old Imperial core, chaos will reign under squalid,
ephemeral regimes controlling limited regions. But the
fugitive Imperial court will be in no position to take
advantage, being occupied with intrigue, factionalism, and
fresh usurpations."

"So that's how it ends?" asked Basil in a dead voice.

"After observing enough history, one comes to the
realization that there are no real endings—only fresh
beginnings. One such will occur at the end of the forty-
first century: the return of the Sword Clans."

"You mean their planet will . . . ?"

"Become uninhabitable, yes. You are already aware of the astronomical death sentence it is under. You also know that, while the Sword Clans supported you in the hope you'd bring about a reunified Empire to welcome them back, their second choice is chaos."

"So Kleinst-Schiavona told me."

"When they can no longer put off their departure from Newhope, they will return to Imperial space proclaiming themselves the saviors of Earth and the human race. After wiping out the Beyonder and Zyungen fiefdoms but failing to conquer the rump Solarian Empire, they will establish their own Earth-centered empire. Their dynasty will die out after a century and a half, to be followed by a couple of short-lived successors. But it will have created the basis for stable consolidation, and the eventual reconquest of the Serpens/Bootes region." (*Gentleness.*) "Yes. The Empire will be reunified and renewed, under a new dynasty that will lead it to new heights of greatness. But it won't really be an entirely new dynasty at all, for the blood of the old one will flow in it. And you will be the link."

"*What?*" Basil struggled to sit up. But it was hard. So hard. "What do you mean?"

"The new society will be dominated at first by a military aristocracy produced by intermarriage of the Sword Clans and the old Imperial populations. The new dynasty will come from such a family. Their Sword Clans side will be descended in part from the Kleinst-Schiavonas—into which your daughter Irena will have been adopted."

"You mean the reunifiers will be descended from her?"

"Yes. So you see why I find it impossible to accept your self-assessment of failure. Furthermore . . ." Omega Prime paused. It was one of the few times Basil had ever known that mental voice to perceptibly hesitate. "You will have another link with the reunification—a more direct one than your daughter's blood."

"*What?*" Basil strove to concentrate. "How?"

Omega Prime explained, and all the pain and defeat

departed from Basil's face as he listened to the voice no one else would have been able to hear.

"Are you still tracking it?" snapped Felix as he emerged onto the bridge, looking disheveled from sleep. They'd only just received the news for which he'd given orders to be awakened.

"Yes, Inspector General," Pym assured him. He pointed to the local-space holo tank, indicating the scarlet vector arrow that had appeared in it. "It is either the same ship we followed to this system or one of the same class. It appeared, seemingly from nowhere, at a point along the course we were planning to search, then proceeded to the brown dwarf's Chen Limit and engaged its drive." He gave an order, and projected courses for the mystery ship and their own cruiser appeared in the tank. "As you can see, we are in a position to intercept it, if you wish us to change course and do so."

"Of course, you blockhead! We can come back and resume our original search plan later. Set in the intercept course now, and overtake that ship. It's very fortunate for you that we can still do so despite your lack of initiative."

Pym kept his face carefully controlled. "At once, Inspector General." He gave orders, and the brown dwarf toward which they'd been proceeding seemed to drift to starboard and vanish from the view forward.

Felix didn't notice the precession of the stars in the screen, for he was trying to puzzle out this development. He'd expected Castellan and his Intelligence Director—both of whom he was certain had been aboard that little craft—to remain in hiding at the orbital construct, trusting in its stealth devices to conceal them. Why was their ship now streaking away from that imagined security?

"Extrapolate that ship's course in the strategic display, Commander," he ordered. The red line appeared in the indicated holo tank, and Felix gave his tight, brief little smile, for it intersected the other scarlet course that marked Silva's retreating forces. *So that's it. They think they can rejoin Silva. But they don't know this ship is here.* An almost sexual excitement surged in him. *I'll return directly to Earth on this ship with Castellan as my prisoner! There's nothing Lothar won't do for me. Later, I can return here and locate that space station, or whatever, at my leisure.* He forced himself not to twitch with anticipation as time passed and the cruiser's green icon crawled closer and closer to the red one in the tank.

They finally drew into a range where even routine sensor scans could not fail to detect a ship under drive, and the quarry began to initiate evasive maneuvers and sensor confusion. Another grim smile touched Felix's lips. Pym had naturally anticipated this, and he and his officers were competent enough within the claustrophobic confines of their specialties. The cruiser and its sensors hung on grimly, closing the range until they were within hailing distance.

In response to Pym's command, the stranger disengaged both drive and impellers. The cruiser flashed up under drive, then went sublight and began to match velocities. Felix, unable to contain himself any longer, shouldered Pym aside and faced the comm screen.

"Give us a visual image at once," he ordered.

The screen came to life, revealing the features of Castellan's Intelligence Director. It was a face very familiar to Felix from intensive study; but some fraction of a second passed before he recognized it, for it was so perfectly unremarkable. It was as though someone had taken photographs of all the humans who'd ever lived and made a composite of them.

"Where is Castellan?" he demanded.

"His Imperial Majesty is not here." The voice was as instantly forgettable as the face. "I am alone aboard this ship."

A spasm of petulant disappointment and frustrated hate shot through Felix. "Where is he?"

"I am neither permitted nor inclined to tell you that."

"Stand by to be tractored and brought aboard this cruiser," Felix forced out through his fury. "I'll deal with you later."

He cut the connection with a vicious motion and turned away from the comm screen.

"Ah, Inspector General," Pym began diffidently, "standard procedure calls for the hostile ship to be held immobilized by tractor beams outside this ship's deflectors and boarded by Marines. As captain of this ship, I am responsible for its safety. So I must insist—"

Felix whirled around and slapped Pym across the face. He gleefully observed the commander's muscle-twitching efforts to force physical control on himself. "Shut up, you stupid clod! I'm the Inspector General. Do you hear me? The Inspector General! Fuck all your 'traditions of the service.' Your status is approximately that of my chauffeur! And I want to interview this 'Intelligence Director' without any unnecessary delays. I will not be obstructed by the petty rules that inferior people like you need to follow in order to perform routine tasks without making messes or hurting themselves. *Is that clear?*" Felix reined himself in, aware that his voice had risen to a scream and annoyed that he'd let his frustration get the better of his self-control. "Is that clear?" he repeated, shakily but at a normal decibel level.

"Perfectly, Inspector General," Pym said through clenched teeth and lips that barely moved. "Your orders will be carried out to the letter."

"See that they are," Felix said shortly, and stalked away, oblivious to the expressions on the bridge crew's faces.

The cruiser's docking bay was smaller than those of capital ships. But the strange ship was a very small one, and in what even Felix had to admit was a very short time it floated on tractors through the atmosphere screen at the pace—about that of a fast walk—at which the low-powered deflector would permit passage of a large solid object. It settled to the deck under the eyes of a Security detail whose members licked their lips and darted furtive glances at each other as they contemplated the new arrival's alien lines.

Felix cared nothing for such things. Marching up in front of the now-motionless craft, he raised a hand communicator. "Come out now—unarmed."

As he gave the command, the enigmatic vessel's flank was an unbroken expanse of silvery smoothness. Then, without even the motion that an eyeblink would have concealed, there was a hatchway in it. A wavering spread along the line of Security guards. "Stand fast!" rasped Felix, who was remembering anew some of the things he'd glimpsed in this system so long ago. *Yes, this cruiser must definitely be lost with all hands in the near future. And I must very definitely get to the bottom of whatever connection this "Intelligence Director" has with that which orbits the brown dwarf.*

He motioned to two Security men to follow him. They obeyed without alacrity as he stepped in front of the inexplicable hatch. The Intelligence Director emerged and walked up to face his captor. A slight reduction in the background hum told Felix that the tractors had been disengaged, now that the prisoner had exposed himself to the docking bay with only the atmosphere screen between his body and vacuum.

"So," Felix began without preamble, "you were trying to contact Silva?"

"Incorrect. I shall in fact do so."

"Oh?" Felix sneered. "How?"

"By means of a message automatically broadcast from my ship when it comes within range." And, as though the mention of it had been a cue, the craft—seemingly too small to call a ship—rose from the deck on contra-grav. And, with the abruptness of its vectored impellers, it began to swing around.

The Security men scattered, falling to the deck as the sleek silvery blade flashed overhead. Felix staggered back, opening his mouth to scream. Before he could form a sound, the craft completed its swinging motion and, with a grinding, rending noise, sideswiped the right edge of the atmosphere screen's opening. The screen flickered, then blinked out of existence. And the metal doors that were supposed to slam shut in an emergency pushed in vain against their bent, crumpled runners.

Felix glimpsed the Security men, and everything else in the docking bay that was loose, rush out into the void, carried by the escaping air. The craft, showing its damage but with fully functional impellers that added their force to that of the gale, flew outward even faster.

Ordinarily, the cruiser might have speared the escaping vessel with energy weapons as soon as it cleared the docking bay. But Pym and his subordinates had other things on their minds—mainly the tornado that was howling through their ship as atmosphere rushed out through the wide-gaping hole in its side. So the Intelligence Director's ship won clear, engaged its drive, and outpaced the photons of the weapons that belatedly clawed for it. But first it ejected a small object.

Felix noticed none of this, for the outrushing air was carrying him irresistibly along, and all at once he was looking at the cruiser from the outside.

He remembered to exhale and leave his mouth open, then reached fumblingly to pull the flexible nanoplastic hood of his civilian space service dress over his head. But before he could complete the motion his arms were pinned to his sides and he was face to face with the Intelligence Director, who was holding him in an unbreakable embrace.

No! he had a split second to think as the cloud of air around him dissipated into the infinity. *You'll die too. . . .*

"No, I won't." The Intelligence Director's lips didn't move, and at any rate his words couldn't have been heard in what was now vacuum. The voice was inside Felix's head, tolling in his mind. "You see, I do not share the human need for oxygen."

Felix was only marginally aware of the telepathic voice, for explosive decompression had begun to boil away his body fluids. The exposed skin of his hands and face became a tracery of ruptured blood vessels, his eardrums burst, and his scream was soundless.

"It was necessary," the Intelligence Director went on, "for me to allow myself to be captured, for you were in possession of information you could not be allowed to have. Just before it engaged its drive and departed to rendezvous with Admiral Silva, my ship dropped a device which produced a brief but very intense electromagnetic pulse. At such short range, it hopelessly scrambled your cruiser's data banks. Its crew may very well be able to return home— by now they will have sealed off the docking bay area and thus halted the escape of air—but they will no longer have the navigational information which might have allowed you, or someone else, to locate the intelligence I serve."

Felix, of course, was no longer listening. He had ceased to trail a cloud of vapor as they drifted away from the cruiser, and the fragile, desiccated husk in the Intelligence Director's arms massed only a few pounds. A slight increase in pressure from those arms and it collapsed into a powder which immediately dissipated. But the Intelligence Director continued as though still addressing him.

"Normally, like any self-aware entity, I seek to preserve my own existence. But, to repeat, this was necessary. And 'death' in your sense is a meaningless concept to me; I can simply terminate my own consciousness at any time, and I will doubtless do so presently. And . . . I confess that the opportunity to put an end to your existence in the process was attractive. It should not have been. But, as I once pointed out to General Bogdan, I am a very complex machine."

The Intelligence Director watched the cruiser vanish into the starfields and smiled.

The impeller-equipped capsule streaked away, curving along a hyperbolic trajectory. With senses beyond the capacity of any human language to describe, Omega Prime tracked that casket's course until it vanished against the flames of the star humans had denominated DM -17 954.

Forgive me, Your Imperial Majesty. A sun—even the home sun of the Luonli—is not enough of a funeral pyre. But it is all I have. It will have to do.

The thought of the Luonli led Omega Prime down new byways of reflection. They were dying rapidly now, spiraling downward toward extinction. Shenyilu was the latest to die, as Omega Prime knew by means it had never felt the need to reveal to any human. *Yes, Your Imperial Majesty, I spoke simple truth when I told you the Luonli are a dying race. But I never explained what that meant to me as the individual I am. For what does a custodian do when the object of its custody dwindles toward nonexistence? No, I never explained—for you could not have understood— the need for a new . . . project. In my case, a younger race.*

Actually, there were several things I never told you. I told you of your blood's role in the Empire's restoration . . . but not your legend's. You would not have believed me. But you, Sonja and Torval will be remembered for your gallant, foredoomed attempt to save the Empire. That tale, growing with the retelling, will sustain those who live through the dark times that are coming, and inspire those who will bring the dawn.

And even beyond that . . . But I did tell you the rest, for you had earned the right to know.

With that thought, Omega Prime shifted its primary attention to a different element of its multifarious sensors and observed a small chamber containing three artificial wombs in cryogenic stasis. The sight shook a recollection loose from Omega Prime's infinite memory: the time three humans had slept in their shuttle, docked within this physical housing—three humans who bore within them the seeds of future myth. Obtaining genetic samples had been simplicity itself. And now three embryos waited for the time when history—the history which had become Omega Prime's ward—would require them and they would be awakened from their frozen slumber. The vast consciousness returned to its contemplation of those embryos.

Is this, Omega Prime wondered, *what parenthood is like?*